a table by the window

A Table by the Window

THE GRESHAM CHRONICLES

The Widow of Larkspur Inn
The Courtship of the Vicar's Daughter
The Dowry of Miss Lydia Clark

TALES OF LONDON

The Maiden of Mayfair
Catherine's Heart
Leading Lady

Visit *www.lawanablackwell.com*

a table by the window

LAWANA BLACKWELL

BETHANY HOUSE PUBLISHERS

Minneapolis, Minnesota

Published by Bethany House Publishers
11400 Hampshire Avenue South
Bloomington, Minnesota 55438

Bethany House Publishers is a division of
Baker Publishing Group, Grand Rapids, Michigan.

Printed in the United States of America

ISBN 0-7394-5397-1

To
Penny, Kristine, and Heather . . .
the beautiful women my sons
had the good sense to marry.

LAWANA BLACKWELL is a full-time writer with eleven published novels, including the bestselling GRESHAM CHRONICLES series. She and her husband have three grown sons and live in Baton Rouge, Louisiana.

chapter 1

Soft raps upon a door were creepy at 1:00 in the morning. Especially when a person lived alone. Pulse pounding, twenty-five-year-old Carley Reed set the pan of *Gnocchi alla Giordano* on the stove and tossed the oven mitts to the table on her way through the kitchen.

"I'll see who it is, Jim!" she called in the empty living room of her apartment. She closed her left eye to squint through the peephole with her right. An aged face loomed out of the dim hallway.

Oh dear. Carley turned the latches on the knob and dead bolt, unfastened the chain, and eased open the door.

"Mrs. Kordalewski," she said, softly this time. "I'm so sorry. Did I wake you?"

"You did not. I had to get Shimon some Tylenol for his hip. I heard you in your kitchen."

"Is he all right?"

"He is just old. Like me. You have a visitor?"

"No," Carley replied sheepishly. "Just pretending . . . just in case."

The old woman cackled. "In case I was a bad guy."

She was frail and spotted, with a hand wrapped around the curve of a cane and collarbones jutting above the white roses embroidered on a pink chenille robe. Her Polish accent was thick, even after half a century in San Francisco, but Carley figured anyone tenacious enough to survive the Treblinka extermination camp could speak any way she pleased.

9

"I had trouble sleeping," Carley explained. Cooking was her alternative to pacing the floor or wringing her hands.

Mrs. Kordalewski raised her chin, sniffed. "Spaghetti?"

"Gnocchi."

"Smells good. You make with potatoes?"

"Yes." Easing the door a little wider, Carley felt compelled to ask, "Would you care for a taste?"

"Is too late. No good for digestion."

"Of course. Well . . . sorry again for—"

A bony hand shot out and caught the door. "A taste is all right. I have Tums."

Three minutes later Carley was moving aside a stack of papers to clear a space at the table. Tums or not, she knew to dish out only small servings of the oval-shaped potato dumplings and marinara sauce. "I worked my way through college at an Italian restaurant. DeLouches, in Sacramento. I was a waitress, but I helped out in the kitchen when they were shorthanded."

Her neighbor picked up a fork, but her watery eyes studied Carley's face. "Do you not have to go teach in the morning?"

Carley glanced at the clock over the ancient stove. In five hours she would be rising. That is, if she ever managed to grab some sleep. Exhaustion clung to her so heavily that even her eyelids seemed attached to weights, but her mind, just as exhausted, could not cease running a treadmill of scenarios.

"What keeps awake a girl who needs her sleep?"

Automatically Carley glanced at the stack of papers just beyond her right elbow—her second-hour English Literature students' compositions on "Symbolism in Dickens' *Great Expectations*." The four on top were almost identical, word-for-word. It had taken her only twelve minutes of searching the Internet to discover the source of those students' "research."

"Just a little problem at work. You haven't tasted it. Careful, it's hot."

Mrs. Kordalewski blew on the morsel impaled upon her fork.

She nodded after the first nibble. "Is very good."

"Thank you. All I need is enough to pack for my lunch, and you may have the rest. I'll bring it to you when I get home from school."

Which might not be a good plan, she realized after the words left her mouth. One did not simply send a note home with a student guilty of cheating. There would be parent-teacher conferences, perhaps as early as right after dismissal. "On second thought, I'll pack it up now and carry it for you when you've finished."

The old woman leaned her head to eye Carley's oversized gray T-shirt and baggy plaid flannels. "I don't know. If my Shimon is still awake, I don't want him to see you in your pajamas and get ideas."

"Mrs. Kordalewski!" Carley sputtered, half choking on a gnocchi.

She then noticed the ghost of a smile. "You're teasing."

"Maybe a little," Mrs. Kordalewski said with a pleased look, spearing the last gnocchi on her plate. "I thank you. Our granddaughter, Julie, visits tomorrow, and we will have something good to feed her. Remake your bed."

Carley blinked at the abrupt change of subject. "Remake my bed?"

"Put your pillow at the foot. You will sleep like a baby."

After accompanying Mrs. Kordalewski to her apartment with the promised container of gnocchi, Carley's longed simply to flop into her twin-sized bed, but she followed her neighbor's advice. Whether from some principle of ergonomics or simply the power of suggestion, ten minutes after crawling under the rearranged sheets, she began floating into gauzy slumber.

"It's a cool fifty-two degrees out there on this Tuesday morning, the fourteenth of January, with highs expected in the upper fifties. . . ."

She pushed back the covers and reached for her bedside table, only then remembering she had reversed her position. Swinging feet to the floor, she felt for the lamp switch. Light flooded the bedroom.

It was furnished simply, for San Francisco apartments were not cheap, even south of Market Street, where the deceptively named Bridgeview Towers was tucked among warehouses and nightclubs. Over the years, Carley had collected a mission-style dresser, mirror, and chest from a consignment shop located—appropriately—on Mission Street. The rest of the furnishings were a mismatched collection that Carley had gathered. A framed, vintage-style poster of the Orient Express from Target. A wicker armchair bought on clearance at Cost Plus World Market. A faded and frayed Turkish rug the former tenant had left rolled up in a corner with a note inviting the next tenant to keep it or throw it away.

"... *very light scattered showers until late this morning. . . .*"

After two pieces of toast with Earl Grey tea, Carley showered and turbaned a towel around her head. She could not skip the blush-mascara-lipstick ritual, for she considered her face to be as bland as white bread, with its twin slashes of reddish brows over eyes the color of gravel, nondescript nose, and thin lips. Her assets in the looks department were good straight teeth—thanks to a dentist who repaired years of neglect in exchange for tutoring sessions with his daughter during Carley's first year of teaching in Sacramento—and chin-length, layered hair of such an unusual natural blending of auburn, copper, and light brown that it drew occasional compliments from strangers of both sexes.

In the bedroom she pulled a teal green sweater and skirt over her five-foot-five frame and zipped her feet into black suede boots. She fluffed her bangs with her fingers; took up coat, briefcase, and lunch bag; and stepped out into the third-floor hallway.

When the doors parted, the elevator was already half-filled with commuters from the three upper floors. A tall, thin young man with chill-pinked nose and cheeks and a blondish crew cut stepped out before Carley entered. Carley was in too much of a hurry to pay much attention to the questioning look he gave her, but once inside the elevator she happened to notice that he was heading toward the right, where there were only three apartments. The elevator doors closed as she was trying to decide whether to exit.

Rats! she thought as the elevator emptied into the lobby. She pressed the third-floor button. Sure enough, when she stepped out into the hallway the man was turning away from apartment 3C.

"Excuse me . . . that's my apartment." She sighed at the rumbling sounds of the elevator doors closing behind her.

The man winced. "Sorry about that."

The maturity in his voice made him seem older than her first impression, perhaps thirty. He wore a tan corduroy blazer over a green checkered shirt and dark brown pants. Long legs grew from white sneakers as big as loaves of bread. "Would you happen to be Carley Reed?" he asked, advancing a couple of steps.

Carley shifted her lunch and briefcase to her right hand and pressed the elevator button again. "May I ask what business you have with her?"

There was no reason to be paranoid. The Nikolaouses in 3A were awake. Faintly she could hear Katie Couric's televised voice, smell the aroma of strong Greek coffee. But then, there were the tennis shoes with dress slacks. Would any sane man dress in such a way?

He caught her downward glance and gave her a sheepish smile. "I forgot to pack my Oxfords."

"Oh." Carley relaxed a little. "Yes, I'm Carley Reed. And you are . . ."

"Dennis Wingate." Taking the remaining four steps to her, he dipped long fingers into a coat pocket and fished out a business card. "I'm a private investigator."

She scanned the address on the card. Sacramento, California. "Why. . . ?"

"You might prefer to discuss this inside."

"No," Carley said, torn between curiosity and the need to get to work early. "I have to catch a bus. You'll have to walk me to the stop."

"Yes, of course."

As they waited for the elevator, he explained that he had been hired by a Tallulah, Mississippi, attorney by the name of Stanley Malone. He took another card from his wallet. "He's handling Cordelia Walker's estate."

"My grandmother's dead?" A lump rose in Carley's throat while a hazy scene materialized in her mind. Herself, very small, sharing a bench and carton of animal crackers with a soft-voiced woman. "How?"

"A heart attack. She went peacefully in her own bed, if it's any consolation."

It *was* consolation. Nice to have that image in her head, rather than the one she carried of her mother's final moments on earth— cursing doctors and nurses as if they had caused the cirrhosis of the liver themselves.

"Why Mississippi? My grandparents live in Washington State."

"Mrs. Walker moved to a little town called Tallulah after her husband died, according to Mr. Malone. I believe it was four years ago."

Another pang, even though Carley had no memory whatsoever of her grandfather. Her mother only spoke of her parents while drinking, when Carley's main mission was to stay out of range as much as possible. All she knew was that Sterling Walker was a machinist for the Port of Tacoma, Cordelia Walker, a housewife.

"Sorry to have to break the news." Mr. Wingate said.

She nodded as the elevator stopped and doors parted. Stepping back to make room were the dental hygienist with whom Carley sometimes chatted in the laundry room and the gray-haired man from the fourth floor who jogged every morning. Carley absently returned their good-mornings.

You have no more family, she told herself. And the only contact she had initiated with her grandparents was after her mother's burial almost a year ago, when she sent a note to the address she found while cleaning out her mother's belongings. It had seemed the decent thing to do.

But she had signed it with a simple *From Carley* with no return address. Looking them up was filed in the "Perhaps One Day" category. *Family*, as defined by the examples in her childhood, made her skeptical.

Which was why, at twenty-five, she had never allowed herself to sustain a relationship beyond a few dates. Why join her life with someone who could turn out to be a frog instead of a prince? How many times did her mother bring home a new man who was going to change their lives for the better?

Once free of the elevator and other sets of ears, Carley motioned Mr. Wingate toward the alcove where thirty-two mailboxes were set in the wall. "When is the funeral?"

Discomfort washed across the clean-shaven face. "It was in October."

"Three *months* ago?"

"I would have found you sooner, but the name I started out with was 'Walker'. That was two names ago. . . . ."

Carley ignored the implied question. Mr. Wingate was a nice man, but that did not give him a right to her entire life history. She offered her hand instead of an explanation. "Thank you for telling me about my grandparents."

"You'll contact Mr. Malone, then?" he said with a resigned expression.

"Yes. And I have to hurry, or I'll miss my bus."

He nodded and turned toward the lobby door. "I can do better than that. Let me hail you a cab."

"That's not necessary," she said, following. "I still have time."

He looked back at her. "Please, I insist. I'll add it to my expense account, so you'll ultimately be paying for it anyway."

"What do you mean?"

The open glass door allowed in the traffic noise of Harrison Street. "Well, from your inheritance."

The Yellow Cab was a welcome respite from thirty-eight minutes of commute involving two buses and walks totaling three blocks.

Inheritance, Carley thought as the driver turned north onto Van Ness. Would there be enough—minus Mr. Wingate's fee—to pay off the $4,359 remaining of her student loan? The $1,700 she still owed Visa from her mother's burial?

Wouldn't it be wonderful to be debt free!

But the thought would have to wait, for the taxi was slowing to a stop at the corner of Vallejo and Webster Streets.

Emerson-Wake Preparatory School sat behind scrolled wrought-iron gates in Pacific Heights, San Francisco's most exclusive neighborhood. The 12,900-square-foot Queen Anne style house had been built in the early 1900s for Amiel Herschel, a Polish Jew who immigrated to San Francisco in 1890, started out in the clock repair business, and expanded into copper mining.

It was a given that parents willing to pay an annual tuition of twenty-four thousand dollars would be involved and supportive. Carley did not have to purchase her own supplies, nor did she worry about school shootings or being robbed in the restroom. With only a bachelor's degree and three years' experience teaching in inner-city Sacramento, she was fortunate to be employed in such a prestigious institution.

That was what she told herself every morning. She had even believed it for the first week or two.

She paid the driver with the ten-dollar bill Mr. Wingate had pressed into her hand, telling him to keep the change. The grounds were quiet, the brick walkway damp from misting rain. Students would not begin arriving for another forty-five minutes. In the attendance office, Faye Wyatt looked up from her keyboard and raised her eyebrows.

Carley's pet peeve. She had once walked out of a shoe store because the sales clerk did the same eyebrow-thing without bothering to speak. The DeLouches would have fired the woman on the spot for treating a patron so condescendingly.

"Is Dr. Kincaid in yet?"

Faye's eyebrows continued to levitate.

"This is important."

The receptionist gave up and pressed a button upon her telephone. "Dr. Kincaid?"

"Yes, Faye?" came through in a metallic tone that was not entirely the machine's fault.

"Carley Reed asks to see you."

"Send her in."

Carley thanked Faye, who had resumed typing, and went on to the door beneath a brass plaque reading *Headmistress.*

"Good morning, Carley," Dr. Georgia Kincaid said from her desk. She had olive skin with few lines and wore pale pink lipstick. Jet black hair flowed from a square face into a French twist, the same way it did almost four years ago when she was principal of Sacramento High School and Carley was a teacher fresh out of California State University.

Two years later, Dr. Kincaid had left for San Francisco. Carley did not cross paths with her former boss until last June, when she happened across Dr. Kincaid and her husband under the refreshment canopy at the California Shakespeare Festival outside Oakland. Dr. Kincaid mentioned looking for a replacement English literature teacher and encouraged her to apply. She remembered how hard Carley had worked in Sacramento and guaranteed she would love Emerson-Wake.

It sounded like a good move to Carley, eager to get out of Sacramento, where there was always the chance of bumping into certain ghosts from the past.

"Good morning, Dr. Kincaid," Carley said. "I'm afraid I have bad news."

Dr. Kincaid lay down her pen. "Uh-oh. Please have a seat."

Carley sat in the chair facing the desk and unlatched the briefcase in her lap. "I almost telephoned you last night. But it was so late."

"What's wrong?"

"Four of my second-hour students copied their assignments

from the Internet." She leaned forward to hand the papers over the desk.

"This isn't good," Dr. Kincaid groaned, flipping through the stack.

"Would you like to see the Web site?"

"Yes, later. But it's clearly plagiarism." She set aside the first paper, looked at the name on the second, and blew out a longer stream of breath. "Ryan Ogden. His grandfather will be livid."

Retired four-star general Avery Ogden, author of several science-fiction novels, grandfather to three Emerson-Wake students, was the preparatory school's most generous contributor.

"But he has no cause to be angry at *us,*" Carley pointed out. "Not at the school."

Without replying, the headmistress scanned the papers again. At length her mocha-colored eyes met Carley's. "I want you to take the day off."

Carley shook her head. "I'm not about to skip out and leave you to handle this alone."

"I insist." She pressed a button on the speakerphone. "Faye, will you round up someone for gate duty? And I'll need to see Melinda when she arrives."

"Yes, Dr. Kincaid," came through.

Graduate student Melinda Pearson was one of two "floating" aides and substitute teachers. She had taken Carley's classes for two days back in November, when Carley had an especially fierce migraine. She was highly competent.

But very unneeded this morning. At least in Carley's opinion.

"Why are you doing this?" she asked.

"It's best if I handle this myself." Dr. Kincaid picked up her pen and began rotating it with fingers tipped in the same pink as her lips. "Did you ever explain to your students what plagiarism *is,* Carley?"

Desperation had entered her tone.

And something else . . . faintly. Accusation.

At me? Carley leaned forward again in an attempt to catch her eyes, but they were fastened hypnotically to the pen-turning process.

"They're high school sophomores," Carley reminded her.

"But did you—"

"*Explicitly*. What English teacher doesn't? And besides, it's spelled out in the handbook they signed." Disappointment surged through her. "You can't be thinking of dropping this."

"Of course not. But a negative grade in this class would destroy any chance at a good college." Finally her eyes met Carley's again. The brittle voice softened. "I realize that second-hour class has been a difficult one for you, Carley. But if we allow vindictiveness to cloud our—"

"You think I'm being *vindictive?*" Carley cut in, unable to believe her ears.

A hand released one end of the pen long enough to rake the stack of papers. "Could you really live with knowing that Erin Baine missed out on Harvard because of one childish lapse in judgment?"

It seemed as if Carley's lungs could not pull in enough air. "And so you propose we look the other way while she *cheats* her way in? So she can become a doctor or lawyer? Or how about a senator?"

Redness slashed Dr. Kincaid cheeks. "Of course not. I propose . . . I *insist*, we give them another chance. This once."

Clarity struck Carley like a swift, silent bolt of lightning. "This isn't about Erin, is it?"

"It's about all four of them."

"You're afraid of losing your job if General Ogden stops his support."

She flinched when the pen slammed against the desk.

"I'm sorry," Dr. Kincaid said right away, but in the next breath added, "Take the day off, Carley."

A foghorn sounded from the west, where white mists shrouded the Golden Gate Bridge's lofty piers. Other sounds met Carley's ears: seagulls' incessant *ky-eows*. Laughter from uniformed elementary students at the antics of the barking sea lions. The chatter of Japanese tourists snapping photographs of each other with Alcatraz over their left shoulders. The rustle of waxed paper as she dug out the remaining chocolate morsels from a bag of Blue Chip cookies.

No San Franciscan in her right mind would seek consolation from a damp bench at the end of Pier 39, but it was one of the few places from childhood Carley could recall being happy. At least for part of one summer day.

Her mother's boyfriend-of-the-month, a construction worker named Maxwell, had driven them from Sacramento. Even at nine, Carley had doubts about most of Maxwell's claims—that no cousin of his had ever scaled the TransAmerica Pyramid in special suction shoes, nor was another cousin Clint Eastwood's bodyguard—but his generosity more than made up for the lies. He trailed behind Carley's mother through one shop after another, paid for Carley to ride the carousel four times in a row, and then treated them to dinner at Neptune's Palace restaurant.

"See Angel Island?" he had said, pointing a Dungeness crab claw toward the Bay on the other side of the glass. "My Uncle Jim dug up a chest full of gold coins when he was stationed there."

"What did he do with them?" Carley had asked for politeness' sake.

He had looked over his shoulder, in a furtive manner that made Carley halfway believe him, and then leaned closer. "He hid them in his basement and sells a handful now and then to a coin dealer. Always a different dealer, mind you."

Then Maxwell sat back in his chair and winked. "He's got over a million dollars in the bank now."

Linda Walker was still pretty at the time, though chain-smoking and drinking were turning her voice as husky as a man's. She rolled her green eyes and asked why Maxwell drove a ten-year-old Tempo with a broken radio and stuck passenger door, if he had a million-aire uncle. Carley knew that was the beginning of the end, even before Maxwell's face clouded.

By Christmas Linda was married to Huey Collins, an accountant at the California State Capitol. It was a promising move up—from a duplex on H Street to a three-bedroom brick rambler in Citrus Heights. In a rare show of maternal caring, Linda pressured Huey into adopting Carley, reasoning that she did not want her daughter playing second fiddle to his own two girls. Later, Carley overheard Linda confide to a girlfriend over the telephone that the adoption was so Huey would have to pay child support, should there be a divorce.

Nonetheless, Carley reveled in the relative normalcy of the situation. She was enrolled in a school that did not post guards on the playground and hallways. Collection agencies ceased telephoning. The family attended church. Linda quit her job at Safeway and even developed an interest in cooking beyond frozen microwave meals. The stepsisters, ages eight and nine, were fun playmates on their third-weekend-per-month visits. Huey was a kindly father. For a while.

And then Linda, bored with domesticity and having to ask for spending money, took a job as a counter clerk at Best Western. She worked Saturdays and Sundays, which suited her even more, for the stepdaughters got on her nerves when they visited. That left Carley and Huey alone at home for three weekends out of every four. He would take her to IHOP after church on Sundays, as if to make up for the torment he was beginning to inflict upon her at home. She began wetting the bed and making poor marks in school. Linda had no idea, for Carley had been doing the laundry since age seven or so, and when had Linda ever kept a parent-teacher conference appointment?

Huey was arrested the following October, after his eldest daughter confided in a teacher. When the social worker and police officer visited the house in Citrus Heights, Carley knew instinctively how she was expected to reply to their questions. In spite of her fervent denials, they brought her to a clinic to be examined by a woman doctor. Huey was sent to prison for five years after his attorney made a deal with prosecutors who wished to spare the girls from having to testify. The run-down duplex Carley and Linda moved to on 23rd Street seemed a refuge.

Her mother did not bring any more men home to live with them until Carley was fourteen. That was when Linda became pregnant by Wayne Ross, part-time bartender and singer in country-western clubs. Wayne played funny songs on the guitar, pasted up new wallpaper, fixed the drip that had etched a brown inverted *V* beneath the bathtub faucet, spent eight hundred dollars to retrieve Linda's car from the repossession lot, and spoon-fed her soup after she miscarried the baby. But he was insanely jealous, once even beating up a UPS driver for supposedly giving Linda the eye while delivering a package to the family who shared the duplex. He slept days, and his ears were as sharp as sonic radar. He woke at the faintest noise to rant and rave.

In spite of the migraines that were beginning to plague her, Carley began staying outdoors after school and on weekends, and gravitated toward a half-dozen other adolescents who found the streets more welcoming or interesting than their homes.

Her new friends taught her how to shoplift and smoke

cigarettes—even pot whenever they could get it. She dyed her hair and fingernails black. One spring day, a boy she had a crush on stole his father's Aerostar van, and the group set out for San Francisco. For three days they managed to evade authorities in Golden Gate Park. The police returned the other children to their parents with stern warnings but kept Carley in custody when Linda met them at the door with a black eye and bleeding lip. She refused to press charges against Wayne, and so Carley was sent to a foster home in Yuba City, fifty miles from Sacramento.

The Woodleys had a fine house, but it took Carley only days to realize her position as housemaid and sitter for four undisciplined children under the age of seven. When she slipped away five months later with a credit card and twenty-three dollars plus change from Alice Woodley's purse, two policemen met her at the Sacramento Greyhound station. She spent eight days in juvenile detention, then was sent to a group home in Redding, California.

There, the snarls in her life began untangling. She was enrolled in Pioneer High School. Her grades improved. She made the basketball team and gave up cigarettes after the coach threatened to kick her off if he smelled tobacco again. The migraines eased from at least one a week to one every four or five months. One of the group home's counselors, Janelle Reed, provided a sympathetic ear to her railings about Linda's choosing a man over her and failing to protect her from Huey Collins. But more importantly, she gave Carley a glimpse of what her future could be.

"Learn from your mother's failings and you won't end up like her," Janelle had said, time and time again.

Carley's first official act upon turning eighteen was to legally shed the name *Collins* with money she had saved for just that purpose. It was bad enough to have memories of her stepfather stored in the back of her mind. *Reed* seemed the logical choice, even though by this time the counselor had moved to Alaska with her husband to train sled dogs. It cost not a cent more to get rid of *Rainbow* in favor of simply no middle name. After mulling over several possibilities, she decided to keep *Carley*. Her mother claimed to have named her after singer Carly Simon—though in typical Linda-fashion she had paid no attention to the correct spelling—but it was still a nice, normal name, and she could not imagine having to adjust to a new one.

She unsuccessfully tried for a basketball scholarship at California State University and so put herself through school by waiting tables thirty-plus hours weekly. Linda died in Mercy General Hospital on March 3, 2002. And even to the end she maintained that she was a good mother who had simply made a few mistakes. Wasn't the fact that her daughter was a college graduate proof enough?

How easy it would be, Carley thought as she got up from the bench, to sit back and allow a handful of rich kids to bend the rules. After all, she had done her duty by reporting them to the head-mistress.

She shook her head. It was a nice try, but she could not make herself believe it. Somehow, over the course of institutionalized living and working her way through college, she recognized that certain people stood out from among the masses by virtue of their character. Like Janelle Reed. The DeLouches. Having had most of her childhood wrecked by people with *no* positive character traits, she did not take that virtue lightly. How slippery was the slope from winking at a handful of cheaters to breaking the law? Or ruining someone else's life?

Or becoming like her mother? Her worst fear.

You can't back down on this, she told herself.

Back in her apartment, Carley averted her eyes from the answering machine's blinking light. Just because she had decided to stand firm did not mean she was looking forward to the confrontation that would result. The telephone rang at half past seven as she was stretched out in pajamas and slippers in front of *America's Funniest Home Videos* reruns, trying to lighten her mood. She rested the half-finished peanut butter and jelly sandwich on the plate upon her stomach and angled an arm to reach for the cordless receiver on the wicker sofa table.

"I've been calling all day, Carley," came Dr. Kincaid's brittle voice before Carley could say hello.

The concern in the headmistress's tone was gratifying. That meant she regretted her course of action.

"I had to get away and think," Carley said. "It wasn't right for you to send me home like that."

A sigh came through the receiver. "Do you think I enjoyed handling it this way? But you have to understand that the school can't exist without donations."

"Are you saying you gave them another chance?"

"With the condition that they turn in new compositions by Friday. With notes of apology to you for misunderstanding the ru—"

"And those students who followed the rules?" Carley cut in, making a row of little pinches along the bread crust.

"This doesn't affect them. My hands are tied on this one, Carley. I'm ordering you to let this go."

Carley took a deep breath. "I can't do that, Dr. Kincaid. We both know that's not fair."

"What we both *know,* is that I went out on a limb to hire you, with only three years' experience and no master's degree." Dr. Kincaid's brittle voice sharpened. "You're a good teacher, Carley, in spite of your inability to maintain discipline in some of your classes. But frankly, I'll sacrifice you if you force my hand."

You can't back down, Carley reminded herself.

And then, misgivings. *She did go out on a limb. You've never been fired. If you can just hang in there for five more months, you'll have the summer—*

"Carley?"

You're a coward, Carley said to herself.

And what she said to Dr. Kincaid was, "All right."

"I appreciate that," the headmistress said before breaking the connection.

Wiping her eyes with her paper napkin, Carley set aside her sandwich. Throbbing in her right temple warned of an impending migraine. She buried her face in a sofa pillow. Was she any better than the students who had cheated? So much for her seemingly high standards of integrity. Integrity was easy when there were no personal risks involved.

On leaden feet she carried her dish into the kitchen. She had just swallowed two Excedrin tablets to ward off pain and half of a Dramamine tablet to ward off nausea, when the answering machine's blinking light caught her attention again. She may as well clear the messages.

"Carley, this is Dr. Kin—" She pressed the Erase button.

"If you're there, I need you to pick up." Erase.

"Miss Reed, this is Stanley Ma—" Erase.

Too late her mind registered the baritone drawl. In all the emotional turmoil of the day, her mind had simply shelved the news of her grandmother's death. She returned to the living room and took the two business cards from the coat folded across the back of the chair. The attorney's card listed both office and home telephone numbers. Her finger was poised over the dial buttons when she considered the time difference between California and Mississippi. Two hours, three? Whichever was correct, it was at least 9:45 P.M. on Mr. Malone's end. She propped his card against the telephone. She would have to wait until tomorrow afternoon.

Sleep was again elusive for hours, in spite of medication, and she was too exhausted to get up and reverse the bedding. She woke to the telephone's ringing, five minutes before her clock radio was set to go off. *Dr. Kincaid,* she thought, trying to clear the fog from her mind as her feet felt for slippers. Thankfully, no headache. She reached the kitchen as the baritone drawl from the night before was speaking through the answering machine.

"Miss Reed, this is Stanley Malone, in Tallulah, Mississippi. Would you please give me a ring when—"

"Hello, Mr. Malone," Carley said, snatching up the receiver. "I'm sorry I didn't call yesterday."

"There's no need to apologize, Miss Reed. I'm just glad Mr. Wingate found you. And *I'm* sorry about your grandmother. Miz Walker was a fine lady."

"Was she?" Carley asked, a little surprised by the wishfulness in her own voice.

"She certainly was. And she left you her house and most of its furnishings. And some money, in the neighborhood of a hundred and sixty thousand dollars."

Carley pulled a chair from the table and sank into it. Surely her sluggish mind had misinterpreted. "Did you just say a hundred and sixty thousand?"

"Before certain expenses, but those are comparatively minimal. I gather most of the estate comes from what remained from your grandfather's life insurance."

"How did he die?"

"Heart attack, same as Miz Walker."

Tears welled up in Carley's eyes. "They didn't even know me."

"That wasn't your doing, Miss Reed," he said with sympathetic tone.

"I could have tried harder. All I did was send a note after my mother died. It probably didn't even reach my grandmother."

"But it did. She had asked the people to whom she sold the house in Washington to forward any mail addressed to her, just in case your mother or you would wish to contact her. It was thoughtful of you to send it."

"Thoughtful," Carley echoed bitterly, a lump rising in her throat.

"She never blamed you, Miss Reed," Mr. Malone said. "If anything, she blamed herself."

Carley wiped her eyes. "For what?"

There was a hesitation. "I don't wish to speak ill of the dead. . . ."

"My mother, you mean? Nothing would surprise me about her. Tell me."

Over the line came the sound of his throat clearing. "The Walkers attempted to gain legal custody of you when you were very young, thereby causing your mother to flee Washington. At least when your mother lived nearby, they were able to see that you were clothed and fed properly. To a degree. She . . . apparently used you as leverage sometimes."

"I can believe that," Carley said flatly.

"I'm sorry to hear it." His voice became businesslike again, but in a gentle way. "Would it be possible for you to come down here and settle the estate?"

"Can it not be done long-distance?" Carley asked. Too late she realized how cold her tone sounded. But then, her only link with Tallulah, Mississippi, had been deceased for three months.

She was about to explain herself when he said, with no judgment in his voice, "Yes, that's an option. You would simply need to retain an attorney on your end. We have a couple of fine Realtors here who can sell the house and oversee shipping the furnishings to you or send them to a consignment shop here in Tallulah. But it was Miz Walker's deepest wish that you come have a look at the house before you dispose of it."

"Well, of course. If that was what she wished. But did she say why?"

"I believe it comforted her to know that you would have a reason to meet your relatives."

"What relatives? My mother was an only child."

"But your grandmother wasn't. Her sister, Helen Hudson, was the one who persuaded Miz Walker to move here and help her run her little antique shop. And the Hudsons' youngest daughter and her husband and two boys live here as well."

"My mother never mentioned any family besides my grandparents." That information changed everything. The cord stretched as she walked over to the calendar on the refrigerator door. Her students would be on a field trip to Chabot Space and Science Center in Oakland on Thursday, the thirtieth. And she would probably have no problem getting permission for a substitute teacher for Friday, given that the date was over two weeks away. That would allow four days, two for traveling. She asked, "Would the end of the month be all right, if I can clear it with my boss?"

"That would just be fine, Miss Reed," he said warmly. "Just give me a ring when you've made the arrangements."

chapter 3

Long-standing frugal habits died hard. By Friday, when it had finally sunk in that her financial situation was about to improve dramatically, Carley still walked to her usual stop at the corner of Market and Grant, rode Muni Rail Bus #5 to McAllister and Fillmore Streets to catch #22 to Fillmore and Broadway, then another two blocks on foot.

She traded good-mornings with faculty members on her way to the classroom with briefcase and mug of tea. At first bell, fourteen chattering homeroom students filtered through the doorway and soon settled down to discuss Arthur Miller's *The Crucible*. American Literature II—Twentieth-Century Literature was an honors class made up of seniors focused upon getting into Ivy League colleges.

"Why do you think John Proctor did not wish to be involved when the girls started making accusations?" she asked, standing before the rows of desks.

Three hands raised. She called upon Vishal Patel in the second row.

"Inertia," he said, then frowned at the laughter his answer prompted.

Carley smiled at the student, son of Indian immigrants. "Would you care to explain?"

He nodded. "Why is it that so many people don't vote? Inertia. They don't want to be involved with anything outside their comfortable routines."

Five hands launched and a debate began. Sometimes heated, but mannerly for the most part. Were every class like this one,

Carley thought as the students filed out of class, she would have no complaints about teaching.

But it had taken her only a few months out of college to realize the truth of what she had heard during the course of her education studies; classes have personalities. The seventeen students entering the room and filling the desks could not have been more different than those of the first hour. Or at least the majority. Those who wished to learn kept low profiles, more afraid of their peers' scorn than a teacher's disappointment.

And the ringleader was Ryan Ogden. He did not even meet her eyes as he approached to drop his rewritten composition on a corner of her desk. Tall and tanned, he took nothing seriously except for soccer, cheerleaders, and his midnight blue BMW 330Ci convertible. But then, why should he care about his studies when no one at Emerson-Wake dared hold him accountable? Teachers were a dime a dozen. Multimillionaire contributors were rare.

The three other students who had cheated placed their compositions in the same spot, with only Erin Baine mustering at least a sheepish look. But no notes of apology materialized.

Was she even surprised? Carley blamed herself. From the first day she had felt intimidated to be standing in front of students who paid more for tennis shoes and pocket computers than she paid for rent. She was able to hide that anxiety fairly well. Or so she had thought. But she made the mistake of pretending not to notice little challenges of authority, for fear that she would have to impose discipline and ruin the rapport she thought they had. Like predators, they had smelled the fear, and it was downhill from there.

"Why do you suppose Shelley's earliest works were so dark?" she asked after reading aloud the first eight lines of *Queen Mab* while the students presumably followed in their texts.

"Because his parents named him *Shelley*." This quip did not come from Ryan Ogden, but it may as well have, for the speaker was a lesser player on the soccer team who twisted around to look at the back row for approval.

"That was his *surname*, Clayton." Her voice was shrill to her own ears, over the guffaws. "His given name was *Percy*."

She regretted those words as soon as they left her mouth, for the next wave of laughter led to socializing.

"Class, I would appreciate your attention!" she said above the din, advancing to just inches from the front-row desks.

There was an encouraging little lull, into which she interjected, "Why does Shelley refer to sleep as 'death's brother'?"

Riley Runnels continued showing off an ankle tattoo to Daniel Hall. Shawn Armstrong was mouthing something across the room to Tiffany Giles. In the third row, a hand crept upward.

"Yes, Alton?" Carley said.

A few heads turned in that direction. Crimson stained the boy's peach-fuzz cheeks. Like Carley, Alton was new to Emerson-Wake, his father having transferred from a computer-networking company in San Jose to head a similar company in San Francisco. Shyness and an extra eighty pounds doomed Alton to social ostracism. But he said, bravely, "Because they're related, in a way. Both overtake us, sooner or later."

Carley nodded. For Alton's sake, she did not allow *too* much approval to enter her expression. "Overtake us?"

"You can only fight sleep for so long. It's the same with death."

"How do we fight death?" Carley asked, pretending not to notice a hushed conversation going on in the last row or the odor of an open bottle of nail polish.

"With pills and doctor visits and stuff like that." Alton replied, sitting a little straighter. After a second's thought he added, "And exercise."

"You could sure use some!" came from the back row.

The laughter was explosive and cruel. Alton shrank into his chair as much as his girth would allow. Even from several feet away, Carley could see tears glisten in his eyes. Ryan Ogden smirked as Mark Green leaned to pound his shoulder.

"And you could use some manners, you arrogant jerk," she muttered, as laughter snowballed into socializing.

Only a few of the students in the front row heard, and they gaped up at her after some hushed whispers.

"Sh-h-h!" someone hissed. Murmurs rippled along the rows, faces turned to stare. Ryan Ogden ceased chatting with his girl-friend to send Carley a puzzled look.

"What did you say?" he demanded, eyes narrowing.

"She called you a jerk." A stage whisper from one of Ryan's toadies.

Silence dropped into the classroom like a lead soccer ball.

Carley felt her heart pounding in her chest. She scolded herself, *Why couldn't you keep your mouth shut?*

A corner of Ryan's mouth quirked.

She could read his mind. He had decided that this was some-thing he would enjoy. He held absolute power. Everyone in the room knew it. Carley had crossed a line she should not have crossed, but perhaps—just perhaps—she could keep her job if she were to kiss his Birkenstock loafers and beg forgiveness.

Not for a million dollars!

"And it's a shame, with all you have going for you," she said evenly. How ironic, that in this moment all second-hour ears were finally tuned in her direction. *I should have done this on the first day.*

She was not finished. "What would you do if you didn't have an old man fighting your battles? If you weren't allowed to get away with cheating? You haven't a clue what the *real* world is like."

"Oh, and you have, Little Miss Schoolteacher?" he said with brows raised mockingly.

"More than you can know."

He muttered something back, too low for her ears to catch, but the titillated shock on the faces in his immediate vicinity gave her a clue.

Suddenly Carley saw herself as if she were a fly on the ceiling. Here she stood trading insults with a boy whose popularity would only increase because of the altercation. As for warning about the real world, Ryan Ogden and his ilk had no need to worry. Wealth insulated them from that world and protected them from consequences in this one. Family donations would ensure acceptance in at least some private college, as well as into the best fraternities and sororities. Those same financial connections would propel them up corporate ladders or into profitable marriages, and into homes on golf courses.

Only the Alton Terrises would still have to struggle.

She felt immense regret for adding to the boy's already low status, but dared not do further damage by sending him an apologetic look. The students were still staring, as quiet as held breath, hoping for more fodder for hallway gossip.

She would not oblige them. She went to her desk and pulled out the top drawer. Conversations began with renewed vigor. Hostility rolled towards her in waves. But it did not matter. Three minutes were all she needed. Long enough to pack her personal belongings into her briefcase, slip on her coat, and walk to the door. Then they would be out of her life for good.

Still, her heart sank at the sounds of applause and hoots as she stepped out into the hall. The door to the history classroom opened. Fellow teacher James Hurley stuck his crew-cut head out and eyed the briefcase in her hand. "Is there a problem?"

"Not anymore. I'm going home," she replied, moving to the far side of the hall, half afraid he would somehow force her back into the classroom.

Calm voice, calm voice, Carley ordered herself on her way through the outer office. She ignored Faye's elevated eyebrows and subsequent "Carley?"

Dr. Kincaid had the telephone receiver to her ear. She looked up and said into it, "Pardon me, but something's just come up and I'm going to have to call you back. Yes, I have your number."

"What is it, Carley?" she said after breaking the connection.

"You'd better send Melinda to my classroom."

"What do you mean? What happened?"

"I called Ryan Ogden a jerk."

"You *what?*"

"I know, it was childish. But he humiliated Alton Terris." She took in a deep breath. "I appreciate your hiring me, Dr. Kincaid. But if you have any compassion, you'll call Alton's parents and recommend they put him in a school that doesn't cater to bullies."

The headmistress pushed out her chair and stood, color flooding her face so that her lipstick looked ghostly white. "How dare you . . ."

"Then I'll do it myself. I quit, by the way. But when the general calls, tell him you fired me. May as well make yourself look good."

Carley had not raised her voice during the whole exchange. Still, in the outer office, Faye gaped up at her as if she had lost her mind. "Oh, lower your eyebrows," Carley muttered on her way past her desk. "You're getting wrinkles."

Anger-fueled adrenaline propelled her through the gates. By the time she reached the McAllister-Fillmore stop, she felt as if she had set aside a heavy load.

I never have to go back! So what if teaching jobs were hard to come by in January? She was about to inherit a hundred and sixty thousand dollars! If she had to wait tables for a while, so be it. Some of her fondest memories were of the bustle and aromas and interaction with customers at DeLouches. A break from teaching would be refreshing, and in upscale restaurants, tips were nothing to sneeze at.

She telephoned Mr. Malone from the desk wedged into a corner of her living room. "Would it be all right if I flew down there on Monday?"

"The twentieth?"

Carley smiled at the surprise in his voice. Her initial impulse had been to try to book a flight that very afternoon, but she supposed she should take a couple of days to wash clothes and pack, bring refrigerator perishables to Mrs. Kordalewski, inform her landlord, and arrange for the post office to hold her mail. "I've had some free time fall into my lap."

"That'll be just fine," he said warmly. "Have you booked your flight?"

"I wanted to check with you first."

"I appreciate that. But we're pretty flexible down here."

"Then I'll get on the Internet and call you back."

But first, she had another call to make. After two rings, a woman with a Hispanic accent answered. Carley identified herself and was asked to wait. Mrs. Terris's voice came on a minute later. "Yes? Miss Reed?"

Carley knew Jan Terris fairly well. She volunteered in the library on Mondays and Wednesdays, obviously and mistakenly hoping this would help her son fit in.

"Alton had good friends back in San Jose," Mrs. Terris said after Carley relayed the facts to her. A sigh came through the line. "He begs us every day to let him move in with his grandparents during the school months. It's tearing me up. But shouldn't he be learning to face problems instead of running away from them?"

Oh, that poor boy, Carley groaned inside. So just throw him to thugs, so he can spend his adult life trying to overcome the emotional bruises and inferiority complex?

"Mrs. Terris, imagine yourself working in an office where your co-workers take great pleasure in tormenting you. Would you stay in the interest of learning to face problems? Or find a job in a friendlier environment?"

"I would leave," came back to her ears, just above a whisper.

"Why do we force children to eat garbage we wouldn't eat?"

A silence, followed by a crisp "Thank you for calling, Miss Reed."

Carley's heart sank.

But her spirits soared when Mrs. Terris said, "I have to go get my son now."

Replacing the receiver, Carley sat back in her chair and

concentrated on breathing deeply, slowing down the adrenaline rush. She would not have to live with the guilt of knowing she had made Alton's school days at Emerson-Wake even more difficult. Was she being vindictive? She did not think so. Were Alton her son, she would hope someone would care enough to do the same.

She turned on her computer. She had never been inside an airport, nor did she know where Tallulah was located. But she knew how to navigate the Internet. In less than a minute, she discovered that Tallulah's closest commercial airport with flights from San Francisco was in Jackson, Mississippi.

Frontier Airlines offered the cheapest round-trip ticket, leaving at 6:35 Monday morning. The trip would take over nine hours, counting layovers in Denver and Houston, and the two-hour time difference would put her in Jackson after five in the evening.

How long to stay? Surely the legal issues and becoming acquainted with relatives could be taken care of in one week. If they turned out to be anything like her mother, a week would be too long.

She chewed her lip, finger poised on the computer mouse. Two weeks? If Tallulah proved intolerable, she could simply return to Jackson, check into a cheap hotel, and vegetate. Read novels. Rent movies. Find a Kinko's or library and update her résumé.

Ten days, she thought, compromising. And once she entered her Visa information and clicked the mouse again, the deed was done. No time to entertain doubts.

She rang Mr. Malone's office on the cordless telephone. A female voice asked her name and said, "I'm going to have to put you on hold for just a second, honey."

Carley smiled. The image her mind conjured belonged more to old antebellum movies than to the twenty-first century—the receptionist in a sprigged gown, fanning herself while sipping coffee from a flowered Wedgwood cup.

Elevator music gave way to Mr. Malone's courtly drawl. "You've bought your ticket, Miss Reed?"

Now in motion, Carley's mind next pictured a Colonel Sanders clone. White suit and goatee, and smiling eyes. The image evaporated as she gave her attention back to the matter at hand. "I'm afraid I won't be in Jackson until Monday evening. May we meet on Tuesday?"

"Absolutely. Now, if you'll just give me your flight information, we'll meet—"

"That's very kind of you, but I'll be renting a car." In the space between *car* leaving her mouth and a breath entering, she was certain he was about to protest. Preemptively she said, "It'll be fun to drive again. I sold my car before I left Sacramento."

Actually, the 1989 Toyota Camry had died of natural causes and went to a junk dealer. But the two hundred dollars she was paid still qualified it as "sold."

"Then you would be wise to spend the night in Jackson, rather than be on unfamiliar roads after dark. The car rental people can direct you to a good hotel. And bring warm clothes. The thermometer dipped down to twenty-one last night."

She thanked him and asked when she should come by his office. He replied that one o'clock would give her ample time to drive down and have lunch. "I would invite you to join Loretta and me, but we already have a luncheon engagement. There's Dixie Burger and Tommy's Pizza on the south end of town, but I recommend Corner Diner. You'll see it on your left, about halfway down Main Street."

Carley wheeled her carry-on bag from Jackson International Airport Terminal, meeting forty-five-degree breezes scented with jet fuel instead of the magnolias she had hoped for. At the Budget rental counter, a woman with mahogany skin handed her the keys to a cherry red Chevrolet Cavalier and recommended the Pine Belt Inn. "It's just off I–55, honey. And you can get a nice room for about seventy dollars."

There it was. The "honey" again. Were all Southerners as quaint and accommodating?

The brunette behind the hotel counter dispelled that notion. "You want two doubles or a king?" she asked, annoyed at having her telephone conversation interrupted. Nonetheless the room was clean, and the king-size bed seemed like such an extravagance that the first thing Carley did was stretch out on it crosswise just to see how it felt. She ate a foot-long turkey sandwich from the Subway next door, showered, and then propped herself upon pillows to watch the Food Channel on cable, another extravagance.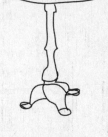

Tuesday morning when her eyes met the 9:08 A.M. on the clock radio, she bolted up in bed. *Time difference*, she remembered. Her body clock was set at seven. After a hurried shower, she pulled on her spice-colored marled turtleneck and tan corduroy slacks and draped her black wool coat across her purse on the Cavalier's passenger seat. The morning clerk made up for his predecessor's rudeness by showing

Carley the route to Tallulah on the map from Budget Rental.

"You'll go about seventy miles once you're on the highway," the older man drawled, a finger tracing the red line. "Be sure you keep it under sixty-five, now. The law's been crackin' down on speeders, on account of them lumber trucks barreling through."

Mississippi in the grip of winter was greener than Carley had imagined. Highway 49 South unrolled like a great gray ribbon, over low rolling hills with red clay banks and winding rivers with white sandy banks, past fruit stands and cattle grazing in pastures of emerald rye grass, and through pine forests and little towns with names like Magee, Florence, and Mount Olive.

At 11:15, Carley was starting to wonder if the morning clerk had given her the wrong directions, but then, through her windshield she read the sign *Poloma River* attached to a bridge over water the color of weak tea. Fifty feet or so past the bridge rose another sign: *Tallulah. Population 1,280.*

Finally! Carley thought. In her haste, she had not taken advantage of the hotel's complimentary breakfast and had simply brewed a cup of tea in the room microwave to have with a package of airline peanuts, so she was ready for lunch.

Signs of urbanization cropped up—a Dollar General store and Henderson's Grocery. The Old Grist Mill restaurant looked promising, but the parking lot was empty. The highway rose ahead to a flashing light at the crest of a hill, then sloped down and melded into Main Street. Flanking both sides behind parallel-parked automobiles were attached shops of weathered brick and stucco and wood. Stenciled onto wide windows or etched into signboards were such names as *Odds & Ends, Peggy's Pastimes, Corner Shoppe Antiques.* Canopies stretched out over boarded sidewalks upon which a surprising number of people strolled in and out of shops.

To her left, two blocks past the stoplight, rose a modest-sized white Greek Revival building with four columns: *Tallulah Town Hall* read the bronze sign. And just beyond, on the opposite corner, a brick building with *Corner Diner* stenciled upon both windows. Tables and people were visible through the glass.

"Not a moment too soon," Carley murmured, waiting for a blue truck to pass so that she could make the left turn. She drove past Tallulah Courthouse and nosed the Cavalier into a space across from a Laundromat with *Kangaroo Washaroo* on the signboard. She was digging in her purse for change when it struck her that there were no meters. She stepped away from the car feeling like a privileged lady.

The diner's interior was quite expansive. Green-checked vinyl covered two dozen or more square tables and booths, most occupied. Men outnumbered women by a fraction. Carley had halfway expected farmer-types in overalls, but the only person thus clad came around from behind the cash register counter—a young woman with short brown hair and silver hoop earrings the size of bracelets. She led Carley to a small table and handed her a well-worn menu covered in plastic. Despite the bent corners and an ink stain, everything listed looked delicious in Carley's state of starvation. Except for the fried chicken liver special.

"What would you like to drink, honey?" asked the waitress, a stout woman with graying hair caught up in a ponytail. She wore a green striped apron over a pink T-shirt and jeans.

Carley smiled at the third *honey* to meet her ears in two days. "A Coke, please." What she really wanted was tea, but she did not care for iced and did not see "hot" on the menu. When the waitress returned, Carley ordered meat loaf, mashed potatoes, gravy, and green beans. Comfort food.

With only three waitresses, service was slow, but no customer seemed anxious. Neither was Carley, for she had plenty of time. She scanned faces, careful not to stare. Were any of her relatives here? Would she discover, when they were finally introduced, that they had lunched only a few feet apart?

She looked to her right. Two men in light-gray police uniforms shared a booth with a woman with shoulder-length brown hair. The older policeman and the woman sat with elbows touching and plates of food before them. The younger man was eating a sandwich from a brown bag. He looked about Carley's age. But the tanned face, close-cropped sandy hair, eyebrows, and lashes made it hard to guess his age.

Watching the three converse like old friends, Carley was seized by a wave of loneliness. Puzzling. Having spent most of her life watching out for herself, she could usually sit among strangers without feeling alienated. And being raised in such a roughshod way toughened a person in some aspects.

She imagined the loneliness was because she owned property here, had relatives here, but did not belong to this town or to these people. A year ago that would not have bothered her. A person with roots firmly planted elsewhere did not have to grieve over not belonging to some temporary place. But losing a mother—such as she was—and now the act of quitting her job had shaken those roots once firmly embedded in California soil. Did she belong anywhere?

Stop thinking that way! she ordered herself. She had set out on an adventure. Once she met Mr. Malone and her faceless relatives, she would feel more at home, have a pleasant stay, and then return to San Francisco to start sending out résumés.

The waitress brought a platter of food large enough to feed two people and refilled Carley's glass. "Enjoy your meal, honey," she said. The meat loaf was tasty and the potatoes fresh instead of instant, with real butter and bits of pulp, the way she liked them. But the green beans were canned, cooked too long, and tasted strongly of bacon grease. The DeLouches' chef would have had a conniption, she thought.

Every table was occupied now. Two men waited just inside the door to be seated. Scraps of unhurried conversation met Carley's ears. Vowels were fluidly elongated and sometimes even two distinct sounds, such as a mother addressing a small tot as "Be-in," and a man ordering a double portion of "co-urn bread." The occasional *g* was dropped, as when her waitress told someone that her father had had to stop "drivin'" after dark because of his eyes. And an extra *r* cropped up now and again, as when the busboy called to the cashier that the booth by the "winder" was cleared.

She sensed someone watching, looked to her right and met the blue eyes of the sandy-haired policeman. He gave her a sheepish little smile and turned back to his companions. Embarrassed as well, Carley gave attention to her own meal. She consumed half the meat loaf, a token couple of green beans, and all of the potatoes— and contemplated ordering more on the side. When she ventured a glance to the right again, the trio had been replaced by a young man and woman.

The waitress gave her directions to Mr. Malone's office. For the courtesy, Carley left a four-dollar tip even though her check only amounted to $7.50. She took her place beside three patrons waiting at the register. Absently she studied a bulletin board positioned behind the counter at eye level. Tacked to the cork were business cards, advertisements for the Lion's Club's pancake breakfast, a rummage sale in the fellowship hall of First Methodist, the Tallulah High School basketball schedule, a handwritten sheet offering free puppies, and another offering piano lessons. A flyer topped by a color-copied photograph of a woman drew Carley's attention. The woman had coffee-colored skin and curly black hair mussed a bit, as if by the wind. She was smiling, both hands wearing gardening gloves and holding a tray of what appeared to be tomato seedlings.

Large-font words beneath the photograph read:

$5,000 Reward!
for information leading to the arrest and conviction
of
the driver of a red sports automobile
responsible for the hit-and-run death of
Gweneth Brown Stillman
on June 14, 1997

Tallulah, Mississippi
Antique Dealers Association

What a shame, Carley thought. And a double shame, that in almost six years the driver had not been brought to justice, for the poster would surely not still be hanging if that were so.

"Help you, ma'am?"

After the cashier handed back change from a twenty, Carley stepped again onto the sidewalk. 10:50, her watch said, which translated into 12:50 central standard time.

She started the Cavalier and continued in the same direction to circle around the back as the waitress had advised. Fourth Street was shaded with magnolia trees with waxy leaves, long-needle pines, gnarled live oaks, and the bare, moss-draped limbs of red oaks. The majority of houses were wood frame with porches, but no two were alike. Picket fences enclosed some lawns. A brownish-green Christmas tree with scattered bits of tinsel lay between sidewalk and street. A man tossed pinecones into a basket beside a pale pink stucco house. Another walked a golden retriever down a sidewalk. A woman unloaded groceries from the trunk of a car in a driveway.

Fourth Street ended at the stop sign at Poloma Street. Tallulah Library, with painted gray clapboard and rust-colored shutters stood to her left. Across the street were the long red-brick building, playground, parking lot, and gymnasium of Tallulah High. Carley thought of the good students she had left. Did they feel betrayed?

How could staying and having a nervous breakdown have helped them? she asked herself.

Moot speculation anyway. Dr. Kincaid would have fired her for the "jerk" episode, had Carley not beat her to the punch by resigning. She turned left in front of the school. The first-hour honors students would probably learn just as much in the capable hands of Melinda Pearson. She found that she did not particularly care who taught the other classes.

Fifth Street had the same flavor as Fourth Street. Frame houses, porches, shade trees. Stanley Malone's office was in a converted yellow frame house. The gravel lot was apparently once a driveway, now widened. She parked a polite distance away from a dark blue

Lincoln Town Car. Stepping across the porch, she opened the wooden door and stepped into a reception area in what was probably once a living room. A coatrack stood to her right. Two green damask settees faced each other; a table held a stack of magazines. A framed print of Van Gogh's *Sunflowers* graced one wall. The floors bordering a red Oriental rug were shiny parquet. Beyond the sitting area was a desk, oak filing cabinet, and a woman watering a large ficus plant. She set the watering can on the top of the filing cabinet.

"You're Miss Walker, aren't you?" she asked, advancing. Before Carley could speak, the woman corrected herself. "I mean, Miss *Reed*."

Carley was not surprised, for Mr. Malone was expecting her. And really, how many clients could he have in such a small town? But just having someone recognize her by name lifted the loneliness a bit. Returning the smile, she said, "Guilty."

They shook hands. The woman had short brown hair flowing from a widow's peak and tucked behind ears with small silver knot earrings. She was petite, with slender wrists. "I'm Loretta Malone, Stanley's wife. And please call me Loretta."

"If you'll call me Carley."

"Good enough. How was your flight?"

"Interesting, but long. I'm glad I thought to bring a book." *Cranford,* by Elizabeth Gaskell, a novel Carley had read in her freshman year of college but which seemed fitting for the occasion, with its sketches of life in a country village.

Loretta nodded. "Losing two hours has some sort of psychological effect. Your trip back will seem much shorter."

"You've been to California?"

"Only to Los Angeles, decades ago when my little sister was trying to break into acting. She couldn't lose the drawl and was hired only once, for a *Shake 'n Bake* commercial. But it was probably for the best. She and her husband own a dinner theater in Branson now."

Already Carley liked Loretta Malone. But then, she was drawn to older women. And remarkably enough, they seemed drawn to her. Janelle Reed, Margarita DeLouche, Georgia Kincaid. Even Mrs. Kordalewski. Did older women possess some sort of maternal radar that honed in on the fact that she was an orphan long before her mother died?

"Your red hair gave you away," Loretta went on. "When Mrs. Walker came to have the will drawn up, she brought a photograph of you as a little girl."

"Really?" Carley longed to see it. There were so few mementos from her childhood, save some uncut sheets of school portraits, with gaps in the years that Linda forgot to send a check before the deadline or simply ignored the order form.

It dawned upon her that the photograph was probably in the house she was inheriting. She had not given it much thought but suddenly was anxious to see it. It was a link to her past—no matter that neither she nor her mother had ever lived there.

"Let's see if Stanley's off the phone," Loretta said, sending a glance toward the buttons on her own telephone. "Good."

Heels clicked as she led Carley to an oak door. She gave it a couple of gentle raps and stuck her head through.

"Miss Reed is here."

"Come on in." A man in an olive dress shirt and striped tie came around his desk. He was not a Colonel Sanders clone after all. A fringe of salt-and-pepper hair circled his scalp from ear to ear, and thinning strands were combed across the top. His nose was slightly bulbous at the tip, and his smile sent crinkles from the corners of his brown eyes to his jawline, like a pair of parentheses. He asked about her flight and offered her the leather chair beside his desk.

Loretta had left the office, but entered again to hand her husband a file. "Would you care for some coffee or tea?"

"Hot tea?" Carley asked hopefully.

"I have Lipton and English Breakfast."

"English Breakfast would be nice. And plain, please."

"Stanley? More coffee?"

"Better not," he said after a longing glance toward a brown mug. He opened the file and perched a pair of reading glasses upon his nose. "My next appointment is at two, so we have plenty of time. There's no reason why we can't look over the will now, as the others have already been taken care of."

"That's fine, thank you," Carley said automatically, as her mind ran over his words. "The others?"

"Your grandmother left some things for other relatives. For example, her 1998 Honda Accord went to one great-nephew, and some money to save for college to another. Some furniture went here and there." His eyes, above the reading glasses, met hers. "But the bulk of the estate still goes to you."

Heat rose to Carley's cheeks. He had misunderstood the reason for her question.

"I'm actually relieved she included them," she said, for she felt a bit like an interloper, inheriting most of the estate over people with greater emotional investments in her grandmother's life. "I just thought all heirs had to be together before a will could be opened."

Mr. Malone smiled. "Ah. Only on television."

"What would have happened if you hadn't found me?"

"Well, there is a provision that everything passes on to your great-aunt Helen's side of the family if you don't come forward to claim your inheritance after seven years. That's the same amount of time necessary for a person to be declared legally dead in Mississippi, by the way."

"Will they be disappointed?"

"On the contrary. Miz Hudson was quite pleased when I informed her we had found you. It was she who advised your grandmother to have me hire a private investigator, back when we were drawing up the will."

The attorney's eyes returned to the open file. "Miz Walker left you one hundred and fifty-nine thousand, four hundred and eight dollars, and forty-three cents on deposit in Lamar County Bank. There is a house at 5172 Third Street, and all its furnishings. She purchased it outright, and so selling it will be easier than a house with a mortgage, if that is what you decide to do."

Of course she would have to sell it. But the thought was unsettling.

"Do you think she would have minded?"

"Not at all. Miz Walker struck me as a very practical person. I recommend Kay Chapman when you're ready to speak with a real estate agent, by the way. I do closings for her. I'll ask Loretta to give you her card."

On cue, his wife returned, perching cup and saucer on the edge of the desk. Carley thanked her and moved both to her left.

"You're left-handed?" Mr. Malone said.

"Yes."

"So am I."

Loretta groaned. "You're not going to give the poor girl *the speech,* are you, Stanley?"

"Of course not," the attorney replied, but the disappointment in his expression betrayed that he had been poised to do that very thing.

"What speech?" Carley asked.

Sending his wife a glance laden with reproach and apology, he said, "It's simply a documented fact that we lefties lose an average of seven years of our lives, just because of the frustrations of living in a world geared to righties."

"Tell that to your Grandpa Malone," Loretta said. "Ninety years old and still mows his own lawn."

"But has he ever tried to use a pair of scissors?" Carley asked. "Or a manual can opener?"

"There you go!" the attorney chortled, and Loretta even smiled.

Carley decided she liked Mr. Malone as well. It took her a little longer with older men, for childhood had left her with a thick streak of cynicism. But even the horror months with Huey Collins had not quenched the longing for a father, which had been with her for as long as she could remember.

When Mr. Malone asked Loretta for one of the Realtor's cards, she offered to go ahead and make the appointment. Through the door came the squeak of a chair and, presently, her barely audible voice. Stanley passed a fee sheet across his desk, showing the hours he had worked for the estate, and payments made to Mr. Wingate, an insurance company for homeowner's insurance, and Lockwood Funeral Home.

"That last statement is so high because they shipped Miz Walker's body up to Washington after the memorial service, to be buried alongside her husband. He had a prearranged policy, so there's no bill from up there."

"I see." Carley stifled the surge of disappointment by telling herself that the memory she would carry back to California would be of where her grandmother had actually spent the last four years of her life, rather than of a headstone.

"You okay?" the attorney asked, studying her.

"Yes."

He nodded and continued. "There is no inheritance tax in Mississippi on estates less than a million dollars. Combined, everything reduces the cash portion of your estate to one hundred and thirty-nine thousand, seven hundred and thirty-three dollars." He smiled. "And six cents."

Carley shook her head in wonder. "And I was hoping for enough to pay off my student loan and credit card."

"I gather it's enough to do that?"

"Way more."

"Well, you'll still want to check those figures yourself. I'll give you a calculator and a little privacy."

"I'm sure they're accurate," Carley said.

"Never assume anything when you're dealing with finances, Miss Reed," he advised, pushing out his chair. "Money can bring out the worst—in people you would never suspect."

chapter 5

"Is it all right if Kay Chapman comes by the house at nine in the morning?" Loretta asked after Carley signed the papers.

"That's fine, thank you."

"Very good. Let's take my car to your new house, and I'll bring you back for yours later."

Loretta steered the Town Car on what she called the back way, toward the school, then south, followed by another right turn onto Third Street. She turned into the driveway of the third house on the right, sending a trio of squirrels scattering. Carley stepped out of the car.

The house was white frame with forest green shutters. Concrete steps rose to the left side of the covered porch, flanked by two iron pots of winter-blooming yellow daffodils. Above the steps was a white door with long glass panels on either side and a transom overhead. At the right end of the porch, a wooden swing hung by chains, faced sideways in front of a window.

A delightful aroma wafted Carley's way. She drew in a lungful and turned to Loretta.

"Sweet olive," Loretta said before she could ask. She nodded toward a tall green shrub with tiny white blossoms between the driveway and house. "They bloom in winter, and folks plant them by their porches because they smell so good. By the way, the Paynes live there on your left. Stanley gave them a key and asked them to keep an eye on the house. They refused payment out of respect for your grandmother."

Carley looked at the two-story pale green wooden house, the empty driveway parallel to hers. "How kind. I'll be sure to thank them."

On the porch, Loretta unlocked the door and handed Carley a ring with two identical keys attached. She smiled. "You first."

"All right." Carley stepped into a long living room with braided rug on a hardwood floor, blue toile print sofa and wing chairs heaped with pillows, a coffee table and two end tables with lamps. Floral prints decorated ten-feet-high buttery yellow walls.

Loretta, coming in behind her, flicked on the light switch. "Good. I called the utility company yesterday. You should have gas and water too."

"How thoughtful of you."

"That's the beauty of small-town living. But I'm afraid the telephone goes through Hattiesburg. They can't turn it back on until next week, so I said never mind. All you young girls have cell phones anyway."

"Actually, I don't," Carley said, smiling at the "young girl" reference. A cell phone was one of those expenses she could not justify in the past, not with debts still hanging over her. "But I'm sure there are pay phones?"

"In the library. And you're welcome to come to the office and use ours." Loretta ran a finger through the dust on an end table. "That's what happens when a house sits empty. I'll give you the number for my cleaning service if you like."

"I kind of enjoy dusting."

"Then you'll have a good time." She motioned to a brown space heater sitting out a bit from the back wall. "We have more cold weather coming. Do you know how to light them?"

Carley was vaguely familiar with their workings, for a couple of the houses her mother had rented had had them. "I think so."

"I'll just refresh your memory before we leave. I'm sure there are matches in the kitchen. The piano must have sat between the windows. Mrs. Walker left it to the senior citizen center. That's where her television went too."

They meandered about the house. Leading off the living room was a bedroom with a black iron bedstead, a chair upholstered in sage green, and a chest of drawers.

Beyond that door, a short hallway ended at a bathroom, with doors on each adjacent side. The room to Carley's right had no bed, just a long table, a wooden chair, and tall piece of furniture with drawers and a mirrored door. "That's a chifforobe," Loretta said. "They're very sought after by antique collectors. This was probably Mrs. Walker's sewing room. I do recall that the serger machine went to Mrs. Hudson."

Through the open doorway of the opposite bedroom, Carley looked at the afghan folded over a quilt at the foot of a cream-colored iron bedstead. A hairbrush and bottle of Jergens lotion sat upon an old bowfront dresser with round mirror. Goose bumps prickling her arms, she turned and walked back down the hall with Loretta following.

Against the back wall of the living room, an open arched doorway led to a kitchen three times as roomy as the one in Carley's apartment. The refrigerator doors were propped open with a broom. Loretta helped Carley roll it out so that she could plug it in.

"The china cabinet must have gone here," Loretta said of the empty space beside it. That went to Sherry."

"Sherry?"

"I forgot, you're still learning who everyone is. Sherry Kemp is Mrs. Hudson's youngest daughter. I'm not sure how many other children there are." She twisted the cold water faucet. After a sputtering noise, water ran from the tap. "Good. But you'll need to leave it dripping during nights when the weather's below freezing. I noticed a thermometer on a porch post."

"Dripping?" Carley joined her at the sink.

"Just enough to keep it moving." She turned the cold water so that a long drip plopped from the tap every half second or so. "Most frame houses have exposed pipes. They're probably wrapped, but even so, you don't want to take a chance on their freezing and bursting."

Beyond the kitchen was a wide sunny room housing a sagging sofa and chair of faded green velveteen, and a washer and dryer. Carley was looking out the back window when she heard, "Come see, Carley."

She followed the voice to her grandmother's bedroom. Loretta stood in front of a chest of drawers against the near wall, out of sight range from the hall. Three photographs in identical silver frames were arranged on an embroidered scarf. Loretta handed her one of two white-haired women with arms linked, standing in front of a shop window. One woman smiled as if on the verge of laughter, the other smiled only with her eyes, as if struggling to maintain decorum for the photographer.

"This is your grandmother," Loretta said, tapping the glass over the more serious-looking woman.

"Really? And my Aunt Helen with her?"

"It is indeed."

The framed portrait in the center was of an older man with strong chin and eyeglasses. "He must be my grandfather."

"Hmm. Probably so." Loretta took it from her and handed her the last frame. "Look at this one."

Linda, smiling and beautiful, stood beside a mechanical horse as she held an unsure-looking red-haired child in the saddle. Tears stung Carley's eyes.

Loretta patted her shoulder. "This isn't the one Mrs. Walker brought to the office. Would you like me to help you look for more?"

As tempting as it was, Carley had a more pressing wish. "Thank you, but I've kept you here long enough. But do you think you could show me where to find my aunt before we go back for my car?"

"Why, of course," Loretta said. "I have all the time in the world. That's the beauty of having your own husband for your boss."

Auld Lang Syne Antiques sat shoulder to shoulder with The Katydid and Three Sisters Antiques, on the west side of Main Street between Second and Third Streets. A bell tinkled softly over the door as Carley followed Loretta inside. Shelves and glass-fronted cases displayed everything from ironware to wooden bowls, depression glass to pottery, toys to silverware. They gave off faintly musty aromas mingled, appropriately, with that of potpourri. At the counter, an angular-faced woman with chestnut hair was wrapping tissue around a bowl and pitcher for a woman wearing a cranberry-colored cloak.

"Pam Lipscomb," Loretta whispered of the woman behind the counter. "Works for Mrs. Hudson. Her daughter's in Iraq, bless her heart."

"Miss Helen?" Pam said over her shoulder.

A curtain moved to the side and a woman of about seventy came through a door carrying a box. "This should do it, Pam."

"We have more customers."

"Oh." The woman handed her assistant the box, looked up, and went stone-still.

"Hi, Mrs. Hudson," Loretta said, gently nudging Carley forward. "This is Carley."

The customer turned with bemused expression as Carley's great-aunt hurried around the counter and opened her arms. "Oh, goodness, child!"

"It's good to meet you, Aunt Helen," Carley said, caught off guard by the embrace.

"And it's wonderful to meet you." Aunt Helen's silvery hair smelled of a fresh perm, her shoulders of Estée Lauder's White Linen. "What I wouldn't give to have Cordelia here!"

"I'm sorry I never . . ."

"Shush now. None of that." She stepped back a bit, holding Carley at arm's length. She was full-figured, an inch or so taller than

Carley, and wore a black wool sweater and gray skirt that stopped between calf and ankles. Below the tear-lustered hazel eyes, her soft cheeks were faintly rouged. Pearl earrings clasped her earlobes.

"Aren't you pretty as a picture!" she exclaimed. In spite of the "shush," her voice bore no trace of a Southern accent. It had a strained texture that sometimes comes with age, but was nonetheless pleasing to the ears.

"Mr. Malone said you talked Grandmother into looking for me. Thank you for that."

"Oh, but it didn't take much talking, child."

It was as if a piece of the hodgepodge puzzle that had made up Carley's life so far snapped into place. She had a history extending beyond Linda. And perhaps it was a good history after all. Her happiness mingled with sadness . . . over what might have been. But this was not the time for rumination. Not with her aunt's arm around her shoulders.

"Will you be comfortable in the house?" Aunt Helen asked. "Because you're more than welcome to stay with us."

Carley had to think about that one. The oddness of staying in an unfamiliar house where her grandmother had died, versus a home that would surely be as warm and hospitable as was her aunt. But for over a week?

She had only one experience as a houseguest. During her first year on staff at Sacramento High, co-worker Diane Paxton invited her to share Easter vacation in her parents' rustic cabin near Lake Tahoe. The Paxtons were lovely people, but the lone bathroom was an add-on—right off the living room, with a two-inch gap at the bottom of the door. Evenings trips to the bathroom were torture, with six people sitting about a Monopoly board and no TV set to provide background noise and at least the illusion of privacy.

That would probably not be a problem at Aunt Helen's. But what if her husband smoked? She could not afford to spend a couple of days in bed because of a migraine. And once she accepted, she would be locked in for the remainder of her visit. It seemed safer just to thank her and say, "I'll get more work done at the house if I just stay there."

"I understand," Aunt Helen said.

The bell jingled. Two women entered, chatting. Aunt Helen excused herself and went over to greet them. Loretta nodded at Carley as if to say, *Perhaps we should leave?*

Carley nodded back. As the women started browsing shelves, Aunt Helen returned to invite her for supper the next day. "I wish we could tonight, but Patrick—our grandson—has an away game in Purvis. You're more than welcome to come with us."

"Thank you, but tomorrow would be great," Carley said. "I can take my time unpacking and make some plans."

"Of course. I'll just come for you after I close up shop."

"How about if I just drive myself? Then no one has to bring me home."

Which meant she could leave as soon as politely possible if the evening proved a disappointment. But she hoped that would not happen.

Aunt Helen showed no offense, and took a business card and pen from the counter. "I'll write my address on the back."

"Why don't I just show her?" Loretta offered. "I have to drive her over to the office anyway."

"That's very kind of you," Aunt Helen said, but still handed Carley the card. "Just in case you get lost, dear."

A person would have to have no sense of direction whatsoever for that to happen in this town, but it was nice to be fussed over. Loretta drove back up to Fifth Street and took a left in front of an ice-cream-cone-shaped sign that read *The Sweet Tooth* in front of a white shop. Four houses down, Aunt Helen's was tan brick with white shutters and doors. A black Dodge Ram pickup truck occupied a space in the double carport.

"Mr. Hudson's home," Loretta said, turning the Town Car into the driveway. "Would you like me to introduce you?"

"May we not?" Carley said. "I'd rather wait until Aunt Helen is here."

"I understand." As Loretta backed out the car and nosed it toward Main Street, a yellow sedan came from that direction. The woman behind the wheel and Loretta exchanged waves.

"Do you know everyone in town?" Carley asked.

"Just about."

"That must be nice."

"Mmm-hmm," Loretta said, stopping at the stop sign and looking in both directions. A pickup truck advanced from the north, a red Volkswagen from the south, so she waited. "Most times it is. But with Stanley being the only attorney in town, that's not always nice. Shared inheritances sometimes bring out the worst in people."

"Does he only handle wills and real estate closings?"

"Goodness no. He does it all, even criminal defense. Thankfully, we have so little crime that he hardly ever sees the courtroom." She sighed. "But there are the few rotten apples. A few years ago a minister's wife, Gwen Stillman, who served on the Keep Tallulah Beautiful committee with me, was picking up litter in front of their church when someone in a car hit her and kept on going. Her baby girl was sitting in a stroller just a few feet away . . ."

Her voice trailed to silence as she pressed the gas pedal to cross Main Street.

"I saw the poster in Corner Diner," Carley said.

"They're all over town. People take this very personally. After all this time, it doesn't look like even Dale will solve this one. It had to have been someone passing through, someone who knows to stay clear of here."

Before Carley could ask, Loretta looked at her and said, "Forgive me. Dale Parker is our chief of police *and* statewide hero. He brought in the Highway 98 serial killer seven years ago. You're probably too young to remember, but it was all over the national news."

"I'm afraid I didn't watch much news when I was younger." At eighteen, schooling and work had dominated Carley's life.

"Warren Knap is his name." Loretta pulled up in the driveway of the law office, switched off the key. "He was from Tylertown, mind you. Not here. And his *current* residence is Parchman Prison. He killed four women in five years; three in their houses after following them from businesses along the highway, and another in the woods after she ran out of gas. He left a McComb church secretary for dead with ten stab wounds, but she recovered after weeks in critical care."

"How was he caught?" Carley asked.

"Dale was just a rookie policeman in Hattiesburg—it's a college town thirty miles southeast of here. He recognized the suspect in Shoney's, even though the composite sketches weren't all that detailed, *and* the man was wearing a toupee. Anyway, after Dale brought him in, he could have been elected governor of Mississippi. He was given the Police Medal of Honor and thirty-thousand dollars in award money. Our chief of police was retiring, and so our Board of Aldermen offered him the position."

Carley thought of the uniformed men in Corner Diner. She spoke of the older one, of course.

"He made *Newsweek* after that," Loretta went on. "They said he was the youngest chief of police in the country. Only twenty-two years old at the time."

But then again, he could have been the one with the sack lunch.

Or neither. It really did not matter, although Carley was glad to hear of a monster being put away. But she found herself saying, "There were two police officers in the diner."

"Well, we only have three on the force, and one's a woman. Did one of the men have blonde hair and blue eyes?"

"I think so," Carley said, irritated at herself for being so vague when she knew full well that he did. She thought, *What are you, in the sixth grade? Afraid someone will think you're interested in a boy?*

"That would have been him." Loretta pulled the key from the ignition. "And Stanley heard at the courthouse last week that Dale and his debutante girlfriend in Atlanta had a parting of the ways. I guess it was just too hard, long-distance courting. I'm sure the news has already spread like measles among every eligible woman in the county."

She gave Carley a little smile. "It's a shame you're going back to California. I could introduce you. I just love playing matchmaker."

Carley smiled back. "I wouldn't want all those women mad at me anyway."

As impulsive as the act of flying to Mississippi on practically the spur of the moment was, Carley was an almost obsessive believer in making lists. Seeing her responsibilities in print gave her a measure of feeling in control of her own life. She supposed even some good habits could be gleaned from the flotsam and jetsam of a turbulent childhood.

And so before looking for more photographs and possibly other family mementos, she brought pen and notebook from her purse to the table. As the list grew, she wondered if it could all be done in ten days. Eight, actually, minus travel. She needed to unpack, dust furniture, meet with the real estate agent, find a source for boxes and cartons to pack whatever she decided to ship home, arrange for that shipping, figure out what to do with the rest, and visit the bank to transfer her inheritance to Bank of California.

Shop, she wrote. She could do this tomorrow. This was definitely soup weather, and a big pot of minestrone would last for days. Within her main list, she began a grocery list.

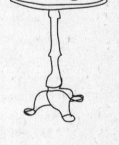

> *canned tomatoes*
> *onions*
> *dried lima beans*

The doorbell interrupted. A slender woman with shoulder-length dark ash-blonde hair introduced herself as Gayle Payne, and held out a dark plastic-wrapped loaf.

"It's zucchini bread. I chaperoned the third grade field trip to the Mennonite bakery today."

"How thoughtful." Carley took the loaf. "Won't you come in?"

"Thank you, but I have to cook supper." She wore a blue denim jacket, white turtleneck, and brown skirt. High cheekbones narrowed her hazel eyes into horizontal crescents, and she had a slight overbite, but nonetheless she was very pretty.

As gracious as her visitor was, Carley felt relieved when she declined her invitation. She did want to finish her list and look for photographs. "I appreciate your looking after the house."

"We were happy to. I'm so sorry about Mrs. Walker. She was a sweet lady."

"Thank you. I'm glad she had good neighbors."

"Oh, *she* was the best neighbor. She didn't fuss about the children's noise, and even let them climb her fig tree. Dean—my husband—wrapped the trunk with an old blanket when the cold snap hit, by the way. And he cut back the muscadine vines after Christmas."

"Muscadine?"

Gayle smiled. "Purple grapes with thick skins. Most people make jelly from them, but they're good for snacking too."

Carley assumed both fig tree and grapevines were in the backyard, which she had yet to explore. *Thank you* seemed suddenly inadequate. "I'd like to cook something for your family one evening and bring it over."

Gayle protested, but feebly, and ended up saying, "I'm sure everyone would love a change from my cooking." She smiled again. "*I* would love a change from my cooking."

"Do you like chicken cacciatore?"

"I'm not sure we've ever had it. So that will make it a double treat."

They agreed upon Thursday, which would give Carley time to shop and orient herself with the kitchen.

"Oh, by the way," Gayle said. "Sherry Kemp still has the key Mr. Malone gave us. Her husband and boys moved some stuff out of the house during Christmas break. She called last night and said you were coming in today and that she would just give it to you."

"Sure, that's fine," Carley said.

Though the refrigerator was empty, the cabinets were fairly well stocked with cans and cartons, as well as a set of copper-bottomed thick stainless cookware. She found tea bags in a canister and took down a mug with *Natchez Trace Parkway* and a tree etched in green. The zucchini bread was moist and laden with raisins and pecan chips. That gave her an idea. She added cream cheese and pecan chips to her grocery list. She would make an Italian cream cake to bring over to Aunt Helen's tomorrow evening.

The second ring of the doorbell came from a woman who introduced herself as Byrle Templeton, from next door opposite the Paynes' side. Bundled in a brown cloth coat, she was stoop-shouldered, with a face as wrinkled as old parchment. Her gray hair was drawn back into a bun and covered with a paisley scarf. She thrust out a plastic grocery bag containing two pint jars.

"Mayhaw jelly," she drawled when Carley took out one with ruby-colored contents. "And the other's figs. I'm eighty-two years old and still do my own cannin'."

Carley could do no less than invite her inside. But she declined.

"My boy, Chester Junior, and his wife, Joy Nell, is carryin' me over to my sister's in Lumberton in a little while. Your grandmother used to give me rides to the senior citizen center every Friday. That's when we do quilting. I can't hold a needle anymore, but I can sort pieces. We sell them at the Fourth of July fair."

"Really? Did my grandmother make the quilts on the beds here?"

"She did." The aged eyes watered. "Don't seem right—her just not getting up one morning like that. I kept pushing the door-bell. . . ."

"I'm glad she had you for a friend," Carley cut in, fearing her visitor would break down into tears.

Mrs. Templeton seemed to draw something from her own reserve. She blinked, nodded, and asked where Carley lived.

"San Francisco."

"My, my. You ever been through one of them earthquakes?"

Carley smiled. "Not any that were strong enough to notice. But I've only lived there six months."

"Well, I don't think I'll be visiting you there. At my age, it's hard enough to stay upright when the ground is still." She declined Carley's offer to escort her home but did consent to having her elbow held down the steps. On the ground, she offered the use of her telephone any time Carley wished.

"Thank you, Mrs. Kordalewski."

"Who?"

"Mrs. *Templeton,*" Carley corrected.

Having had two neighbors call seemed to put a stamp of authenticity on Carley's right to stay. She brought in her bags to the front bedroom. The double bed would not be as luxurious as the Comfort Inn's king-size mattress, but it was more roomy than the single beds and sofas she had slept on from her earliest memories.

She hung some clothing in the empty closet, folded the rest in a drawer, and carried her toiletry case to the bathroom. Lighting the white porcelain wall heater, she wondered if people got used to the inconvenience. But then, not heating the entire house for one person appealed to her innate sense of frugality.

She set her toiletries about on the counter, and smiled at a half empty bottle of White Linen. Which sister had influenced the other one? In the chilly back bedroom, she tried not to imagine her grandmother's lifeless form on the bed. She pulled out a dresser drawer and caught faint aromas of sachet and Downy. Flannel and knit nightgowns were folded with precise corners. Carley ran a hand along their softness.

Three months, she thought with a lump in her chest. Ships passing in the night. What if Mr. Wingate had found her before her grandmother died, *before* she knew anything about the will? Would she have been persuaded to come? She hoped she would have had the decency to do so, especially after learning her grandfather had died earlier.

From the chifforobe she took out a yellowed pasteboard box with *Women's Slippers, Size 8* printed on the end. It had the weight and rustle of papers inside. A peek under the lid was rewarded with the sight of photographs, almost to the top.

She carried her treasure to the kitchen table. Fortunately, names and dates were penned on the backs. Most were of Linda. Even her mother's baby pictures were recognizable from the shining cap of blonde hair. A black-and-white strip from a photograph booth showed a much-younger version of the man in the dresser portrait, pressing cheeks with a pretty young woman with fair hair and a wide smile. *Sterling and Cordelia, 1950* was written in faded blue ink. There were a few black-and-white snapshots of Helen and Cordelia as girls.

Many photographs were of a child with wisps of fiery red hair. Carley came across one of the tot sharing a bench with an older woman who smiled self-consciously for the camera. *Carley and Cordelia, Garfield Park, June 1981* read the back. And there on the seat between them, a small red carton.

Animal crackers, Carley realized. She set that one aside, and when finished looking at the rest, placed it on top of the collection before closing the lid. She would frame it back in California.

Evening had crept up on her, she realized, looking out at the shadowy form of the Payne house from the kitchen window. She still had to dust the furniture. But she had a problem. She had not thought to pack casual clothes for cleaning and packing, so she changed into her plaid flannel pants, the long-sleeve T-shirt she used as a pajama top, and slippers. She found a can of furniture polish beneath the sink. The doorbell rang as she was attempting to get it to spray.

"I'm Ruby Moore, from just across the street" drawled a fortyish woman holding a quart-sized covered casserole by the handles with hot pads. She wore a thick beige fleece jacket over a pink knit sweat suit and tennis shoes. Graying brown hair, cut short in a wedge shape, emphasized her flushed cheeks.

"Please, come in," Carley said with a backward step.

She did, and moved aside so that Carley could close the door. "And I'm so sorry about Miz Cordelia. She was a good neighbor."

"Thank you." Carley introduced herself, though her visitor obviously knew who she was. "May I make you some coffee or tea?"

"I just had a Dr. Pepper. And you look busy."

"I'm *trying* to be busy. The nozzle's clogged."

"That's because it hasn't been used for a while. It happens a lot at my house for the same reason, if you get my meaning. Do you have some rubbin' alcohol and a needle?"

"I saw a safety pin in a dish in the bathroom," Carley said. "I'm not sure about alcohol."

"*All* us *old* people have rubbin' alcohol," Ruby said, with a wink. "I can't stay long. My parents are coming for supper in about an hour. I'd invite you to join us, but they're bringing about three hours' worth of videos of their Florida vacation, and trust me, you'd rather pass. But I have you some chicken-tortilla casserole here."

"Why, thank you." Carley followed her into the kitchen. "I was going to open a can of tuna."

"You're welcome." Ruby set the casserole on the stove. "I hope it's good. I got the recipe off the Internet. Now, go get that pin and alcohol, sweetie."

She was sitting at the table with an empty teacup when Carley returned after finding both items in the bathroom. While the nozzle soaked in a little alcohol, Ruby asked what Carley did in California.

"I'm an English literature teacher," Carley replied.

"Well, we're both in education, aren't we? I work in human resources for the Lamar County School Board."

Partly to deflect questions about teaching, but mostly because she was interested, Carley asked how long Ruby had lived in Tallulah.

"All my life. My daddy has a farm about five miles southwest of town."

"What does the town's name mean?"

Ruby proved herself the right person to ask. "It's Choctaw for 'Leaping Waters' because of the springs about a half mile beyond the middle and high schools. Daddy has a cigar box filled with arrowheads *his* daddy found while plowing his fields, so you know they lived all over here. But the federal government forced out most of the Choctaw to Oklahoma in the early 1800s, and those who stayed didn't do well. Fortunately, I don't think that's the case any more. The tribe owns several businesses around Philadelphia, Mississippi. An industrial park, golf course, and the like."

Ruby fished out the nozzle with two fingers and began working on it with a pin. The town, she explained, started out as a general store at the crossroads of what later became Highway 42 and Main Street, owned by a former Union officer, who decided he had had enough of Minnesota winters. "Addison Lockwood was his name. He married a local farmer's daughter, a Margaret Moore."

"One of your ancestors?" Carley asked.

"My ex-husband Don's. A great-great-great-great aunt or something like that. Our telephone directory—such as it is—has more Lockwoods and Moores than any other name. Even Smith, my maiden name."

She said a town gradually grew around the store, helped along by lumber mills cropping up in the region, and especially when Lovely Lady Lingerie opened up a garment factory in the early 1950s. But Tallulah hit a recession in the late sixties when the factory closed. In the mid-seventies, the remaining residents began meeting in the fellowship hall of First Methodist to figure out a way to revive the economy and stop the exodus of families.

Bart Lockwood, owner of Lockwood Funeral Home, had a vested interest in the matter. He pointed out how a fair number of people still came to shop for antiques at Red Barn Emporium, owned and run by retired Tallulah High School principal, Harold Moore, and his wife, Nadine. Hattiesburg was booming, with its university, hospitals, and industries, as was the gulf coast. There was no lacking for customers in Mississippi. What if more such shops were to open?

Rather than feel threatened, Harold and Nadine understood that more shops would draw more customers, thereby increasing their own business. They gave classes on what to look for during buying trips up north and to Dallas and Atlanta. Landlords realized it was in their best interest to entice budding entrepreneurs into empty buildings by offering extremely favorable terms. Most shops were founded by women whose husbands were already employed, or retirees of both sexes who already had sources of income.

The experiment went dismally slow for three years but then took off after Bill Moyers aired a segment about the Mennonite community and bakery in nearby Columbia, Mississippi, and devoted three minutes to Tallulah and its antique shops.

"There's a plaque in the lobby of Town Hall dedicated to Bart Lockwood," Ruby said, replacing the nozzle onto the can. "But the poor fellow passed away of a stroke before he got to see the results of all his hard work."

She aimed the nozzle at the inside of the cup, gave it a quick spurt, and smiled. "And there you have it."

"I'll remember that trick," Carley said, taking the can from her.

"It also works to switch out a nozzle from a can of hair spray or air freshener," Ruby said, and winked. "But then you don't have an excuse to visit."

By ten o'clock, Carley had finished dusting the furniture and dry mopping the hardwood floors. At ten-thirty she lay curled on her side on the soft mattress of the front bedroom. Loretta had warned against leaving any space heater burning overnight, and so the dark air was growing chill. An owl, perhaps two, hooted from somewhere not far from the east window. But Carley drifted into sleep easily, her stomach filled with offerings from thoughtful neighbors, her body warm beneath a sheet, two blankets, and two quilts stitched by her grandmother's own hands.

Wednesday morning after breakfasting on zucchini bread and tea, Carley showered, applied makeup, and dressed in her V-neck coral sweater and favorite slacks of soft black twill. The clock read 8:30, a half hour before Kay Chapman was to arrive, so Carley pulled on her coat and went through the room off the kitchen, and out the back door.

Slate-colored clouds canopied the sky. The air was colder than yesterday's and smelled of rain. Steps led from a small porch to a patio of old brick, upon which sat two iron and wood-slat benches and a medium-sized round wooden table. Frozen dew glistened on the lawn, where an empty bird feeder hung from a pole, and a con-crete birdbath had collected twigs and leaves in a ring of brownish water and ice. Four weathered landscape posts rose up to hold a square of lattice strips. Dry brown vines clung to the posts and were woven through the lattice. The muscadines, Carley assumed.

Grass crackled as she went around to the side yard between her grandmother's house and the Paynes'. In a patch of sunlight stood a tree about ten feet high with leafless, spreading branches. The grayish trunk was indeed wrapped with a blanket and some rope. The tree did not look much like anything worth protecting, but she supposed if it gave pleasure to the neighbors' children, it was worth the precaution.

She rather regretted that this was not all happening in warm weather. Not because of the space heaters, for she was becoming used to them. But for just a little while, it would have been nice to enjoy the sensation of relaxing out in her own backyard with a book and cup of tea.

But that can happen. Once she sold the house, she would have enough money to buy one in California. Probably not in San Fran-cisco, but there were the bedroom communities connected to the mass transit system, such as Pleasant Hill and Concord. She could live as a woman of modest means rather than a student or newly hired teacher scraping along. Perhaps she could have dinner at a nice restaurant once in a while. And this time, in the dining room instead of the kitchen.

"I'm afraid you're going to be disappointed when you hear my appraisal," Kay Chapman said after a tour of the warmed house. "The median home value here in Tallulah is seventy thousand dollars. Quite different from San Francisco."

They sat in the living room, Mrs. Chapman on the toile-print sofa, Carley in the adjacent chair. The real estate agent looked to be in her early thirties. Brunette hair fell to just below her ears and fanned out a bit in a subtle flip. Her full figure was clothed in a business suit of gray with black trim and collar, and a knee-length skirt.

"I understand that," Carley said. She envied Mrs. Chapman's full lips, obviously not the result of the collagen injections that were becoming somewhat popular among California women. *You can afford them,* she told herself and squelched that notion immediately. Her fear of needles was stronger than her vanity.

"But we can be very safe in asking eighty thousand for this one," Mrs. Chapman went on. "And that gives prospective buyers room to negotiate. Everyone likes to feel he's had a hand in getting a good deal."

She took a sheet of paper from her briefcase. "All I need is your signature on the contract."

"Contract?"

Mrs. Chapman's smile did not mask the puzzlement in her eyes. "It's standard procedure, giving our agency the exclusive right to sell the house for six months."

This was moving too fast.

"Um . . . I'm just not one hundred percent sure yet that I want to sell."

Carley surprised even herself with this revelation. Perhaps the seed had been planted last night during the course of dusting, moving from room to room handling everything that her grandmother had handled. She had developed an affection for the house. Besides, she had not even had the opportunity to confer with Aunt Helen or the others she had yet to meet. Should she not consider their feelings? What if a relative wished to buy the house before it was put on the market? Didn't normal families ask for input before making permanent decisions such as this one?

"Would you rather rent it out?" Mrs. Chapman asked. "We could keep it filled. There aren't that many rental properties here."

"I don't think so," Carley replied. "I'll need the money to buy a house in California. But this is all too new for me, frankly. I only learned I owned this house a week ago. I should have thought about it longer before having you over. Sorry for wasting your time."

"My time wasn't wasted." Mrs. Chapman slipped the paper back into her briefcase and snapped it shut. "Why don't you sleep on it a couple of days? It's best to be certain anyway. Once you sign, you can't change your mind for the six-month period."

"Really?"

"I take that back. Of course you may change your mind, but we would be forced to charge a penalty for our time and inconvenience. You don't want that, and we wouldn't want to have to do that either."

"Have you ever had to?"

"Once, when someone backed out after we'd already found a buyer for his property." She wrinkled her nose. "I feel guilty every time I run into the guy. But even *he* isn't immune to contract penalties."

Carley was curious why the emphasis on the *he*. But there was no point in asking, as she knew so few people in Tallulah by name.

"As I said, it's best to be certain," Mrs. Chapman went on. "You just call when you're ready. How is that?"

"Yes, thank you," Carley said, and was swept with a great surge of relief.

Her visitor had stepped over the threshold when Carley remembered something she had intended to ask. "Do you know where I can get some boxes?" There were several things she wanted to ship home, such as the Blue Willow dishes.

"We actually sell them, for the same price we pay at Office Depot in Hattiesburg," Mrs. Chapman said as cold air flowed in around her. "As a service to our customers. Just come by the office any time. You'll just have to assemble them yourself, but that's easy."

"Thank you." Carley hesitated. "But I'm not a client yet."

"That doesn't matter. And besides, you'll probably be a client one way or the other, sell or rent. You can't very well chain the house to your car and drag it to California, can you?"

That made Carley laugh. "No, the Budget Rent A Car people would be very upset."

Henderson's Grocery, west of the flashing light, was about half the size of a Safeway supermarket. Almost every customer Carley wheeled past gave her a curious smile or at least a shy nod. Canned beef stock was on her list, but on impulse she put a small roast into her cart. Being on the short road to freedom from debt was cause for celebration. That was also her rationalization for a half gallon of Breyers mint chocolate chip ice cream.

"Is the chicken salad fresh?" she asked a bald, white-aproned man at the small deli counter.

"I mixed it up only two hours ago," he drawled, spooning some on a melba toast round. "Here, try it."

She chewed. Minced celery and egg as well as chicken, and not too heavy on the mayonnaise. Her own recipe called for a bit of curry powder, parsley, and sweet pickle, minus the eggs, but she would not have time to make a batch before lunch. "It's good. I'll have a pound. Um, make that a pound and a half."

"You ever try it on raisin bread?" drawled a young woman with medium brown curls and a serious-looking infant strapped to her chest.

"Chicken salad?" Carley smiled at the baby.

"You'd be surprised how good it is. Even with tomater and lettuce. I like your hair. It's not dyed, is it?"

"Thank you. No, it's all natural. Boy or girl?"

"She's a girl," the woman said proudly. "Her name's Megan."

"Bye, Megan," Carley cooed, and was rewarded with a gummy

smile. In the small bakery section she thought, *Oh, why not?* She could always have the raisin bread with cream cheese for breakfast. But just in case, she also placed a loaf of whole wheat into her cart. The only item on her list not in stock was fresh oregano, so she bought a bottle of dried but asked about it at the checkout counter.

"Try Fresh Pickin's at the flashing light." The clerk was about fifty, with dark blonde hair piled high upon her head and no makeup or jewelry. The badge on her smock read *Anna Erwin.* "Miz Bell grows herbs in her greenhouse."

"Thank you. I'll do that."

"I have two gin-nee pigs," came from Carley's right.

While unloading her cart and counting out payment, Carley had not really looked at the young man bagging her groceries. But now she noticed his head was small for his body, and was made to look even smaller by the navy blue knit cap pulled down over his ears. The top button to his flannel plaid shirt was fastened, and he wore high-top black tennis shoes and corduroy slacks belted high around the waist.

"Do you?" Carley said.

Moss-colored eyes brightened in his face. His words came out thickly, as if formed by an oversized tongue. "My sister, Hayley, gave them to me for my birthday. I named them Bugs and Daffy. Do you know who Bugs Bunny and Daffy—?"

"Neal, honey, let me give the lady her change," the checkout clerk cut in pleasantly. Into Carley's hand she counted, "Five . . . six . . . seven dollars and fourteen cents."

Carley thanked her, dropped the money into her purse, and said to the young man, "Yes, I know who they are. Those are good names. And happy birthday."

"It's not my birthday." He wheeled the loaded cart around and took hold of the bar. "My birthday's March-the-first. Do you know my sister?"

"No, I'm new in town. But here, I can get those."

He shook his head. "It's my job. I have on a termil shirt under here. What's your name?"

"Carley Reed." She followed through the automatic door and caught up with him. Above the squeak of wheels on concrete she said, "And you're Neal?"

"Neal, yes. Henderson is my other name. What's your other name?"

"Reed," Carley repeated. When he blinked at her, she realized his ears had picked up *Carleyreed.* More slowly, she said, "My first name is Carley. And my other name is Reed. Your father owns this store?"

"My daddy's store, yes. Grandpa did too, but it was littler and in a different place. I don't remember it much, just the candy. Do you like SweeTarts?"

She opened the Cavalier's trunk. "Sorry, not really. But I used to love Milk Duds."

Candy was a major contributor to her need for extensive dental work in her teens. She was fortunate that money was tight most of the time when she was a child, or she would have diabetes by now.

Neal hefted a plastic grocery bag by the handles. "Milk Duds are good. I can't have too much candy. That's because of the sugar. If you eat too much, then you have to buy teeth like Grandma Milly. Do you know her?"

"I'm afraid I don't know a lot of people here."

"Because you're new in town?"

"That's right."

He shook his head at the five-dollar bill Carley offered. "Daddy says we don't make people pay extrey for service. I have to go back in now. G'bye."

Carley smiled. "Good-bye, Neal."

She watched him push the cart up the small parking lot at a half trot and then return the wave of a man climbing from the cab of a dusty white pickup. Fresh Pickin's was an open-air stand with wide strips of thick clear plastic hanging from sides of the roof to the concrete floor, to conserve some of the heat of the electric heaters set about. *Miz Bell*, blonde and thirtysomething in jeans and sweat-shirt, looked nothing like the mental picture Carley had conjured.

"You ain't from the South, are you?" she asked as Carley dug her wallet from her purse to pay for the oregano and a red tomato that looked more appealing than the winter-anemic one from Henderson's. "Ah can tell by yore accent."

My accent? Carley thought as she handed over a five-dollar bill. "I'm from California."

"I'll be dawg." Gray eyes appraised her in a friendly way. "I'll bet you drink yore tea hot."

Carley smiled. "Scalding."

The woman laughed, counted out her change, and asked her to wait a minute. She disappeared into a wooden building connected to the back of the stand, then returned with a plastic bag of slender green leaves. "Lemon verbena. Try a few in yore tea."

But when Carley started to take out her wallet again, the woman shook her head. "It's on me."

"Why, thank you."

The dashboard clock read 1:55 as Carley pulled into the drive-way. She was buttering a pan when it struck her that, though she might not belong to Tallulah—nor did she really desire to—she no longer felt like an outsider.

It wasn't that San Francisco or Sacramento residents were not friendly. Far from it. The difference here was small town versus big city. Having tens of thousands of residents, tourists, and commuters stifled curiosity. There was little novelty to meeting an unfamiliar face when another would be coming along a second later.

A three-quarter moon sat above distant treetops in the dark sky as Carley walked out into the driveway with her grandmother's alu-minum cake container in hand. On Main Street, lights shone down on empty shop fronts. Customers were visible through Corner Diner's well-lit windows.

A white Roadmaster station wagon with wood-grain side panels occupied the space beside the truck in the Hudsons' carport on Fifth Street. Behind that was parked a silver minivan. Carley knocked at the front door. A second later the sound of barking came from the other side.

"Hush, Tiger!" A woman's voice said as the knob turned.

Carley instinctively took a backward step. The door swung open. A woman in navy slacks and white knit shirt smiled up at her as she crouched to hold the collar of a full-grown collie. "See? She's not a burglar."

That satisfied the dog, who stayed put when released. Straightening, the woman smiled and said, "I've been looking forward to this ever since Mom called. I'm Sherry, your first cousin once removed."

Plump in a healthy sort of way, she had chin-length honey-blonde hair loosely parted on the right side and flowing back a bit from her face. Her aquamarine eyes were enhanced by blue frames running along the top of a pair of otherwise rimless lenses. She looked to be in her midforties, a bit older than Linda would be if she were still alive, though her unlined face bore none of the ravages of fast living.

"It's so good to meet you too," Carley said, smiling as she stepped into the foyer.

"And this is Tiger, which proves Mom and Dad should never have let a grandson name their dog. You didn't have to bring anything. But I hope that's cake."

"Italian creme."

"Yum. Here, let me hold it while you take off your coat. Just put it on that chair right through that door."

After surrendering the cake server, Carley took a couple of steps through a doorway into a dark living room, draped her coat over a chair back, and laid her gloves on top. Back in the entrance hall, the dog sniffed her hand.

"Tiger . . ." Sherry warned.

"It's all right. I like dogs," Carley said, stroking the animal's head. The fact that he did not jump up on her raised his esteem in her eyes.

"Well, he's got to share you with everyone else." Sherry took the container's top handle so that she could link arms with Carley. Tiger led, paws clicking on ceramic tiles. Unlike the living room, the den looked well used. It was large enough to accommodate two sofas, three chairs, and a recliner, lamp tables, a television, and a fireplace. Tan carpeting stretched out to mist-green walls. Savory aromas wafted from a kitchen door.

A man and teenage boy ceased watching *Cops* and stood—the man lowering the volume with the remote control. Sherry introduced her husband, Blake, and son, Patrick.

"Well, hello, Carley." Blake Kemp stepped around a coffee table and offered his right hand. "Now, tell us truthfully . . . are you a nut, a fruit, or a flake?"

"Blake . . ." Sherry warned, and even the boy looked embarrassed.

"I beg your pardon?" Carley asked, hand still clasped by his long fingers.

"You know the saying . . . California is like a breakfast cereal?" He released her hand. "I'm just pulling your leg. It's a pleasure to meet you. But I have to admit, I just wish it were seven years later."

Seven years. . . ? He was chuckling at his own joke, but Carley recalled a saying she had read somewhere: *Many a truth is wrapped in jest.*

She smiled politely and gave herself a mental pat on the back for having the foresight to drive herself over.

The boy stood as tall as his father, his face a mass of freckles topped by carrot red hair. Carley wondered about the red hair connection, but then noticed that his father's was the dusty-strawberry color that bright red sometimes fades to over the years.

"It's nice to meet you, Miss Carley," he said shyly.

"Oh, you don't have to call me *Miss*."

"Well, I'm not allowed . . ." Patrick looked at his mother.

"It's a Southern thing, Carley," said Sherry. "My family had to get used to that when we moved down here. But now, even *I* can't bring myself to call anyone older than me by only their first name."

"Even if you're related?" Carley asked.

"Hmm." Sherry looked at her husband.

"She has a point there," Blake said. "By the way, we have another son, Conner. He's at the University of Birmingham on a golf scholarship."

"Is he the one who named the dog?" Carley asked.

"He is," Sherry replied. "Patrick would have named him after some NBA player. Wouldn't you, son?"

"I'm not sure," the boy replied. "I was only eleven. I probably would have named him something like Batman."

Carley laughed with the others. "How did the game go against Purvis?"

He looked surprised that she should know about the game, grateful for her interest, and disappointed to report the results. "It was a washout. One of our guards broke his sports glasses and had to sit out the last half. We lost by fourteen points."

"But we'll be ready for Seminary," Blake said. "They're our biggest rivals. It's a home game. Maybe you could come Friday night?"

His remark about the seven years still left a bad taste in Carley's mouth. She was about to say that she would probably still be packing, when Patrick gave her a smile wide enough to show braces on his upper teeth.

"I hope you'll come. They've beaten us four straight years, but we're ready for them this year."

"I'll try," Carley promised, smiling back.

Aunt Helen came through a door drying hands upon a dish towel, fussed over the cake container, and swept her into the kitchen. "Come meet Rory."

A man was holding a long fork over a sizzling black pot upon the stove. He had a full scalp of steel-gray hair combed back from his forehead, and a pink-tinged, lined face. Eyeing Carley, he said, "Do you like catfish, little girl?"

"I'm not sure I've ever tasted it."

"Well, you've never had 'em the way I cook 'em, anyhow."

His secret was to dip the fillets in a thin batter of Dijon mustard, egg, and canned milk before rolling them in seasoned cornmeal flour, he explained over a delicious, cholesterol-saturated supper that included fried potatoes, pieces of cornmeal dough called hush puppies, black-eyed peas with bits of bacon and small okra pods, and coleslaw. They sat around a long table in the vast kitchen, Helen confessing that the formal living and dining rooms were essentially wasted space.

Tiger, well trained, lay watching with his head resting on his leg in the den doorway. In the course of conversation, Carley learned that Blake owned the only barber shop in town, that Sherry met him when the Hudsons moved to Tallulah during her senior year of high school, and that she taught middle school science.

"Mr. Malone says you're a teacher too, Carley," Aunt Helen said, buttering a hush puppy.

Patrick's eyebrows lifted in a friendly way. "What do you teach?"

"High school English literature," Carley replied, sending the boy a smile before diverting everyone to a more pleasant subject. "But what I don't understand is . . . what brought you here from Washington?"

"Rory was stationed at Fairchild Air Force Base," Aunt Helen replied. "He came to our school play with a girl in my junior class. I had a lead part in Thornton Wilder's *Our Town*."

"And once I saw Helen flip that blonde hair," Rory said, "I said to myself that she was the girl I was going to marry."

"I wish you wouldn't say such things in front of Patrick, Dad," Sherry scolded affectionately while salting peas. "We're trying to teach him that you're not supposed to fall for a girl just because she's pretty."

"Well, you weren't around to warn me, were you?"

That made Patrick chuckle. Aunt Helen gave her husband an indulgent smile and continued. "Anyway, that was in 1947. We moved all over the country. Rory retired from the air force with twenty-five years when we were in Biloxi."

"Keesler Air Force Base." Blake passed Carley the ketchup after she glanced in that direction.

Aunt Helen went on to say that Rory was hired at Mississippi Mortgage there in Biloxi and was transferred to the Tallulah branch six years later, in 1976. "People were just starting to open up the antique shops."

It was all interesting, for Carley was still a bit in awe of being able to share a pleasant family meal, just as normal people did all over the world. But what she wanted to know most was what she could not ask at the table. What caused her mother to turn out to be the way she was? And did they have any inkling as to the identity of her father?

Dessert was banana pudding, with Italian creme cake on the side. Carley asked only for banana pudding, having heard of it but never tasted it. Banana slices were layered with broken vanilla wafers in custard, with toasted meringue on top.

"This is dreamy," said Carley.

"So's this cake," said Uncle Rory.

"Are you going to sell the house?" said Blake.

Carley cringed inside. She had planned to broach the subject when it seemed the appropriate time. But silence was hanging, so she said, "I can't keep a house here, living in California."

"'Course not," Uncle Rory said.

Aunt Helen nodded. "It's yours to do with as you please."

"We might like to buy it," Blake said.

Sherry set down her fork and groaned. *"Blake . . ."*

He gave his wife a pleading look. "It can't hurt to *talk* about it."

"But we decided . . ."

"I know, I know," he said, raising placating hands. "But how much longer will interest rates be this low? It's a great investment. We could rent it out."

"Well . . ." Sherry said with uncertain expression.

That encouraged Blake to turn to Carley again. "You haven't signed with a Realtor yet, have you?"

"No. Kay Chapman came by this morning, but I asked for a little time."

"And how much did she appraise it for?"

"Eighty thousand dollars. With room for negotiation."

"So, that means midseventies. And minus Kay's six percent commission, if we arrange a private sale."

"Is that ethical?" Carley asked. "After she's been to the house?"

"It's the nature of the business," Blake assured her. "I used to dabble in real estate on the side."

"And obviously he wants to do it again," Sherry said. Husband and wife locked eyes for a few seconds, his pleading and hers long-suffering. At length she blew out her cheeks and asked Carley, "Will you give us a couple of days to talk about it?"

"Of course."

Uncle Rory cleared his throat. "Bad idea, mixing family with finances."

"Dad, Blake isn't Uncle Dewey." Sherry turned again to Carley. "Dad cosigned a car loan thirty years ago and got stuck with the payments."

"I agree with your father," Aunt Helen said quietly.

Blake nodded. "I understand, Miss Helen. But if we got a regular bank mortgage, how would that be any different from anyone else buying it?"

"Yes, Dad, how would it?" Sherry asked.

All eyes went to Uncle Rory. He shrugged. "I guess that would be all right. If you meet with Stanley Malone first, get a purchase agreement all legal-like."

"Of course," Blake said.

"May I have another slice of cake?" Patrick asked.

Thankfully that brought an end to the discussion. Carley's relief in finding a possible buyer so soon and keeping the house in the family, was tainted slightly by her first impression of Blake. Would he try to pressure her into a deal that was not in her best interest? If only she knew more about real estate.

Everyone helped clear the table, raking scraps into the trash can, loading the dishwasher, covering leftovers. Then Sherry apologized for eating and running, that she had papers to grade.

"I'm so glad we had the chance to meet you," she said, catching Carley up in an embrace.

Patrick, hanging back a bit as if he feared he might be expected to do the same, said, "Please don't forget the game."

"We'd offer to pick you up," Sherry said, "But we go early and help stock the concession stand. You'd probably enjoy the walk anyway. It's just a stone's throw from Aunt Cordelia's house."

"From *your* house," Blake corrected, shaking Carley's hand. And it was said in such a friendly way that Carley warmed up to him a little. For that, and the ketchup.

And then he ruined it all by adding, "Admission is three dollars—which shouldn't be a problem for an heiress, right?"

"Don't say such things!" Aunt Helen scolded, swatting his arm lightly with a carton of tall kitchen trash bags.

Carley held her breath, but Blake merely grinned and said, "Sorry!"

When the three were gone, Uncle Rory shooed Carley and Aunt Helen from the kitchen. "I'll get the pots," he said, fingers testing the temperature of tap water.

They shared a den sofa. With Tiger flopped on the rug at her feet, Aunt Helen said, "Please don't pay Blake any mind. He's a decent man, good to Sherry and the boys. His mouth just runs away with him sometimes."

That took a weight off Carley's mind. "Thank you. And maybe it'll be better for you . . . keeping the house in the family."

"I can think of my sister whenever I drive by, no matter who owns it. But I appreciate your giving them this chance. Whatever works out, do plan to stay with us, once the furniture is all packed up. Or whenever you feel like it. You're always welcome here."

"Thank you, Aunt Helen." By now, Carley had no qualms about accepting her hospitality. "Is there anything of Grandmother's you'd like to have?"

She shook her head. "I have the things Cordelia left me in her will, like our grandmother's tea set and her serger sewing machine. And we made copies of some of each other's photographs a couple of years ago. You'll probably want to donate the mattresses and pots and pans and such to the Salvation Army. They'll come out from Hattiesburg for them. We have a consignment store here that could sell some of the good furniture for you. They'll come for it too."

"Would you like her clothes?" Carley asked carefully.

"I couldn't bring myself to wear them. Give them to the Salvation Army."

Carley had handed dollars to bell ringers outside shops ever since she began making her own money. But her grandmother's clothes?

"Don't worry," Aunt Helen said, reading the discomfort on her face. "I rather like the idea of spotting something that belonged to my sister on someone who needs it."

"I like knowing that about you." Realizing there was still much she did *not* know, Carley said, "Where are your other children?"

Her aunt replied that Deanna, who lived in Indianapolis, was a pastor's wife, piano teacher, and mother of three grown children. Kenneth, born a year after Deanna, was an electrical engineer, married, and living in Raleigh.

"They all come at Christmas. Ken and his wife, Glenda, stayed with Cordelia the three years before last. She loved having someone to fuss over."

"I met some of the neighbors. They said she was a fine person."

"She was. And I'm glad her last years were good ones."

"What do you mean?" Carley asked, absently fingering the fringe on a throw pillow.

Aunt Helen hesitated. "When I flew up to Washington when Sterling died, I ended up handling the funeral arrangements. Thankfully, he had a burial policy as well as good life insurance. Still, it all overwhelmed Cordelia to the point where she could not make a simple decision."

"She must have loved him very much."

"Yes." Another hesitation. "But it wasn't just grief that made her unable to function. She had never even balanced a checkbook or made a house payment in her life."

"Why?"

"Well, one reason was that Sterling was so hardheaded. Rory referred to him as 'Archie Bunker.'"

"Who?"

Her aunt smiled. "That was before your time, wasn't it? He's a television character. Sterling was good to her in his own way. He liked to buy little gifts, surprise her. I'm just saying he had strong opinions and insisted on controlling everything. The fact that he was eleven years older contributed to that. She was seventeen when they married. . . ."

"Seventeen?"

"Those were different times. I was only sixteen when I married Rory three years earlier. Our parents had passed on, and we were being raised by our aunt Maude, on a pension, so it was a way of relieving the load on her.

"Anyway, after we helped Cordelia move down here, I took her to see Doctor Borden here in town. He suspected clinical depression, and that she had probably had it since her teenage years. He referred her to a woman psychiatrist in Hattiesburg. It took some begging to convince Cordelia to see her."

"Why?"

"As I said, we were raised in different times. Seeing a psychiatrist meant you were either crazy or not a good Christian. And I'm sure Sterling had reinforced that notion."

"But she went. . . ?"

"Eventually. She was put on an antidepressant, and within a couple of months her whole outlook changed. Working in the shop, seeing people every day, helped too. She became the fun sister I . . ."

Voice trailing, Aunt Helen dabbed her eyes with her fingertips. Tiger rose from his nap to nuzzle her other hand and study her with worried brown eyes. Aunt Helen scratched between his ears.

"I'm afraid I let Cordelia down, badly. We moved from one duty station to another, even to Germany, and had three children to raise. There were some years when all we did was exchange birthday and Christmas cards. I wish I had it to do over again. I would have kept in closer contact, perhaps I could have helped her with Linda."

"You think my mother inherited Grandmother's depression? Was that what made her the way she was?"

"I believe it contributed," Aunt Helen said. "We talked about it when she moved down here. Linda had a big dose of her father's stubbornness, and Cordelia lived too deep inside her own misery to give her the attention and boundaries she needed. Sterling worked a lot of overtime, so he wouldn't have been much help. You give a child like that enough rope and she'll hang herself."

"She tried that," Carley said flatly.

"What? Hanging herself?"

"When I was a sophomore in college. A neighbor found her just in time."

"My, my . . ." Helen shook her head. "Poor Linda. And what a terrible life *you* must have had."

Carley shrugged. "It helps to understand why she was that way. And she could be loving at times."

Such as when Linda took her to see *The Princess Bride* and out for banana splits afterward. Those sorts of memories were bittersweet for their extreme rarity—and when juxtaposed with the harsh fact that her mother had failed to protect her from the evil people in their lives.

The second question she had wanted to ask during supper came again to her mind. "Did Grandmother have any idea who my father was?"

Her aunt gave her a pitying look. "I'm afraid not, dear. She said Linda dated so many boys since she was fourteen that they had no clue. She was living with a man when you were born, but neither of them claimed he was your father."

"I don't remember him."

"Well, I'm sure that relationship lasted about as long as the others. Do you remember living with Cordelia and Sterling when you were about three?"

"Vaguely. Where was my mother?"

"In . . . jail, for assaulting a woman one of her boyfriends left her for."

"Mr. Malone said my grandparents tried to sue for custody."

"And that was why Linda left the state with you. Cordelia always regretted that they didn't go about it another way. But then, who was to say that she would have had the energy for you that she didn't have for Linda? I'm sure that drove her deeper into depression."

"So many regrets," Carley sighed.

Her mother's instability and failure to protect her. Her grandmother's depression. Her own painful childhood memories. Aunt Helen's not keeping closer contact with her younger sister. That she herself had not looked up her grandparents.

"That's just how life is, Carley," Aunt Helen said. "But I've lived long enough to see how God can make good come from our regrets."

That sort of talk, as well as the "Christian" reference earlier and prayer before supper, made Carley uneasy. She was not an atheist. In fact, when she heard the Gospel message at age ten, she embraced it wholeheartedly and was baptized three weeks later.

Believing in God was not the issue. Understanding Him was.

One major barrier to understanding was constructed from memories of people who claimed to believe. At the head of that list was Huey Collins. Second was the congregation who held him in such high esteem that they elected him deacon, not taking the trouble to notice the terror in a little girl's eyes.

And then there were her foster parents, the Woodleys, with their picture of Jesus in the dining room and fish symbol on their car.

The church choir group who left a five-dollar tip and gospel tract after consuming over three hundred dollars' worth of food at DeLouches.

The woman whose bumper Carley's Camry had barely nicked while dodging a runaway shopping cart in front of the Safeway. She sprang from her Volvo praising Jesus that no one was hurt, and then sued for back injury, settling out of court for seven thousand dollars, thus running up Carley's insurance premiums.

The mortar that held those memories together was made up of what Carley perceived to be the nature of God himself. Was He paying so much attention to the sparrows and lilies that he could not see what was going on under Huey Collins' roof, nor hear her stomach growling on the days Linda could afford cigarettes and Johnny Walker but not cereal and milk?

When talk got around to religion, Carley usually started making excuses to leave. She was about to do so when Uncle Rory came into the room and eased into a chair.

"Your back hurts?" Carley asked, relieved at the opportunity to change the subject but concerned about the pain that washed over his face. "I should have helped you finish."

He smiled and shook his head. "It aches just the same whether I'm working or loafing. But I'm afraid I'm no good at lifting anything heavier than a cooking pot, or I could help you pack."

"Please don't worry about that. I'm only boxing up small things. Loretta Malone gave me the name of a shipping company for whatever I send home."

That led to questions about Carley's life in San Francisco. When Aunt Helen asked how she was able to take off so many days from teaching, she found herself telling the whole story. It was cathartic to get it all out.

Especially when her aunt shook her head and said, "I would have done the same thing. You shouldn't have to compromise your values just to keep a job."

"And there's no virtue to being miserable when you can do something about it," Uncle Rory added.

"Thank you for saying that," Carley said, warming to both of them even more. At length she glanced at her watch. Ten o'clock. Not too late for someone whose body still assumed it was eight, but late for two elderly people who had spent hours in the kitchen and antique shop.

Both walked her through the hall, where Aunt Helen embraced her again. Carley drove back down Main, past sidewalks virtually empty. Most houses on Third Street had at least one window illuminated. For as long as she could remember, such a sight could bring on melancholy, a feeling of being excluded from whatever the people inside were doing. She did not feel this way tonight.

Instead she felt a wave of pity for the students who had given her so much trouble, even Ryan Ogden. The ski trips to Aspen, diamond jewelry, and sports vehicles for sixteenth-birthday presents, surely diluted their capacities to enjoy simple things. There was no entertainment or material possession on earth, on this cold starry night, that could match her sense of well-being from simply being embraced by her family.

"Is it possible to transfer the balance to this Bank of California account?" she asked on Thursday morning.

The Lamar County Bank officer turned blue-shaded eyes back to her computer screen. "I'll take care of that rat now."

Right now, Carley's mind translated for her startled ears.

"When do you think the funds will be available in California?" she asked when the tattoo of fingers against keyboard slowed.

The woman smiled and jabbed a key with an index finger. "It's there as we speak, Miss Reed." She opened a cash drawer. "Now, how would you like your change?"

In no way did Carley envision spending five hundred dollars in the six days she had remaining in Tallulah; in fact, she still had most of the three hundred from an ATM in the San Francisco airport. But the officer had suggested that the shipping company might balk at an out-of-state check.

The fact that Carley's checkbook lay in a dresser drawer in her apartment made the advice even more practical. Still, she would probably have more than enough left to pay cash for the rental car instead of charging it as she had planned.

Visa, your days are numbered, she thought.

A man was entering the bank as she approached the exit. Caught up in her own enthusiasm, she barely glanced at him.

"I *thought* you might be here."

That voice! Carley looked up at Blake Kemp's grinning face. But before she could say that she did not appreciate his insinuation that she could not wait to get her hands on the money—even though that was essentially the case—he spoke again.

"Do you have a minute?"

"Um-hmm." Carley moved over to the counter where deposit and withdrawal slips were kept.

This time he gave her a nervous smile. "We'd like to buy the house."

"Oh. Sherry too?"

"Of course." He looked about, lowered his voice. "Will you take seventy-two thousand? And leave the major appliances for future tenants?"

As little as Carley knew of real estate, she had absorbed enough from television and newspaper financial columns to know that she was supposed to make a counter offer in sort of a bidding ritual. But she still harbored a sense of guilt, having swept into town and inherited the bulk of her grandmother's estate over people who had actually spent time with her. And they *were* family.

"All right," she said.

He blinked, and his pleased expression faltered. "Ah . . . really?"

She could read his thoughts—he wondered if she would have agreed just as quickly if he had offered even less. As little as she cared for Blake, she decided to spare him some torment.

"But that has to be my bottom price."

He looked relieved. Taking a cell phone from his pocket, he said, "Sure, that's fair. Since you're not going to be in town much longer, do you mind if I see if Mr. Malone will draw up the purchase agreement today?"

As it turned out, the attorney said he could see them right away. Carley followed Blake's white Mitsubishi mini-truck over to the attorney's office, and fifteen minutes later the paperwork only needed Sherry's signature to take effect. "I'll bring it over to the school and then go back to the bank," Blake said, pumping Mr. Malone's hand and then Carley's.

The Cavalier's heater had no time to put a dent in thirty-degree weather. But the Tallulah library was warm and smelled of old books and wood and polish. The lone computer sat on a desk between the books-on-tape and magazine areas. Librarian Edward Juban said Carley would need to have a library card in order to access the Internet.

"But bein' as you have an address here, I can fix you up with a temporary one. My condolences on Miz Walker, by the way." He was a soft-spoken, pear-shaped man, with dark brown hair, gray eyes, and a mustache that partially concealed a repaired cleft palate.

"Thank you," Carley said. "Did she come here often?"

"Pretty often. She was a very gracious lady."

Every compliment directed toward her late grandmother sent a little stab to her heart. *By the time you were old enough to contact her on your own, you had almost no free time,* she tried to rationalize as Mr. Juban typed out her card.

And so now memories of her grandparents would always be secondhand. After death was a terrible time to try to catch up.

"What sort of books did she read?" Carley asked after signing her card. There were only a handful at the house. Besides a worn Betty Crocker and even more worn Bible, she had come across a crossword puzzle dictionary, an oversized picture book of quilting patterns, a collection of quotations, and a guide to Southern landscaping. One other title had made Carley smile.

The Independent Woman's Guide to Minor Automobile Repairs.

But no fiction.

Discomfort crossed Mr. Juban's face, as if he were a physician who had just been asked to breach patient confidentiality. "Well, romance novels, mainly. Miz Hudson brought back a half dozen that Miz Walker had checked out before . . ."

"Really?" Carley was stunned and touched. Stunned, because the picture Helen had painted of her grandmother's married life was bleak. And touched, because there must have been at least some mutual affection, for her not to have soured on romance over the years. Thanking the librarian, she sat at the computer and logged in with her new library card number. She entered her password in the Bank of California Web site. The transfer had indeed gone through. With a few clicks of the keys, she paid off the school loan and credit card balance, which included the cost of her round-trip airline tickets two days ago.

Lovely, lovely zero, she thought. Such an underrated digit. Her next item on the list was to telephone Kay Chapman and the shipping company in Hattiesburg. She walked back to the counter as light-footed as if walking on the moon, and asked Mr. Juban the location of the pay telephone.

He pointed to an arched opening past a couple of study tables. "I believe there's still someone on it, but she usually doesn't take long. Do you need the directory?"

Carley reached into her purse for her notebook and the roll of quarters from the bank. "No thanks."

No sound came from the doorway as she drew closer. She came to a halt just before an alcove. A woman leaned against the wall, speaking with hushed voice into the receiver of a wall telephone between two doors stenciled with *Ladies* and *Gentlemen.* She was some years older than Carley but dressed younger, in tight jeans with bleach lines and a black leather motorcycle jacket. Straight, blunt-cut black hair fell in different lengths to her shoulder blades, her eyebrows were invisible behind bangs, and eyeliner was thick on both top and bottom.

". . . just going to have to be patient. You think this is—"

She looked up at Carley and stopped.

Sorry, Carley mouthed, taking a backward step.

The woman shot her a sour look and turned toward the wall.

Carley gaped at the *Harley Davidson* on the jacket's back. *How do you know I wasn't going to the restroom?*

She moved over to wait by a display of books by Mississippi authors. So that Her Redneck Highness would not have the satisfaction of knowing her rudeness had affected her in any way, she picked up a book and began leafing through it.

Soon her anger turned inward. *You just paid off all your debts, and you're going to let one person ruin your day?*

Intellectually, she was aware that her reaction was not just about being snubbed by a stranger—just as she was aware that she could not spend the rest of her life blaming her mother for everything. But a childhood of having to fend for herself had stamped into her earliest psyche the notion that she was an inferior person. Certainly not good enough to mingle with classmates with smiling moms who made cookies and ironed their clothes and fathers who pitched baseballs on manicured lawns. Homes where the Easter Bunny and Santa Claus came *every* year, not just hit or miss.

Any slight, such as a clerk's lifting her eyebrows, worked its way into fissures that were already there. That sense of unworthiness was probably the biggest reason she had so few close friends. If a person did not believe in herself, who else would?

Or maybe you're just obnoxious. Carley smiled at her own droll thought, for as low as she could feel about herself sometimes, she did not think that was the case. But then, being unaware of one's own obnoxiousness was probably the first characteristic of an obnoxious person.

"Someone returned that one just an hour ago," Mr. Juban said, beside her. "It was on the *New York Times* list for three months. It won't sit here long."

Carley closed the book to look at the cover. For all the attention she had given it, it could have been a manual on raising poultry. *Camellia Street,* by Bertram Norris. A contemporary murder mystery, said the blurb on back. "And he lives in Mississippi?"

"Well, Nashville, actually, but he graduated from USM in Hattiesburg, so we claim him. He came to Books-A-Million back when his first book, *Delta Dreams,* came out, and he signed my copy. I have it stored in my closet—his first-edition books will be worth a fortune one day, just like Grisham's *A Time to Kill.* It was an excellent read, but this one's my favorite."

He was so willing for her to check it out that Carley hesitated before saying carefully, "I've just never cared for mysteries. When the suspense builds too high I end up peeking at the last chapter, and then my interest is gone."

Mr. Juban's brown eyes widened, as if she had confessed to stealing lunch money from schoolchildren. "We don't read simply for the endings, Miss Reed. A book is like a train trip. The journey is as important as the destination."

What could she say? She was finished with *Cranford* and needed something to read. "I can put this on my temporary card?"

He smiled. "That's what it's for, Miss Reed."

As he scanned the book at the desk, Carley caught movement in the corner of her eye. She looked to the left. The woman was standing just outside the alcove with arms folded, as if waiting for another call.

And yet, the way she stared made it almost seem as if she were waiting for *her.* The last physical altercation Carley had gotten into was at fifteen, when a cheerleader called her "reform-school trash." She had no intention of getting into one again, and especially not with a motorcycle-jacketed woman who could probably rip out her hair with one hand. When Mr. Juban handed her the book, she thanked him and walked over to the slanting magazine racks to wait for the woman to take her call or leave.

She did neither, but approached.

Oh no, Carley thought.

"Sorry about that," the woman said, unsmiling, but not looking threatening.

Self-talk or no self-talk, Carley felt better. "No problem."

"That was my brother. Dad disowned him. My boy and I live with my folks; Dad checks the long-distance bills, so I have to call from here."

"Oh. I'm sorry."

"Yeah. Me too." The woman turned and walked away, sending Mr. Juban a wave on her way out. Carley let out a long breath and went to the telephone.

Kay Chapman answered after the first ring, and was very understanding. "That's how the business is," she said, echoing Blake's sentiment. She offered some advice. "I wouldn't take a dime less than seventy-four thousand, if I were you. And do remember me if the Kemps' loan doesn't go through. I can always fax a contract to California."

Carley had not even thought of that. Relieved to have a backup plan, she thanked her. She telephoned Van Dyke Freight Company in Hattiesburg next, and arranged to have a truck out to the house on Tuesday morning between 8:00 and 10:00. *Five days away.* Surely she could be finished packing and sorting by then. She *had* to be, for the flight home was the following day. For a town so laid-back, time certainly raced.

While a pot of minestrone simmered on one burner, the sauce for cacciatore on another, Carley started going through closets and dresser drawers. She decided to keep such things as Grandmother's Bible and Betty Crocker cookbook—both with handwritten notes in some margins—and the book of quotations. A blue calico apron. A wonderful maple dough bowl. The quilts. Two sets of hand-embroidered pillowcases with crocheted edging.

As Aunt Helen had suggested, she began packing her grand-mother's clothing into boxes labeled *Salvation Army*, saving out a mauve flannel shirt, soft and roomy. She buttoned it over her gray flannel slacks and imagined that her grandmother would have been pleased to know that she would wear it one day.

She planned to speak with someone at Renaissance Consign-ment Furniture about the few pieces of like-new furniture. The two iron bedsteads and her grand-mother's dresser, chest, and chifforobe would be shipped back to California.

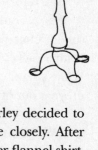

She worked fast, stopping only long enough for a chicken salad sandwich—delicious on raisin bread after all—and to bring the finished caccia-tore next door, politely declining a grateful Gayle Payne's invitation for her to join her family tonight. The packing tape ran out at two-thirty. Carley decided to walk to the drugstore and explore the town more closely. After brushing hair and teeth and pulling her coat over her flannel shirt, she set out westward.

At Main Street she looked south toward the row of shops where Auld Lang Syne was located. Should she drop in to say hello to Aunt Helen? A group of women were getting out of an SUV parked in front. *Maybe on the way back.* She went a block north, crossed to the other side at Corner Diner, and walked another block, occasionally weaving around shoppers and feeling more inclined to stroll and window-shop than hurry for packaging tape.

Shop windows displayed vintage merchandise. Taped inside some corners were the same fading posters of Gweneth Stillman. It appeared that no one wanted to be the first to give up the hope that her killer would come to justice. Or perhaps, hope had died long ago, but no one wanted to be the first to take down the poster and give weight to that fact. Either way was touching—and contradicted what she had imagined about race relations in the South.

Shouldered between Peggy's Pastimes and Tallulah Drugstore was what apparently was once a café. Curious, Carley moved closer and cupped her hands to peer through the grimy window. A counter came into focus in the murky darkness. Beyond that, boxes were scattered upon the floor and tables and chairs were stacked haphazardly.

At the sound of footsteps she automatically took a step back. The younger policeman from Corner Diner was strolling her way from the drugstore.

"Hi," he said.

She returned his smile. "Hi."

He was only a couple of inches taller than Carley's five-feet-five, solidly built with muscular shoulders obvious even through the leather jacket over his light-gray uniform shirt. "That was Emmit White's hamburger place until mismanagement and Dixie Burger drove it out of business about eight years ago."

"What a shame."

"Well, he rakes in a fortune by owning the only auto repair business and gas station in town, so I can't spare him too much pity." Uncertainty entered his blue eyes. "Uh . . . Miss?"

"Yes?"

He pointed to the left corner of his mouth. "You have . . ."

"What?" She touched the same corner of her own mouth.

"No, other side."

She felt the crust of dried toothpaste, focused her eyes at her reflection in the dark window. Heat rose to her cheeks as she wiped the dime-sized spot away with a moistened finger. "Thank you."

"I'm sorry if I embarrassed you."

"No, I'm grateful. And now I understand some of the funny looks I've gotten."

His laugh carved deep dimples in his cheeks. Carley smiled and held out a hand. "I'm Carley Reed."

"Dale Parker." They shook hands, and releasing hers, he said, "You're Miz Walker's granddaughter?"

"Why, yes."

"I'd heard a granddaughter from California was down here to sell the house," he explained in an easygoing drawl. "I just took a guess. Most of the antique hunters are older."

"Did you know my grandmother?" Carley asked.

"Not really," he said as uneasiness washed across his face. "I had to go in through a window after her neighbor Miz Templeton called."

Kindly, he spared her the rest. "I'm sorry about what happened."

"Thank you."

"Hey, Chief!"

Carley looked to her right. An athletic-looking man, about fifty and bald, was jogging toward them from across Main.

"I have no idea who that is," Chief Parker murmured.

"Bet you don't remember me," the man said upon reaching the sidewalk.

Chief Parker grinned and offered his hand. "Well . . ."

"Wayne Golden, from Picayune."

"Ah, yes I do remember," Chief Parker said, and introduced Carley.

"You're the reason I spotted Chief Parker, little lady." Mr. Golden nodded toward two women and a man standing outside Enchanted Attic Antiques. The women waved. "My wife, Nancy, noticed your pretty red hair all the way across the street."

"Thank you." Carley smiled and returned the women's waves.

"But I don't want to trespass upon your conversation. Just tell me a convenient time to drop by the station."

"Why don't I just . . ." Carley began.

"Wait, please," Chief Parker said, touching her sleeve. He turned to Mr. Golden again. "May as well save yourself some time. I'm afraid I haven't changed my mind about the property."

Carley's forearm still felt sensation, even through layers of wool and flannel and even though his arms were now folded.

"And yet my brother says you haven't sold the timber either," the older man said. "Wasn't that why you took it off the market?"

Chief Parker's smile was beginning to look strained. "Well, timber doesn't stop growing."

"True. But look, I'm still willing to buy the land. Just sell your timber now, so I'll have time to replant before I retire."

"I'm sorry."

"Then half. I'll give you a good price."

"The land goes too deep for two tracts to get decent frontage. And you'd want the half with the pond, right?"

"Well, yes. That was the plan, to build on it."

"That's my plan too, one day." The younger man shifted his weight, folding his arms. "Look Mr. Golden, I'm sorry I backed out. But there's other land out here. You'll find a nice place before you retire."

Mr. Golden sighed, shook his head. "All right. Sorry to disturb you."

"It's not a problem. And I'll tell your brother if I hear of any other deals."

"Thanks," he said halfheartedly, before catching a lull in traffic to sprint back to his party.

"Sorry about that," Chief Parker said to Carley. "When I first came to Tallulah, I had some money in the bank I wasn't sure what to do with."

Reward money, Carley thought, impressed that he did not mention that fact.

"I'm a total ignoramus about stocks. Our sheriff, Amos Price, said a forty-acre tract was about to go to auction—that an investment like that would pay double in just a few years, and he put me in touch with the owner. But I kind of fell in love with the land."

"That's nice. Anyone owning forty acres in the Bay Area would be a multimillionaire."

"Yes? Well, if that were the case here, I *might* have been tempted to sell. Is this your first visit to Mississippi?"

Carley nodded. "It's my first time in the South, period."

"Too bad you didn't wait 'til spring. It's only this dreary for a couple of months."

"I don't find it dreary. And the people are very nice. But I have to confess I'm a little disappointed."

"Why?" he asked, raising sandy-colored brows.

"I've been here three days, and I haven't heard a single *ya'll.*"

That brought another smile. "Well, now, that's because *ya'll* is plural. If I were to say 'It's a pleasure to meet ya'll, Miss Reed,' that would be true, but grammatically incorrect."

"Thank you," she said with a smile. It was a charming thing to say, and she understood why women chased him, as Loretta had said. She should leave now, she told herself, lest he assume she was hoping to be among those ranks. She nodded toward the drugstore. "It was a pleasure to meet you too, Chief Parker. I'd better do my shopping."

"You have a good day now, Miss Reed."

"And you too."

She purchased three rolls of tape and a small radio with

batteries. As she walked back down Main Street she found herself wondering about his former girlfriend. Even *she* knew that Atlanta was a long way off, and so distance was surely a factor in the breakup. But it seemed that two people who genuinely cared for each other would solve that problem. There had to be other issues. Perhaps his good looks and reputation as a local hero? Was it that having women fall all over him was too much of a temptation?

In which case, she would not blame the Atlanta former girl-friend one bit.

It's none of your business anyway, she told herself, and as a sidebar acknowledged that women were just as capable of running around as were men. That led to depressing thoughts about her mother, so she pushed the whole subject from her mind and looked at the contents of the shopwindows again. The SUV was still parked out-side Auld Lang Syne, so she decided to go on home.

On Third Street, a boy and girl in jackets and kneepads were roller-skating up and down the sidewalk. She moved to the edge every time they fell into single file to pass, and they drawled timid thank-yous. They happened to be in front of Carley's house when she was halfway up her driveway.

"Do you live here?" one called.

Carley turned and smiled. "Only for a few days."

The boy's blonde hair peeked beneath a knit ski cap. "Was Miss Cordelia your grandmother?"

"Yes, she was. My name is Carley Reed."

"We're sorry she died," said the girl.

The boy, obviously her brother, nudged her and said something under his breath.

"It's okay," Carley said. "I'm sorry she died too. Thank you."

"You're the lady who brought our supper over?" the girl asked.

"Um-hmm. What's your name?"

"Kimberly. I'm eight." She had a reddish brown ponytail, ear muffs, and hazel eyes that became slits when she returned Carley's smile. "And Micah's nine."

The boy nodded. "Our brother Lane's eleven months old. Do you have any kids our age?"

"I'm afraid I don't have any children at all."

He looked disappointed. "There are lots of kids on this street, but they're either too little, like Lane, or teenagers."

"I'm sorry."

"It's not your fault," the girl said magnanimously. "Besides, we have friends on other streets."

"Sometimes Mom drives us over, or they come here," Micah said.

"Well, I'm glad."

The pair gave her shy good-byes and returned to the sidewalk.

After fiddling with the radio for a few minutes in the kitchen, Carley found the public radio station. *All Things Considered,* a program she usually enjoyed, was just coming on. But she found herself listening more for the sound of skates passing than to the interview with opera tenor Salvatore Licitra. Finally she turned off the dial. When she had not heard the children for a while, she stepped outside. *They must have gone in for supper,* she thought.

Mrs. Templeton was scattering something under the magnolia tree in her front yard. Carley went over to her side of the porch.

"Sunflower seeds," the old woman said after an exchange of greetings.

"There's a bird feeder in my backyard I'll never use."

"No thank you, dearie. I had a feeder, but the squirrels always robbed it. This way, they all get a little something."

"Would you like me to bring over some soup?" Carley asked impulsively.

"Oh, you don't have to do that...."

"I'd be happy to. I made a huge pot."

"Well, thank you, dearie. You're a nice girl."

Back inside Carley ladled minestrone into a container. She became aware that she was smiling, for no particular reason.

———

With gravel snapping below and siren wailing above, Dale steered the patrol car up Deerpath Road. Headlights painted the tree trunks ghostly white. Through gaps he spotted flashing blue lights.

Happy Acre Park did not quite live up to its name, with its dozen or so mobile homes, in various stages of rust, and tiny weed-choked lots. His tires spit gravel as he braked to a stop, inches from the first patrol car on the scene. He stepped out and Marti Jenkins hurried over.

"Sorry to call you out, Chief."

On the force for the past two years, Marti was tall and lanky, with short brown hair and a wide mouth that revealed more gums than tiny pearl teeth. She had been a court reporter until, sick of the indoors, she enrolled in the police academy. And it was obvious that she would like the two of them to be more than co-workers. Dale never let on that he noticed her moonstruck looks. She was a capable deputy, but simply not his type.

"No, you did right," he said, even though only three forkfuls of white beans and brown rice were warming his stomach. He wore the jeans and sneakers he had changed into after his shift, and had simply zipped his leather jacket over his sleeveless undershirt.

Which makes me appropriately dressed for this place, he thought wryly, for undershirts were mandatory dress for wife beaters. At least most times. The last time he had come out to arrest him, Elroy Chavers was naked as a fish. Wrestling and cuffing a sweaty, naked, drunken man was not high on his list of fun activities.

The rule, that he instituted himself, was that two officers must respond to domestic disputes, for they could be as dangerous as an armed robbery. He unstrapped his holster and jogged to the plank-and-cinder-block steps leading up to the twelve-by-sixty trailer with Marti on his heels. Elroy's rants and Connie's wails came clearly through the tiny windows.

"Get on inside, now!" he ordered the foursome standing on the porch of the neighboring double-wide, one of the few mobile homes in the park that actually had skirting and a tidy lawn. To Marti, he said over his shoulder, "What are they doing, hoping the kids'll see a murder?"

"I heard glass breaking a minute ago," she called back.

Dale sprinted up the wobbly steps, tried the knob, and pounded on the metal door. "It's Chief Parker, Elroy! Open up!"

"YOU RUN AROUND WITH YORE SISTER ALL DAY, AND THINK YOU KIN JUST OPEN UP A CAN OF SOUP FOR MY SUPPER?"

"PLEASE STOP HURTIN' ME, BABY! I TOLD YOU, I THOUGHT WE HAD A PACK OF CHICKEN BREASTS IN THE FREEZER!"

"Elroy!" Dale shouted. "Don't make me break down the door!"

"GIT OUTA HERE, CHIEF. AIN'T NONE OF YOUR BUSINESS!"

Rats! Dale thought. It was impossible to back up enough on the wobbly plank to kick in the door, so he leaned into it with his shoulder and pushed. Fortunately, Elroy had done a sloppy job of repairing since the last time Dale paid a visit, and the whole frame gave way.

In a living room surprisingly unscathed, save a coffee table on its side and broken overturned lamp, a fully clothed Elroy Chavers turned from his wife to lunge at Dale, giving Connie the opportunity to sprint through the tiny kitchen and down the hall.

The alcohol in Elroy's bloodstream caused him to make stupid moves. His fist swung past Dale's nose with a good eight inches to spare. Within seconds, Dale had him in a hammerlock so that Marti could cuff him.

"We was just talkin'!" Elroy roared, attempting to wriggle free.

"Got him!" Marti said.

Dale shoved the cursing and slobbering man to the sofa, harder than necessary, so that Elroy's legs skidded across the vinyl floor. He leaned down, screamed into his face, "CALM DOWN, YOU STUPID HICK!"

With a whimper, Elroy turned his face and raised a shoulder.

"Chief?" Marti said tentatively.

Pulse pounding in his temples, Dale straightened. He had forgotten she was in the room. "Go see about Connie."

"Sure," she said, but hesitated, eyeing him.

Dale sighed. "Look, I lost my cool for a second. I'm not gonna hurt him."

She nodded, and had taken only one step, when Connie launched herself from the hall, with dark hair flying and bare feet slapping the kitchen floor. "Don't ya'll hurt my husband, you hear me?"

"Connie, we don't need you in—"

She hustled into the living room, fell at Elroy's side on the sofa, wrapping arms around him and pushing his head to her shoulder.

"I didn't mean to hurt you, baby," Elroy sobbed.

"I know, sweetie," she sobbed back. Turning a tearful, triumphant look up at Dale, Connie said, "Ya'll can go now. We was just horsin' around. He didn't lay a hand on me."

"Yeah?" Marti said. "How'd you get the busted lip?"

For a second the woman looked rattled. "I ran into the door."

However inclined Dale was to leave the two to each other, he was forced to follow the letter of the law. Besides, he did not care to be called back an hour later when the argument resumed.

"Come on, Connie. You know the routine."

"You ain't takin' him," the woman said, wrapping arms tighter around her husband. "I won't press charges."

"We don't need you to this time. We saw him hit you. Move away now, or we'll have to bring you in too, for obstructing justice."

It was Elroy who convinced her, slobbering and weeping about how sorry he was, that she should go to her mother's so she wouldn't be alone.

"I'll come for you in the morning, sweetie," she said through her tears as Dale pulled Elroy up from the sofa.

"You'll come in a week," Dale said.

"Aw, come on, Chief!" Elroy said. "I got to work."

"You should have thought about that earlier. I'm sick and tired of being called out here."

"Okay, I'm heading back to my supper," Dale said a half hour later, while Elroy cooled his heels in one of the two cells.

"I . . . have enough spaghetti to share," Marti said, her doe brown eyes not quite meeting his. "The sauce has mushrooms, not meat."

"No thanks." To lighten the rejection and spare himself the sight of pain across her face, he added, "You need all the calories you can get."

When he returned home, his answering machine was blinking. Dale pressed the button, released his brother's voice.

"Hey, Shorty! The girls have Presidents' Day off from school next month, and we're gonna visit Peggy's folks in Mobile. We could drive on over to see you on Sunday the sixteenth, if you could arrange to be off duty."

A small jolt of panic quickened Dale's pulse. He glanced at his watch and picked up the receiver. Was 9:48 too late to telephone a household with schoolchildren?

Time zone, he remembered with sinking spirits. There was no doubt 10:48 was too late to be calling anybody but policemen.

He's talking about three weeks away, he reminded himself, and felt better. Between now and tomorrow, he would have time to concoct a story of why he would not be in Tallulah that weekend. Perhaps even agree to fly down to Tallahassee for a visit in early spring, so Chad would not be tempted to schedule another trip. His brother never met a stranger, and the last thing in the world Dale needed was to have him down here, running his mouth and asking questions.

One question in particular. The thought ran goose bumps up his arms.

He carried his supper from the kitchen and ate it, cold, in front of the *Tonight Show.* Switching off the television at midnight, he looked at the telephone again. Four days since he'd last dialed Riley's number. He *had* to hear her voice again.

You can't keep doing this to yourself! he thought, even while opening his wallet.

One more time, and that's it.

The long-distance card routed all calls through Colorado, so that his number would not show up on her caller ID. Of course she would know it was him, but would not be able to prove it without great pains, if at all.

It was 1:00, Atlanta time. Even better, for he liked her voice best when it was thick with sleep.

But instead, his ears were affronted by a recorded message, a tinny-voiced operator stating that the number had been changed to an unlisted one.

He slammed the receiver and paced the floor with face burning, heart pumping against his rib cage, cursing himself for the short-sightedness that had caused him to jump at the first high position offered in the heady days after bringing in serial killer Warren Knap.

How could he blame Riley, with her model face and figure, fine soprano voice, and big dreams of Broadway once she graduated from Oglethorpe University this spring? He would have gladly followed her—law enforcement officers were needed everywhere, and he did not even have to be the head guy. Being with her would have been enough.

But no. He was tied to Tallulah, where an exciting night meant hauling in a drunken wife beater and then cleaning vomit from the back of his patrol car. He was more of a prisoner than Elroy Chavers, for even Elroy could look forward to being released.

chapter 10

Aunt Helen's Roadmaster pulled into Carley's driveway at a few minutes before noon on Friday. "I promised Patrick I would remind you about tonight's game," she said as she stood just inside the living room.

"I'll be there," Carley said. "Here, let me take your coat."

Her aunt shook her head. "No, I'd rather you go get yours. My second reason for coming is to treat you to lunch."

"That sounds great," Carley said. "But I have minestrone and a ton of chicken salad. Ever try it on raisin bread?"

"I can't say I've had that pleasure," her aunt said after a moment's hesitation.

Carley laughed, helping her out of her coat. "I have whole wheat too."

"Oh, why not have an adventure? Anyway, your kitchen will be a lot more peaceful than the diner." She looked at several sealed boxes stacked in the corner. "My, you've been busy."

"It was easier than I thought it would be," Carley said. "I'll just have some last-minute things to box up before the movers come, like the quilts on my bed."

"Well, our guest room is waiting for you when you're ready. I'm glad you're not bogged down with clutter. Cordelia wasn't a pack rat, and she got rid of a lot of things before moving down here."

Carley made iced tea. Aunt Helen wanted to try the raisin

bread—but only half a slice, just in case. She was not as enthusiastic as Carley was, and followed with another sandwich on whole wheat with her soup. She spoke of a trip her family had taken to San Francisco, years ago when Rory was stationed at Nellis Air Force Base in Nevada.

"Muir Woods was my favorite place. There was something ethereal about those sequoias."

"Why don't you both plan on another trip there?" Carley asked. "You can stay with me, and I'll be your tour guide."

"That's very sweet of you, but I don't know if we'll ever take you up on it. I had enough of traveling when Rory was in the air force. And the shop keeps me so busy." Ice clinked as she set her glass down. "Which reminds me . . . I need to pass along a message."

"Yes?"

"This is probably silly. . . ."

"Why don't you tell me, and let me be the judge?"

"Well, all right. A good friend, Marianne Tate, asked if I thought you might be interested in staying on a couple of weeks longer."

Why? raced from Carley's mind to her lips, but having essentially given her word that she would listen, she kept them closed.

"She and her daughter, Jenna Moore, own Grandma's Attic across from my shop. Naturally I had told them about you. Marianne and Jim fly to Miami tomorrow to visit friends and take a Caribbean cruise for their fortieth anniversary. Only their granddaughter, who was to help Jenna run the shop, called from McComb this morning to say her morning sickness is worse, and asked if they would find someone else."

"But I already have my return ticket," Carley said.

Aunt Helen nodded. "Marianne said she would pay the penalty for changing it. And your salary, of course, as well as the loan of her car. They would turn in your rental car for you at the airport. All shops are closed Sundays and Mondays, so you'd still have some time to pack. But don't feel pressured. There's always the temporary agency in Hattiesburg. I've used them myself during emergencies."

Thus, problem solved. "Why would she want me at all?" Carley asked. "She wouldn't have to pay the airline penalty or lend out her car, if she used the agency."

"Well, she liked Cordelia very much. And I mentioned that you were just as personable."

"Really?"

Her aunt smiled. "Don't be so modest, dear. As far as your airline penalty, it would work out to about the same amount as hiring a temp. Frankly, new shop clerks start out at minimum wage. The agency charges us two dollars an hour more so they can make a profit. And you never know if whomever they send will be good with customers. That's asking a lot of you—minimum wage and delaying looking for a job. I'm just being selfish. I'd like to have you stay longer."

Carley chewed on a bite of sandwich, and the idea. Minimum wage was not an issue, not for two weeks. And without knowing when she would manage another trip this way, it would be nice to spend more time with her newfound family.

Still, she needed to be looking for a permanent job. But what sort of job? She was not ready to take on teaching again. Perhaps it would be good to have a little productive space in which to think about her future, to download *San Francisco Chronicle* classified ads in the library and see what was available.

The doorbell chimed. Carley went through the living room and welcomed Blake Kemp, who settled the matter.

"It's going to take about seven working days before we find out if our loan came through," he said, accepting Carley's offer of a bowl of soup. But he declined a sandwich on either of the two breads.

Why not just wait it out here? Carley thought. She could pay her February rent and utilities online. She would just have to telephone her landlord to hold her mail once the post office started delivering again, then ask the freight company to come later, so that she would be certain of being back in San Francisco to receive everything.

"Oh, by the way," Blake said, hitting his forehead. "Sherry wanted me to give you the key we borrowed from the Paynes. But I forgot it."

"You may as well keep it, since you're buying the house," Carley said. "I have a spare on my chain."

"On the same chain?"

"Well, yes."

"Hmm." He chewed thoughtfully, swallowed. "Now correct me if I'm wrong . . . but isn't the point of having *two* keys, to keep them apart in case you lose one?"

"Smarty britches," Aunt Helen said, but smiling.

Carley smiled too. He had a point.

———

"Here we go, Bobcats, Here we go!"

Tallulah trailed Seminary by five points, but for the past nineteen minutes of game time, the lead had changed hands seven times. Players and referees were sweating, coaches and cheerleaders could barely be heard above the continuous roar from both sides of the gymnasium.

"What are your favorite colors? Red and white, red and white!"

"LET'S HUSTLE, BOBCATS!" Sherry called out from Carley's left.

When the half-time horn bleated, both sides rose and cheered players on their way to locker rooms.

"I'm drained!" Carley said over the din. "I'd forgotten how exciting a basketball game can be. And I can't imagine how it must be to watch your own son out there."

Sherry nodded, her face flushed. "I have to cut back on caffeine on game days, or I'd be out there slapping referees."

"Would you care for something from the concession stand?" Aunt Helen asked from Sherry's other side. Uncle Rory was leaning forward as if poised to go. Blake, an unofficial coaching assistant, was in the locker room with the team.

"No, let me," Carley said. Her offer had nothing to do with the fact that she had spotted Dale Parker enter in civilian clothes shortly after they were seated. But she could not help but hope that he would happen by the concession stand at the same time.

Sherry nudged her side. "We'll both go."

A sign over the stand read *Sponsored by Tallulah High Beta Club.* Teenagers and adults worked the long counter. Sherry had informed Carley earlier that she and Blake and four other parents with sons on the team did not work the stand during the games, but they were in charge of setup and cleanup. A tall girl wearing a red baseball cap gathered two cartons of nachos, a hot dog, popcorn, and napkins on a cardboard tray for Carley. Sherry's tray held the drinks. Carley insisted on paying and was relieved when Sherry's expression betrayed no resentment of her inheritance.

Dale Parker did not materialize. But as she received her change, Carley noticed another friendly face behind the counter. Other customers blocked her from moving sideways, so she leaned forward to call, "Hi, Neal!"

Neal Henderson scanned faces, stopped at hers. "Hey . . . uh . . ."

"Carley!"

"Oh yeah! Carleyreed! I'm the potato chip man!"

There was a ripple of laughter, none of it cruel. A man with a mullet haircut said, "Hey, Neal, how's about you quit flirting with the pretty lady and give us some service?"

Neal grinned at him. "Okey-dokey, Mister Chuck!"

Forty-five seconds after the start of the second half, one of Tallulah's seniors made a three-point shot, bringing the score to thirty-three to thirty-five. Patrick struggled to guard a player with two inches of height advantage, but at times, by talent or sheer determination, was able to block several shots and produce points on the offensive end of the court.

"Go, Patrick!" Sherry called, while a half carton of nachos grew cold from inattention in Carley's lap. With the score tied and twelve seconds on the clock, Coach Sullivan called a time-out and brought his players together for one last huddle. Then as the ball was inbounded, Patrick and the other forward stepped into the path of the covering guard. The Tallulah center rolled around the pick, was fed the ball by the point guard, and with a simple lay-up, the game was over.

"Yes!" Carley exclaimed amid the roar. She hugged Sherry, Uncle Rory, Aunt Helen, and the woman and child behind her. After so much excitement, she was too stoked with energy to go home to her quiet house, so she stayed and helped Sherry and Blake and two other sets of parents clean up the concession stand. When they were almost finished, they divided the last of the hot chocolate into Styrofoam cups and sat in a circle in metal chairs reliving the best moments of the game and simply enjoying one another's company.

"Why don't you just stay down here, Carley?" asked Lynn Hall, mother of the point guard. "We could introduce you to my husband's cousin. He's a dentist in Hattiesburg and looking for a wife."

"His *fourth* wife," said her husband, Ron, a chemistry and physics teacher.

"I thought polygamy was illegal," Blake said, wide-eyed.

Carley joined their laughter. In their state of euphoria and exhaustion, they would have chuckled if someone had commented upon the weather.

———

Soon after arriving at Grandma's Attic, Carley realized that shop-clerking was similar to being a waitress—answering patrons' questions about any given menu item, showing gratitude that they had walked through the doors, yet giving them space and not fawning over them.

As to the merchandise, Marianne Tate had a system.

"Every item has a number on its tag or in the display case," her daughter Jenna had explained during a lull, pulling out a drawer of an old mahogany library card catalog. She was a short woman in her late thirties, well under five feet tall, with a wide smile, beautiful teeth, and very curly brown hair. "When someone asks you about an item, you simply look up its card to find out more about it."

Each card contained penned notes from either Jenna or her mother, and sometimes taped photographs or magazine clippings. But on the first day on this job, Carley simply straightened merchandise, dusted shelves, and allowed Jenna to do the selling.

The Hudsons had invited her for supper, so she brought over the pesto pasta salad she had prepared before work. Sherry, Blake, and Patrick were in Birmingham visiting Conner. Uncle Rory placed on the table a platter of what appeared to be beef pot roast, surrounded by potatoes, carrots, and onions.

"Venison," he said proudly.

"Oh," Carley said dully.

He smiled understanding. "Not sure about that, are you?"

"Well . . ."

"You don't have to eat it," said Aunt Helen.

"Thank you," Carley breathed, and just in case she had hurt Uncle Rory in the slightest way, she added, "The vegetables look delicious."

He winked. "And they don't remind you of Bambi, do they?"

Later, in the living room, Aunt Helen and Carley looked over the photographs while Uncle Rory worked the *Hattiesburg American* crossword puzzle, with Tiger dozing at the side of his chair.

"What's a seven-letter word for *scoundrelly*—begins with a *k* and ends with an *h*?" he asked, raking the end of his pen through his mustache.

"Knavish?" Carley guessed after mentally counting letters.

"That's it!"

"It pays to have an English major on hand," Aunt Helen said.

Carley felt so close to the two, so grounded in family, that she thought she would not wish to be anywhere else.

Until Aunt Helen said, "We have a nice little church, Grace Community. Would you like to come with us tomorrow?"

"Thank you, but I'd rather not," Carley said.

She waited for the "why" that was hanging in the air.

But instead her aunt nodded, and Uncle Rory asked for a word starting with *m* for *cryptogram.*

"Mystery," Aunt Helen said, giving Carley a thoughtful little smile.

"It was made by James Powell and Sons in England, in 1921," Carley said on Thursday while rain fell outside. Her fingers trembled slightly as she unlocked the case that held a Venetian-style pedestal bowl of clear green glass for a middle-aged couple named Fletcher.

"Ninety-five dollars, Dave," the woman mused.

"Like you said, it would look elegant on the console table," her husband said. Both were originally from Kansas, they had told Carley, and now lived at Keesler Air Force Base, where Major Fletcher was stationed.

"Well, yes . . ."

His hand held out the pewter jam pot, priced at twenty dollars because of a dent along the base. "We'll put this back, if it would make you feel better."

She thought about it and smiled. "All right."

Carley was pressing tissue paper around the sides of the bowl when Jenna returned from lunch, propping her umbrella in the stand at the door. After the Fletchers left she said, "I can't wait 'til Mom calls. How did it feel, making your first big sale?"

"It felt great," Carley said.

But the sale that gave her the most satisfaction occurred the following morning, when a trio of women with heavy Southern accents entered. They were from Foley, Alabama, they said, another Southern antique Mecca. Only the woman wearing thick bifocals had been to Tallulah before. They were looking for Depression glass, old clocks, vintage aprons, and salt and pepper shakers. Jenna asked Carley to help the woman seeking the latter.

"Oh goodness, here she is!" the woman breathed after scanning the shelves. Almost reverently she picked up a four-inch pepper shaker in the form of a little nun with folded hands.

Having just dusted those shelves the previous afternoon, Carley said, "I'm afraid we don't have the salt shaker. That must be why it's only three dollars."

"I would have given three hundred," the woman said, rubbing her thumb over the smooth ceramic. She turned luminous eyes to Carley. "I already have the salt shaker. Our cat knocked the pepper shaker off a shelf about ten years ago, and I've looked all over for a replacement, even on eBay. My son Robert bought me the set at the dime store when he was a little boy. We aren't even Catholic—he just liked the look of them."

There was clearly far more to that story. Carley took the shaker reverently from her hands. "Let me find a box for it."

By the time Carley returned from the storeroom, the two other women had joined their friend at the counter. They wanted to see the shaker. One embraced the new owner, who was wiping her eyes with a tissue.

"You're not from around here either, are you?" the woman shopping for clocks asked Carley, while Jenna rang up two Depression glass juice glasses.

"Guess where she's from?" Jenna said before Carley could answer.

"Hmm . . ." she said. "California."

Jenna laughed. Carley gaped at the woman. "How could you tell?"

The woman gaped back while her companions joined in the laughter. "You mean I'm right? I threw out a wild guess."

"Why don't you go to lunch now, Carley?" Jenna said when the trio had exited.

For the past three days, Carley had spent her free hour reading *Camellia Street* over a bowl of minestrone or a sandwich in the tiny kitchen off the upstairs storage room. Mr. Juban had not exaggerated about it being a great read, and she was rather proud of herself for resisting peeking ahead. But this morning, just before the shop opened for customers, Aunt Helen had stopped in to ask Carley to ring her shop when she could get away to meet her at Corner Diner.

After telephoning, Carley bundled into her coat. The three women from Foley were coming out of Three Sisters Antiques.

"Can you recommend a good place for lunch?" one asked.

Carley nodded. "Corner Diner is just up the street. I'm heading there now if you'd like . . ."

The bifocaled woman gave her an apologetic look. "I've been there. We were hoping for something not quite so heavy."

That ruled out Dixie Burger and Tommy's Pizza on the south end of town. The Old Grist Mill had a salad bar, she had heard, but they only opened for lunch on weekends.

"Don't you have a soup and sandwich shop tucked away somewhere?" asked the woman who had guessed Carley was from California.

"You can probably get sandwiches made at the deli at Henderson's Grocery. It's just a few hundred feet west of the flashing light. But I'm afraid there's no place to sit."

The bifocaled woman apologized for detaining Carley. "I guess we'll do pizza. Thank you."

Carley glanced over her shoulder before entering Corner Diner. The trio were getting into a dark blue sedan.

"You know, someone should open up a sandwich shop here," she said to Aunt Helen over identical plates of the special of the day—grilled pork chops, baked sweet potatoes, and turnip greens.

"Why don't you?" Aunt Helen asked while her knife trimmed the fat from her chop.

Carley smiled. "Seriously, I think one would do well. There's nothing here for older women."

Her aunt cocked a playful brow at her. "*I'm* an older woman. And this pork chop suits me just fine."

"But you're also a local. The shop clientele are mostly older women in groups." She looked around at the filled tables. "Even the men shoppers usually accompany wives. This place is too busy, and the hamburger and pizza places aren't suitable for sitting around making pleasant conversation."

She was about to add that San Francisco and Sacramento had quaint little bistros on practically every block, but she feared sounding like the city mouse talking down to the country mouse.

"You might have a point there," Aunt Helen said thoughtfully.

"That place next to the drugstore would be the perfect location too. Is the owner just going to let it sit there empty? I didn't see a *For Sale* sign or anything."

"I guess Emmit's too busy to bother with it. But I doubt Tallulah's ever had a sandwich shop like those in Seattle."

Carley had forgotten her aunt was more well-traveled than she was. "That's what Blake should think about investing in, instead of a rental house."

Aunt Helen winced. "I love my son-in-law, but for Sherry's sake I would appreciate your not putting that bug in his ear. A rental house would be a fairly safe investment, but another business besides the barber shop would be just too risky."

"I understand," Carley said and dropped the subject.

Dropping it from her mind proved more difficult, she discovered while preparing an omelet for supper. Tonight's basketball game was in Picayune, almost eighty miles away, and Sherry had offered her a ride. But asking Jenna's permission to leave a couple of hours early would have been embarrassing, with less than a week on the job.

Earth-tone colors, she thought, chopping green onions. *Quaint, but trendy, like a Parisian cafe. Sandwiches and soups on the menu, and light meals like pasta salad.*

Idle pondering, like chewing gum for the brain. But fun to imagine anyway.

chapter 11

The deaths of seven astronauts aboard the space shuttle *Columbia* put everyone in a somber mood on Saturday. Jenna brought a small portable television to Grandma's Attic to keep up with news coverage, and shoppers conversed in reverent tones, almost as if at a wake.

Even conversations between patrons at Corner Diner were subdued.

"Carley dear, forgive my nosiness, but I just have to ask something," Aunt Helen said as they lunched together.

Carley sprinkled pepper on her chicken and dumplings and braced herself for what she suspected was coming. "Sure."

"Do you never think about death?"

"I think about it," Carley said.

"What about God?"

"I believe in God. I'm just . . . not sure what to think about Him."

Aunt Helen nodded, brows denting. "But shouldn't that make you want to find out more?"

The worry mingled with affection in her expression made Carley want to pat her arm and agree to do whatever it would take to reassure her. But she owed her aunt no less than honesty. "I did  at one time. But then some things happened, and I wondered how He could love me enough to send His son to die for me and yet not protect me."

"What happened, Carley?"

"Just some things, I really can't talk about. But you can imagine what sort of men my mother attracted."

The aged face was a study in sadness. "You poor baby."

Carley turned her head to blink tears. When she had composed herself, she went on. "And please don't take offense—you and Uncle Rory are salt of the earth, but my most rotten experiences have been with religious people."

"I'm sorry to hear that," Aunt Helen said. "And I'm not even surprised. There are always wolves among the sheep. And often, even the sheep aren't all we should be. But you mustn't blame God. He surely must have put some good people in your life. Look where you are now."

"Well, yes." And was it fair to blame God for Huey Collins and not thank him for Janelle Reed and Aunt Helen?

"God gives us all free will to choose, honey, and some people make terrible choices, live terrible lives. Would you want to give up your free will in exchange for everyone behaving as they should?"

"No, of course not," Carley said. "But why didn't God put good people in my mother's life?"

"I'm convinced He did. We have teachers all around us. But some people, like poor Linda, are so focused on themselves that they never notice them."

That made sense, Carley conceded silently. At length she took her aunt's hand. "Thank you for caring enough about me to bring this up. I promise, I'll think about what you said. But as for church, you're going to have to give me some time. I don't want to be disappointed again."

"Then, I won't pressure you," Aunt Helen said, squeezing her hand. "God wants your heart, more than your body in a pew. But worshiping with fellow believers is still very important. I hope one day you long for that fellowship enough to give church another try."

"One day," Carley said, and qualified it by adding, "Maybe."

Later that afternoon, Carley and Jenna stepped out onto the sidewalk to wave at a flushed-faced bride and groom leaving First Baptist in a reconditioned Model T. When Patrick stopped by with a supper invitation from his mother, Carley asked about the game, and congratulated him on the victory over Picayune. "Tell her I'll bring Caesar salad," she said, and hurried over to Henderson's after work for the ingredients.

The Kemps lived in a two-story mixed-brick house about a quarter of a mile southeast of town on Mill Creek Road. Blake grilled chicken, Sherry stirred together a potato salad, and Aunt Helen tended a pot of butter beans while Carley made the salad and iced the glasses. After supper, Patrick left for Hattiesburg and a movie with friends, and Sherry loaded the videotape of *The Sound of Music* simply because during the meal Carley had mentioned never having seen it.

"How do you solve a problem like Maria. . . ." Carley sang all the way home.

———

With shops closed Monday, Carley felt no guilt over staying up late Sunday night finishing *Camellia Street*, but she grumbled when the doorbell woke her at 8:45. *I should have packed my robe,* she thought, pulling her coat over her pajamas. Or even bought one, once she decided to stay longer.

"I'm sorry, did I wake you?" Blake asked as Carley let him in.

"That's all right." But she did not ask him to sit, hoping his business would be brief so she could return to bed.

"I just came from the bank."

"Umm-hmm?" Carley ran her tongue over her teeth, imagining how foul her breath must be.

"They denied our loan. They said we owe too much on our house and my shop."

It was Carley's turn to say, "I'm sorry."

He ran a hand through his dust-colored hair and took a breath.

"But it would still work, if you'd finance the house yourself."

"I can't do that, Blake." She was glad for a legitimate excuse. "I'll need the full amount to buy a new one back home."

"It would work out the same," he argued. "You'd just have to get a loan, and apply our monthly payments to it."

"I would have to pay interest," Carley said, fishing.

"But you'd earn interest at the same time. It's a minor inconvenience. You still have a huge chunk of money for the down payment, so your notes should be small."

"Blake . . ."

"We'd do it for you."

She was left with no more excuses. Only a reason that she could not say, not without hurting his feelings—that even though he was family, even though there were times that she liked him, he was not the sort of person with whom she could engage in business with total confidence. And so she said, simply, "I'm sorry, Blake. I'd rather not."

He was hurt anyway. Angry, actually. "Well, that's just great!"

"I'm sorry, Blake," she said for the third time, wishing he would leave.

For three seconds he stared at her. As if measuring his words, he said with bitter tone, "You know, Sherry did more for Miss Cordelia than you ever did."

His meaning was crystal clear. She had snatched the inheritance away from people more deserving. She felt heat rise to her own face, needle-prickles in her sinuses. "My grandmother had a choice."

"You never even bothered to look her up."

"You need to go now. Please."

"Yeah, all right," he muttered, but paused halfway though the door to throw back, sarcastically, "You'll want to get Kay Chapman over here right away. Sorry we delayed your getting your hands on even more money."

Sick at heart, Carley made a mug of tea and sat in her coat in the chilly kitchen. Sleep would be impossible, and she did not feel up to visiting the library, the first item on today's list. The worst part of it was that there was no one in whom she could confide, even from the pay phone. Janelle Reed had her hands full in Alaska. Former co-worker Diane Paxton, close enough of a friend to ask Carley to be a bridesmaid in her wedding two years ago, had faded into the land of matrimonial bliss and had yet even to send a thank-you note for the Wedgwood place setting.

And she certainly could not go to Aunt Helen. As close as they had become, her loyalty would still naturally be to Sherry and Blake.

Sherry came over a half hour later, after Carley had changed into slacks and her grandmother's flannel shirt and was halfheartedly wrapping dishes in newspaper.

"I'm on my free hour, can't stay long," Sherry said at the door. "Blake called. I'm so sorry he was upset. But thank you for not agreeing to finance the house."

"Then, you're not angry?" Carley asked, afraid to breathe.

"I'm totally relieved. I didn't want to buy it anyway."

"But you told Uncle Rory . . ."

"Because that's how it is when you're married to a man with big dreams. I shoot so many of them down that once in a while I just have to go along."

"Oh dear." Tears blurred Carley's eyes again. "I was so worried."

Sherry took both her hands. "Well, put it out of your mind now. Blake'll get over his grumps. I'll talk with him. Really, Carley, it's not a big deal."

"Thank you."

"No, thank *you.*" Releasing her hands, Sherry looked over her shoulder. "Now, I have to leave in fifteen minutes. What do you have for a raging sweet tooth?"

"Do you like mint chocolate chip ice cream?"

"Does Popeye like spinach?"

When she was gone, Carley's mood was so much lighter that she showered and pulled on her black slacks and teal sweater and headed for the library.

"Thank you for recommending this," she said, handing *Camellia Street* over to Mr. Juban. "I enjoyed it."

He gave her a cautious look. "You didn't . . ."

It took her a second to catch on. "Peek ahead? Not even once."

"I'm so proud of you," Mr. Juban beamed. "Now, let's see. . . . You should read *Delta Dreams* next—start at his first book."

"You're talking about Bertram Norris?" came a man's voice. Dale Parker stepped up to the counter and smiled. "Hi."

"Hi," Carley said back, struck again with the blueness of his eyes.

"Bert and my brother were in the same fraternity at USM."

Mr. Juban's eyes widened. "Then you went to his signing a few years ago?"

Dale shook his head. "I missed it. I was in Florida for my parents' thirtieth anniversary."

"I wouldn't have time to finish another book," Carley said. Of the five more lunch breaks remaining at Grandma's Attic, she would probably spend at least a couple with Aunt Helen. And with the trucking company scheduled for Thursday, she could not devote any evening hours to reading. "I'll just wait and buy it in San Francisco."

"You're leaving soon?" Chief Parker asked, as his blue eyes revealed what seemed to be genuine disappointment. Or perhaps he was simply being a gentleman.

"Next Monday."

"But that leaves you with a week with nothing to read," Mr. Juban said, as if that were the most terrible tragedy he could imagine. "Since you're going to buy a copy over there anyway, just check one out here and turn it in just before you leave. Then you can finish later."

"I wouldn't be able to leave it alone," Carley said, touched by the librarian's solicitousness. "And I still have packing to finish."

"Order a copy online," Dale Parker suggested. "You'll have it waiting in your mailbox back home."

"That's a good idea."

Mr. Juban brightened. "Yes, a good idea. But you'd better do it right away, while no one's on the computer."

Carley had hoped it would be available anyway, so she could look over the classified ads in the *Chronicle*. But reluctantly she stepped away from the counter.

"Well, thanks," she said to both men.

Chief Parker nodded. "Have a good day, Miss Reed."

"Same to you."

On her way to the computer, Carley heard him ask Mr. Juban for state and federal income tax forms. A reminder that life would continue on here as before after she returned to California. That brought a surprising little stab of pain.

She ordered *Delta Dreams*, halfway fearing Mr. Juban would come over and scold her if she did not take care of that first. In the *Chronicle* classified section she noted three promising positions geared to her education: proofreader for a medical transcription business, editorial assistant at a publishing house, and enrollment services counselor at a business college. She brought up her résumé from her e-mail account, then switched to the word-processing program to write a cover letter and résumé.

"I have six printouts," she said, placing them on the counter beside six older copies of *Southern Living* she would scan for recipes during snippets of free time.

"That'll be sixty cents," Mr. Juban said. "Did you remember to order the book?"

Carley had to smile. "I remembered. May I leave these here while I use the telephone?"

"Of course."

She dialed Kay Chapman's number. "I'm going to need to put the house up on the market after all," she said.

Thankfully, Kay did not ask for details. "How about if I stop by in the morning with the contract?"

———

"Why didn't you tell me about that FBI recruiter?" Deputy Garland Smith asked back at the station.

Dropping the tax forms on a bare spot on his desk, Dale replied, "What's to tell? I'm not interested."

"Sure," Garland said with a shrug. In his midforties, he had dark hair graying at the temples, a salt-and-pepper mustache. He was a decent man, not one to sulk, but the round dark eyes could not conceal his disappointment.

Who could blame him? Twelve years on the force, and then to be passed over in favor of a rookie who'd had a lucky break. Dale had no illusions that the Board of Aldermen had not hoped the publicity of his appointment would benefit the antiquing businesses. He probably had helped put Tallulah on the map.

And I'd jump at the FBI in a minute, if I could! he thought, pulling out the wooden desk chair on rollers. Or last summer's invitation from the Dallas police force, to join their Criminal Investigation Division. He glanced at Garland, now printing out his duty report. *At least you can leave this Disneyland for Antique Collectors.*

Suddenly, the office seemed to close in on him, just as the town had closed in on him years ago. He took clipboard and citation pad from his desk drawer and pushed out his chair again. "I think I'll go up to 589. Catch some speeders."

Garland's brows lifted. While Dale would make traffic stops when infractions took place under his nose, he usually consigned the speed traps to the two deputies. One of the perks of being chief. But today he needed to be away from the probability that some citizen would stroll in any minute to complain about a pothole or leaning stop sign or, worse, want to simply make small talk.

"You don't have to do that," Garland said. "I'll go."

Dale went to the coatrack for his jacket. "Just hold down the fort. The girls all say I look handsome with flushed cheeks."

The deputy laughed, and the tension cleared.

Turning the cruiser onto Main Street, Dale passed Carley Reed driving the Tates' 2003 platinum-colored Cadillac DeVille. She returned his wave.

She would have gone out with you if you had asked, Dale told himself. She was a pretty woman, and he could tell by the light in her eyes that she had a sense of humor. It was a pity she was returning to California. Two weeks had passed since he had last attempted to telephone Riley. Incredibly, being forced to give up on the hope of ever hearing her voice again had softened the knot in his chest somewhat. And a woman who could make him laugh would speed the healing. But she would have to be a woman content to stay in Hickville, and obviously Miss Reed was not.

She reads Bertram Norris, he thought with a dry smile, pulling to the side of the highway behind a kudzu-draped telephone pole. Was that irony? He never quite grasped the meaning of the word. But of one thing he was certain—if Bert had decided to become an architect or engineer, he himself would be in a posh office with a view of a skyline, instead of on the side of the road, waiting to ruin some trucker's day.

Or, to divide the blame further, if only Chad had not sold him the '67 Mustang.

His older brother had bought the firethorn-red fastback from a neighbor during high school and restored it into the envy of every jock at Lincoln High. It was a chick magnet.

So, during their parents' thirtieth anniversary celebration six years ago, when Chad mentioned needing a more family-suitable automobile, Dale pounced on the offer. The wasted return airline ticket did not matter. Nor did it matter that he would have to sell the three-month-old Chevy Camaro waiting in the overnight parking garage of Jackson International Airport. He owned the car he had lusted over throughout his teen years!

"You're gonna have to buy a repair manual," Chad had advised. "The one in the glove compartment's so old it's missing pages."

The seven-hour drive from Tallahassee to Hattiesburg was sheer joy. It was while Dale was refilling at the Citgo Station on Highway 98 that he glanced over at the Books-A-Million, a parking lot away. He had planned to order the manual online, but decided he may as well stop in. The afternoon was still young—1:30, now that he had gained an hour changing time zones.

Had he *known* the impact that decision would have on his life, he would have continued driving. Or better yet, flown back as originally planned. What good was the car doing him now, rusting at the bottom of his pond?

Bertram Norris, Chad's fraternity brother and fellow big man on campus was just packing up after a signing for his first book, *Delta Dreams*. "I'm starving," he had said with arm loped around Dale's shoulders. "Let's go next door, you big hero, and I'll buy your lunch."

It took very little persuading. Dale had only eaten an apple during the drive, and he was especially fond of Chinese food with all its vegetarian choices. But he should have refused when Bertram ordered drinks while they waited for their entrées, and then thrice again during the meal. That much alcohol after a two-year abstinence was lethal.

Literally.

Six years had passed, but he could still hear the sickening thud, just over the hill past Mount Olive Church. He had not seen Gwen Stillman until he backed up to see what animal he had hit. His ears had caught the sound of a motor advancing between the shrieks from the infant in the stroller three feet away. Sweating and shaking, he shifted back to first gear and took back roads, making a circle, approaching Highway 42 and then Black Creek Road from the west.

He had no idea what damage had been done other than cracks webbing his windshield on the passenger side, could only hope it was not extreme enough to attract attention. He hid the Mustang in bushes on his land. Faintly he could hear the sirens as he lay huddled in the back seat suffering from heat and grief.

At sunset he jogged across country northward toward Highway 589, slapping at mosquitoes. He hot-wired an old pickup truck outside a farmhouse with no lights in the windows. He abandoned the truck in a Circle K parking lot in Jackson and continued four miles to the airport on foot, grateful for the daily running and strength workouts.

Still, he was exhausted by the time he drove the Camaro into his driveway, after midnight. There were eleven messages on his answering machine. He listened to the most recent, from Garland, took a quick shower to wash away all evidence of a cross-country trek, and then dialed the station.

"Yeah, Garland, what in the world's going on?"

"Aw, Dale, where've you been? I called your folks' house and paged you three times at the airport."

"My folks left for Gatlinburg this morning, and I never heard any page. The car wouldn't start, and I had to have the Chevy people send a tow truck to the parking garage so they could fix the alternator."

The news of Gwen Stillman's death hit him like a ton of bricks, even though he had witnessed the awkward way she lay. Doctor Holden, the county coroner, had already ascertained that a red vehicle was involved. Fruit stand owner, Dana Bell, had called in to report seeing a damaged red sports car speeding eastward on Highway 42 this afternoon, while on her way home for her asthma inhaler.

"I'm on my way," Dale had said, rubbing the bumps on his cheek. Even those could be explained. A person coming from Florida without mosquito bites simply had not had a good time.

He worked diligently on the investigation, coordinating information with the state police, putting in extra hours. It was the least he could do. Most of Tallulah turned out for the funeral. Thankfully, the casket was closed, but the framed photographs on the table beside it were just as haunting. Gwen Stillman, from infant to gap-toothed schoolgirl, from adolescent perched in a horse's saddle to cap-and-gowned teenager holding up a diploma, from blushing bride to beaming mother.

"I hope you catch that monster like you did the last one," was expressed to him several times. The sense of community outrage was almost palpable.

Turning yourself in won't bring her back, he had reminded himself. And the thought of becoming the target of all that outrage had given him nightmares, terrifying him to the point of nausea. Especially after basking in all the attention and adulation. Those same newspapers and magazines that had lauded him as a rescuer of women would not hesitate to decry him for hit-and-run murder.

There was no way he was going to be able to have the Mustang repaired—as if he cared for the accursed car any longer. But he could not leave it to be discovered during hunting season, even though when he slipped out there to retrieve his suitcase, he had removed the plates, wiped it down, and scraped off the vehicle identification number. His land had been on the market for four months. He could not see Kay Chapman wading through shrubs and briars, but any savvy potential buyer would surely do so.

The urgency heightened when Kay telephoned the station the morning of July fifth. "Remember Mr. Golden, who looked at your land back in May? He's decided he wants it. We'll be writing out a bid today."

It was routine for Dale to leave the station and make rounds. And no one would have blinked an eye at his swinging by his own property to give it a quick check. Still, paranoia had caused him to park the squad car behind a thick stand of pines. Setting the Mustang afire was not an option, for the smoke would be visible for miles around.

The pond on his property was not a natural pond—it had been formed when the previous landowners dammed a valley. His only solution was to drive it along the dam, cut to the right, and jump.

The low shrubs would spring back, covering tire tracks. The water was at its deepest there, fourteen feet waiting to swallow all evidence.

The only hitch was the thought of anyone slipping back there to fish or swim. But, he had reassured himself, if the Mustang happened to be discovered before it rusted into mud, it would simply indicate the guilty person had panicked and sought out this hiding place. By then, someone else would be handling the investigation. He planned to get out of Dodge as soon as possible.

The best laid plans of mice and men go oft astray, Dale thought, frowning. Faintly he could hear the engine roar of an advancing log truck. He touched the keypad of the dash-mounted Stalker ATR police radar to measure oncoming-vehicle speed. He had a feeling he would use up his ticket book today. It was either this or give vent to frustration by going home and screaming into his pillow. Which did absolutely no earthly good. How well he knew!

Not only did Kay Chapman bring a contract in the morning—she also brought a sign for the front yard.

Well, that's done, Carley thought as Kay's Lexus pulled out of the driveway. Ruby Moore, checking her mailbox, crossed the street.

"Oh dear, are you leaving soon?"

"Next Monday. Thursday I'll be moving in with my aunt and uncle."

"Then I insist you come for supper tonight."

"You've already done enough," Carley protested.

Ruby waved a hand. "I have to eat anyway. I'm just going to bake a chicken in my clay roaster and steam some broccoli."

But she also prepared something new to Carley's experience: grits. Not served with butter, as she would have supposed, but in a casserole with melted cheddar and garlic. They were quite good, once Carley became used to the texture. They played UNO afterward, something Carley had not done since leaving the Redding group home.

Mrs. Templeton brought over another jar of figs the following morning. Carley gave her a paisley silk scarf she had decided should go next door instead of in the Salvation Army box. And Gayle Payne telephoned her at Grandma's Attic with an invitation to supper.

The rest of the week sailed by. A truck from Van Dyke Freight came for the four pieces of furniture and two boxes on Thursday morning. Carley moved in with Aunt Helen and Uncle Rory after work, returning to the house Friday morning to meet the truck from Renaissance Consignment. The two workers carted off everything but the appliances, as Kay had advised keeping them would make the house more marketable.

Tallulah lost to Oak Grove by one point that evening. Voices were hoarse from yelling, spirits subdued as Carley helped the Beta Club parents clean the concession stand. She had volunteered simply in the hopes of making amends with Blake. To her relief, he was cordial. But he did not apologize for the harsh things he had said. Perhaps he was embarrassed.

And perhaps that was the real reason for his not coming over to the Hudsons' the next evening for Carley's lasagna.

"He has a little headache," Sherry said, not quite meeting Carley's eyes.

Even though Jenna had already given Carley a paycheck the day before, she brought over a coral necklace Sunday afternoon as a thank-you gift, and Stanley and Loretta Malone stopped by to wish her a safe flight.

As Uncle Rory backed the Roadmaster out of the driveway Monday morning, Carley opened her mouth to ask him to drive over to Third Street before leaving town. She closed it again. That was already his intention, she realized instinctively as Main Street's stop sign drew closer. And sure enough, he turned right instead of left.

Aunt Helen did not ask why they were heading south, nor did she seem surprised.

So that's what it means to have a family, Carley thought, eyes filling. People who knew the desires of her heart, because they cared enough to imagine what they might be.

"Don't pull in," she asked as they neared the house. She wanted to see it all and, from a distance, have a picture in her mind to go with the one Kay Chapman had promised to send from the listing. But there was no point to getting out of the car. As her bond with the house grew, she had kept in the back of her mind that she would have to let it go. Another lesson from childhood. However deep she allowed affection to go, would be how deep she'd feel the pain later. One fond look and then detach.

Detaching from her aunt and uncle proved more difficult. As she embraced both dear old souls, she found herself promising to come back for a visit in a year or so.

"I'm praying for your safe trip, Carley," Aunt Helen said.

Carley did not mind. If God indeed listened to prayers, surely those of Aunt Helen found His ear.

"Did you have a nice holiday?" Mrs. Kordalewski called from the mail alcove after Carley wheeled her carryon into the lobby on Monday afternoon.

"Very nice, thank you," Carley called back.

"Wait and I will go up with you—so we can visit."

At this final leg of the long journey, Carley desired nothing more than to get up to her apartment. But she waited.

"We have missed our schoolteacher friend," the old woman said when the elevator doors closed.

Feeling guilty for her impatience, Carley thanked her and asked, "How is your husband?"

"Ah, that man! He bought four of the movies called *Rocky* at the synagogue rummage sale for fifty cents each, and so he asked our granddaughter to find us a good deal on a VCR."

"Why don't you just borrow mine? I never use it."

"Thank you, but we would not like to do that. What if it breaks? And anyway, Julie bought the VCR already. Only she tried to get Shimon to get a new kind of machine she says is better."

"A DVD player?"

Mrs. Kordalewski nodded. "Shimon asked if he could watch his *Rocky* movies on the DVD, and Julie said no, but we could buy the same ones better on . . ."

"Disks," Carley supplied.

"Yes, that was it." The elevator doors parted, and they stepped out into the hall. "And then Shimon asked what he would do with the movies he bought, and Julie said they were cheap, just to throw them away. He said that was no good, such a waste, just get the VCR."

She passed a spotted hand over her face. "He wanted to fight in the ring when he was a young man, but his father made him go to pharmaceutical school. And so now he watches the *Rocky* movies, sometimes two in the same day. He is hard of hearing, you know. I already came to check the mail two times, even though I knew it was too early, just to get away from the noise."

Carley would have found the situation comical if not for the distress in Mrs. Kordalewski's face. An idea popped into her head. "Did you know that you can buy earphones for televisions? He would be the only person able to hear it."

The sparse brows raised hopefully. "And where can you buy such things?"

"Any electronics store. I tell you what, I have to run errands tomorrow. I'll pick up a set."

"How much do they cost?"

"They're very cheap. Not more than two or three dollars."

You're such a liar, Carley chided herself inside her living room. She was discovering that the best thing about having money was the freedom it gave her to do something for someone else. But she understood Mrs. Kordalewski's pride, that she would insist upon repaying her.

Telemarketers took up most of the space on Carley's answering machine. But there were two messages from Jan Terris. Weary as she was, Carley picked up the receiver and dialed.

Please let it be good news, she thought, leaning against the counter, listening to the first, second rings, and the *Rocky* theme song coming through the wall.

"Alton is so happy, back in his old school," Mrs. Terris said. "He rejoined the choir and the drama club—he was too intimidated to do anything that stood out at Emerson-Wake."

"I'm so happy to hear that," Carley said as her fatigue evaporated.

"I promised Alton I would check on you. When you didn't return my calls, I called the school. The secretary said you'd resigned. We've been worried."

Carley explained where she had been for the past three weeks. "I just walked in a half hour ago. It was kind of you to worry."

"Well, I'm just glad you're safe and sound. Alton will be too. But what will you do now?"

"Look for a job. And a house across the Bay within commuting distance."

"I hope you find both," Mrs. Terris said.

Tuesday, after signing up for the civil service examination at the State Employment Agency, Carley had an excellent turkey avocado sandwich on eight-grain bread at a little café on Hyde Street. She admired the art-deco layout of the menu and the warm colors of the decor, the soothing, unobtrusive background music and relaxed atmosphere.

Tallulah really needs one of these, she thought, munching on a kosher spear. Surely one day someone besides Blake would come up with the idea.

She bought earphones at RadioShack, groceries at Safeway—and indulged in the luxury of a taxi ride home instead of struggling with bags on the bus. The answering machine blinked with another message from Jan Terris, asking Carley to call.

"A friend of my husband's, a Bruce Temple, is CEO of a software company, and they have a position open for a catalog proofreader. He says it's yours if you want it."

"Just like that?" Carley said.

Mrs. Terris laughed. "That's how it is in business."

"There are seven people in our catalog department," said Bruce Temple, a fortyish man with family photographs in his office at Pragmatic Software, Incorporated, on 43rd Avenue. The position paid eighty-seven dollars a month more than teaching at Emerson-Wake, and Carley was assigned a quiet cubicle with only the clicks of fingers against keyboards and piped in soft instrumental music as background. Even if the job—combing software instructions and advertisements for any grammar or punctuation or typographical errors—was boring, at least she did not have the stress of maintaining discipline over anyone but herself.

"You have saved my life!" Mrs. Kordalewski popped in to say with a coconut cake in her hands. "Shimon, he says he hears better with the earphones, and so we are both happy."

"I'm so glad," Carley said.

With three and a half months remaining on her lease and no place for the items that would be arriving from Tallulah, she rented a unit in a personal storage facility on the corner of 11th and Mission Streets. And because, in May, she would have to sign another lease for at least six months or move before June first, she spent every free hour house hunting across the Bay.

They were far more expensive than she had imagined. For under two hundred thousand dollars, she could only hope to buy a small condominium unit. By April's end, Whitney Martin, the agent from Tanner & Associates had alerted her to two possibilities in Walnut Creek and Concord. Whitney possessed none of Kay Chapman's constraints against applying pressure, but Carley had made it clear that she would not sign a purchase agreement until her house had sold.

Becoming debt free was the most exhilarating experience she had ever known, and she intended to stay that way for as long as humanly possible. Lodged deep in her memory were the times she had had to screen telephone calls for her mother, lying to collectors and enduring their verbal abuse. Owing money gave other people power over your life. Too many people had held that power in her life. She would be her own woman, or die trying.

There were a few bites on the house, back in Tallulah. A young family signed a purchase agreement but failed to secure a loan because of extensive credit card debt. An older couple made three walk-through appointments, but ended up buying a mobile home on ten acres. A man from Jackson who invested in rural properties bid sixty thousand. Kay did not even bring the offer to Carley.

"I knew you wouldn't want to *give* the house away," she said over the telephone.

Carley agreed.

"Don't be discouraged," Aunt Helen consoled on Saturday, the nineteenth of April. They took turns telephoning, every other week or so. Though Carley had called just last Tuesday, she was the one to call again this time.

"Life just moves more slowly down here," her aunt went on. "People take a long time making up their minds."

"My real estate agent keeps telling me I should go ahead and buy a condominium, then pay it off when the house sells."

"Well, that's an option. There's nothing wrong with that."

"Would you do it?" Carley asked.

"No."

"Why?"

"Because I've lived long enough to look back and regret almost every decision I allowed fear to pressure me into making."

Carley was about to reply, respectfully, that fear was not the issue, when she realized that it was the *only* issue. Fear of losing the condominiums to another buyer. Fear of how long it might be before any others came on the market that she could afford. Fear of having to extend her apartment lease. Even fear of annoying the real estate agent.

She was not even especially fond of either condominium. The one in Walnut Creek was short on closet space, and the kitchen in the Concord unit was as small as her apartment kitchen and had counter tiles the color of Pepto-Bismol.

"I should wait, shouldn't I?" Carley said. Just the thought unclenched the knot in her stomach.

"Perhaps you should, dear."

Carley's throat thickened. "I'm so glad I have you in my life, Aunt Helen."

There was a pause. Perhaps her aunt was experiencing the same emotions, for her voice was softer when she replied, "You're a dear girl, Carley. And it's as if God is giving me a chance to make up for neglecting my sister."

Whitney Martin called three evenings later. "You've lost out on Concord. The loan officer at Guaranty Bank says you can get a mortgage for the Walnut Creek unit based on the equity on your house with no prepayment penalty, over the telephone in less than a week."

"I don't want to borrow any money," Carley reminded her.

"Then, why didn't you wait until *after* you sold your house to start looking?" the agent said crisply.

It was a fair question. Carley admitted, "I should have done that."

"Don't you realize that once you've paid a hundred and thirty thousand dollars down, you would have only a seventy thousand dollar mortgage? The notes would be far lower than the rent you're paying. And with the interest being tax deductible, you would still come out ahead even if your house took years to sell."

That made sense. *There's nothing to fear about this,* she reasoned with herself. *If you don't like the condo, at least you'll have a piece of property you can sell later when something better comes along. Better than throwing money away on rent.*

So why was her stomach beginning to cramp again? Carley said, "I just can't do it that way."

Photographs and a letter from Janelle Reed arrived on Saturday, May 3, along with a card from Bank of California inviting her to move her checking account options up a notch, now that she qualified for the "Over Twenty-five Club." She was grateful for her former counselor's thoughtfulness, even to the bank for at least recognizing that this was her day. But after twenty-six years, hope had still not died that her birthday would be different from most other days, an occasion to remember.

You have the money, she told herself midway through cleaning her oven. *Treat yourself.* She telephoned for a reservation at Rose Pistola on Columbus Street, and ironed the special-occasion black dress. That evening she had a lovely meal of grilled swordfish with fennel, potato, olive tapenade, and strawberry cheesecake for dessert, then took a taxi on to Gill Theater for the University of San Francisco production of *Much Ado About Nothing.*

"Ah . . . excuse me?"

Carley turned. The man behind her in the ticket line had a handsome angular face and collar-length brown hair.

"I just have to tell you . . . you have great hair."

She smiled. "Thank you."

"So, how come your date's making you get the tickets?"

"I'm by myself."

He glanced off to his left, so automatically Carley did too. A young woman in black dress and silvery fringed shawl stood studying a poster. Lowering his voice, leaning close enough to give Carley a whiff of mint mouthwash, he said, "I happen to have the best view from a hot tub in North Beach. Do you like sushi?"

"I've never met her," Carley said before stepping out to move to the back of the line. Her ticket was in the nosebleed section, which was not such a terrible thing because, in spite of her healthy bank account, she felt a little guilty for spending so much on her meal.

Back in her apartment building she left the elevator to find a semi-flat postal package outside her door with the Hudsons' return address. She smiled and opened it inside the living room. Along with a birthday card with Uncle Rory's signature and Aunt Helen's penned, *Dearest Carley, may this year be a great adventure for you,* was a handcrafted backpack of royal blue bandanna cloth. She hugged the bag to herself and went into the kitchen, where the answering machine blinked with two waiting messages. Sherry's voice first, wishing her the happiest of days, the second from Aunt Helen, hoping she was out having a good time. Carley played them again. She had not even realized they knew her birth date. She did not know theirs, a mistake she intended to correct tomorrow.

A tear rolled down her cheek, and she wiped it with the edge of her hand. She lay staring at her dark bedroom ceiling a half hour later and asked herself, *Can you do another year of this?*

Her job was not what she had expected. However friendly and helpful her co-workers were, most were married or engaged, so their social lives revolved in those directions. Contact during work hours was limited, as she spent most of her day poring over copy in her cubicle.

You can look for another job. The Terrises would understand, especially if she gave notice. Not every position was suited to every temperament. She was more of a people person than she had realized. Grown-up people. And she particularly missed the friendly association with the clientele of Grandma's Attic.

She mulled over that thought, reminded herself that had been a temporary position, no longer available even if she were to return to Tallulah. But there were other jobs, if not in the small town, in nearby Hattiesburg.

Or she could look into opening that café.

A shiver ran through her as she realized that notion had never been far from the back of her mind.

There were other things she missed about Tallulah. Sharing a dinner table with family. Returning neighbors' waves while leaving for work. Hearing owls at night. The aromas of pine trees and chimneys and sweet olive blossoms. Having people greet her by name at the bank, the grocery store, the library. Feeling connected to her grandmother as she pottered about the house.

What's stopping you from having that again? Even asking herself that question brought an ache to her chest. She wanted to go back. And there was no reason why she could not.

She would be charged a penalty for taking the house off the

market, but living mortgage free would more than make up for that. The furniture in storage would need to be shipped across country again, along with her computer and pieces of apartment furniture worth salvaging, but again, one month's rent that she did *not* have to pay here would probably cover that cost.

Still, she waited three days before taking any action. She wanted to be certain hormones or loneliness were not goading her into making a decision she would regret.

———

"When do you leave?" Mrs. Kordalewski asked three weeks later, when Carley went next door to break the news. Plugged into the television, Shimon nodded from his lounge chair and turned back to a boxing match between Sylvester Stallone and a muscular black man with a Mohawk haircut.

"Next Friday," Carley said.

"But what will we do without our dear friend?"

"You'll do fine. I met the new tenants down in the office. They're an older couple, the Solareks."

Mrs. Kordalewski's spindly fingers probed the hollow of her neck. "I knew a Solarek family back in Krakow, when I was a girl. Nice people. The boys threw rocks at some bullies one time, and made them go away. Perhaps they are related?"

"Wouldn't that be something?" Carley said.

Midmorning on the last day in May, Carley turned off the ignition of a rented Volkswagen in the driveway of 5172 Third Street and smiled.

This was the right thing to do.

That thought was reinforced when she let herself into the living room. The empty space she had left now boasted a brown corduroy sofa and two mismatched upholstered chairs, table with lamp, coffee table, and braided rug. In her bedroom were a double mattress and box spring on a bed frame with two pillows and bedding, as well as a dresser and mirror. One yellow and one blue towel hung in the bathroom, a half dozen washcloths of assorted colors were folded in the cabinet.

In the kitchen, a vase of fragrant white gardenias sat in the middle of a slightly battered oval maple table surrounded by four chairs—two maple and two folding metal. There were assorted dishes, pots, and utensils in the cabinets, and faded towels in a drawer. In the refrigerator—plugged in and humming—were two casseroles with warming-up instructions from Gayle and Sherry, and a pot of soup from Uncle Rory.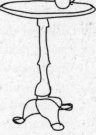

"Everyone cleaned out storage sheds and attics," Aunt Helen explained when she dropped by on her lunch break. "We made it into a party. When your things come, you can give what you can't use to the Salvation Army."

Kay Chapman stopped by that afternoon. Carley wrote the

agency a check for three percent of the home's appraised price.

"I feel terrible about this," Kay said, closing her briefcase.

Carley, her stomach pleasantly digesting Gayle's chicken-and-rice casserole, shook her head. "That was the best twenty-four hundred dollars I've ever spent."

———————

"I know I dropped a couple of pennies down here yesterday," Carley said on the sixth of June, fingers probing the bottom of her purse. She did not want to hand checkout clerk Anna Erwin another crisp twenty dollar bill from the airport ATM, not for a grocery total of twenty dollars and four cents.

"Don't worry about it, honey." The cashier scooped up pennies from the Shoal's Chewing Tobacco can on the side of the register.

"Hi, Carleyreed," Neal said. "Where did you go?"

"Hi, Neal." Carley smiled and hooked the two bags over her arm. "I've been away in California for four months."

"Oh. I found a kitty in the parking lot. She was so hungry she drank a whole can of milk. Dad says I can't give her a name until we're sure nobody lost her. Did you lose a kitty?"

"No, I sure didn't."

"Okay. Well, bye."

Carley's smile lasted all the way home. Tallulah in June was a feast for the senses. She almost wondered if it was against the law *not* to cultivate a flower garden, for all the geraniums and roses, impatiens and periwinkles, lilies and gladiolus, petunias and begonias sprouting from lawns. The air was heady with scents of magnolias and gardenia and jasmine.

And fresh-cut grass. Patrick, who earned pocket money with his lawn mower, had been by that morning.

And there were the vegetable patches. A family of five would not be able to consume all the tomatoes and cucumbers that had magically appeared upon her porch during the past week.

"What do you do with white squash?" she asked Mrs. Templeton at the roadside mailboxes. A bag with a half dozen of the vegetables that looked like flying saucers had turned up just that morning.

"I slice 'em crossways and batter fry 'em," her neighbor said.

"Batter fry?" Carley said, disappointed.

"Or you put 'em on a neighbor's porch."

Carley assumed she was hinting. "Sure, I'll bring them over."

"No, dearie." The woman gave her a knowing little smile. "I had my turn. Now it's yours."

Gayle Payne was glad to get them. Carley invited Ruby Moore over for pasta salad and rosemary chicken that evening.

"Petal High School's taking applications through this month for an English Lit teacher," her neighbor said.

"Petal?"

"About twenty-two miles east. The principal's my ex-husband's cousin, so let me know if you decide to apply, and I'll put in a good word for you."

Tactfully Carley said, "Would that really be a good plan?"

Ruby laughed. "Don and I get along fine now. It's just that while we were married he got along fine with *other* people too, if you catch my drift."

After Ruby walked back across the street, Carley wrestled with the idea of returning to teaching. Security and benefits, versus the idea growing in her mind like the begonias in the Paynes' yard. Like the grime on the window of Emmit White's empty café.

Fear, she recognized. She was not ready to go back into the classroom, and so fear would be the only reason to apply. Take the safe route, and then she could look back in her old age and wonder what might have happened if she had followed a dream.

You can do this, she told herself.

But what if she failed, lost all her money?

You'd still have a house, still be out of debt.

That is, if she determined not to borrow a dime and set aside a buffer amount to live on for six months if the place was not successful.

That meant doing her homework.

When Tallulah library shelves could produce only two books on starting a small business, she drove to Hattiesburg Saturday morning. It was a fairly large city positioned at the fork of the Leaf and Bouie Rivers, boasting two hospitals, a university, and two Super Wal-Marts. Inside Books-A-Million she saw a display of Bertram Norris's latest bestseller, *Thompson's Crossing*. Carley made a mental note to ask the clerk when it was due to come out in paperback, but then impulsively put a copy in her hand basket. She could afford it, she told herself.

She purchased four other books, two specifically on running small cafés. In the parking lot she caught a whiff of food being prepared and noticed the *Closed* sign being flipped to *Open* in the window of China Garden Restaurant. She usually avoided Chinese restaurants; not even the most delicious meal was worth the migraine triggered by the *MSG* many added to their dishes. But then, a second sign hanging in the window caught her eye—*No MSG*. She put her bag into the Volkswagen, saving *Thompson's Crossing* to skim, including the final chapter, at her table. She needed to concentrate on learning the restaurant business, and what Mr. Juban did not know would not hurt him. Besides, he would be thrilled to have another copy donated to the library.

The waiter was a young Asian man, probably a graduate student. "You read Mister Norris," he said, handing her a menu.

Carley touched the book jacket. "I've read a couple, but just bought this one. Do you?"

He shook his head and pointed to a dozen or so 8x10 frames, arranged in two rows upon the opposite wall. "We have his picture with my father."

There were no other customers yet, so Carley pushed out her chair. The matted photographs were of local and national celebrities: Johnny L. DuPree, first African-American mayor of Hattiesburg; Brett Favre, Green Bay Packer's quarterback and USM grad; a humorist named Jerry Clower. All smiled while standing beside an elderly Asian man. Even without Bertram Norris's autograph, Carley would have recognized the author from the photograph on the book jacket. He was tall, with goatee and dark hair combed back from high forehead. An arm was casually loped about the shoulders of the Asian man. *The best pepper steak in the South,* was penned beneath his autograph.

She smiled at the waiter. "I guess I'm having the pepper steak."

Later that afternoon she ran into Loretta Malone outside the bank, and learned that Chief Dale Parker was dating an accountant/former beauty queen who lived in Pascagoula. Loretta scolded lightly, "See? You should have moved back earlier."

"I'm not a police groupie," Carley said back just as lightly, in spite of the twinge of disappointment as she headed home.

The living room was her classroom of choice for studying the restaurant business, for she could close up the rest of the house and allow the attic fan to pull a minor gale through the screened windows. Locals complained about the heat, but she was not inconvenienced by it enough to get estimates on central air conditioning. Perhaps later, when there were not so many other things to do. Besides, the windows brought in soothing sounds of crickets trilling and tree frogs chorusing and people chatting on porches, as well as the aromas of green pine needles and jasmine.

At the east end of Third Street, Harold Cooper, manager of the Dollar General store, had a blue Ford Contour GL, loaded, with 57,000 miles on the odometer and a *For Sale—$3,800* sign in the window. Uncle Rory advised that it was a good deal but recommended she have it checked out mechanically.

"Be my guest," Mr. Cooper said, handing Carley the keys.

Emmit's Texaco and Garage dominated the corner of Main and Highway 42, just past the flashing light and across Main from the Tallulah Fire Department. A young man with grease-stained fingers and coveralls wrote out a work order and directed Carley to a waiting area with a dozen chairs, coffeepot and soda machine, television bolted to the wall, and the not-unpleasant smell of tires from a display rack.

She recognized Mr. White by the *Emmit* on the badge affixed to his blue chambray shirt. He was reed thin, as if working burned up all his food fuel, and had the hunched bearing—chin thrust forward, peripheral vision alert—of a woman intent upon being first to a sale table.

But however greedy, he was shrewd enough to do honest work, Uncle Rory had said. He might own the only garage in town, but most Tallulah residents would drive or tow their cars to Hattiesburg before allowing themselves to be cheated.

Carley devoted her attention to *The Complete Idiot's Guide to Starting Your Own Restaurant* while she waited. The temptation was strong to walk up to the counter and ask about the abandoned café, but she felt instinctively it was not a good plan to show her hand too early to a person with a reputation for greediness.

"Miss Reed?" he said finally.

Carley crossed the room, leaving the book in her seat.

"The GL needs the tires balanced, but it's a good car. Regular oil changes, never been wrecked."

"That's good to hear. Can I get the tires done now?"

He shook his head. "Not until it's your name on the registration."

It seemed a silly rule. She could understand it if she was getting a paint job or altering the car's appearance, but she did not think there were many vandals who went around fixing other people's cars.

The GL became hers three days later. Stanley Malone notarized the transaction, and she registered and paid the sales tax at the Department of Motor Vehicles in Hattiesburg on Monday and shopped online for car insurance in the library that afternoon. Her telephone was installed, so she would no longer have to use the library computer once her belongings arrived on Saturday. Still, it was always a pleasure to chat with Mr. Juban, even though she had to dodge questions about plot twists in *Thompson's Crossing*.

On Tuesday, her cousin Sherry followed her up to Jackson to turn in the rental Volkswagen. Carley treated her to lunch in Nora's Tea Room, a converted Victorian house.

"This is wonderful," Sherry sighed after a bite of chicken mushroom crepe. "I wish Tallulah had a place like this."

Carley stared at her. "Did you get that from your mother?"

"Well . . . no." Sherry's lenses magnified the confusion in her aquamarine eyes. "You bought it."

"Not the *crepe*," Carley laughed. She remembered, then, her promise not to put any bugs in Blake's ears. She had no way of knowing how much information wives shared with their husbands, even wives who did not want their husbands to start new businesses. Carefully and evasively she said, "I just remember telling Aunt Helen that Tallulah needed a quaint little café. Let's save room for dessert. The praline pie sounds heavenly."

When Sherry dropped her off at the house that afternoon, Carley telephoned Stanley Malone's office and asked to pay for an hour of his time.

"You're not in trouble, are you?" Loretta joked.

"I may be getting into some," Carley replied. "I'd like his advice on starting a business."

"Interesting. How about two o'clock Thursday? And don't worry about the fee. If you go into business, you'll need Stanley at some point anyway."

And so on the twenty-sixth of June, Carley sat again in Mr. Malone's office. She asked Loretta to stay and give her perspective as well. After spelling out her plan, she asked, cautiously, "What do you think?"

Stanley pressed steepled fingers to his chin. At length he said, "I think that's an idea waiting to happen."

Loretta nodded. "I agree. Someone's going to do it sooner or later. Stanley and I've discussed how the dining establishments here haven't kept pace with the shops. We lose a lot of business to Hattiesburg."

"But you don't want to go barging into something you might regret later," Stanley cautioned. "You need to see if it's financially feasible. We need to draw up a business plan."

"I've done that." Carley reached for the briefcase at her feet.

Husband and wife looked at each other.

"I've been studying," Carley explained, handing a manila folder across the desk. "I ordered a restaurant accounting software program online. And Aunt Helen gave me some information about the local laws for small businesses."

The attorney balanced his reading glasses on his nose and scanned the pages. "I'm impressed. It's all here. Projected sales, projected food and labor costs, projected profitability. . . ."

"But it's based entirely on my *not* having to borrow money. And the only way I can see to do it is to rent that building Mr. White owns."

Stanley looked doubtful. "Emmit White is a stingy old cuss."

"That's putting it mildly," Loretta said after a sip of her own tea. "He would charge a fortune."

"Even if he's not using the building?"

"It's not hurting him, sitting there idle," Stanley said.

"It's hurting him if he isn't collecting rent. Low rent is better than none."

"But high rent is better than low; that would be his way of thinking."

Loretta asked, "Why can't you start fresh somewhere else, Carley?"

"Because he already has equipment and furniture. And I'm assuming his place already meets building codes and zoning laws or he wouldn't have been able to open up in the first place."

"Well, yes," Stanley said. "I filed the papers for him. And I see your point."

"It can't hurt to pay him a visit, Stanley," Loretta said to her husband.

"Very well. I'll go sometime tomorrow."

———

"He doesn't want to lease it," Mr. Malone telephoned to say the following afternoon. "He said he'll sell it to you, with all the equipment and furniture, for a hundred and ten thousand dollars."

Ouch! Carley thought. "If he wants to sell it, why hasn't he listed it with a Realtor?"

"I'm sure he doesn't want to pay the fee, just figured someone like you would come along and offer one day."

"I can't pay that, not with the operating expenses I've projected until the profits come in."

"I agree. He lent me a key. Shall I give it back?"

Carley thought that one over. "How long can we keep it?"

"As long as you need it," Stanley replied. "The building's not going anywhere."

Uncle Rory was off on a fishing trip with some of his Lion's Club cronies, Aunt Helen said over the telephone, and would not be home until Saturday evening.

"That's all right, my things are coming Saturday anyway. But I'd like to ask him to look over Emmit White's place with me the first chance he has."

First, she respected her uncle's life experience, and second, the thought of entering a building that had been empty for eight years was creepy.

"How about after church Sunday?" Aunt Helen said with no trace of deviousness. "I'd like to see it myself."

"I'll meet you at the Old Grist Mill for lunch first," Carley said. "My treat."

———

The truck from Van Dyke Freight Company backed into the driveway a few minutes after 11:00 Saturday morning. Carley had been up since 7:00, pushing the pieces of donated furniture that she would not need into the back room. Two men in blue uniform shirts carried in her furniture, including Grandmother's belongings that had now come full circle. Afterward, Carley gave each a ten-dollar tip.

The fading sound of the truck's engine came through the open windows as Carley stripped tape from the box containing her computer. An hour later, she was at her desk in the space once occupied by Grandmother's piano, plugging the computer cord into her telephone jack.

Houston, we have control, she thought as the Internet screen popped up on her monitor.

———

The dining room at the Old Grist Mill was spacious and the decor decidedly rustic, with wide-planked floors and split-log walls decorated with old advertising signs. Punched-tin light fixtures illuminated red-checked tablecloths. Only half the tables were occupied, but Aunt Helen had said there would be people waiting in the lobby once the Methodists and Baptists let out.

As if on cue, the Kemps, members of First Methodist, showed up. Conner was home from Birmingham University for the summer, working weekdays in the pro shop at Canebrake Golf Club in Hattiesburg. He was a handsome boy, not as tall as Patrick, nor as blonde as his mother.

The waitress and busboy pushed another table over. When Carley asked that the Kemps be included on her ticket, Sherry protested. "No indeed, we're not going to let you—"

"Hush, Sherry, this girl's loaded," Blake said before ordering rib eye with two extra sides and encouraging his sons to do likewise. After the drinks were brought out he leaned his elbows on the table and said, "So Carley, I hear you're wanting to buy Emmit White's old hamburger joint."

Carley swallowed an ice cube, Sherry nudged her husband, and Aunt Helen rubbed the space between her eyes.

"Where did you hear that?" Carley asked when she could speak.

"Even Emmit gets his hair cut."

There was no point to being evasive. "I can't buy it. I hope he'll change his mind about renting it, if it's worth renting."

"We're going to check the place out after we leave here," Uncle Rory said.

The brothers exchanged looks.

"Mind if we tag along?" Patrick asked.

Conner lowered his voice. "They say Old Man White sealed the bodies up in the wall."

"That's why he let the place sit locked up for so long," Patrick said. "They needed time to decompose."

"Boys . . ." Aunt Helen and Sherry warned in unison.

Patrick glanced at the nearest table, where a family of five were involved in their own conversation. "But you gotta wonder. Tammy Giles said he bought two big sacks of quicklime that summer she worked at Green Thumb."

"Emmit's wife grows a garden." Uncle Rory dumped a packet of Splenda into his tea. "Lots of folks around here buy quicklime."

"It neutralizes soil that's too acidic," Blake explained to Carley.

"And it helps dead things decompose quicker," said an unrepentant Conner.

"There aren't any bodies there," Aunt Helen said firmly. "Now, how about finding a more pleasant subject?"

Carley waited until conversation turned to baseball and leaned closer to Sherry, on her left. "What bodies?"

Sherry murmured behind a cupped hand, "Several years ago, Emmit went to the lumber mill where his son-in-law worked and threatened to kill him for cheating on his daughter. Soon afterward, he disappeared with the girlfriend, leaving not only Emmit's daughter but a seven-year-old son. Nobody's heard from either one since. This being a small town, there are about a dozen theories."

As it turned out, everyone wanted to see the old café.

"Whew!" Conner wrinkled his nose, stepping over a pile of rags. "This place is a sauna."

"Spider webs," Sherry said. "I hope you like to dust, Carley."

Carley ran a finger along the chair railing. "I thought I did."

The building, though narrow, was roomier than it appeared from the outside. There was space for about a dozen small square tables, and four booths lined the south wall. The counter boasted a cash register, but the coating of dust would have to be removed before Carley could tell if it still worked. In the kitchen, stainless pots and pans were stacked on metal shelves. The ice maker, freezer, and walk-in cooler were shut off and their doors were propped open. The kitchen led to a small office with a gray metal desk and filing cabinet, and to a storage room with a door that accessed the gravel service lane running behind the shops.

After a while Patrick and Conner, tired of tapping on walls, left to walk home and watch baseball.

"It's structurally sound." Uncle Rory crouched to press a wall beneath the sink. "No sign of termites. But it needs an exterminator for the other critters."

Carley wheeled around from inspecting the grease-grimed grill. "What critters?"

Blake's foot shot ahead to stomp on the terra-cotta tile. He looked at the underside of his foot and grinned. "Just the usual eight-legged critters. Probably some with four too."

That was discouraging. As were the mildewed plastic brew baskets of both six-gallon iced tea machines.

"Hot water and bleach will clean those up." Sherry said.

"But are you sure you want to do this?" asked Aunt Helen.

Carley looked around, catching a vision of what it could be. Bathrooms scrubbed, the grout between the tiles bleached, the broken mirror in the men's room replaced, potpourri beside the sinks in both. The tables and curved-back chairs given fresh coats of varnish. The peeling wallpaper with multicolored-balloons stripped away, so that the walls could be painted a warm olive or teal green.

Carley's Café on a sign over the door.

"Carley?"

She blinked at her aunt. "Sorry. And yes, I'm sure. If the price is right."

chapter 14

Carley was waiting outside Emmit White's garage Monday morning at 7:45.

"You're too early, but you might as well drive it around to the dock and come wait inside," Emmit said peevishly. "Leave your key in the ignition."

That was what Carley was hoping for. Once inside, she approached the counter. "May I ask your advice, Mr. White?"

"I already told you, the Ford's a good buy."

"This isn't about the car. This is the final day Petal High will accept applications for a certain teaching position. Do you think I should apply?"

"Why are you askin' me?" he asked, staring across at her as if she were insane.

"Because from what I've learned about you, you had a similar decision. The owner of the Chevrolet dealership in Tylertown wanted to promote you to manager of the repairs department, but you had this dream of owning your own garage here in Tallulah."

His eyes narrowed. "What does a schoolteacher know about runnin' a business?"

"What did *you* know?" Carley asked.

"More than a schoolteacher knows, young lady."

"But I'm studying, every spare minute. And I'm a hard worker. I believe I can turn that empty building into a successful café, if you'll lease it to me."

"Nope." He opened a stapler by its hinges, filled it. "You got my price."

"I can't afford to buy it. Not until I've saved up enough profit."

"Profit!" Snapping the stapler closed, he said, "If you know that much about me, you know my son mismanaged that place and blew my whole operating account in the Biloxi casinos. I had to pay back wages and back taxes out of my own pocket. I ain't gonna be landlord to another failed business and give folk somethin' to laugh up their sleeves at again."

No wonder he was so bitter, Carley thought. This, and a daughter abandoned by her husband. "I didn't know about your son," Carley said. Stanley Malone was the source of her information, and he was not inclined to gossip. "Honest."

"Well, now you do."

"I'm sorry he hurt you. I know how you feel."

He snorted. "You can't know how I feel!"

"Yes, I can. Because my mother robbed me."

Suspicion narrowed the hazel eyes again. "What are you talkin' about?"

Carley had not expected the conversation to branch off in this direction. Too late to ponder if she should be so transparent. "There are givers and takers in this world, Mr. White. My mother was a taker, like your son. She robbed me of my childhood. But I'm determined to have a good life anyway. And I can do that teaching school, if I have to."

"Well good. Then you don't need my building."

"No, I don't. But the café has become my dream, Mr. White. Have you forgotten what it's like to have a great big dream?"

He stared at her for a while longer, then cleared his throat. "I'll rent you the place for a thousand a month. Not a penny less."

"I can only offer four hundred. I asked around, and that's about the norm for small businesses here."

"You're talkin' crazy. The shops don't have kitchen equipment. And it just needs cleanin'."

"It's not going to be a hamburger joint. It needs total refurbishing."

"Refurbishing!" he snorted. "Seven hundred."

Ordering her voice to stay steady in spite of knees turning to Jell-O, Carley said, "I'll make you proud of that place, Mr. White. But I can't go higher than five hundred."

This time his eyes widened, plowing deep furrows into his forehead. "She wants it for five hundred," he muttered to empty air.

Carley took a breath. "But I would have to ask for a five-year lease for that same price."

Emmit White snapped a work order into a clipboard and slapped it upon the counter. And just in case that was not enough drama, he slapped a pen beside it. "Here, fill out the top for the repair."

"But—"

"We don't have nothin' else to talk about. And you're keeping me from my work!"

The fury in his expression brought warning needle-prickles to Carley's sinuses.

Don't cry, don't cry, don't cry, Carley willed on her way to a chair. It simply was not meant to be. As soon as the car was ready, she would collect her résumé from the house and drive over to Petal. And if she did not get that teaching job, she would make other plans. She did not have to scramble, thanks to Grandmother.

But she could not squelch the disappointment rising up from the pit of her stomach. Her eyes teared, blurring the print on the work order. Dabbing them with her fingertips, she hoped Mr. White would not notice, and that no one else would enter until she regained her composure.

When she could no longer breathe through her nose, she grabbed her purse from the chair beside her. But not fast enough. She could not hold back a sniffle.

Oh no . . .

Carley sent a worried glance toward the counter, where Mr.

167

White studied her with arms folded. She lowered her eyes, took out a tissue, and blew her nose.

"Come on now, miss. No call to be doing that," he said in a worried tone.

She placed clipboard and pen in the empty chair. No way could she manage to walk up to the counter. Eyes averted, she mumbled, "Sorry. *Sniff.* I'm going to have to come back later. Sorry."

"Wait," he said when she reached the door.

She stopped without turning, tried to speak, but all that came out was a tight, "Hmm?"

"Look, I'm sorry for yellin' at you."

"It's all right."

"Come on, turn around and talk to me."

Carley turned.

He beckoned her close and propped his folded arms on the counter. "It's just that that building's a sore spot. My wife wanted to give Randy a chance to make something of himself after he kept gettin' fired from other jobs, but I warned her against it. If you think you can make a go of it . . ."

Carley waited.

He blew out his hollow cheeks. "You can have it for five hundred."

"Really?"

His frown hinted at self-disgust for caving in. "Under one condition, missy. You name it after my wife. She's had to put up with a lot. It would make her feel good."

"Thank you!" Carley gushed. "I mean, I'm sorry about your son, but thank you so much! You won't regret it!"

He was trying hard not to grin. "Oh well . . ."

The relief flooding through Carley froze, though she tried to keep her smile from faltering. Having her name over the door meant more to her than she had realized. But she had no choice. "And um . . . what is her name?"

"Annabel."

Annabel's Café.

Carley tried to imagine it on the sign. *It's . . . different. Count your blessings. You got the place, and for a good price.*

"Her mother named her after some poem or another she read in school," Emmit went on.

"Annabel Lee?" Carley said cautiously.

"Well, yeah. That's her name."

Annabel Lee. A tragic poem, but with some beautiful lines by Edgar Allen Poe.

A teenage boy walked in, asking about having a flat tire fixed on his father's truck. Carley returned to the chair in a creative daze.

> *It was many and many a year ago,*
> *In a kingdom by the sea,*
> *That a maiden there lived whom you may know*
> *By the name of Annabel Lee;*
> *And this maiden she lived with not other thought*
> *Than to love and be loved by me.*

She drew up another mental picture of the sign. *Annabel Lee Café.* It would be the better side of different. It would be unique.

"You're kidding!" Stanley said.

"What made him change his mind?" Loretta asked.

Carley took a breath, then told them.

"You women," Stanley said, shaking his head. "You don't play fair."

"I didn't intend to cry. I wasn't trying to manipulate him."

Loretta patted her shoulder. "Never be ashamed of a few honest tears. These men think with their heads too much. Sometimes you have to aim for the heart."

But there was no more time to bask in victory. There was a lease to draw up, forms to fill out. The IRS for starters. No aiming for the heart there.

———

Burt Lockwood from Pest Begone Exterminators said the building would need to be left alone for a week after his initial spraying and laying out of traps on July 3, and that he would need to come back after the cleaning and painting to begin preventative maintenance.

The Fourth of July celebration began with a pancake breakfast sponsored by the fire department at the elementary school cafeteria. Main Street was barricaded for the 10:00 parade, with beauty pageant winners and runners-up waving from the backs of convertibles, the Tallulah High School marching band and drill team, tractors pulling homemade floats advertising local businesses, and decorated pickup trucks bearing people of all ages who threw candy from the beds.

Afterward, cloggers in red gingham shirts square danced to the fiddles and guitars and banjo of *The Okatoma River Gang*. Tallulah Middle School cheerleaders sold lemonade and soft drinks. Blake and Uncle Rory worked the Lion's Club booth taking orders for care packages to be sent to Mississippi military serving in Iraq and Afghanistan. Tallulah Pentecostal sold barbecue plates to pay for a church bus; Mount Olive Church sold cups of homemade ice cream to benefit a youth choir trip; and businesses gave away such things as American flag pins, balloons, paper fans, and potholders. Mayor Dwight Coates' speech was titled "Carrying Liberty's Torch." Shops were closed, but at two in the afternoon an auctioneer for the senior citizen center auctioned off quilts. All were purchased, some by out-of-towners who came for that express reason, according to Mrs. Templeton.

Carley, Aunt Helen, and Sherry watched most of the goings-on from folding chairs set up outside Auld Lang Syne. Several people stopped by for a chat, and when introduced to Carley, expressed interest in the café.

It was most encouraging—but surprising—this early in the plans.

"Small towns," Sherry reminded her. "You can't even keep secrets from yourself."

Carley spotted Emmit White briefly through the sea of bodies. She excused herself and found him at the booth where a male medical technician was checking blood cholesterol. Emmit was accompanied by two women; one with white hair combed into a knot and carrying a straw purse large enough to hold a watermelon, and the other wore tight pink shorts, a white tank top, and baseball cap over her long dark hair. Carley recognized her from the near-confrontation by the library telephone back in January.

Still a little leery of the younger woman, Carley addressed the older—which was what had propelled her over. "Hi . . . you must be Annabel."

The woman gave her a pleasant, blank smile. Emmit nodded at Carley and leaned closer to his wife. "That's the lady who's renting the café. Miss Reed."

"Please call me Carley."

She held out her hand and the woman hesitated, then laid a soft hand into it.

"This is my daughter, Mona Bryant," Emmit said, not smiling but not unpleasant.

Mona detached her attention from the bandstand in the center of the street to give Carley a bored "Hi."

"Hi." Carley released Annabel's hand slowly, for fear it would simply drop to the woman's side—which it did.

Clouds rolled in from the west, along with distant rumbles of thunder, as family groups were already heading over to Lockwood Park with lawn chairs and ice chests for the Lion's Club fireworks display. "Oh well, there's always next year." Uncle Rory said.

They were closer to Fifth Street than Third. Aunt Helen said, "Come on home with us, Carley."

"Thanks, but I think I can beat the rain." Carley said. "I'll see you all later."

She smiled at herself. She had *almost* said *ya'll.*

Dale Parker and Marti Jenkins were loading two sawhorse barricades from the Third Street intersection into the bed of a Tallulah Public Works truck. Sherry had introduced Carley to the female deputy at the ice cream booth a couple of hours ago.

"Better hurry!" Dale called to Carley.

She waved and continued on, the first sprinkles pelting her bare arms. She had only seen Dale twice since returning to Tallulah. Once he had waved from behind the wheel of the patrol car. The second time it was she who drove past as he chatted with a woman outside Town Hall. She wondered about the Pascagoula girlfriend. For all her sentiment about not wishing to date any Don Juan, she was a little disappointed that he had not at least asked her out once. Not that she would have *accepted,* but it would have been nice to have been asked.

She used the remainder of the weekend and following week to experiment with menu items. Aunt Helen accompanied her to the Mennonite bakery near Columbia, where Carley sampled bread slices—three-seed barley, Italian herb, twelve-grain, oat bran, buttery white, tomato basil, raisin. The owners agreed to a substantial discount if she purchased in bulk. Perhaps later, when she owned the building free and clear, she would buy a commercial mixer and oven. Dana Bell of Fresh Pickin's agreed to the same discount on produce that she gave Corner Diner, the Old Grist Mill, and the two fast-food places.

Carley chopped, sautéed, and processed in her home kitchen for two days. Aunt Helen and Uncle Rory, the Kemps and her neighbors were her first guinea pigs. They ate all the samples and declared them outstanding.

But then, they were biased, and most did not fit the profile of the clientele she was aiming for. She asked the nineteen women who quilted Fridays at the senior citizen center to allow her to bring refreshments.

They were more objective.

"This is very good, dearie," Mrs. Templeton said of the pesto pasta salad. "But there's a mite too much salt."

Carley tasted it and realized that a heavy hand with the Parmesan cheese was the problem. Which was a better problem to have, for cheese was more expensive than salt.

She was surprised by the tepid reviews of the roasted turkey and cranberry sauce sandwich, one of her favorites.

"It's very good, but just doesn't go with summer," said Polly Dearman, retired librarian, prompting nods of agreement. Carley made a mental note to reserve it for November and December, if at all.

The soups—creamed broccoli, tomato basil, minestrone, potato cheese—were big hits. In fact, she judged the experiment a success, for every pint of soup, every sandwich square disappeared. Even the turkey and cranberry.

She saved herself the trouble of conducting test trials of the three desserts she planned to offer. Anyone who did not like at least one of the selections of Italian creme cake, chocolate mousse, or strawberry cheesecake would be just too hard to please.

chapter 15

Early Monday, husband and wife team Billy and Leigh Ann
Moore, who cleaned the Old Grist Mill, the courthouse, post office,
library, and a couple of other businesses, arrived with rags, buckets,
industrial-sized bottles of cleanser, and a CD player. Carley, hoping
that her help could shorten the job to two days instead of the three
predicted, volunteered for chores out of direct range of the old-
time country-western music. She was out on the sidewalk washing
the front windows when a man wearing a suit stopped to ask if she
had hired a painter.

"Stand by your man . . ." floated from inside.

"Not yet." Carley dropped the squeegee into the bucket and
wiped her right hand on her 49ers jersey shirt.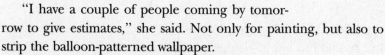
"I'm Carley Reed."

"Averil Stillman," he said as they shook hands.

"Oh." Her mind went blank but for a certain
poster. "I'm uh—sorry."

"Thank you," he said with a gracious little nod.
He was thickset, about forty, with ebony skin and
hair cut so close to the scalp that Carley had first
thought him to be bald.

"I have a couple of people coming by tomor-
row to give estimates," she said. Not only for painting, but also to
strip the balloon-patterned wallpaper.

"May my brother come by as well?"

"Is he a painter?" Carley asked, then realized how foolish a question it was. The tragedy of the death of the man's wife was a distracting presence.

Mr. Stillman did not seem to notice or, if he did, was kind enough to ignore her rattled state. "He's a good painter. Winn Stillman's his name. And he can give you plenty of references."

"Sure. Just have him come by today to set up a time, or call me this evening. Do you have paper and a pen?"

His smile revealed beautiful white teeth as he took a small spiral notebook from his coat pocket. "A preacher always has paper and a pen."

Winn Stillman came over at two, in paint-stained but clean and pressed khaki shirt and slacks. He introduced his son John, home for the summer from teaching art at Piney Woods School near Jackson. The Moores were considerate enough to turn off the music box while Carley explained to the Stillmans her ideas for color.

"I'd like the walls to be medium olive green," she said, showing them paint cards from Lowes in Hattiesburg. For wainscoting and trim work, she had chosen caramel brown, an earthy dark red called Pepper Spice, and parchment white.

"I'll want to add crown molding later, if I see that I can afford it," she said.

"Annabel Lee . . ." John Stillman mused aloud, studying the south wall.

"What are you thinking?" Carley asked.

He waved his right hand across, as if his fingertips could brush against the space where wall met ceiling. "What if, instead of crown molding, we painted about eight inches of that parchment color, then stenciled some of the poem's lines in red script with brown shadowing? It would add to your theme while saving you a lot of money."

"I love it," Carley said when the picture was clear in her mind. But she had to give the other painters their turns, so she said she would contact the two later.

"By the way," she asked Winn back on the sidewalk. "Your brother. . . ?"

"Averil," Winn supplied.

"Yes, Averil." Carley's hesitation had come from wondering if she had the right to ask, rather than having forgotten the name. "The baby girl . . ."

"Samantha. She's fine. Seven years old, and going into the second grade."

"Uncle Averil finally married again last year," John said. "Rita's a sweet lady, good to Samantha."

"I'm so glad," Carley said. "I hope you don't mind my asking."

Winn smiled. "Of course not, Miss Reed. People here held our hands through that nightmare. We'll never forget Gwen, but life has to go on."

———————

An affable young man named Skeet Barnes, with mullet hair-cut—short sides, long back—came by at 9:30 Tuesday morning. His estimate was forty dollars lower than Winn Stillman's, and he could start Thursday instead of the next Monday, but the way his eyes dipped several times during the course of their conversation made Carley uncomfortable.

My face is up here! she wanted to tell him.

"I'm just on my way to a job in Collins," he said, penning digits along the bottom of his business card. "But here's my cell phone number."

"Yes, thank you," she said back, gritting her teeth when his eyes strayed again.

As soon as he was gone, she tossed the yellow legal pad sheet with his estimate in one of the cleaners' black trash bags. Leigh Ann Moore, wringing a sponge over a bucket, gave her a knowing wink and began singing,

"Yore cheatin' heart . . . will tell on you."

The third painter simply did not show.

When Carley drove home for lunch, she telephoned Skeet Barnes' house so that she could let him know her decision, hopefully on the answering machine. The answering machine obliged.

"Thank you for coming by," Carley said, "but I've hired another painter."

And then realizing that was not yet so, she dialed Mr. Stillman's number and left a different message on still another answering machine.

The place was sparkling, inside and out by five o'clock. Drained, Carley paid the Moores and drove home. The air had cooled to seventy degrees. Carley sat on her porch swing with feet propped on an overturned packing crate, eating cold spaghetti and marinara sauce from a Tupperware container. The shadow from the oak in the Paynes' yard crept over Carley's driveway. Crickets trilled and frogs sounded like rusty hinges, and from somewhere up the street came the choppy notes of piano practice. Presently Micah and Kimberly Payne drifted over to show her a jar containing a praying mantis they had caught in the yard.

"What are you going to do with him?" Carley asked.

"Mom says we have to let him go before bedtime," Micah said, disappointed.

"Or he'll die," Kimberly reminded him.

Carley glanced toward the street, where an approaching automobile seemed to be slowing. Sure enough, a white patrol car pulled into her driveway.

"Cool!" Micah exclaimed, but when the door opened, he crouched to ask Carley, "Did you *do* something bad?"

"I don't think so."

The children hurried over to the steps. Rising, Carley caught sight of the sandy head of hair.

"Good evenin', Miss Reed," Dale Parker said as he strode up the walk.

Carley rose and joined the children. "Good evening."

"You're the Payne kids, aren't you?" he asked.

"Yes, sir," Micah said.

"Their names are Kimberly and Micah," Carley said.

Kimberly, dumbstruck, held out the jar.

"Now, what have we here?" Chief Parker paused at the bottom of the steps to reach out for the jar and hold it out to the ebbing sunlight. "How did you catch him?"

"With Daddy's baseball hat," she whispered, blushing under his smile.

"Baseball *cap*," her brother corrected.

"Micah . . . Kimberly . . ." floated from next door.

"Supper," Micah said. "We've got to go."

Dale handed the boy the jar, and drawled, "Better not run with this. You don't want to fall. And the bug would probably appreciate not having its brains rattled to death."

Micah grinned. "Yes, sir."

"It's good to know there are still places where children can play outside in the evenings." Carley said, stepping back to allow him on the porch, watching the children hurry past the front of her car.

"Yes, it is. But I'll bet they cleared it with their mother first. These days you have to be careful, no matter where you live." He eyed the container of spaghetti in her hand. "I'm interrupting your supper."

"That's okay. I'm finished."

"Looks like I should have come earlier and done you a favor."

"It's not that bad. I made it myself two days ago."

He winced. "I'll bet it tastes better than my foot tastes right now."

"Having never tasted your foot, I'll take your word for it."

That made him smile. "Do you have a few minutes, Miss Reed?"

"Certainly. Would you like to come inside?"

The alternative was to invite him to share the porch swing—and sitting so close would make her nervous. The sofa, pushed against the wall below the window, caused the open curtains to billow like sails instead of flapping like flags. "Please make yourself comfortable," Carley said. "Would you care for a glass of tea?"

"Just ice water, please."

Bending to her distorted reflection on the side of the toaster, Carley checked her teeth for stray bits of basil and fluffed her hair with her fingers. When she returned to the living room, he was flipping through pages of *Managing for Results* and set the book back on the coffee table.

"Don't get up," Carley said as he started rising from the sofa.

"Oh, but my momma would tan my hide if she heard I didn't." He stepped forward to take the glass and waited until she had settled into a chair before sitting again.

"This hits the spot," he said after three long gulps. "I carry bottles in a little Igloo in the patrol car but ran out today. I guess this heat is even harder for you, not being used to it. You sort of skipped over our springtime, didn't you?"

Carley wished she had changed from the jeans and jersey she had worn while cleaning, and she hoped her deodorant was still hanging in there. "It hasn't been bad, so far."

"That's the spirit," he said. "A trooper."

Don't blush, don't blush, Carley thought as heat spread through her cheeks. *Change the subject, change the subject!*

What subject?

Lamely she asked, "Is your office in Town Hall?"

"Nope, the backside of the courthouse building. You can see the bars in the windows from the parking lot. I wish we were in front so we'd have a better feel of what's going on outside, but at least we've got ample space. You should come over and let us show you around sometime."

"Thank you, but I don't think I'll be doing that."

He looked both disappointed and amused. "Why is everyone so intimidated by a jail?"

"Well, I don't know," Carley said, much more comfortable with banter than personal observations. "I guess because it has a different connotation than, say, the *mall*."

His laugh dimpled his cheeks. "That's not how the fifth graders feel on their annual 'Don't Let Peer Pressure Lead You Here' field trip."

He downed the rest of the water. Setting the glass on the braided rug out of the way of his shoes, he rested his hands on his knees and said, "I should have called, Miss Reed, but when I saw you on the porch I thought I'd take a chance."

"What is it?"

"Well, I'd like to speak with you about the café you're opening."

Her pulse jumped. "According to Mr. Malone, we've filled out all the right forms."

"I'm sure you have. No, this is about the menu. I wonder if you'd consider including some vegetarian dishes."

"You're vegetarian?"

"Vegan, actually. I get tired of brown bagging it, and it would be nice to just be able to stop in somewhere and get a decent meal that I didn't have to cook. Even in Hattiesburg and Jackson, the vegan options are limited. And you can get burnt out on salad bars."

"So you don't eat eggs or dairy products either."

"Not since I was twenty."

"You'd find lots of places to eat in San Francisco."

"That's what I hear," he said with a wistful expression.

"May I ask why you became vegetarian? Was it for religious reasons?"

"Not at all. I'm agnostic." He cocked an eyebrow. "I hope that doesn't offend you."

"It doesn't offend me."

"It was for my health," he said. "I had started working out, lifting weights, but had no stamina because of asthma. So I started reading books on nutrition. I took the whole plunge—gave up sugar, white flour and white rice, food additives. My asthma not only got better, but my complexion cleared. And with the increased stamina, I lost sixty pounds."

She was trying to imagine the *before* picture when he read her thoughts and smiled. "No, I was never in the 'in crowd' at school."

"Neither was I," Carley said. But she was not about to volunteer information about her bad teeth.

And however badly she wished to accommodate any potential customer, she had to think of the business. She could not afford to cater to every whim. What if someone asked her to include kosher dishes? Atkins meals? Organic?

Reluctantly, she shook her head. "I truly wish we could help you out, Chief Parker."

"Dale, please," he said.

"Dale. But what can you eat that would appeal to mainstream customers? Forgive my saying this, but they're not going to want to order sprouts and berries."

He nodded as if anticipating that argument. "And that's why I'm here. To ask you not to make up your mind until you've had a chance to try out some vegan dishes."

"But you just said there are no restaurants."

"At my house." The sandy eyebrows raised hopefully. "Saturday evening?"

Say no, she thought. His offer to cook sample dishes was essentially a pick-up line. He had either grown weary of the Pascagoula girlfriend or she had dumped him.

Her less cynical side reminded her of the sack lunch at his table in Corner Diner.

He's not making up the vegetarianism.

Or perhaps it was her *more* cynical side, reminding her that a local hero who dated beauty queens would not be inventing excuses to date *her.*

Both sides caved at the hopefulness in his blue eyes. She got to her feet. "All right. I'll get a pen and—"

"Why don't I just come for you?" he said, rising as well. "I could bring the patrol car. You've probably never ridden in one."

"No, thank you," Carley said. And he was wrong. She had ridden in three over the course of her childhood. And given the memories associated with those rides, she could not share Micah's sentiment that they were "cool."

———

Tables and chairs needed to be scrubbed clean in preparation for varnishing, so Carley went to the café Wednesday morning while most of Tallulah was still in bed. At noon, Aunt Helen brought lunch over from the diner.

"Oh, just in time," Carley said, raising a Styrofoam lid. Green liquid sloshed on her navy T-shirt already damp with furniture soap—but she was more interested in the contents of the container than her appearance.

"Mustard greens?" She asked. They could not be turnips because of the absence of small chunks of root. She was learning.

"Collards," her aunt replied.

There was also roast chicken and O'Brien potatoes. Carley pulled two dry chairs up to a table. "As long as they're greens. I've been craving them all morning. They must be addictive."

Aunt Helen smiled. "You're turning into a true Southerner, Carley. Next, you'll be craving corn bread and pot likker."

"Come again?"

"It's country slang. Corn bread soaked in the 'gravy' from field peas. Rory loves it, but I never developed a taste for it. Would you be a lamb and run to the Coke machine next door? I didn't have an extra hand for drinks."

"If you like, but I have lemonade and cups in the ice chest."

"Even better."

While they ate, Carley updated her aunt on the café's progress. "The Underwoods are coming this afternoon to talk with me about the sign."

"Very good." Aunt Helen had been the first to recommend

Clifford and Vera Underwood. They had designed and carved the sign for Déjà Vu Antiques as well as for many of Tallulah's businesses, including the Old Grist Mill.

But it was a Steve Underwood who showed up at 1:30. About six feet tall, he appeared to be in his early thirties, with short ink-black hair, a faintly bronze complexion, dark brows and lashes, and a square jaw. As he shook Carley's hand, he said, "I help my folks with their business during the summer months."

"What do you do the rest of the year, Mr. Underwood?" Carley asked.

"Teach history at USM."

"Oh . . . should I have said 'Doctor'?"

"How about just 'Steve'?"

"All right." Carley offered him the chair Aunt Helen had vacated. Another Southern gentleman, he waited until she sat first. "Are you familiar with the poem *Annabel Lee*?"

He shook his head. "I avoid poetry at all costs. But it's by Poe, right?"

"Yes. And that's to be the name of the place. I was wondering if we could incorporate that into the sign somehow."

"I'm sure we can. Have you a copy here?"

"No, I don't. I should have thought of that."

"That's all right. I can look it up online. But do you happen to have it memorized?"

"Well, yes."

"How does it go?"

Carley began quoting, a little self-consciously. It helped that he did not stare at her, but made little scribbles in a spiral notebook.

I was a child and she was a child, in this kingdom by the sea. . . .

"I'm impressed," he said when she had quoted all forty-one lines.

"Thank you. I was an English Lit major."

"Oh." He scribbled some more, a little dent of concentration between his dark brows. "Sorry about what I said about poetry."

Carley smiled, even though he was not looking up at her. Leaning forward on folded arms, she said, "That's all right. I'm not married to it. May I see what you're drawing?"

"One . . . second." He made a couple more marks, then turned the notebook and passed it to her. A sketch of a woman took up the page, looking off to the right with waist-length hair and the hem of her long skirt rippling as if in a stout breeze. *Annabel Lee Café* was penned in classic flowing letters.

"This is perfect," Carley said as shivers ran down her arms.

"The only drawback to showing her whole body like that is that we won't be able to show her facial expression with any fine detail."

"But you captured the longing and waiting, just by her posture. I would have thought you were an art professor, if you hadn't said history."

He smiled. "Thank you. Drawing has been a hobby since I was a boy. But my mom's the real artist in the family. She'll do the etching on your sign."

"I can't wait to see it."

"Well, you won't have to wait long. Two weeks, at the most. And . . . we have to ask for a fifty-percent deposit."

"Of course." She took checkbook and pen from her purse. "Do you enjoy working with your parents?"

"I do. They're great people."

It must be nice, being able to say that, she thought with a little stab of envy. "My aunt Helen says your father also builds furniture for Pine Woodworks."

Steve nodded. "He always has several pieces on consignment."

"I plan to take a look once the painters start. I'll be needing a deacon's bench for a little waiting area beside the counter."

"Will you be using these?" he asked, twisting to run a hand along the curved back of his chair.

"After I've cleaned and varnished them."

"Then I wouldn't recommend pine. Dad can make you an oak one that'll blend with the style."

That sounded wonderful. And expensive. "How much would it cost?"

He smiled again. "I let my dad do his own pricing. Furniture's kind of his sideline. But everyone says he's reasonable. Just call out to the house when you're ready, just to make sure he's in his workshop."

About an hour after Steve left, Carley heard tapping and turned toward the half-glass entrance door. A figure stared back at her, leaning close to the window with hands cupped at the sides of his face—*her* face, Carley realized, beckoning.

The knob turned and a girl entered with tentative steps. She was big-boned and overdeveloped for her age, which looked to be sixteen or seventeen. Charcoal liner circled green eyes, and four dime-sized hoops dangled from each earlobe. Blonde hair streaked with unnatural orange sprouted from her head in spikes, as if she had been electrocuted. A red tank top revealed a long pale scar on her right forearm; low-cut faded jeans revealed a pierced navel.

"Yes?" Carley said, hoping this girl was not seeking a job. She had read the booklets put out by the Equal Employment Opportunities Commission, and was aware that she must tread lightly. In theory she did not believe in judging a book by its cover. But her conservative customers surely would. Besides, she had to question the common sense of a person of any age who would look for a job dressed in such a manner.

The girl cleared her throat. "I hear you're gonna open a restaurant here?"

"Well, a café," Carley said with a polite smile.

"Oh. I need a job now."

"Sorry. I won't be hiring for another couple of weeks."

"I can help you clean those chairs, paint the walls. . . . Whatever you need doin'. I'm a hard worker."

"The painters are already lined up. And I'm afraid I don't need any other help right now."

The disappointment in the green eyes moved Carley to ask, "What's your name?"

"Brooke Kimball."

"Why don't you try Hattiesburg?"

The girl shoved both hands into her pockets, a feat Carley would not have thought possible.

"I don't have a car. Just my bike."

She was standing there, still hoping against hope, and Carley had to remind herself that she could not afford to allow compassion to get in the way of good business sense.

Her conscience prodded, *But what if someone had judged you, during your black fingernail phase?*

And Carley answered back, *My shoplifting, black fingernail phase?*

Conscience won out in the end, if only by not allowing her to crush the girl's hopes completely. And there was the EEOC to consider. "Look, I don't have any applications printed yet, but you're welcome to drop off a résumé any time."

"A résumé . . ." she said with a resigned nod. "Okay. Well, thanks."

Thursday morning Carley spread out pages of the *Hattiesburg American* collected from neighbors and family, propped open the café's front door with a gallon bottle of pine cleanser, and lifted the lid of a quart-sized can of varnish. *Should have bought a footstool,* she thought, four chairs later, when shifting her weight did not lessen the impact of ceramic tiles upon her knees.

"Anybody home?"

Carley looked toward the door, where a uniformed Dale Parker was entering. The older man who had shared his table at Corner Diner came in behind him, identically clad.

"Good morning," Carley said, smiling up at the two. Her knees creaked as she rocked back to sit on her ankles.

Dale shook his head. "Guess you never heard that all work and no play makes Jack a dull boy."

"I wish you'd send him over here," Carley said.

Both men chuckled, and Dale introduced Deputy Garland Smith. He had dark brown hair, graying at the temples, a salt-and-pepper mustache, and dark eyes as round as buttons.

"Don't get up," the deputy said as Carley started to balance her paintbrush onto the rim of the varnish can. He stepped past Dale and leaned down to shake her hand. "I hear this fellow's tryin' to talk you into serving granola and tofu."

"Tofu." Dale grimaced. "No way. Well, we'd better go save the town from bad guys. We just saw your door open and thought we'd check on you."

Other people also saw the open door as an invitation, and she was delighted to have them do so, for the job quickly became monotonous. Uncle Rory brought over a Coke after picking up a prescription in the drugstore. Gayle Payne and her children, buying earplugs on their way to the pool at Lockwood Park, stopped in for a quick hello. A brown, black, and white multi-breed dog nosed his way in, but was either too shy or too put off by the smell of varnish to visit. He answered Carley's beckoning by wagging his tail and then turning and trotting out.

Which was a good thing, Carley realized, as he took one last look at her through the window. Dog hairs and wet varnish did not mix. She was having enough trouble picking out the occasional bristle from her paintbrush.

You don't have to be so cheap about everything, she scolded herself.

Brooke Kimball stepped through the open doorway. Instead of the cropped tank top, today she wore a tight yellow shirt long enough to cover her pierced navel. Not that people would notice, Carley thought, for their retinas would be burning from the sentiment expressed in hot pink letters across the front: *Objects Under This Shirt Are Larger Than They Appear.*

"May I help you, Brooke?" Carley asked, stifling a sigh while an absurd thought flitted across her mind. This girl could be a spy for the Equal Employment Opportunity Commission, wired with a tape recorder.

But how would she hide it?

Blue rubber thongs flopped as the girl advanced. She dug into her back pocket. "You said I could bring this by."

"Your résumé?"

"Yes, ma'am."

She unfolded a sheet of notebook paper with ragged edges.

Why am I not surprised? Carley thought.

"Mr. Juban said the computer was bein' worked on, so I

couldn't type it. I hope that's okay."

"It's fine. Just put it on that chair by the kitchen door." She remembered her purse was hanging on the back of the chair, so she watched the girl walk over to it, marveling that anyone could be comfortable in jeans so tight.

And the shirt!

You would have loved to have had one like that when you were her age, Carley reminded herself. The writing would not have been *true,* in her case, but still, it would have attracted the attention she so desperately craved.

Just as this girl was doing, she realized.

"Thank you," Carley said when Brooke returned. Another bristle was clinging to a wet chair leg. She picked it out with her fingernails while saying, "As I explained last week, I won't be hiring for a while."

"Yes, ma'am."

But when Carley looked up after rubbing the stray bristle into a rag, the girl had made no move to leave.

"I could help you do that."

"Thank you, but I'm doing fine." Carley admired the girl's tenacity. The expression on the young face was so familiar. Where had she seen it?

She had not seen it, she realized, but *felt* it when she stood before Emmit White asking for a chance to prove herself. Again softening her tone, she explained. "I couldn't allow you to help me without paying you. It would break the minimum wage law, and I would be fined and probably lose my business before it even opens. But I can't *pay* you, because I haven't received my tax ID number yet."

"Yes, ma'am." She nodded. "Thank you, Miss Reed."

For what? Giving you false hopes? "Take care, Brooke."

The girl returned less than twenty minutes later with a small paper bag. "Mr. Marshall says this is the best brush they have for varnish."

Carley blinked up at her. "Mr. Who?"

"He owns the hardware store."

Which you would already know, if you'd bought your brush there instead of off the drugstore rack, Carley told herself. But she could not accept this favor, even if she repaid the girl, and even though she would end up going to the hardware store to buy the same brush herself. Accepting would only fuel the false hopes the girl already had.

Carley rested the defective brush on the varnish can rim again. "I'm very impressed that you did that, Brooke. It shows real tenacity as well as creativity and will serve you well."

The girl brightened, but cautiously, as if not able to believe her ears. "Really?"

"Yes, really." Carley sighed, "But you'll have to get your money back. I can't accept that brush—even if I pay you back—because it makes you think you have a good chance of getting a job here. And I'm sorry to say it, but that's probably not going to happen."

"Oh." Brooke bit her lip. Even from the floor, Carley could see the sheen over the charcoal-rimmed green eyes before the girl turned away.

Carley shifted her hips to the left, unfolded her legs, and got to her feet. "Just a minute, please," she said, grimacing, shifting her weight back and forth as needles prickled her calves.

Brooke returned from the doorway. "You all right?"

She nodded, and when she could walk, pulled out two unvarnished chairs. "My legs fell asleep. Will you sit with me for a minute?"

The girl waited until Carley was seated, to perch upon the edge of the second chair with shoulders slumped.

How do I even begin? Carley thought. Not only could she see her own reflection from not too many years ago, in that jaded/naive, hard/tender, tough/fearful face, but she imagined her own mother was once like this Brooke Kimball. What would she say, were she able to go back in time and speak with her?

"Do you know what I'm planning to open here?" Carley said.

Brooke hesitated, obviously wondering if this was a trick question. "A café?"

"Not only a café, but a serene little place where people can relax, visit with their friends, and soak up some atmosphere as well as good food. I'm not targeting teenagers as patrons, although anyone of any age who walks through the door is certainly welcome. My main focus is on older women, the shoppers you see on the sidewalks."

Carley watched the girl for any sign that she was going too fast. But Brooke seemed to be absorbing. At least her green eyes did not wear the glazed look of some of her former students.

"Anyway," Carley went on, "Older women are usually very conservative. And they're more comfortable around young people who are dressed modestly."

"I have a dress," Brooke said quickly. "And a denim skirt. You don't have to let me wait tables. You can put me in the back, washing dishes."

"That's not the point. Besides, we'll have uniforms here."

Then, what *was* the point? She was rambling, unfocused, when the girl needed some concrete advice. Carley sighed again. "Brooke, how old are you?"

"Seventeen."

"Has no one told you how to dress to apply for a job?"

The girl stared back, chewing on her bottom lip. At length she shook her head.

"Well, you know what I said about the customers who'll be coming here? It pretty much applies to most business owners. If you dress like you're . . . hanging out with friends, for something as important as job hunting, business people won't take you seriously."

The green eyes narrowed thoughtfully. She looked down at her shirt, then glanced away.

Carley's heart went out to her. Against her better judgment she said, "Brooke, did you list any references on your résumé?"

"Yes, ma'am."

"Please don't call me ma'am. I know it's a Southern thing, but I'm only nine years older than you are, and my Western ears just aren't used to it."

"Yes, m—." She closed her eyes for a fraction of a second before correcting herself. "Okay."

"I'm not promising you a job, but I will contact those people. Do you understand?"

The girl's shoulders straightened. "Thanks!"

"And your guidance counselor too, if she's not on your résumé."

"I'm not in school," Brooke said.

"I know. But they work summers too."

"I mean, I'm not in school."

Carley looked at her. "You dropped out?"

"Back in March."

"But why?"

She shrugged. "I was gonna fail eleventh grade anyway."

"Oh." And yet the girl was clever enough to spot Carley's problem with the paintbrush and try to solve it in the hopes of getting a job. She obviously had *some* sense.

Carley glanced again at the letters on the shirt. *In some areas.*

"Yeah, she worked real hard for us the past two summers. The kids just loved her," said LPN Arleen Fielding over the telephone that evening. One of two references on Brooke's résumé, she lived off Highway 44 and was employed at a clinic in Seminary.

"Why did you terminate her employment?" Carley asked at her kitchen table while tearing salad greens.

"Well, I didn't really terminate it. I just don't need her this summer. My boyfriend's mom—Roberta—moved in with us 'cause her old man's fishing buddies were always laying around in her living room drinkin' beer. She told him to choose them or her, and he chose his buddies."

"Oh. I'm sorry to hear—"

"Roberta isn't. She said she'd rather clean up after three kids than a half dozen big ones, and it's saving us the baby-sitting money we'd have to pay Brooke."

"Would you say Brooke is honest?" Carley asked.

"As the day is long. She got here on time and never stole a penny."

The second name on the résumé caused Carley to smile. She did not telephone this person, but drove over to Henderson's early Friday morning.

"Just leave that in the buggy, hon," cashier Anna Erwin said, reaching the scanner around to read the bar code on the 48-pack of bottled water.

"Hey, Carleyreed," Neal pulled the shopping cart through the checkout lane as she was replacing the wallet into her purse.

"Hi, Neal." She did not *need* the water today, for the painters would not be coming until Monday, and she was content with tap water herself. But she did not want to make Neal uncomfortable, or hinder his work, by showing up with the sole intent of asking about Brooke Kimball.

"Are you having a good day?" she asked, unlocking the Ford's trunk.

"I'm havin' a good day," he echoed. "Gabe and I played dominos last night. Do you know Gabe?"

"I don't think so."

"He's my cousin. He's twelve." He swung the water into the trunk. "They live in Prentiss, and we made peach ice cream. Do you like ice cream?"

"I love ice cream. May I ask you a question?"

"Okay."

"I met a girl named Brooke Kimball the other day." The car rocked when Carley slammed the trunk. "Do you know her?"

"I know Brooke. She has a basket on the front of her bike. She wants plastic bags, not paper. She ties them to the basket so they don't bounce out."

What to ask now? "Is she nice to you?"

He grinned, nodded. "She's nice. She's my friend."

Next, to Tallulah High School, where the guidance counselor, Mrs. Sparks, was a short, softly rounded woman with white cheeks and permed auburn hair. Carley remembered her, vaguely, from the basketball games.

"You're the young lady who's opening the café," Mrs. Sparks said, pumping her hand. "The whole faculty is excited. We get burned out on lunchroom meals, and take turns going for takeout two or three times a week. Only we get sick of fast food, and you can't call in orders ahead of time to Corner Diner."

Telephone takeout orders. Carley had not considered the idea, assuming most of her patrons would be out-of-town visitors. And she did not even realize that Corner Diner didn't offer that service. The vision she had for Annabel Lee Café suddenly grew. Was it possible that it would be even more successful than she had originally thought?

They sat in an office with Wedgwood blue walls, Carley taking her up on an offer of a chocolate-covered mint from a candy dish. "Brooke Kimball has applied for a job at my café. Would you recommend her?"

Mrs. Sparks nibbled a bit of her own mint thoughtfully. "Yes and no, frankly."

"I guess I should hear the bad news first."

"When she was here, she wouldn't study, cursed like a sailor, and dressed like a tramp." She sighed. "None of that seems to have changed, from what I can see and hear."

And none of that was surprising. Still, it was enough to reinforce Carley's initial misgivings. But as long as she was here, she asked, "And the 'yes'?"

"She'll work like a field hand if you encourage her. I tried that, and was beginning to make some headway with her, but there was no reinforcement from home." Defensively, she added, "It's almost impossible to do your part if the parents refuse to do theirs."

"I understand," Carley said, without explaining just how well.

The figs were ripe, but Carley had no time for them, beyond filling a cereal bowl in the mornings for breakfast. She invited the Paynes to pick them, and suspected it was not by happenstance that they overlooked the ripest figs on the lowest branches. Nice, when friends, as well as family, took pains to be thoughtful.

"I hear you have a date with a certain chief of police," Gayle called over the sheets on her clothesline Saturday morning as Carley filled her bowl.

Carley made a face at her. "It's not a date."

Gayle laughed, but then came around the sheets. "Just be careful, Carley. He's a nice guy but a real Romeo, from what I hear."

"Really, it's not a date. He's cooking some vegetarian foods in the hopes of my putting them on the menu. But thanks for looking out for me. And that goes for leaving the best figs too."

"Well, it's your tree! Besides, you need them. They're loaded with zinc."

Zinc? Carley thought on her way into the house. She hoped it made a person stronger, for today she had to carry sixty chairs into the storage room in preparation for the painters coming Monday. She would have to leave the tables for them to move, but wanted to get as much out of their way as possible beforehand.

She did not telephone the Kimball home; she wanted to speak with Brooke in person and figured the girl would show up again. Sure enough, she arrived a few minutes after Carley. In a concession to modesty, she was wearing a simple white cotton shirt with all buttons fastened. But the denim skirt fell only midway down her heavy thighs.

How did she ride her bicycle without causing a scene?

"Hi, Miss Reed," the girl said.

"Hi, Brooke."

"Um . . . I was wondering . . ."

"You're here about the job," Carley said, lowering a chair to the floor. "I've checked your references."

"Yes, ma'am?" the girl said hopefully, then flushed. "I mean—"

"It's okay if a *ma'am* slips now and then. I've been called worse. You have the job."

"Oh, thank you!"

Carley held up her hand. "Wait, hear me out. You have the job, providing you agree to three conditions."

"Anything!"

That almost made Carley smile again, but she forced herself to assume a serious expression so that the girl would understand the gravity of the situation.

"First . . . you must understand that the *only* job I'm offering you is as dishwasher. I've done it before—it's hard work. If you don't think you can handle it, or if you think you might be tempted to complain later, I'd rather get someone else."

"I can handle it," she said. "I won't gripe."

"Good. Second, when we order uniforms, you'll get your correct size, with room to move around in, and you will not shorten or alter it in any way. Do you get my drift?"

"I'm not sure . . . "

Carley sighed and conjured up an image of suit-and-tie EEOC investigators lurking outside the window. "My patrons will need to feel comfortable here."

The girl nodded, but with enough glaze over her green eyes to cause Carley another sigh. "Brooke, frankly, I don't want anyone coming to work here looking like a Hoochie Momma. Now do you understand?"

The green eyes widened with comprehension. "I'll wear a gunnysack if you say to."

Now Carley could not help but smile. "Maybe it won't come to that. And number three is that you get along with your fellow employees. Keeping customers fed and happy will be stressful enough. We don't need drama in the kitchen. No fights, no cursing."

"I can do that," Brooke said.

"Are you sure?"

"I can. You won't be sorry, Miss Reed."

Carley recalled having said the same thing to Emmit White. She hoped both predictions would come true. Lifting the chair again, she said, "Okay, now if you'll excuse me, I need to finish here."

But when she walked back in from the storage room, the girl was still standing, leaning her head thoughtfully.

"Is there something else?" Carley asked.

"Is it against the law for me to help you do that?"

"Yep." Carley hooked her arm through the curved back of another chair. "You're still a minor, and I still don't have my tax ID number."

"You wouldn't have to pay me. I got nothing better to do."

"Thank you, anyway. We'd better play by the rules."

The girl hesitated, then picked up a chair.

"Brooke, I said you can't help me."

"Uh-huh. I heard you say that." Brooke started carrying the chair toward the propped kitchen door.

Had the girl lost her mind? Suddenly uncertain if she should have agreed to hire her, Carley was about to order her to stop, when Brooke turned and gave her a little smile, "But if I won't listen, how are *you* gonna get in trouble?"

chapter 17

Remembering her protests to Gayle that this was not a date, Carley nonetheless rationalized that the desire to wear something other than grubby work clothes was reason enough for a dress. But a casual dress, a three-year-old lime green sleeveless knit with polo collar trimmed in white, and tan sandals.

Dale's directions were simple enough. A white frame house on Second Street on the west side of Main, three houses down from Green Thumb Nursery. The only house on Second Street with a squad car in the driveway, parked behind a Mustang coupe in a dark metallic blue. He answered the door wearing jeans, a knit shirt almost the color of her dress, and a navy apron featuring a cartoonish pig wearing wings and a halo, beneath *Heavenly Pig Barbecue House.*

"A gag birthday gift from my brother, Chad, a couple of years ago," he said before she could ask. "It's an actual restaurant in Tallahassee. But why waste a good apron?"

"Do you give him gag gifts?" Carley asked on the way through a tidy living room with tan canvas sofa and recliner, big-screen TV, and pine bookcase.

"Of course." He paused before an arched doorway. "Ah . . . I didn't have time to clean up."

The kitchen was indeed a mess, with bowls in the sink, vegetables littering the counter around a cutting board, a light brown mixture congealing in a blender, open jars of mustard and soy mayonnaise, and cellophane bags of bread. But he had taken great pains with the presentation of his food, for the table boasted an impressive two trays of sandwiches, plates, and soup bowls for whatever simmered in two pots on the stove.

"I understand," she said, even though she herself was obsessive about cleaning up as she went along. "Everything smells so good."

"Really?" He rubbed palms together and pulled out a chair. "Well, I hope you came hungry."

"I did." But the fact that he had such variety frightened her. Had she not made the point that she could only devote a small portion of her menu, if any, to vegan foods? She said, "You cooked so many dishes."

"I wanted to give you a good selection," he said, settling in the chair beside her and placing half a sandwich on her plate. "Let's start with avocado-cucumber. Easy and delicious."

He was correct about the delicious part, and she had no reason to doubt the easy. Simply cucumber and tomato slices, pepperoncini, mashed avocado, and alfalfa sprouts sprinkled with olive oil and vinegar, on whole wheat bread spread with tofu mayonnaise.

"Very good," she said, nodding after her second bite.

The anxiety in his expression lessened. He took the sandwich from her. "Save some room for the rest, please."

The rest included:

Spinach wrap with chopped vegetables and sunflower seeds
Olive spread on barley
Veggie burger on multigrain bun
Grilled eggplant sandwich
Roasted portobello mushroom, zucchini, red bell pepper, and chopped basil on white
Mediterranean hummus—the contents of the blender—with pita bread
Mushroom-wild-rice soup
Tomato-vegetable soup

"How did you learn to do all this?" she asked, raking up more hummus into her bread before he could take the plate away.

"Necessity—cookbooks and the Internet. I couldn't even fry an egg before I went vegan." He tilted his head thoughtfully. "Which means I've never fried an egg, come to think of it."

She did not care for the grilled eggplant sandwich, and so privately ruled it out. A perk of being one's own boss. Both the soups were delicious.

"You do understand that, as good as everything is, I can't promise how many will go on the menu?" she warned, even though she already knew that the hummus was a keeper.

"I understand," he said. "And it's really good of you to at least consider them."

She insisted upon helping clean the kitchen.

Clearly tempted, he said, "But I don't have a dishwasher. . . ."

"Neither do I. But I have a system. I'll wash and rinse, you can dry and stack."

"Only if you'll wear my apron," he said, reaching back to untie the strings. "Since you have the messiest part."

He helped her slip it over her head, then tied it for her. The simple courtesy unsettled her a bit, and she covered it by scooping up the almost-empty bottle of Dawn on the back of the sink. "Do you have any more of this?"

"Here, I'll get it," he said, and she stepped aside so that he could open the cabinet. He handed her the dish soap, and as she tested the hot tap water she asked about the two framed photographs on the windowsill.

"My family last Christmas," he said of the one on the right. "My parents, Alvin and Ginger, brother, Chad, and his wife, Peggy, and their three girls."

"But where are you?" she asked.

"Taking the photograph."

"And that's you and your brother?" she asked, nodding toward the one on the left. The two boys in different softball uniforms had identical heads of platinum hair.

He nodded. "I was nine, so Chad would have been twelve. I was in coach's pitch and he was in junior fastball."

"What do your parents do?"

"Mom keeps house, and Dad's still a ranger at Florida Caverns State Park."

She handed him a dripping plate. "With such a close family, what made you go to college in Hattiesburg?"

"Well, I followed Chad. I had done so all my life, and so I didn't even think hard about it, even though he was a senior when I entered as a freshman. He had an academic scholarship; I had a burger-flipping-ship. Chad moved back home after graduation, and I planned to do the same. But by the time I earned my bachelor's in Criminal Justice, I was dating a junior in Marketing."

Carley wondered if he was referring to the Atlanta socialite fiancée.

"My first girlfriend," he went on. "Diane. That was after I got in shape. By the time she dumped me for a premed student, I was working for the Hattiesburg Police Department."

So, she was not the Atlanta fiancée after all. Carley said, "And you became a hero."

"Well . . . I have to give some credit to vegetarianism. Back in my carnivore days I wouldn't have gone near a salad bar."

Carley loved his modesty and self-effacing humor. "I hope Diane was good and sorry."

"That thought did cross my mind once or twice," he admitted with a little smile.

"Your family must be proud of you."

"I hope so. They all came when I was sworn in as chief of police."

"Do they visit often?"

He shook his head. "It's easier for me to go there, what with Chad's family and Mom's rheumatoid arthritis. And I do, about once a year. We aren't the Cleavers, but we're pretty close."

"The Cleavers?" Carley asked while unscrewing the base to the blender.

"You know . . . *Leave it to Beaver*?"

"Is that a TV show?"

"It *was*," he said. "Now it only comes on cable reruns. I can't believe you've never heard of the 'Beave.'"

"I didn't watch a lot of television growing up." Even the times they owned one, watching TV conflicted with her main goal of staying out of range of Linda and, sometimes, certain other people.

"Well, that's probably good," Dale said. He gave her a sidelong grin. "So you were the studious sort, were you?"

"Not really. Just your typical girl."

"Barbie dolls and tea sets?"

"Sometimes."

Their fingers met again as he took the blender handle from her hands. He frowned. "No fair, Carley. You let me rattle on about my family, and now you clam up when I ask about yours. Were you secret agents or something?"

Just the idea made Carley smile. "You're right."

"You *were* secret agents?"

This time she laughed. "No, about my being evasive. The truth is, I didn't have a very good childhood. And so it's not a pleasant subject of conversation."

The towel stopped moving in his hand. "I'm sorry to hear that."

She gave him a grateful look. "It's over now."

They worked in silence for a little while, but not an awkward one. Presently he asked how the restaurant business was going.

"I hired my first employee today," she said. "Sort of."

When she told him the name, he shook his head. "I strongly advise you to reconsider. Forgive my crudeness, but the Kimballs are plain and simple white trash. Melvin Kimball's living on disability for a supposed back injury. And you'd never know this was a dry county from looking at the heap of bottles in his yard."

"How can he buy liquor in a dry county?"

"He gets it from Hattiesburg."

"What about his wife?"

"The way I hear it, she ran off with another man when the girl was very young. I don't know much about Brooke Kimball, except that she puts on a parade when she rides that bike through town. She's never been arrested, but you can tell just by looking at her that she's going to be trouble one day."

That could have been said about me, Carley thought. "I do appreciate your concern, Dale. But I'd really like to give her a chance."

He shrugged. "Okay, but don't say I didn't warn you. I've been in law enforcement long enough to know that it's true—the saying that fruit doesn't fall far from the tree."

But the fruit doesn't have to lie where it falls, she thought.

He wrapped half of the sandwiches in cellophane and spooned soup into plastic containers. When he presented her with a grocery bag, she said, "Don't you want to save these for your lunches?"

"There's enough for both of us. Besides, that's half the fun of cooking—sharing with a friend."

He sounded sincere, not as if this was a subtle warning that she should not entertain any romantic notions about him. Carley met his eyes and smiled. She liked the idea of being Dale Parker's friend.

She would not be a woman if she did not wonder if friendship would lead to romance sometime in the future. But if so, the future was where it belonged. If he were to broach that subject so soon, her old cynicisms would creep into the mix. She was content to keep them at bay for now.

———

There was nothing Carley could do in the café while it was being painted, so she devoted Monday morning to house cleaning and exchanging e-mails with the graphic designer in Sacramento who made DeLouches' menus so unique. After lunch she drove to

Turtle Creek Mall in Hattiesburg and bought a summer nightgown and robe set and a bottle of White Linen for Aunt Helen's seventy-fifth birthday party, to be held at Blake and Sherry's tomorrow evening.

Tuesday morning she stacked and refrigerated two long pans of lasagna before telephoning the Underwood house to ask about a deacon's bench.

"We'll be home all day," said a woman who identified herself as Vera Underwood over the faint whining of an electric motor. She gave Carley directions, adding, "If no one answers the door, just come around back to the workshop. The dog won't bite."

Three miles east of town on Highway 42, Carley spotted the white sign pointing toward Tallulah Pentecostal Church. Old Salt Road wound through pastures and piney woods. The Underwoods lived in a log home with a porch that stretched across the wide front. As Carley got out of the car, a young beagle sprinted from around the side with ears flopping. He barked until Carley said, "Nice doggie." Then he wagged his tail and trotted beside her up the steps.

Vera Underwood answered her ring. She was an elegant woman, with high cheekbones, brown hair combed into a loose knot, and a light bronze complexion enhanced by an embroidered turquoise cotton shift.

"Good morning, Miss Reed."

"Carley, please."

"Lovely. I'm Vera. Won't you come in?" Her accent was the female counterpart of Stanley Malone's. Graceful, almost melodic. To the dog, she said, "Sorry, Mickey, not you."

Honey-colored beams were stacked from sky-lit cathedral ceiling to slate floor. A stone fireplace reigned over one wall. The furniture was obviously handcrafted, with red Indian-blanket-print cushions.

"I just stepped inside to make lunch," Vera said. "But I'll show you to the shop."

"I didn't realize it was so late," Carley said, even though she was certain the GL's clock had read only 10:30 when she turned off the ignition.

Vera smiled. "We're early birds, but just aren't ready for breakfast at six or so in the morning. So we have late-breakfast/early-lunch, whenever we decide we're hungry. I realize *brunch* is correct, but we backwoods country people just don't speak that way, or our friends would accuse us of putting on airs."

"I've never been in a log home. It's so serene. And cool. Almost like being inside a cave."

"That's because it's so well insulated. The boys built this themselves—my husband and Steve—from trees on our land. The fireplace was an extravagance, with our having to order stones from Tennessee, but I've wanted one ever since my family stayed at Old Faithful Lodge when I was a girl. And since the logs were free . . ." She smiled again. "But I didn't mean to go on so."

"No, it's very interesting," Carley assured her. "I would love to see the rest sometime."

"I love to show it off. Why not now?"

"Don't you have to make lunch?"

"It won't take long, especially now that I have a helper. You'll stay, won't you?"

Carley was still not accustomed to such open hospitality from essential strangers. "Are you sure?"

"But of course."

Vera led her through the wide doorway into the kitchen. The long table and chairs were so richly polished that they gave a mellow amber sheen. Vera said, "Clifford made most of the furniture."

That included their four-poster king-size bed frame. A guest room with black iron bed frame was situated between the Underwoods' room and Steve's room. Steve lived here only during summers and university holidays, Vera said, for he had a Hattiesburg apartment for the academic year.

When Carley had seen even the bathrooms, she followed Vera down a hall and out the back door. A brick path led from the porch to a brown frame building with long screened windows. She could hear hammering as well as the buzz of a power tool. The inside smelled of freshly cut wood, machine oil, and varnish. Stacks of plywood rested against one wall. At a long worktable, Steve Underwood was running an electric router around the inside of a thick piece of oak. Several feet past the table, a man with a gray crew cut was rubbing stain into the unfinished wood of a massive pine bookcase.

Steve saw Carley first and switched off the router.

"Good morning!"

"Good morning," she said back.

Vera introduced Clifford, who closed the lid on his bucket of stain and showed Carley a sketch of a deacon's bench that matched the bentwood café chairs.

"Steve said you might be by, so I went ahead and drew this up. Is about five feet wide what you have in mind? That would be a little longer than those in homes, but not too long to ruin the aesthetic appeal."

"That sounds good," Carley said.

"I can have one made in a week and a half," Clifford said. "How does two hundred sound?"

"It sounds reasonable," Carley said. Truth was, she did not have a clue how much a deacon's bench should cost. Perhaps she should have researched on the Internet. But Aunt Helen and Uncle Rory would not have recommended the Underwoods if they were not honest, and so she would have to rely on their judgment.

Vera showed her how far along she was with the sign. The letters were routered, and the figure of the woman outlined with pencil. Steve was correct in saying his mother was the artist of the family. "It's going to be beautiful," Carley said.

"Thank you." Vera took her arm. "Now, let's go make lunch."

"Mother . . ." Steve said as Mr. Underwood chuckled.

"I'm happy to sing for my meal," Carley assured both men.

Breakfast/lunch was simple: Mexican corn bread, and chef

salads made with mixed greens, boiled eggs, garden tomatoes, cheese, and strips of leftover grilled chicken. Peeling eggs, Carley asked how the Underwoods had gotten into the business of woodworking. Vera told her that Clifford was a civil engineer and that she taught art history at USM until they both decided at age sixty to make their hobbies their avocation. "We had saved all our lives for this, and it just seemed the time to do it."

"That took a lot of courage," Carley said.

"And so does opening up a café," Vera said, handing her a cutting board and knife.

"I've never thought of myself as courageous," Carley told her.

"Hmm. So you have no fear about starting your own business?"

"Well, yes. Plenty of fear."

"But you're doing it anyway. That makes you either courageous or foolish, and you don't strike me as being a fool."

"Thank you, Vera," Carley said, and once again thought about how glad she was to have moved here. Was Tallulah unique in its number of nurturing women? It was almost as if God looked ahead years ago and decided this was the place where she would get the most healing from the past.

Her cynical side asked that if God was that involved in her life, why had Huey Collins been allowed to torment her? She thought about Aunt Helen's words about free will. If her stepfather could be programmed, like a robot, that would mean she could be as well. Would she wish that?

The men came into the kitchen and offered to help.

"We should have company more often," Vera said before reminding them to wash their hands.

"I can't find the salad dressing, hon," Clifford asked at the open refrigerator.

Vera winked at Carley and crossed the room. "Perhaps I can."

"Your parents are great," Carley said as Steve opened a drawer for napkins.

"Thank you. I'm sure yours are too."

Carley returned his smile. "Will you hand me those tomatoes?"

Over lunch the three asked about her plans for the café, even down to the colors the Stillmans were currently rolling on the walls. Over dessert of watermelon slices, Carley learned that Vera was one-quarter Choctaw, Steve therefore one-eighth, and that Clifford was the grandson of sharecroppers. She left with a bag of homegrown tomatoes and an invitation to come back and visit again. It was one of those niceties people said, of course, but she had enjoyed their company and the way the hands of the clock were not too much of an issue here in the piney hills.

She backed the GL out of her driveway that evening with the pans of warmed lasagna, wrapped in foil and dish towels, on the floorboard and Aunt Helen's gifts on the seat. Lights were still on in the café, so Carley parked behind Winn Stillman's truck. She could smell paint from the sidewalk.

"Perfect timing, Miss Reed," John said, gathering rags into a bucket.

Winn smiled, folding a ladder. "Well, what do you think?"

Carley turned slowly, taking it all in. The olive green was even more soothing on the walls than in the sample square, and it balanced out the brown, red, and parchment trim work. Running along the tops of the four walls, in elegant script that must have been extremely difficult to stencil, were lines from the poem's final stanza:

> For the moon never beams without bringing me dreams
> Of the beautiful Annabel Lee;
> And the stars never rise but I feel the bright eyes
> Of the beautiful Annabel Lee.

The Stillmans were waiting. The first word to pop into Carley's mind was one she had grown sour on while teaching school, after hearing students use it to describe movies, earrings, the latest hip-hop song, even a brand of chewing gum. So she smiled at the two and used another adjective that was just as appropriate. "It's wonderful."

She regretted not having left the house earlier, for the Stillmans were as eager as she was for her to see the rest of their handiwork. By the time she turned down Mill Creek Road, six vehicles were parked two-by-two in the driveway, and five were parked alongside the road. Along with family members were neighbors from Fifth Street, some members of the Hudsons' church, and fellow shop owners—including Marianne Tate. Almost everyone brought at least a token gift in spite of Sherry's having penned *No gifts please . . . Mom will consider your presence gift enough* on the invitation.

"Did you misspell *presence?*" Blake quipped while scooping ice into glasses, and Sherry assured him that she knew how to spell. Still, with worried expression later, she asked Carley if she had her invitation in her purse.

"It's on my refrigerator," Carley said. "But you didn't spell it wrong. It's just that everyone loves your mother."

Aunt Helen glowed with pleasure, but the fact that some guests had followed Sherry's instructions and some had not, posed a dilemma. "I don't think I should open them until everyone's gone," she whispered to Sherry and Carley as people were settling into sofas and folding chairs with plates of food. "I don't want to embarrass anyone."

"Well, you'll have to open *one*, Mother," Sherry said, while Blake and Uncle Rory exchanged a secret smile. "Go look in our bedroom."

The surprise was Deanna Hudson Wood. She was an older version of her sister, Sherry, but with brown hair and Uncle Rory's dark brows and lashes. Mother and daughter came up the hall arm-in-arm, Aunt Helen wiping her eyes.

When the guests were gone, Sherry shooed Aunt Helen, Uncle Rory, and Deanna from the kitchen to the den and shooed Conner and Patrick in the opposite direction. Carley was scrubbing pans at the sink when Conner came into the kitchen and asked if the painters had finished.

"Just before I came here," she said.

"How does it look, Carley?" Sherry asked.

"They did a wonderful job."

The kitchen clean and dishwasher humming, everyone rejoined the Hudsons and Deanna. Aunt Helen opened her gifts, and then Sherry divided the rest of the cake onto paper plates.

"Well, that was fun," Uncle Rory said, covering a yawn as Blake went around with a trash bag.

"Me, too, Dad," Sherry said, covering her own yawn.

Carley managed to stifle hers. She rose, went over to Aunt Helen, and leaned down to wrap her arms around her shoulders. "I'm glad you had a good birthday."

Aunt Helen touched her cheek. "Thank you, dear."

Deanna rose to embrace Carley. "I'm glad we finally got to meet, cousin."

"Me too."

After farewells were exchanged, Carley was halfway to the door when Uncle Rory said, "By the way, Carley, did your painters finish?"

"They did," Sherry said before she could answer.

Deanna got again to her feet. "I want to see it."

"So do I," said Aunt Helen.

The group loaded up into Sherry's SUV, with Carley following so that she could drive on home afterward. Proudly she unlocked the door, turned on the lights, and ushered everyone inside. As they wandered around the place, reading lines from the poem, marveling at the cleanness of the kitchen and bathrooms, and praising her choice of colors, Carley drank in their compliments and decided she had severely misjudged the word *awesome*.

chapter 18

Wednesday evening, Dale changed in the station bathroom to shorts and his *1999 Hattiesburg March of Dimes 10K* T-shirt, drove to the high school, and ran four miles around the track. At home, he showered and changed into jeans and another T-shirt, then ate two veggie burgers and several carrot sticks in front of *Law and Order* on cable.

Putting it off's not gonna make it any easier, he told himself at the close of the episode. He switched off the remote and picked up the cordless telephone. The ten-digit Pascagoula number appeared several times in the caller ID. Pressing the *Dial* button, he leaned back in his recliner.

Stephanie answered during the first ring, as if she had been waiting.

"Dale?"

"Yeah, hon, it's me. Sorry I didn't call sooner. There was an overturned tanker truck on Highway 42, and I had to assist the highway patrol."

"Really?" she said, her voice a mixture of hope and mistrust.

"These truckers take those curves like they're still on the interstate. He's lucky to be alive." He softened his voice. "Did your sister drive you?"

"Yes."

"How was it?"

There was a hesitation, then she barely whispered, "It hurt."

"Really?"

"I'm still cramping. They sent me home with pain pills."

"Poor baby!" He blew out an audible breath. "I feel like a major heel for not being there. When you only have two deputies, and one is out with the flu . . ."

"It's all right, Dale," she said dully. "You explained."

"I just want you to know I thought about you all day." He waited one second, two. "Did you . . . get my check?"

"Yes, but I don't need—"

"Please, Stephanie. We agreed, remember? This was my problem as much as yours."

He heard faint sniffling.

"Stephanie?"

"I just didn't know how depressed I would feel . . . afterward," she blurted thickly.

"Well, that's only natural," Dale soothed. "You'll feel better tomorrow, when you don't have this hanging over you. And as soon as I can get down there, we'll drive to Mobile and have dinner at Gambino's, then find you something special at the mall."

There was another hesitation, another sniff. "Really, Dale?"

"Well, of course, baby. Why do you even have to ask?"

"You were . . . so upset."

"I know." He sighed again. "I acted like an idiot. But I'm proud of you, for being a real trooper. And we'll have a half dozen kids when the time's right."

"I love you, Dale," she said.

"I love you. But, hey, now that I know you're all right, I'd better get out of this uniform—the fumes are making me nauseous. Got some gas spilled on it at the wreck."

"You should have done that first thing." Worry sharpened her tone. "Will you be all right?"

"I'll be fine, baby. Don't worry about me. Just take what the doctor gave you and get some sleep. Promise?"

"I'll try."

"That's my girl."

Once the connection was broken, he held the cordless to his chest and closed his eyes, overcome with a great surge of relief. Shotgun weddings may be a thing of the past, but thanks to DNA technology, a man did not have to walk the aisle to be trapped. Just the thought of eighteen years of court-ordered child support gave him chills.

He did feel pity that she had had to go through the ordeal without him. But it was her own fault. Especially after that false alarm back in April. She had assured him she was taking precautions. Once could be chalked up to an accident. But twice? He looked forward to marriage and a family. But on his own terms, in his own time.

Which ruled out a woman like Stephanie Long. Great eye candy, and fun to have on his arm. There was nothing better than watching the envy in other guys' eyes. But a compulsive shopper with no less than seventy-eight pairs of shoes in her closet, five full sets of china in her cabinets, and so many stacks of catalogs beneath her coffee table that her postman surely was in danger of a hernia. He wanted a woman with whom he could hold a conversation about something other than the latest fashions for home and body.

As he washed the few dishes at the sink, he thought of Carley Reed, wearing his apron, actually asking questions about his family, how he became interested in vegan cooking and the like. Passionate about her little café, charmingly ignorant of pop culture from her own generation, and with a refreshing sense of humor. Not as beautiful as Stephanie or Riley or some of the others. But certainly cute.

He smiled. *And shorter than me.*

He had never given much thought to divine providence, especially after the horrible accident with Gwen Stillman and the dominos that fell in its aftermath. But it certainly was a remarkable turn of fate that such an outstanding woman would show up twice in Tallulah, just as he was emerging from painful breakups.

"Yeah . . . hullo."

Mr. Kimball's vocal cords were made of steel wool, Carley decided with the telephone receiver to her ear Thursday morning.

"May I speak with Brooke?"

"She ain't awake," the voice grumbled. "Don't be callin' here so early."

Carley had put off telephoning until just before leaving the house; nine o'clock seemed more than an appropriate time for a weekday. Still, she said, "I'm sorry," and got halfway through the *sorry* when the connection broke.

"And good-day to you too, Mr. Manners," she muttered, replacing the receiver.

As she neared the café five minutes later, she could see Brooke's blue bicycle leaning against the lamppost, the girl looking through the window.

"I just called your house," Carley said, stepping up on the sidewalk after parking. "Your dad said you were still asleep."

The girl rolled dark-rimmed eyes. "I'm surprised he answered. He doesn't roll out of bed 'til noon or so."

She wore the same tank top and skintight jeans she had worn on her initial visit, apparently assuming that the dress code was not relevant until she was actually on payroll and assigned a uniform. Or perhaps she did not have any better clothes.

She's nice to Neal and small children, Carley reminded herself.

"It looks great in there," Brooke said.

"Wait 'til you see it from the inside." Carley unlocked the door and waved the girl through.

"It's awesome!" Brooke said, spinning around like Julie Andrews on the mountaintop.

Carley smiled. "Thank you."

"Did you make up that poem?"

"Oh no, not me. I'll bring it from the house and let you read it sometime. By the way, I have my paperwork back from the IRS."

"The who?"

218

"The tax people. Would you like to put in some part-time hours?"

"Would I!"

Carley filled out her first employee time sheet and filed it in her office among an expanding number of files: Shift schedules for heretofore phantom employees. Operating and closing checklists. Employment applications. Brochures and catalogs from restaurant suppliers and wholesale food companies. Product inventory and usage sheets. Income and cash flow statements and balance sheets. Recipes. And the innumerable federal, state, and local tax booklets and forms.

The two moved chairs and tables from the storeroom, arranging and rearranging. Brooke worked tirelessly, and did not complain when Carley stopped for the third time to say, "Um ... I don't know. Let's see if traffic flows better another way."

Two people stopped by to ask for applications. Carley and Brooke stopped only for lunch, which Carley went for herself because she could not stand the thought of sending the girl out in public dressed that way while on the clock. She was just about to step into Corner Diner when Aunt Helen, strolling down the side-walk with Sherry and Deanna, called to her. She waited, but had to decline their invitation to join them.

"I'm just ordering takeout. I have Brooke back there arranging chairs."

"Why don't you go get her?" Aunt Helen suggested.

"Thank you, but it's quicker just to eat back there."

"How's she working out?" Sherry asked.

"Very well, so far."

"Are you still coming tomorrow night?" Deanna asked. She would be leaving for Indianapolis Saturday, and Uncle Rory was cooking a farewell dinner.

Carley smiled at her. "I wouldn't miss it."

She returned to the café with breaded chicken cutlets, German red cabbage, and home fries.

"Hey, we're your first customers," Brooke said as Carley handed her a napkin wrapped around plastic cutlery.

"Isn't that something?" Carley said, not wanting to burst Brooke's bubble by revealing that Aunt Helen had already eaten there. Brooke wolfed hers down and finished the fries Carley had abandoned because they were too greasy.

"Umm, that was good." Brooke pressed a finger into the potato bits too small for her fork. "I get so tired of my own cooking."

"What do you cook?"

"Hamburgers, hot dogs, sloppy joes, mostly. Fried egg sandwiches or grilled cheese. My dad cooks a good pot roast and gravy when he's sober."

"You live there alone with him?"

"His girlfriend, Mildred Tanner, has been with us a couple of years. But I don't touch anything she cooks. She's such a pig. She doesn't shave under her arms, and spends most days watchin' soaps. That's why I need a real job. I want to save enough money so I can get my own place."

"I understand," Carley said.

Disbelief flashed in the green eyes.

She understood that as well. The sense of isolation was not unique to her own childhood, but probably shared by every child with an alcoholic parent. She smiled. "I'm expecting a shipment from the restaurant suppliers tomorrow. Can you help me unpack?"

"Yes," Brooke said, sitting straighter. "What time?"

"Is eight too early?"

"I'll be here. I'll bring breakfast."

"You don't have to—"

The girl shook her head. "You bought my lunch. I'm not a moocher."

"Why do you only put out one ear of corn?" Carley asked from one of the two rocking chairs on Mrs. Templeton's porch that evening. The ear, speared by a nail on a holder about shoulder-level on the trunk of the magnolia tree, was ignored by the four squirrels combing the grass for sunflower seeds in the company of four doves, three crows, a blue jay, a red bird, and several sparrows. It was a scene from a Disney movie, charming and pastoral, but the animals scattered whenever Mrs. Templeton set one foot on the top step or as soon as any person drew near on the sidewalk, any dog or cat approached from any direction, or an automobile approached in the street.

Mrs. Templeton's spindly fingers raked speckled butter beans from their pods into a white enamel dishpan. "Because when the squirrels start eatin' the corn, I know it's time to put out more seed. They like the seed better."

Carley leaned her head, listened. "Is that your phone?"

"No, dearie. I think it's yours."

"See you later." Her footfalls on the porch sent the animals scattering. Entering her house, she went for the extension at her desk. "Hello?"

"Carley! Did I catch you at a bad time?"

"Hi, Dale!" The breathlessness in her voice was mortifying. She faked a cough, cleared her throat, and said in a more formal register, "No, I was next door."

"I looked in the window. The paint job looks great."

The cynical side of Carley, which refused to stay bottled for too long, told her that he was working his way around to asking if she had given more thought to vegan menu items. Before he could confirm her cynicism, she said, "I'm afraid I'm only going to be able to put the mushroom soup, cucumber-avocado sandwiches, and hummus on the menu. But if they do well, I'll see about adding more later."

"Wow! I appreciate that." he said. "But that isn't why I called. I've been meaning to all week, but we've had office inventory going on. Anyway, I was wondering if you'd care to go to a movie in Hattiesburg with me Saturday night."

She allowed one, two seconds to pass, to counterbalance the initial excitement in her voice "That sounds like fun."

"Well, you might want to hear me out first."

"Yes?"

"A gentleman would allow his date to chose the movie, but unless you have a strong preference toward something else, I'd really like to see *The Hulk*."

Carley smiled to herself. She *knew* Saturday morning cartoons. "The big green monster."

"He's not a monster. He's a good guy—and he was my favorite comic-book hero. I sort of owe this to my boyhood self. But I'll let you choose the restaurant. Whatever you like—Mexican, Italian . . ."

"Okay. How about Chinese?"

"Chinese. Ah, sure."

"You don't like Chinese food?"

"It's not my favorite. But I said you could choose."

The forced enthusiasm in his voice made her smile again. "Aunt Helen and Uncle Rory say Barnhill's restaurant has a good buffet. Do they have vegan foods?"

"They've got lots of veggies," he said, voice perking. "And you can get a steak too."

"Then let's go there."

"Good idea. And thanks, Carley."

He had just thanked her for agreeing to go on a date with him. Carley could not recall any man ever doing so. *You are one charming fellow, Dale Parker,* she thought.

And then reminded herself that she was not the first woman with that opinion. She had glossed over Gayle's advice out by the fig tree, but knew that she needed to take it to heart.

————

Carley posted a *Now Taking Applications* sign in the window Friday morning, seconds before Brooke pedaled up with a grease-spotted Dixie Burger bag containing four sausage biscuits wrapped in wax paper, and another with two pints of milk. Not wishing to hurt the girl's feelings, and thankful that she had had her tea and figs earlier, Carley washed down one of the biscuits with milk. Hopefully the calcium would neutralize some of the effects of the saturated fat pouring into her system so early in the morning. It was always a juggling act keeping migraines away, but caution was easier than being bed-bound for three days.

"Thank you," Carley said, dabbing her mouth with her paper napkin. "But you mustn't do this again. You're saving for your own place, remember?"

Brooke, having finished the other three rolls, picked a biscuit crumb from her mercifully loose blue T-shirt. "They didn't cost much."

"It adds up. And it's not ethical for me to be taking anything from you, anyway."

"Oh." The girl nodded. "Okay. I'm sorry."

"Don't be sorry. It was a good treat." Impulsively, Carley reached to pat her arm. Her fingers brushed against a hard ridge of skin and moved away quickly.

"I got hung up in a barbed-wire fence when I was eleven," Brooke said, looking at the six-inch scar running down her right forearm.

"It must have hurt."

She shrugged. "I didn't get stitches. That's why it's so ugly."

"Your dad didn't take you to the doctor?" Carley asked.

"He might have taken me if I'd told him about it, but then he would have beat the tar out of me for being where he said I had no business."

A horn tooted outside. Carley went out to direct the UPS driver to the gravel lane around back. He wheeled six pasteboard cartons to the storage room and produced an automatic clipboard that resembled an Etch-A-Sketch for her signature. After locking the back door again, Carley took scissors from her desk and cut the packing straps to the carton sitting nearest to the kitchen door.

Wrapped in flexible Styrofoam sheets were six-dozen seven-and-one-eighth-inch plates. Carley took out the first. *Wide-rim rolled-edge American white, classic and sturdy, three-dozen for $11.99,* the catalog had read.

"Whoa, that's pretty," Brooke said.

"You think so?" Carley said, handing the plate over the open carton.

"Hmm." The girl rubbed her hand over it, pantomiming washing. "Yeah. It's good."

Carley laughed. "Well, they're not going to unpack themselves."

She had to leave Brooke to the task two hours later when a man from South Central Bell arrived. Telephones were set up in minutes at the outlets in the front counter and office. A wall telephone for the kitchen took over an hour.

"You want to test it out?" the man said.

"Yes, thank you." Carley knew just who to call, had already looked up the number in one of the potholder-thin telephone books. She only hoped Tommy's Pizza had no qualms about sending a fourteen-inch Canadian bacon with black olives to the soon-to-be competition.

Three people came by for job applications in the afternoon. Two cartons remained when Carley called it a day at 5:00. "You did good work," she said to Brooke.

"Thank you." The girl looked down at the floor but could not conceal the pleasure in her expression.

Odd, Carley thought, how she could be so bold at times and timid at others.

"I led you to believe this would be part-time. I can finish up tomorrow, if you'd like to take the weekend off."

"No, I'll be here in the morning," Brooke assured her.

chapter   19

Uncle Rory prepared Creole jambalaya in an iron pot, yeast rolls, and green salad for Deanna's farewell party, followed by hand-cranked ice cream flavored with the last of the figs from the Hudsons' tree.

"I'll see you at Christmas," Deanna said when Carley embraced her and wished her safe flight.

Early the following morning, Carley unhooked her computer and loaded it into the GL. Time to start conducting most of the café business in her office, and Brooke could help with the wiring. She would miss having it at the house, but promised herself she would get another when the business proved itself.

Brooke was waiting on the sidewalk, practically spilling out of the tank top, and stuffed into her jeans. *You have no customers to offend yet,* Carley reminded herself. And she herself wore jeans, albeit loose enough to move around in without cutting off circulation. The girl helped her carry in monitor, modem, keyboard, and printer. They pulled the desk from the wall, and Carley crawled underneath to thread cords through the openings. Brooke had offered to get down there herself, but Carley doubted the jeans could take the strain.

"Okay, can you reach the cord I'm wiggling?"

"I've got it," Brooke said.

"Pardon me." A man's voice that time, familiar though muffled slightly by desk metal. Carley backed from the dark space and rose to her knees. Steve Underwood stood framed by the doorway, wearing light brown corded slacks and a blue chambray shirt.

"Good morning," Carley said.

"Good morning, Carley . . . Brooke."

"Hey, Mr. Steve," the girl chirped.

Small town, Carley reminded herself.

"I can't believe how good the place looks," he said.

Carley smiled and got to her feet. "Doesn't it? And I can't wait to see the sign."

"Do you need help with those cords?"

"No, thank you. We just about have it."

A blanket-wrapped bundle lay on one of the tables. Steve undraped each side. "Protection against potholes and bumps in the road. Well, what do you think?"

Vera's Annabel looked poignantly off in the distance, hand pressed to her bosom as if waiting for her sweetheart. Of all the additions to the café, the sign moved Carley the most. Her dream had a name, carved in wood. Her throat thickened. "Please tell your mother I've never seen anything so beautiful."

"Beautiful," Brooke echoed. "Is that the girl from the poem?"

"It is." Carley looked at her. "I'm sorry, Brooke. I didn't bring it over."

"It's okay. Mr. Juban helped me look it up after I left here yesterday."

For a minute Carley forgot about the sign. "You went to the library just to read it?"

"Well . . . yes, ma'am," she said, clearly embarrassed. "I mean, yes."

Why in the world did you drop out of school? Carley thought. With some education behind Brooke's initiative, she could be president. Or a Mafia don. Clever did not always go hand-in-hand with good, but Carley suspected a streak of decency lay beneath those piercings, the heavy makeup, and outrageous clothes.

"Okay," Steve said. "We'll leave it here for now. My tools and ladder are outside. Once I get the bracket attached, I'll need you to show me how high you want this."

"I'll start unpacking cartons," Brooke offered.

"Good idea."

On the sidewalk, Carley held one side of the folding ladder steady. Steve used a cordless screwdriver to attach an iron bracket over the door. Pedestrians gave them wide berth on their way to and from the drugstore, trading good-mornings and asking the date of the grand opening.

"We're aiming for August twenty-third, thank you for asking," was Carley's standard reply, while dancing inside over the thought of still another potential customer.

When Deputy Marti Jenkins stopped by, she did not mention the opening, just asked Steve how his folks were doing.

"Why don't you drive out there and see for yourself?" he replied.

Marti's laugh showed gums and pearl teeth. "I know, it's been a while. But they don't have to be such hermits either."

"They're afraid someone will force them to take a real job."

The deputy rolled her eyes and finally spoke to Carley. "We're cousins, couldn't you guess?"

Carley felt an odd and faint surge of relief. She supposed it was because the Underwoods had treated her like an honored guest, so it was a letdown to know others were just as honored. Unreasonable, yes, but that was sometimes the way of emotion. But with Marti being family . . . well, people needed to have family over.

"Okay, back up several feet," Steve said after Marti had left.

Carley backed away to stand in front of Peggy's Pastimes. He held the sign at differing distances from the bracket, until she said, "That looks good. What do you think?"

"It works for me. High enough not to bang the heads of us tall folks."

Carley walked back over. "Does that mean you'll try us out sometime?"

He smiled down at her. "Absolutely."

After cutting the chains the proper lengths, he attached them to the hooks and hung the sign. This time they both walked back to admire it from a distance. Not only did the sign give texture to Carley's dream, but it validated her as a businesswoman. No longer was she fixing up "Emmit's old hamburger joint." This was Annabel Lee Café.

"I'll get my checkbook," she said as he folded his ladder. "Come on inside when you've finished."

She could hear the clatter of cutlery outside the kitchen door. When she went through it, Brooke turned from the stainless steel worktable and asked, "How does it look?"

"Go see for yourself," Carley said.

"Okay if I wait a minute? I'm almost done unpacking knives."

"Sure."

As Carley took her café account checkbook from the desk, she noticed the purse she had parked so casually atop the filing cabinet.

She wouldn't.

You don't really know her, went through her mind next.

Cutlery was still clattering. Still, Carley sent several glances toward the doorway while taking inventory of her wallet for cash and her debit card. It was all there. She replaced the purse feeling both relieved and guilty.

"What sort of history do you teach?" she asked in the dining room while writing out the check.

"American, Mississippi, and Civil War."

"I know almost nothing about those last two," Carley confessed. "Only that the North won."

"And rightly so."

When she gave him a look of mild surprise, he said, "Most Southerners feel that way. Slavery was simply wrong. But we're still miffed about having our homes burnt and the severity of restoration." He smiled. "I didn't mean to step up to my lectern."

"It's actually interesting."

"Well, thank you. I wish all my students felt that way." Handing her a receipt, he got to his feet. "This has been a pleasure, Carley."

She rose as well, and held out a hand. "Do tell your parents how pleased I am."

"They'll be delighted." After releasing her hand, he hesitated. "If you're interested, Vicksburg has a Civil—"

Someone was rapping at the door. Dale Parker, framed by the half-window, waved and then turned the knob. He leaned into the doorway to say, "The sign looks great. I guessed it was your folks' work, Steve."

"Thank you, Dale," Steve said, but with the warmth of chocolate mousse.

"Sorry to interrupt your business." Dale smiled at Carley. "But I wanted to warn you I've got a meeting this afternoon and might be a few minutes late."

"That's fine."

"Thanks!" He backed out of the door, waved again on his way past the picture window.

Carley gave Steve an apologetic smile. He was a decent man, she thought, with a nice family. In this case, it was a good thing that the fruit did not fall far from the tree. She had never dated two men during the same time frame, and certainly had little time for romance. But if Steve was working up to asking her for a date, she wouldn't mind.

"I'm sorry, Steve, what were you saying?"

He picked up his clipboard and smiled at her. "Just that there's a Civil War battlefield and museum in Vicksburg you might enjoy visiting sometime. Well, I've got to deliver a sign to Lumberton. I'll give you a call when the bench is finished."

———

What do people here wear to movies? Carley thought at her closet. She decided upon her knee-length, sleeveless dress of subdued pink and white checks. As an afterthought she grabbed her white three-quarter sleeve cardigan. The temperature had reached ninety today and even now had only cooled to eighty-two. But it would come in handy if the theater or restaurant was too cold.

Dale arrived twenty-six minutes late, full of apologies.

"An investigator for the state police was in the office all afternoon," he drawled, steering the Mustang down Highway 589. He looked like a college student, in a yellow polo shirt that revealed the muscles of his tanned arms, and khaki slacks and loafers. "That's why I figured I'd be late. You ever meet anyone in love with the sound of his own voice?"

Carley thought. "There was a girl in Biology 101 who asked at least two questions every lecture. Most had such obvious answers that you had to wonder if she just wanted the attention. You could feel the tension around the auditorium five minutes before dismissal, because that was her favorite time to raise her hand."

"I know that girl!" Dale clicked on his signal light to pass a pickup truck. "She took Intro to Sociology at USM."

That made Carley smile. "We can wait and have dinner after the movie, if you like."

"Oh no, we'll make it."

She had a feeling they would. She could not look at the speedometer without being obvious, but the farms and trees and houses on either side of the road were zipping by too quickly for her comfort zone. *It's just this car,* she told herself. *The chief of police wouldn't speed.*

To distract herself from the curvy hill and solid yellow line ahead, she asked, "Do you work closely with the state police?"

"Sometimes. The guy had what he thought was a new lead on an old case. If he had told us the reason he was coming, we could have saved him the trouble, because the information didn't match our evidence." Dale waved a hand. "He's a good cop. But while he was rattling on, I was getting antsy, just like those students in your biology class. I was afraid we'd have to call off our date."

Another charming thing to say, in his repertoire of charming statements. Carley said, "You mean, you were afraid you'd miss *The Hulk.*"

He looked at her long enough to smile in the sheepish way that had caught her attention in Corner Diner. "Well, maybe that too. The Hulkster's my man."

Carley smiled and looked at the road again. Her heart went up into her throat. He was gaining on a black sedan and signaling to pass. A white van approached in the left lane, with little margin for error. She clenched her fingers, held her breath, and didn't let it out again until they were in the right lane again.

You're being ridiculous, she said to herself as her heartbeat settled back into a less frenzied rhythm. *Are you so flattered that he asked you out that you're just going to let him kill you?*

"Dale?" she said.

"Um-hmm?" He smiled at her again.

"Will you please slow down?"

"Sure," he said, and the car immediately decelerated. "Sorry. I guess I'm still wired from that meeting."

"I understand."

"So, help me to de-stress. Tell me about your day. What did you do besides put up the sign?"

"Well, we hooked up my computer."

"Computer, eh? That's relaxing."

"And put away dishes."

He flexed his shoulders. "I'm feeling better by the minute."

"Flatware too."

This time he leaned his head and feigned snoring.

Carley laughed. "I don't want you *that* relaxed."

"Oh, okay." He smiled back at her. "How's the Kimball girl working out? You didn't let her around the knives, did you?"

"I'll have you know she unpacked the cutlery by herself. And she had access to my purse for a good while."

"And how much was in it?"

"Well, seven dollars."

"She's not foolish enough to risk getting in trouble over seven dollars."

"*And* my debit card."

"Where would she use it? You can't get too far on a bike."

"I believe you're wrong about her, Dale."

"Well, I hope so." His expression sobered. "Just don't be too trusting, Carley. You'll have lots of cash around once the place opens."

"I'll be careful."

Barnhill's was a popular restaurant, judging by the number of parked vehicles. Carley and Dale only had to wait five minutes for a table. The buffet was impressive, with regional dishes such as barbecue ribs and chicken and dumplings, but also teriyaki chicken and spaghetti with meatballs.

And vegetables. Baked sweet potatoes, steamed white potatoes, cabbage, turnip greens, black-eyed peas, and more. Dale's plate was full.

"Thank you for suggesting here," he said, splitting a sweet potato with a knife. "I worked through lunch, as you can tell. It would have been depressing, having to order a salad."

"This seems a good place," Carley said.

"But look around. Mostly families. It's not exactly a date spot. Garland ribbed me about it."

"Well, tell him these ribs are fine."

He laughed. "That's what I like most about you. Your sense of humor."

"Really?"

"Don't tell me you're surprised."

"You're just the first person to tell me that." Carley realized it was one of the nicest compliments she had ever received. Her red hair would fade and turn gray, but a sense of humor was hopefully eternal.

Coming attractions were showing on the screen in Turtle Creek Mall's darkened theater. "I can't see a thing," Carley murmured.

Dale took her hand. "About two-thirds up."

He led her up the aisle. They had to release hands to file side-ways along knees to center seats. Carley found the sarcastic quips of the trio of adolescent boys behind them more entertaining than the plot. But it was nice to be out on a date after so long, and Carley decided she could not imagine anywhere else she would want to be this evening.

"Are they disturbing you?" Dale leaned close to whisper.

"No. They're funny."

"Are you enjoying the movie?"

"Sure."

Five minutes later, he leaned close again. "You're *really* sure?"

She turned to him. "Are you?"

"No. Let's leave, okay?"

Under a clear sky in the parking lot, he opened the passenger door. "I guess it's not a good thing to go back and recapture child-hood. Sorry I've ruined your evening, Carley. "

Carley climbed into the seat. "This is a great evening."

"Liar." He said with a good-natured smirk. He went around the car, climbed behind the wheel, and fastened his seat belt. "I'll make it up to you."

"You don't have—"

"No, really." Starting the engine, he said, "We didn't have time for dessert. Let's go someplace special. What do you feel like? Some-thing chocolate? Or if you'd like a daiquiri or something. . . ."

"I don't drink," Carley said. Not that she found anything wrong with it, in moderation, but if moderation was so easy to maintain, why were there so many alcoholics? A med student she had dated three times during college had told her of studies that suggested addictive behavior could be inherited. When had her mother slipped over that line? There was always the fear that she was more like Linda than she wanted to be. "But if you . . ."

"I don't either. Not since I became vegan."

Carley looked at him. "But there aren't any animal products in alcohol . . . are there?"

He smiled and shook his head. The light at Hardy Street turned green, and Dale steered left toward the city. "My brother, Chad, says everything's black or white with me, and I guess he's right. I just can't see avoiding milk while putting alcohol in my system. And besides, back in my drinking days, all it did was make me sleepy. I would be the one lying on the floor behind the sofa, not the one dancing with the lampshade on his head."

"I know . . . let's go to Shoney's," Carley said.

"Shoney's?"

"I'd like to see where you caught the serial killer."

Easing into a smile, he said, "You would?"

It was an ordinary Shoney's on North 26th Street, within walking distance of the University of Southern Mississippi. No evidence of it being the place where a murderer took his last free meal and a rookie cop became a hero. Carley's eyes scanned the other tables and booths. How many of the diners were even aware of, or remembered, what happened here?

"Tell me about that day," she said, her spoon spreading the whipped cream evenly over her hot fudge cake. "How did you recognize him?"

Dale, having ordered a sensible bowl of mixed fruit, said, "I had studied the composite sketch for hours. Even taped it to my bathroom mirror."

"Loretta Malone said the composite wasn't that good."

"Well, yeah." Dale hesitated. "I don't know if I can explain this."

"Please?"

"It wasn't so much his facial features that caught my eye, but his *expression*." He cleared his throat. "Have you ever exchanged a look with someone and *known* what he's thinking, way down in the pit of your stomach?"

"Yes," Carley said, suddenly eleven again. A shiver ran through her. "Some call it intuition."

"He saw my uniform and looked away," Dale went on. "But in the fraction of a second that our eyes met, I could read his thoughts clear as a bell. He was so clever, in his toupee and dark glasses, so sure he could rub shoulders with decent people, so scornful of the twenty-two-year-old cop waiting for the lettuce tongs. And I knew it was him."

Shivers prickled Carley's arms again. "What happened next?"

"Well, I couldn't call for backup, not with his keeping an eye on me. So I ate my salad, paid my bill, and drove out of the parking lot."

"But why?"

"Because I thought he might look through the window. I was nervous, I guess, paranoid. But I was more afraid of making *him* nervous. I didn't know if he had a gun, didn't want a hostage situation."

"And so you drove around the block?"

"Yep. While calling for backup. But I almost played it too close, for he was walking out the door when I came around from parking in back. I waited until he was too far from the door to run back inside, and ordered him to lie on the ground with his hands outstretched."

"Did he?"

"He did."

"Just like that?"

"Well, I was pointing my pistol at him. I'm just glad he didn't notice how badly it was shaking."

Carley took a spoonful of the neglected cake. "What would you have done if he turned out to be the wrong person?"

"I would probably be pumping gas back in Tallahassee now."

"What was it like to have your picture in *Newsweek*?"

"Oh, it was nothing," he said modestly, but with a glint in his blue eyes. "By the way, it was *Newsweek, Reader's Digest,* and several newspapers around the country."

That made Carley smile. She wasn't the only person at this table with a sense of humor. But she could not return the compliment. As much as she enjoyed his company, she would not allow herself to fall in the ranks of his other nameless and faceless admirers. She had stoked his ego enough by asking about his act of heroism, even though curiosity was her sole motive.

He forked a chunk of pineapple into his mouth and stared at her, chewing.

"What?" Carley said after a minute.

"Once again, you don't play fair, Carley."

"How so?"

"You keep encouraging me to rattle on about myself, but what do I really know about you, other than that you're from California and related to the Hudsons?"

"I . . . have a sense of humor?" she offered.

"Not good enough. Come on, Carley, your turn. Or as Stanley Malone would say, *Quid pro quo.*"

"Okay, okay." She sighed. "My mother died eighteen months ago of cirrhosis of the liver."

"She was an alcoholic?"

"Yes."

"Your father?"

"Not in the picture—whoever he was. I was sent to a foster home, then a group home when I was fourteen, because my mother chose an abusive boyfriend over me."

He looked stricken, his brows dented. "I'm sorry, Carley. You deserve better."

Carley's spoon swirled whipped cream and fudge. "No sympathy, Dale, please. I only told you this because you pressured me. It's not all bad. A group leader at the home helped me through a lot of my teenage angst, and encouraged me to go to college. I juggled classes and waiting tables, taught school for a while after graduating, and now I'm here."

"An entrepreneur," he said.

"Yes. One of those." She hesitated, wondering if she dared prompt another lecture on being too trusting. "And . . . that's why I want to give Brooke Kimball a chance."

Now it was he who hesitated. But warmly. "I understand. I'll just say for the record that I still think it's a bad idea."

"And I appreciate your concern."

She truly did. There was something going on between them that they were both aware of—a budding mutual affection. But when he took her elbow at her front door an hour later, she backed away.

"I'm sorry, Dale. I have a rule about first dates."

A falsehood, actually, for she had dated so few men that it had not seemed necessary to make rules beyond that they treat her like an intelligent person. But she had never been out with a man responsible for so many broken female hearts before. If she wanted to stand out from the adoring masses, this seemed the best way to begin.

"Can we count my cooking for you as the first?" he said good-naturedly.

Carley laughed. "I don't think so."

"Then, how about if I drive away and come back in ten minutes?"

"Good night, Dale."

"Okay, Carley. I understand."

But he did not use that opportunity to ask her out for a second date. "I'll see you later, then."

You did the right thing, Carley told herself as she flossed her teeth at the bathroom mirror. Dale was obviously not like any of the from-prince-to-frog guys her mother had attracted like iron shavings to a magnet. But *she* was not her mother—she wasn't even the Atlanta debutante, Pascagoula accountant, or one of the myriad local beauties hoping their phones would ring.

When Carley's telephone did not ring the whole next week—at least with Dale's voice on the other end—she tried not to dwell upon it. She had learned in college that worry was an energy drain as well as a migraine trigger, and she needed every bit of energy and clearheadedness for Annabel Lee Café.

Interviews from Monday through Thursday had resulted in five employees she would begin training in two weeks. Paperwork consumed the time between interviews, and so she had very little work for Brooke. Still, the girl had pedaled over every morning, just to see.

"Here you are," Carley said on Friday morning, handing her an envelope.

The girl tore the bit of tape on the flap and took out the check. "A hundred and six dollars!"

Please buy some clothes with it, Carley thought, for she was wearing the *Objects Under This Shirt* . . . disaster again. "I took out taxes. The paper-clipped sheet shows how much, and how many hours you worked."

Carley felt competent enough to keep the books, purchase supplies, and compute payroll, but she had taken Aunt Helen's and Stanley Malone's advice and hired a local CPA for serious accounting.

"I'm going to put a bulletin board outside my office for time sheets," Carley went on. "You'll need to make sure I added up the hours correctly every payday."

The girl held the check to her heart. Or rather, to the offensive pink letters. "I trust you, Carley."

"Always double-check, when you're dealing with money," Carley said, echoing Stanley Malone's sentiment of six months ago. She smiled at the girl. "Now, why don't you take it on over to the bank and open an account?"

"Okay!"

Emmit White walked in seconds after the girl walked out. "Then it's true?" he said with a backward frown toward the window. "You hired that Kimball girl?"

"She had good references, and has worked hard for me so far," Carley said. "What do you think of the place, Mr. White? Would you like a guided tour?"

"I walked through the other night. It looks all right."

When Carley stared at him, he shook his head. "You don't think I gave you my only key, do you?"

"Well, no."

"Landlords have rights. Go ask Malone if you don't believe me."

"I believe you." She sighed and pulled a chair from the nearest table. "How about some tea?"

"Not thirsty. But what about that Kimball girl? Did you see that filth on her shirt?"

"She'll have a uniform when we open. And besides, she'll be washing dishes in back."

"She's a tramp. Just like that cousin of hers."

Even though Carley had no idea what the cousin reference was about, she was angry enough at the *tramp* comment to order him to leave. *Entrepreneur,* she reminded herself, drawing in a shaky breath. And an entrepreneur did not allow personal feelings to get in the way of the business.

"Mr. White," she said, forcing steadiness into her voice. "I'll never forget how you changed your mind about renting this place to me. But please remember that you're my landlord, not a business partner. Therefore you have no say over whom I hire. And Brooke

Kimball may look like an adult, but she's still a girl."

He glared and pointed toward the door. "That's my wife's name on that sign."

Carley was opening her mouth to argue further when a quotation from Longfellow slipped out of the mental files of her college education. *If we could read the secret history of our enemies, we should find in each man's life sorrow and suffering enough to disarm all hostility.*

The embittered man before her had suffered—and was still suffering—because of his family. Gentling her tone, Carley said, "And we'll make her proud."

Mr. White looked at her with mouth pressed tight and eyes narrowed.

Oh dear, here we go again, Carley thought.

Until she realized he was not frowning, but struggling to maintain composure. And he lost that battle, for tears meandered down both wrinkled cheeks. Carley hurried into the kitchen and tore off a paper towel.

When she returned he was slouched in the chair.

"Here," she said.

"Sorry," he murmured, wiping his eyes and then blowing his nose.

"Please don't apologize. You have a lot on your shoulders."

"I know it ain't right. Blamin' the girl for what her kin did."

"What do you mean?"

"You don't know?" he asked, tone incredulous. The bony shoulders rose, fell. "When that cousin of hers, Tracy Knight, lived with them, it weren't enough she was sleeping with half the fellers in Lamar County. She went and stole Mona's husband, Rick, and them with a seven-year-old boy."

Brooke's cousin! Carley thought, recalling what Sherry had told her at the Old Grist Mill.

"We had to put Mona in the mental hospital for a while for swallowin' a bottle of pills. Been six years now, and nobody's heard a word from Tracy or from Rick. My Annabel had never got over how our son stole from us, and after Mona tried to kill herself . . . well, that was when Annabel's mind started slippin' away."

He sighed again and closed his eyes. When he did not speak for several seconds, Carley went back to the kitchen for water. When she returned, his eyes were still closed, tears clinging to trembling lashes. She placed the glass on the table. Should she say something? But what? That everything would be all right? She pulled out another chair and sat.

Eventually he looked at her, looked at the glass. He drank half the water, put the glass down again. Embarrassment was obvious on his face, but he said, "Thank you."

I didn't do anything, rose to Carley's lips but she thought better of it. "Did you walk over? Because my car's right out—"

"I'll be fine." A dry smile softened his features, just a little. "Looks like we're even."

That made Carley smile, which made his a little wider.

"All righty-rooty," he said, rising. "I'm going back to work so you can do the same. I'll expect my rent every month with no excuses, little lady."

"Yes, sir," Carley said, like a true Southerner.

———

Steve Underwood delivered the oak deacon's bench Saturday morning and positioned it along the entrance wall adjacent to the counter. "It's wonderful," Carley said, running a hand along the curved back. The oak had a rich sheen against the olive backdrop.

"See how it sits," Steve said, his dark eyes friendly upon her.

"All right." Carley spread both palms on either side to feel wood as smooth as marble. "I love it."

"It's sturdy too. It'll hold up for decades."

"Please tell your father how pleased I am." She had the checkbook ready this time, and invited him to sit at a table. "And may I get you some iced tea? I'm trying to develop a taste for it, now that I'll be serving it."

"No, thank you. I just had coffee. Is everything coming together as you planned?"

"Very well, so far," she said, penning *August 2, 2003* in the date line. "My new staff will start training in two weeks, and if all goes well I should be able to open August twenty-third as planned."

A couple of quick raps came from the window above the door. Dale entered, wearing his uniform and a boyish grin. "I hope I'm not interrupting important business," he said, as if he had not just walked into a *place* of business, passing Steve's truck to do so.

"Well, we *are* kind of—"

"Sure." Still, Dale stood in the doorway. "I keep forgetting to bring your sweater, Carley. But maybe I should hang onto it. I'll check the movie ads—there might be something better this week. How's it going, Steve? When's the fall semester?"

"The eighteenth," Steve replied.

"Ah, I guess you'll be moving back to Hattiesburg soon. Well, my best to your folks."

"Yeah, thanks."

When the door closed again, Carley shook her head. "I'm sorry."

Steve smiled. "You've nothing to apologize for."

"I didn't realize your classes started so soon."

He got to his feet and pushed the chair under the table. "Summer races by, doesn't it? I hope your grand opening's a success."

"Thanks, Steve."

And then he was gone, with a wave at the door.

Ten minutes later, while Carley was proofreading the final mock-up of the menu, Dale returned.

"I'm really sorry," he said, approaching the table with tentative steps. "That was so immature of me."

Carley leveled a look at him. "Well, you just answered the question in my mind."

"You mean, whether it was coincidence that I barged in on you like that a second time?"

243

"What was that about?"

Dale ran his hand through his short hair and pulled out the chair Steve had vacated. He hesitated. "May I. . . ?"

"Suit yourself."

He whistled faintly. "You're really angry, aren't you?"

Carley set the menu on the table and folded her hands. "I don't know that I'm as much angry as confused, Dale. We aren't going together. You're aware that I do business with several people. You don't call for a week—which is your right, because, as I said, we aren't going together—but then act like you're checking up on me?"

"You're right. May I explain?"

Carley shrugged. "If you like."

"Thank you." Elbows on the table, he drew in a breath. "I didn't call because I was afraid."

"Afraid of me?"

"Terrified, Carley. Remember how I said I was a dork most of my life? It was worse than that. When any girl agrees to go out with a short, chubby guy, it's because the prom or homecoming's just around the corner, and she's getting desperate. I had my first girl-friend only *after* I got in shape in college, and even she dumped me, like I mentioned before. But after I made that arrest, women really started flirting with me. Beautiful women. The sort who wouldn't have given me a second look before all this happened."

"I think you sell women short," Carley had to say, and winced inside at her unintended pun. But he had not seemed to notice. "You were older. There is the maturity factor."

"This happened practically overnight, Carley. What else can I think? I was even engaged to a woman like that who was happy to be on my arm when a reporter was present. I can see that, now. Thank goodness she broke it off when I wouldn't leave Tallulah, or I'd always wonder if she really loved me for myself."

Carley had never realized men were capable of such transparency. "But why were you afraid of me?"

"Well, because I like you. More than any woman I've ever met. I got so used to women who were so flattered by dating a hero, that I got lazy. If someone wants to be with you, even when you act like a jerk, what incentive do you have to change? And frankly, how can you respect that woman? I admire how you respect yourself. But this is new for me, dating someone like you. And I don't know how to act."

"Just be yourself," she said, touched in spite of her misgivings.

"I wish it were that easy." He blew out his cheeks. "I thought I'd wait a while, see if my feelings cooled down. But then when I saw Steve's truck . . . well, I got jealous."

That sent a chill up Carley's spine. "I won't date a jealous man, Dale."

"I don't blame you. But in my own defense, all I did was act like an idiot. I didn't threaten Steve. Or you."

It was hard to stay annoyed with him. Carley said, "I'll admit that I'm hypersensitive to certain things."

"Then . . . you'll forgive me?" he asked hopefully

"All right."

His eyes closed for a second. "Thank you, Carley."

"But I'll have to pass on the movie, Dale. I'm pretty busy this weekend." She knew she could have managed to make the time, but this seemed the right course of action.

"I understand." He hesitated. "But you have to eat. Let me take you to lunch?"

"Can't. I'm meeting Aunt Helen at Sherry's house."

"What about tomorrow. Would you consider meeting me at the Old Grist Mill?"

Why not? She still liked him very much. And she could not help but be flattered that she had the power to cause *any* man such emotional stress. "Okay. But is there anything there you can eat?"

"Sure. Baked potato, plain, salad bar." He grinned. "The pleasure of your company will make up for the limited choices. What time do you get out of church?"

"I don't go."

"Oh. I thought since the Hudsons' went to Community . . ."

She shook her head.

"Interesting. That makes us a couple of oddities, here in the Bible Belt. But at least it guarantees us a table before the rush. Eleven-thirty all right?"

"That's fine." She picked up the menu prototype and handed it over the table. "By the way, you might want to see this."

He scanned it and smiled. "Avocado-cucumber sandwich, hummus with pita bread . . . *and* spinach wrap?"

The latter was a last-minute decision. "With cheese, mind you, but all you have to do is order it without. And there's mushroom-wild-rice soup on the other side."

"I'm overwhelmed."

"This was a business decision. They earned their spots."

"There may have been a little bit of pity involved too?"

"Okay." She held up thumb and forefinger a quarter inch apart. "There may have been *some* pity involved. But you'll still have to eat baked potatoes and salads on Sundays, and pack your own on Mondays. We'll only be open the days the shops are open."

"Are you sure that's a good idea?"

She was not sure at all, with so many townspeople asking about the café, and the Old Grist Mill so popular. But other than Brooke, all of her newly hired staff had expressed concern during their interviews over working Sundays. The employee pool was not *that* vast in Tallulah. And coincidentally or not, those applicants who impressed her the most were churchgoers.

She had toyed with the idea of opening for lunch on Sundays, but then tossed the notion. If the day was so important to them, let them have the whole day. Happy employees would surely be productive employees, and she was convinced that her business would be made or broken by the shoppers. She could always change her mind later. She was not out to make a million dollars. Just to support herself with a business that did not demand every waking minute of every day, once it got going.

———

You almost blew it, Dale thought, sending an appreciative wave to hardware store owner Mr. Marshall for slowing his pickup truck to allow him across Main Street.

He stepped to the edge of the sidewalk to circumvent a chattering foursome of elderly women coming out of Enchanted Attic. He recognized one—Mayor Coates' mother. After seven years as chief of police, there was enough politician in his blood to cause him to pause and ask if they were having a good day.

"These are my chums from teaching college, Chief Dale," Myrna Coates said. "We still get together once a year. This year it's my turn to host. Patty here flew all the way down from New York."

"Well, if that doesn't beat all," Dale drawled, shaking one soft hand, then another. "I hope Miz Coates baked you some of her coconut cream pie. It's always the hit of the Founders' Day Picnic."

"I'm afraid your sweet talk is wasted, young man," Mrs. Coates said, taking his arm. "These women can cook circles around me."

"That might be uncomf-table, Myrna!" the woman named Patty quipped in a nasal-sounding hybrid of New York City and backwoods Mississippi. Dale laughed along with the other three, wished them good-day, and continued down the sidewalk.

The same intuition that had helped him recognize Warren Knap in Shoney's had served him well again by telling him what Carley would want to hear. Women loved men who could admit to being vulnerable. And the irony—he was pretty certain the word fit this time—was that he was being totally honest. He *had been* a lonesome, awkward teenager. He *did* appreciate that she seemed to like him for himself and that she would have nothing to do with him if he treated her with less than respect.

Did that not make him a good man?

You are a good man, he assured himself. How many wives, mothers, and co-eds were alive today because Warren Knap was put away seven years ago?

Bad things happened to decent people all the time, didn't they? And lots of good people had skeletons in their closets.

A shiver ran through him, in spite of the ninety-degree heat. *Bad choice of words. Think of something else.*

———

"Do you think I'm being silly, wondering if this raises a red flag?" Carley asked Aunt Helen and Sherry over finger sandwiches, quiche rounds, and raw vegetables left over from last night's middle school faculty planning meeting.

"I wouldn't say *silly*, Carley," Sherry said, swirling a celery stick through ranch dressing. "But maybe you blew it out of proportion. It's actually kind of funny."

"He didn't threaten either of you?" Aunt Helen asked.

Carley shook her head.

"And he confessed to doing it on purpose?"

"He was very repentant."

"You have to understand men, Carley," Sherry said. "No matter how old they get, they never completely leave the school yard. Oh, they may manage to squelch that part of themselves for years, even hide it under a coat and tie, but it's still there."

"Mom?" came from the den. A second later, Patrick stood in the doorway in T-shirt and shorts. "Where did Dad put that fake vomit he bought in Florida? I want to bring it to basketball camp."

"Excuse me," Sherry said, and left the kitchen.

Aunt Helen smiled and passed the tray. Carley smiled back and scooped up a quiche and two finger sandwiches.

"Courtship was much less complicated when I was young," her aunt said. "All we cared about was if the fellow had good manners and a job."

"What about looks?"

She smiled again. "If he was cute, that was a bonus. But looking back, we were too naïve. Romance, hearts, and flowers—that's what was important. We didn't give a thought to the friendship part—

and that's where you learn a person's character."

That made perfect sense, Carley thought. "I turned down his offer of a movie, though I wasn't exactly sure *why* I was doing it. We should work on just being friends for now. There's no hurry."

"No hurry at all."

"I wonder if I should have agreed to meet him for lunch tomorrow."

"That's something friends do." She met Carley's eyes, opened her mouth, and closed it.

"What is it?"

"Just that I hope Steve Underwood tries again. He's a good Christian man, by all accounts, and . . . well . . ."

"You're hoping he'll lead me back into the fold."

Aunt Helen sighed. "I don't pressure you because that's what you've asked. But my Christianity is part of who I am. It comes out in my conversations and interactions with other people all the time. I can't squelch who I am just so you'll be comfortable."

They stared across the table at each other, Aunt Helen's hazel eyes sad and yet firm.

She's right, Carley realized. She had no right to walk around with a chip on her shoulder, especially among family who had accepted her without demanding that she change.

She reached across for Aunt Helen's soft hand, and held it in her own. "I'm sorry."

"It's good to clear the air sometimes," Aunt Helen said, squeezing back.

"Don't stop praying for me, okay?"

She smiled. "As if I would."

The waitress, with *Tiffany* on her badge, was very pretty in spite of two inches of dark roots in her long blonde hair. Setting rolled napkins and glasses of ice water on the table under a battered washboard and aged poster of The Grand Ole Opry, she asked, "Who's minding the jail today?"

Dale smiled up at her. "It's Garland's turn."

"Oh well, his loss is our gain," she said meaningfully, then took their drink orders and left.

In spite of her decision to concentrate on friendship with Dale, Carley felt a disturbing twinge of jealousy. *So, that's how he felt when Steve came over.*

Only Steve had not batted adoring gray eyes, as Tiffany had.

"We rotate Sundays," Dale was saying.

"Hmm?"

"Garland, Marti, and me."

Carley nodded. "Garland was with a woman that time I saw you in Corner Diner. . . ."

"Amy. She's a sweetheart. She teaches their two daughters at home, so it's rare that she gets to join him for lunch. Marti and I tell him he married above himself."

"You don't really."

"Garland agrees. He's a good sport." Dale sobered. "In fact, he's solid gold. He had twelve years on the force when I came here, but never once has he shown any resentment. I don't know if I would have been so gracious if the roles were reversed."

"I understand," Carley said. "But the Board of Aldermen offered you the position. They must have had their reasons for passing him by."

"Well, maybe," he conceded.

Tiffany brought two glasses of tea and took their orders. "Ya'll go ahead and help yourselves to the salad bar," she said to Dale.

But as soon as the waitress walked away, Carley rested her hand on his sleeve. "Wait, Dale. Are you questioning your ability? Because *everyone* says what a good job you're doing."

His blue eyes narrowed playfully. "Who?"

"I can't name names on the spot," Carley said.

"Uh-huh."

"Okay . . . Loretta Malone. She spoke very highly of you my first day here."

"So that explains it," he said, nodding.

"What?"

"Ever since you moved back from California, she's been singing your praises to me."

"Now, why am I not surprised?" Carley said.

He grinned. "I'll have to send her some flowers and a thank-you note."

"Don't you dare."

"Well then, let's get our salads before the Baptists get here." He got to his feet and came around to pull out her chair.

At the salad bar, Carley piled everything but green olives and red onions on her lettuce, spooning honey dijon dressing over the mix. Dale passed up the cheese, croutons, bacon bits and chopped eggs, and poured on oil and vinegar from separate cruets. Tables were beginning to fill. Carley recognized some of Aunt Helen and Uncle Rory's church friends from the birthday party, but she already knew that none of her family planned to come here today.

"Do you mind if I ask why you don't go to church?" Dale said, unfolding his napkin. "You're not an atheist, are you?"

"Not at all." Carley cut a tomato wedge into more manageable pieces. "But church is something I keep putting off—a holdover from childhood. I guess I'm afraid I'll ultimately be disappointed again. What about you? Why are you agnostic?"

Sprinkling salt onto his salad, he said, "My family just wasn't religious. Dad worked weekends, so Mom usually took us to visit my grandparents in Perry."

He raised his eyes to her face as if considering whether to say more.

"What?" Carley asked eventually.

"While I'm not arrogant enough to say God *doesn't* exist, I sort of hope that's the case. Have you ever felt that way?"

"Um . . . I don't think so. Why would you not want him to exist?"

"Oh, different reasons." Brows denting, he gave her a thoughtful look. "How did we get on that track?"

She speared a cucumber slice. "I believe you led us there."

"Then, let's go somewhere else. Tell me, do you miss California?"

"Some things about it."

"Like what?"

"Well, the climate. Buying fresh dates at the supermarket. Chinese restaurants on every corner. Symphonies and theatre." She thought for another second. "And rocks."

"We have rocks."

"Gravel, maybe. Not big enough to climb on."

He ceased chewing. "Are you, maybe, regretting your decision to move here?"

The worry in his expression made her smile. "Not at all. Even after having to pay the Realtor fee on my own property."

"Ouch."

"Well, you did too, didn't you?"

The blue eyes narrowed playfully. "Has Kay Chapman been bad-mouthing me?"

Carley shook her head. "She never mentioned your name. Just

warned me about the penalty fee and mentioned someone else paying one. Since you took your land off the market, I just
assumed . . ."

"Well, you assumed right. So, double ouch." He looked into her
eyes and smiled. "And I don't regret deciding to stay either."

––––––––––

On Tuesday morning the attic fan pulled in the fragrance of hay
from fields skirting the town. Mrs. Templeton, feeding her birds
and squirrels, said that farmers were probably cutting and bailing
before tomorrow's predicted rain.

Uncle Rory brought his rechargeable drill and attached two
hooks to the inside of the café picture window. At three o'clock, an
electrician Stanley Malone had recommended installed a sound system and ceiling speakers.

Wednesday's gray clouds made 10:00 in the morning seem more
like 7:00 in the evening. Carley held the door for Matt Lockwood
of Green Thumb Nursery as he made six trips carrying in a Boston
fern, peace lily, two dieffenbachia, two Ficus benjamina, and two
hanging baskets of English ivy for the window.

After his truck drove away, she loaded *Twenty Years of Beautiful
Music* by 101 Strings into the sound system and moved plants about,
trying to determine the best locations. She was singing to the instrumental track—"Don't cry for me, Ar-gen-tin-a"—when someone
tapped on the window. It was Brooke, standing beside her bicycle.
A lumpy, pillowcase-wrapped bundle bulged in the basket, secured
with four strands of cord.

"Looks good!" she mouthed, pointing up to an ivy basket.

Carley went to the door and stuck her head out. "Thanks,
Brooke. But you'd better get home. It's going to rain soon. Or how
about if I drive you?"

"No thanks. I'll make it."

"But can you manage all that laundry?"

Brooke patted the bundle. "They stay put pretty good when

they're wet. Our washin' machine's broken. But the dryer still works."

Fortunately, the clouds held on to their rain for a couple of hours more.

"Why doesn't her father ever drive her anywhere?" she asked Dale when he stopped by at noon, hinting for a glass of iced tea to go with his peanut butter sandwich.

"Because he knows I'll give him a sobriety test if he so much as swerves an inch. He's had four drunk-driving convictions and would be in prison if Judge McGray wasn't such a wrist slapper. He chewed, swallowed. "Did you know some people have a phobia about peanut butter sticking to the roofs of their mouths? It even has a name . . . arachibutyrophobia."

"Isn't that the fear of spiders?"

"No. You're thinking about arachnophobia." When she gave him a bemused look, he shrugged. "Thanks to the Internet, I'm a treasure trove of useless trivia. But what I can't understand is, why Mildred Tanner doesn't drive her."

"She watches soaps all the time, according to Brooke."

"That doesn't stop her from going to the beauty parlor every Monday."

"Are you *sure* it's her? Brooke says she has . . . hygiene issues."

"Well, yeah," Dale said. "And frankly, if it weren't for the direction the truck was pointing, I wouldn't know whether she was coming or going."

Carley covered a smile. "You're horrible."

"And you're not? Hygiene issues?"

"Okay, maybe we're a bad influence on each other."

"Maybe so." He took a bite of sandwich, chewed, and grinned at her. "Arachibutyrophobia. Look it up."

Friday evening, the Kemps gave a farewell party for Conner, who was returning to school in Alabama in the morning. Mosquitoes made barbecuing on the patio out of the question, and so the guests helped themselves from trays of finger foods, including

Carley's ham-and-colby sandwiches on potato buns from the Mennonite bakery. Most guests were Conner's former schoolmates. Their energy and banter made them fun to watch, and they were not timid about taking turns with a karaoke machine.

"Desperado ... why don't you come to your senses," a pretty girl belted out through braces.

"Patrick's new girlfriend, Tara," Aunt Helen leaned close to murmur.

"Uh-oh," Carley murmured back. They shared the love seat, with plates perched upon their knees. "If they marry, they'd better pass up the honeymoon and start saving for their children's orthodontia bills."

Her aunt laughed and patted her arm.

One of the kids talked Blake into taking the microphone. He sang a surprisingly good rendition of Elvis Presley's "Suspicious Minds." He took a deep bow to the applause and, even more surprising, declined singing another one.

"How about a turn, Conner?" said one of his male friends.

"Not in a million years," he said, smiling, and walked over to crouch in front of Carley. "I just upgraded my computer for school, but my old Dell's still good. Mom says you don't have one at home."

"How much are you selling it for?" she asked. Not once did she assume he was offering to give it to her. After all, he was Blake's son. That did not lower her opinion of him. He didn't owe her anything.

"A hundred and fifty?" he asked hesitantly. "But you should have a look at it first."

"That sounds good." When he moved on, Carley asked Aunt Helen how business was going.

"Very well. I sold the cranberry-glass punch set in the front case to a collector in New York this morning."

"But how?"

"His sister from Mobile came in with a group, took a digital picture with her cell phone, and e-mailed it to him. The man called about an hour later and paid with his credit card. Pam boxed it up and brought it to the post office, and that was that."

"The world is moving too fast," Carley sighed.

"Isn't it? What about you? Did the napkins come in?"

"Yesterday." Carley reached down over the love seat arm for her purse. The soft, thick natural-colored paper, was folded to show the paprika red letters saying *Annabel Lee Café* and the figure of the woman.

"I could only afford the one ink color," Carley said as her aunt held it.

"But it's very nice. You made a wise decision. You won't have time to wash and fold cloth ones every day."

That prompted a thought that had hovered in the back of Carley's mind for three days.

"What would you think of my asking Brooke Kimball if she'd like to move into one of my extra rooms? She wouldn't have to ride that bike back and forth. What's going to happen when winter comes, and it starts getting dark earlier?"

"Carley, please don't."

Carley studied her face. "But why? I thought you, of all people, would love the idea."

"Because I'm Christian, you mean."

"Well, yes."

"Christianity and naiveté aren't the same thing, dear. I'm glad you have a tender heart, but you hardly know her."

Warmed by the compliment, Carley nonetheless persisted, "What if I made her understand that she either goes by my rules or moves out again?"

"Then what will you do if she smokes in the house or breaks some other rule, but turns out to be an excellent employee? You'll still have to see her every day, and how will that affect your work relationship? It's better to go into something slowly, than to move too quickly and have to try to undo what you've done later. That's when people get hurt."

That made sense. "Then you're not saying I shouldn't ever ask her."

"Of course not." Her aunt leaned closer to brush a crumb from Carley's collar. "Just that you should wait until you're one hundred percent sure. And you're *not* there now, or you wouldn't have needed to ask my opinion."

———

"It's no secret that I have no experience in running a café," Carley said to the six people in the café dining room on Monday, August eighteenth. "But what you may not know is that my livelihood is invested. We're not a chain; I paid for every teaspoon and salt shaker myself. If we don't make a profit, I'll not borrow money and risk going deep into debt. We'll simply have to close down."

She had stayed up until two in the morning, preparing many of the menu items to serve double-duty as snacks and visual aids. They were spread out on two tables pushed together, with herself seated at the head. It was after careful deliberation that she decided to be candid before training began.

And yet, she was aware that confessing that her personal finances were tied up was not motivation enough. These people's planets did not revolve around her star, and there were other jobs, some even in Tallulah.

"I'm asking you to make this café as important to you as it is to me. And so I decided you need a higher stake in it. Misters Malone and Laird, the attorney and CPA working with us, have helped me draw up a profit-sharing plan."

There were exchanged glances, nods, and smiles.

"But we can't make a profit without patrons who *want* to come back often. They'll do that if we make dining here a good experience for them, and if we have the attitude that it's a privilege to serve them."

"Miss Reed?"

The speaker was Paula Reilly, age thirty-eight, with short brown hair and bangs. Married to a sawmill worker and the mother of three school-aged children, she had given notice in the hardware department at Wal-Mart to work closer to home.

"Carley, please," Carley corrected.

One bit of Stanley Malone's advice she could not follow, was having her employees address her as "Miss Reed." It went too much against her West Coast grain. She understood that she could not become their friend right away, for what if she had to let one go in a month's time? But surely she could maintain their respect by staying organized, having a plan for every day, leaving her personal life at home, and treating everyone professionally.

Paula nodded. "Carley. At Wal-Mart I told myself every time I waited on a customer that I might be givin' him the only smile he gets that day."

"I like that philosophy, Paula."

Danyell Weathers, the other full-time waitress, nodded. She was tall, with skin like toffee-colored satin and ebony hair pulled into a ponytail with a scarf. Mother of a three-year-old boy, she had moved to Tallulah to live with her parents while her Marine sergeant husband was stationed in Iraq.

Troy Fairchild would work the peak period of eleven to two on weekdays, all day Saturdays, and whenever the computer decided to crash. A friend of Conner's, he took evening classes in computer engineering at USM. He was thin as a rail, all elbows and knees and large feet, with light brown hair and a scattering of pimples. The only son of the pastor at Tallulah Pentecostal, he played bass guitar in a Gospel group—The Singing Fairchilds—with his four sisters,

Carley was encouraged that the white shirt Brooke wore with her jeans was actually buttoned high enough to keep inside what needed to be inside. She sat at the opposite end of the tables between cooks Lisa Gerhard, age twenty-eight, and Rachel Bogart, thirty-one—Mennonite sisters from Columbia. Both were solidly built, with long honey-colored hair; Lisa's flowed from her forehead back into a braid, while Rachel had short bangs and wore silver wire-rimmed eyeglasses.

Carley planned to work the cash register and play hostess. Later, if profits were healthy enough, she would hire someone else for that position. Also, the waitstaff would have to juggle her duties along with their own for about five minutes out of every hour, so she could restock and tidy up the restrooms. It would be a circus for a while. But if training went well, the customers would only see a smooth operation, not the panic attacks back in the kitchen.

She smiled, watching her employees sample the foods on their plates. Future panic attacks notwithstanding, she could not remember when she had felt so alive, so energized.

Thank you, God, flowed through her mind before she even realized it.

chapter 22

As training progressed during the week, Carley realized the smoothness of it had more to do with the quality of her employees than with her little introductory speech. Which was good, because character was more lasting than the adrenaline in the wake of a motivational pep talk.

Opening day, however, was a mixed bag.

The bad began as soon as the clock alarm pierced Carley's throbbing right temple.

"How is it possible to wake up with a headache?" Dale asked a half hour later when he telephoned to wish her luck.

Carley held the plastic bag of ice cubes up to her temple. "My fault," she said. "I kept wondering if we'd forgotten anything. Did I order enough food? What if no one comes?"

"Now, that's not going to happen. Didn't you say folks have been asking you about it for weeks?"

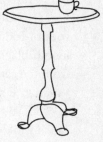

"Yes, but you Southerners will say anything to be polite."

"Okay, we need to get you well, or you'll run customers off with that attitude. I'm gonna call Chester Templeton at the drugstore and see if there's anything helpful I can pick up and run over to you."

"No, thank you. I can't afford to be drowsy. And most prescription medicines have that effect on me."

"Maybe there's something new . . ."

"This isn't the day to experiment." In spite of the pain, she smiled. "Look, it's thoughtful of you to offer. But I took my Excedrin and tiny bit of Dramamine a minute ago, and I'm brewing some tea. I just need to get going."

"Okey-dokey, see you at noon."

Uncle Rory stopped by twenty minutes later with warm buttered biscuits wrapped in a towel, bacon strips, and freestone peach preserves. "Helen was afraid you'd be too busy to eat," he said from the porch.

Carley, clad in her robe with her hair wrapped in a towel, stepped out and kissed the old man's cheek for the first time ever. "Thank you."

Sherry called, and Blake even took the phone briefly to say, "Break a leg! Oh wait, that's in theater, isn't it?"

"Blake . . ." Carley could hear Sherry say in the background.

"Just kidding!" he said. "I've been plugging your place in the shop every day, so don't make me out to be a liar, okay?"

"Okay, Blake. Thank you," Carley said, meaning it.

Gayle Payne sent the children to the door with a half dozen warm biscuits. Carley had not the heart to tell them she had already eaten, so she wrapped them and placed them in the freezer to microwave another time.

Her clothes for the week lay across the bed in the middle bedroom. Today, an azalea pink three-quarter-sleeve blouse, knee-length black skirt, and low black heels. No suits, which would veer from the casual-yet-classy atmosphere she hoped to project. And she would save a ton of money on dry cleaning. Every penny counted.

"So, you're going out to your little restaurant?" Mrs. Templeton called while scattering sunflower seeds.

"On my way!" Carley called back, hopping down the steps. She felt better by the time she steered the GL up Main Street, under a combination of Excedrin, tea and biscuits, and brain endorphins brought on by the all the well-wishers. Figuring she may as well get into the habit and give up her space in front to a customer, she parked in back, several feet from the Dumpster.

In the kitchen, she filled and turned on both tea machines—caffeinated and decaffeinated. Two seconds after she turned on the dining room lights, Brooke's face became visible in the door window, even though staff were not due for another forty-five minutes. Carley unlocked the door and felt a little throb in her temple. Tank top and jeans!

"Brooke, what happened to your uniform?"

Brooke nodded over to her bicycle, leaning against the light post. "I was afraid I'd get axle grease or something on it. But it's in here."

She raised a yellow Dollar General bag. The uniforms were simple—polyester-cotton black skirts or pants for wearability and ease in laundering, caramel-colored, polo-collared knit shirts. And the *coup-de-grace*, paprika-colored aprons with pockets for straws, order pads, and pencils.

From the look of Brooke's bag, it was obvious that the uniform was not folded neatly. Rather than follow her first inclination to scream, Carley took the girl's arm. "Okay, I'll put on a pot of water. We'll steam out the wrinkles."

"But I'm only gonna be in back," the girl said as Carley propelled her through the dining room.

"Doesn't matter," Carley said. "People work better when they look better. Why don't you just keep both uniforms here? You can hang them in that little closet in my office."

"Thank you."

Danyell arrived a few minutes later, followed by cooks Lisa and Rachel, who began laying out cutting boards and knives. The last to arrive was Troy Fairchild, but even he was seven minutes earlier than expected, a good omen of the day to come.

At eleven o'clock, all staff stood in the dining room watching the door. Carley asked Paula to flip the sign in the window to *Open*.

The waitress hesitated. "Maybe you should, this first time?"

"Yes, all right." She could feel six sets of eyes following her across the dining room. At the window she strained to look both ways. No mobs of people hurrying over, but it was still early. She flipped the sign, the staff applauded, and she turned and gave a little bow.

Ten minutes later, a third of the tables were filled.

Mayor Dwight Coates and his wife, Birdie. Stanley and Loretta Malone. Beta Club parents Ron and Lynn Hall. A quartet of older women from Jackson who were directed over from Aunt Helen's shop by her assistant Pam Lipscomb. A husband and wife who had picked up a printout of the menu in Red Barn Emporium. Uncle Rory and Aunt Helen, Sherry and Blake.

The matter of family as customers had come up in the Kemp kitchen two weeks ago, while Carley helped clean up after Conner's going-away party.

"You're going to have to charge us, just like everyone else," were Uncle Rory's words.

"I just can't . . ." Carley had started, but her uncle raised a palm.

"Hear me out, little girl. Only a dime or so out of every dollar will stay in your pocket, with the rest going toward supplies, rent, and wages. You won't stay in business long if you start doing favors for family, and all of us can well afford to go out and eat."

In hindsight, Carley was glad he had spoken so in Blake's company. And, again in hindsight, perhaps it was not by accident that Uncle Rory chose that opportunity. She felt a rough affection for Blake, but allowing him to order "on the house" would probably open an avalanche of problems, with his possibly feeling entitled to treat friends at her expense.

And knowing that he charged Uncle Rory full price for a haircut took away some of the uneasiness over the matter.

"Everything's wonderful," Aunt Helen said when Carley visited their table.

"Wonderful," Blake said, raising his tea glass.

A trio of antique hunters, relatively young women in their

thirties, shared a table. One expressed delight over the vegan choices. "I'll definitely be back," she said to Paula halfway through her avocado-cucumber sandwich.

At about ten minutes before noon, Averil Stillman entered, accompanied by his wife and daughter. Rita was a striking woman, with tawny skin and short reddish hair. Little Samantha's smile revealed a slight gap where a permanent tooth was just sprouting. Her hair, twisted into a barrette at the crown of her head, as well as the iron creases in the sleeve of her tropical-print shirt, gave evidence that Rita was a hands-on stepmother. Carley was glad for the girl.

"Thank you so much for coming," she said, taking three laminated menus from the counter. She was scanning the few empty tables when the girl motioned a finger at her father, who bent down to catch her whisper.

"It's okay to ask," Averil said, straightening again.

"What is it?" Carley asked.

Averil exchanged smiles with his wife and gave Samantha's shoulder a gentle nudge.

"We're trying to help her with her shyness," Rita said softly over the girl's head.

Carley leaned down, held out her hand. "Hi, Samantha. I'm Carley. You sure are pretty."

The girl's eyes widened. In a little voice, she said, "How do you know my name?"

"Because your uncle Winn and cousin John painted all the walls in here. Didn't they do a good job?"

Samantha looked around. "Yes, ma'am."

"What is it you'd like to ask me?"

She chewed her lip, hesitated. "May we have a table by the window? I like to look at the people walk by."

"Well, let's see."

Both window tables were occupied, but the trio of shoppers were digging into purses.

"If you don't mind waiting here on the bench with your parents for about five minutes, we'll have one ready for you."

"Thank you," the girl said, smiling, and the dregs of Carley's migraine finally slipped away.

Dale and Garland came at one o'clock. Dale insisted on ordering the spinach wrap and cup of mushroom soup for both of them.

"I liked them both just fine," Garland said at the counter afterward. "That was great tea, by the way. But I'll be ordering differently when I come back with Amy and the kids. It's just not natural, not having meat in a meal."

Dale handed Carley his Discover card and asked about her headache.

"It's gone," she replied.

"Good! And I'm glad the place is hopping."

The number of patrons filtering in and out seemed evenly divided between townspeople and antique hunters. Carley imagined that percentage would change as the novelty wore off and more shoppers learned of the place. Whatever the dynamics, she would be happy if the tables stayed filled.

The shops closed at five. Her plan was to stop seating customers at six, so that her staff could leave by seven-thirty, after nine hours minus lunch and two breaks. She could always add an evening shift and part-time employees later, after the café had proved itself.

At five after seven the last patrons—librarian Edward Juban and his fiancée, Claire Baker—stood at the counter, declaring their meals delicious and promising to return. The sound of breaking glass came from the back, followed by muffled voices. Troy, cleaning the last table, looked at Carley and hurried for the double doors.

"I guess we'll see how sturdy the china is," Carley said lightly, handing Edward his change. She escorted them to the door with thanks and, not taking the time to lock it, turned and made for the kitchen.

266

Brooke burst through the doors when Carley was but five feet away, and hurried past.

"Brooke?" Carley said.

The girl turned, eyeliner smudged across crimson cheeks. "I'm sorry, Carley!"

By the time Carley reached the door, Brooke was pedaling away. Troy and Paula had come into the dining room.

"She called Danyell the n-word," Troy said.

Carley groaned. "Oh no . . ."

In the kitchen, Danyell and Lisa were on their knees before the sink, picking up shards of china.

"My fault," Danyell said, her own face wet with tears. "I was handing her some dishes, and let go too soon."

"That's no excuse for name calling," Paula said.

Carley nodded thanks at Rachel, returning from the storeroom with a broom and dustpan. "I'm so sorry, Danyell. Here now, move back and let us get it, okay?"

It was fortunate that tomorrow was Sunday. Two days to find someone else. Carley had not been overly impressed with the applicants whose files were in her office, but if they could wash dishes and refrain from using racial epithets, she would have to be satisfied.

Danyell got to her feet, wiped her eyes with the napkin Troy handed her. "She was worn out."

"We're all worn out," Carley said. "But she's gone."

"How do you get along with people of other races?" Carley asked twenty-two-year-old Renee Brown, whose inch-long multicolored nails were out of proportion with her petite body. Hopefully they were not attached with superglue, for there was no way on earth she was going to be able to wear a pair of rubber gloves.

"You mean . . . black people?"

"Well, in this case, yes." Tallulah had only one Hispanic family, the Murillos, who raised cattle on a small acreage out on Highway

42. The only Asian residents were the two young girls that the bank manager, Eric Baker, and his wife had adopted from China.

"I get along fine with everybody," Renee said, her voice high-pitched like a little girl's. "My mama taught me that. You treat other people like you want them to treat you."

Some of the tension eased from Carley's shoulders. "Very good, Renee. I'll let you know by morning."

But her application revealed something odd, Carley realized after giving it closer attention. No local references, just the manager of a furniture store in Hattiesburg and an instructor at Jones Junior College in Ellisville.

Neither reference existed, she discovered by making some inquiries with telephone book in hand Monday morning. She was curious enough to call Dale in his office.

"Renee Brown? Throw the application away, Carley. Better yet, burn it. We've arrested her five times for shoplifting."

"You're kidding."

"She's banned from every shop in town."

Carley breathed a sigh of relief. "Thank you, Dale."

"Anytime." He hesitated. "I've given you some space so you could focus on training and your grand opening but I'd sure like to spend some time with you. Are you up for pasta and a movie on my big screen this evening?"

"It's not *Batman* or anything like that, is it?"

"No way," he drawled. "*Especially* not *Batman*. What kind of superpower does he have? A utility belt and fancy car? And don't get me started on Robin, with his prissy little outfit."

"Okay, okay," Carley said, smiling. "May I let you know? It depends on if I find a dishwasher by evening."

"Then I'll think positive thoughts. What's your favorite movie?"

Carley thought for a second. "*The Last of the Mohicans.*"

"Whoa! Great choice. Now, get busy rustling up a dishwasher so I won't have to watch it alone."

"All right."

But first, she had to telephone Renee Brown, as promised. The woman reinforced Dale's evaluation of her by exclaiming, "Two interviews and I still don't get the job? I ought to come up there and tear your—"

"I'll have you arrested if you come near me," Carley said, replacing the receiver with pulse racing.

Besides four applications from high schoolers seeking only part-time work, there was only Gaye Archer, who had complained during her initial interview about how badly she wanted to quit the video store she was employed in because a "pimply-faced college kid" was promoted manager over her.

"Great, just great," Carley muttered, tossing and palming her key chain. She flipped through the Hattiesburg Yellow Pages to a category she never imagined she would have to look up so soon. *Temporary Employment Agencies.*

However much stress this situation induced, it was mingled with relief that she had followed Aunt Helen's advice about not inviting Brooke to live with her.

The buzzer sounded. Carley walked through the storeroom and paused at the delivery door. She called, "Who is it?"

"It's Danyell."

"I came to ask you to give Brooke another chance," Danyell said in the office.

"But why would you want that?" Carley asked. "You have no guarantee it won't happen again."

She nodded understanding. "Carley, the word she used is one of the biggest insults you can give a person of color. But she's young, and I've heard what her homelife is like. How's she gonna learn how to act right, if people don't give her another chance?"

Carley sighed, realized she was jangling her keys again, and set them back upon her desk. "She *was* a hard worker."

"*I* couldn't have stood at the sink all day like that."

"Are you sure about this?"

"Absolutely sure."

"You're incredibly gracious," Carley said.

"Not really." Danyell returned her smile. "In fact, I'm being a little selfish. When I'm on my knees asking God to watch over my Curtis in Iraq, I want my prayers to get through. I don't want my own unforgiveness comin' between Him and me."

Carley was touched in spite of the discomfort over having Danyell bring up spiritual matters. "I *still* say you're gracious. But if Brooke ruins this chance, you can forgive her all you want, but she won't come back."

She waited until 10:30 to dial the Kimball number, hoping Mr.

Kimball would not bawl her out again. But it was a woman's voice on the line, shrill and grating.

"Brooke ain't here. She toted some clothes over to the washerteria on that bike. If ye see her, tell her she fergot the soap powder here on the table."

"When did she leave?"

"I don't know. Ten minutes ago? Ig-nert girl would ferget her head."

Carley went next door to the drugstore and paid almost twice as much for a small box of Gain than the Dollar General would have charged. She walked a block down Main. No bicycle was parked outside Kangaroo Washaroo. The only person inside was the woman attendant, who sent her an apologetic little wave from the half-door in back and resumed talking on the telephone. A dryer made muffled clanking noises, as if a pair of tennis shoes had gotten mixed-up in the laundry. The place smelled of bleach and detergent, not unpleasantly, though Carley could feel the humidity frizzing the ends of her hair.

"You need some help, honey?" the attendant called with hand over the receiver.

"No, thank you."

From a metal chair she kept watch through the window. Three minutes passed, and then she could see Brooke walking her bicycle, one hand holding steady the white bundle bulging in the basket. Carley opened the door.

"Carley," Brooke said thickly.

"Hi, Brooke."

Inside, the girl dropped the bundle to the tile floor, shook her head. "I'm so sorry I ruined your first day."

Carley shrugged. "It wasn't ruined. It just didn't end very well. Would you like to come back?"

Hope diluted the misery in the green eyes, just a little. "Are you kidding?"

"I wouldn't kid about this. Danyell came over to plead your case, by the way."

Brooke's mouth parted. "I can't believe it."

"The question is . . . can you restrain yourself from any more scenes?"

"Yes! Oh, Miss Reed, I've beat myself up a hundred times for that."

But Carley was not quite ready to close the deal. "What you called Danyell . . ."

The girl's cheeks flushed. "I know."

"That can't happen again, Brooke."

"It won't. I promise."

"Well, maybe it would help if you stopped thinking of her *that way*. And again, if it weren't for Danyell, I wouldn't be here right now."

Brooke nodded gravely. "I want to tell her I'm sorry. Do you know where she lives?"

"Save it for tomorrow. Let her enjoy the rest of her day off." Carley motioned toward the bag in the chair. "By the way, I brought you some detergent."

———

"Just like that?" Dale said, rinsing a colander of whole-wheat penne pasta, cooked al dente.

With a knife tip, Carley scooped the liquid and seeds from a large quartered tomato. Six pods of garlic lay in a corner of the cutting board, waiting to be minced. "Well, there's more to it than that. She's on probation."

"I hope she's learned her lesson." He began wiping baby portobello mushrooms with a wet paper towel. "But you'd better have a backup plan this time."

"Well, Uncle Rory offered to come help me out."

When Dale gave her a sidelong look, she smiled back. "Don't worry. I would hire Renee Brown before I did that to him."

In a large high-sided skillet he sautéed the garlic in olive oil before adding the minced tomato, chopped mushrooms, and several shredded basil leaves. A small bottle of drained capers came next, then he added the pasta to the pan and tossed it until the mixture was warm.

"I bought parmesan cheese too," Dale said, taking the glasses from the cabinet. "Just in case you want it on yours."

"You did that for me?"

"Yes. I violated the sanctity of my refrigerator with a dairy product."

She wondered if all men were so thoughtful. They carried their plates and iced tea into the living room, and Dale loaded the movie into the VCR. The first scene, of Hawkeye and his adopted father and brother chasing a deer through a forest, stirred a memory.

"I'd like to see your land," she said.

"Why?"

"Well, just because. It must be pretty, if you plan to build on it."

"It's a long way from being ready for that." He sighed. "Okay, I'll take you to have a look sometime. But you'll be disappointed."

The movie rolled on. He paused it when the telephone rang.

"A big day here in the sticks," he said, replacing the receiver. "Lassie comes home."

When she gave him a blank look, he said, "Lassie. It was this dog . . ."

"I *know* who Lassie was."

"Sorry. That was Marti, reporting that a farmer on Rocky Branch Road caught a boxer puppy that had escaped from his owners on Fourth Street."

Carley rose and picked up the two plates. "That's good to hear."

"I'll get the glasses. It's just not very exciting."

She turned. "Well, then, here, take the plates instead."

He laughed. "You know what I meant. I'll bet the San Francisco Police Department doesn't get calls about stray dogs."

"San Francisco has over seven hundred thousand people,

Dale." She rinsed the plates under the tap. "But if you want more excitement, why don't you move? You didn't commit to a certain length of time here, did you?"

"Well, no."

"With your resumé, I'll bet you could go anywhere. You might have to start lower than chief, but if it's excitement you want . . ."

"Excitement's not everything." He handed her the towel. "I'm just grousing about my job, like most fellows do now and then. Don't pay me any mind."

"All right." She dried her hands. "I *could* rob the bank for you."

That made him laugh again. His smile remained as he met her eyes. "You're good for me, Carley. You know that?"

She could feel warmth in her face. "Thank you."

"Hence, another reason for me to stay in Tallulah."

He looked seriously poised to kiss her. The quickening of her heartbeat signaled it would not be such a bad thing to happen. She thought of what Aunt Helen had said about moving too quickly. One kiss, and their relationship would jump to another level. If she decided later it was a mistake, there could be no going back to the comfortable friendship they enjoyed now.

She broke eye contact, folded the towel, and set it on the cabinet, pretending not to be aware of what had just transpired between them, even though the knowledge hung heavy in the air.

After the movie he walked her out to her car. And then he did kiss her. On the cheek. Casually, lightly. As one friend might kiss another, but with a smile that said he understood what she was going through. That meant more to her than any passionate kiss at the kitchen sink would have meant.

And he bought parmesan cheese, she thought, backing out of the driveway, watching him raise a farewell hand in the perimeter of his porch light.

———

Brooke arrived at work Tuesday with a package about half the size of a shoe box, wrapped in pink paper sprigged with violets. "It's for Danyell," she explained sheepishly. "I wanted to buy you one too, but you said not to give you gifts."

Maybe this was going to work out after all. Carley smiled approval. "Danyell's the one who deserves it anyway. That was very thoughtful of you, Brooke."

The girl shrugged but looked relieved, and she took her uniform into the restroom to change.

Danyell accepted the gift graciously, even though it turned out to be a garish bisque angel with gilt-dipped wings and exaggerated facial features that spoke more of a foreign assembly line rather than deliberate insult.

"It was the only . . . colored angel they had," Brooke said anxiously.

"She's beautiful," Danyell said.

That set the tone for the day. Business was not quite as heavy as Saturday, but weekends were the busiest times for most restaurants. The good percentage of repeat patrons was encouraging, as well as antique shoppers expressing delight over learning of such a place.

One repeat patron was game warden Don Moore—her neighbor Ruby's ex-husband. He was handsome in a Greek-statue sort of way, with finely chiseled tanned face and wavy dark hair. An oily drawl canceled out his Greek-statue aura. "I hear you're from California," he said with arms folded at the counter, leaning into Carley's comfort zone.

"San Francisco," she replied with a polite smile, handing him the credit card receipt and a pen. "I hope you enjoyed your meal."

He signed his name. "I enjoy the scenery more."

"Thank you." She handed over his copy of the receipt. "The Stillmans are fine painters. Have a good day."

Mrs. Sparks telephoned from the high school. "Are you set up for takeout orders now?"

"I am," Carley replied. In fact, the elementary vice-principal had telephoned twelve minutes earlier. During training, Carley had dropped off menus in the offices of all three schools.

"When will your washing machine be repaired?" Carley asked Brooke after closing.

"It needs more than repairing. And Dad's not gonna buy a new one. Not when they can just send me out."

"Can he afford one?"

The girl's face clouded. "If you can afford two cases of Old Milwaukee every week, you can afford a washer."

Carley reached for the bag holding Brooke's soiled uniforms. "Here, I'll take care of that."

"Oh, no . . ." Brooke said.

"Just listen to your boss. It's no big deal to toss them in with my wash until the situation changes."

It *was* no big deal, as far as the amount of work involved, but Carley understood the tears lustering Brooke's eyes. Having an alcoholic parent caused tremendous pressure that created such things as temper tantrums over seemingly small things—like a broken dish. Little acts of thoughtfulness, even from strangers, were valves that released some of that pressure.

Business slackened during a rainstorm Wednesday at noon, yet some of the town-hall employees sprinted over beneath umbrellas. Averil, Rita, and Samantha Stillman came in on their way to midweek church services that evening. A window table happened to be unoccupied, and Carley ushered them to it before Samantha could whisper in her father's ear. Dale came again with Garland—who ordered the beef Wellington sandwich this time.

Neal Henderson came with his mother for lunch on Thursday. Carley watched the two struggle over what he should order while Paula stood patiently with pad in hand. "This looks good, honey," Mrs. Henderson said, pointing to a graphic of the chicken salad croissant, her fifth or sixth suggestion. "In fact, I'm going to have that."

"What does Brooke like to eat?" Neal asked Paula.

Paula looked up at Carley, who smiled and nodded toward the double doors. The waitress escorted the boy to the kitchen; he returned smiling and ordered a chicken Caesar sandwich. For her extra pains, Paula gleaned a ten-dollar tip.

Business was brisk late Friday afternoon, before Tallulah High's football game against North Forrest High, and then slackened so much after six that Carley sent her staff home early.

On her way home, Carley could hear the cheers and horns from the stadium and learned from her staff on Saturday morning that the score had ended up tied at six points.

Steve Underwood walked in with Clifford and Vera just a few minutes after opening that day.

"The place is beautiful, Carley," Vera said.

"Thank you." Carley gathered three menus from the counter. "I'm honored that you came. But which is this? Early lunch or late breakfast?"

"Whichever you recommend," Clifford said absently, his attention captured by the deacon's bench. He gave a theatrical sigh. "I didn't charge you enough."

Carley laughed. "Well, it's too late now, isn't it?"

"Come on, Dad," Steve said, taking him by the shoulder. "She'll have other customers any minute."

She visited their table after Troy took their orders, and asked Steve how his classes were going.

"Very well, thank you," he replied. "And I don't have to ask you how the café business is going."

"Oh, but it would be nice to be asked." Realizing the subtle-but-meaningful distance between what had just left her lips and what she had intended to say, she cleared her throat and said, "I mean . . . it's always nice to be asked."

They did not seem to have noticed her gaffe. Or, at least Clifford and Vera gave no sign. As for Steve, she had no way of knowing because she could not bring herself to look him square in the face. "I'll see if Troy is bringing out your drinks."

Only half the tables were filled an hour before closing, but there were five takeout orders to make up. Kickoff for the USM away game was at five-thirty, and radios all over Tallulah were tuned to WXRR Hattiesburg. Reluctantly, Carley allowed Paula to plug in her little radio so that she and Troy, the die-hard fans, could keep up during trips to the kitchen.

"You know, you'd get more business if you played it out here too," Troy said as Carley helped him bus a table.

"Nope," Carley said. "Serenity is our theme."

And if she *were* inclined to broadcast a game, it would not be this one—USM at University of California at Berkeley. She was especially glad for her decision by closing time, for Paula and Troy wore melancholy expressions over the 34–3 loss that she would not have cared to see in the faces of her customers.

But even their expressions lightened when Carley spoke the magic phrase. "Okay, time to pass out paychecks!"

———

"Do you have an umbrella?" Uncle Rory asked, coming around the side of the house with bucket in hand on Tuesday morning.

"It's in the car," Carley said, locking her front door. As she walked to the steps she could see sprinkles dotting her car windshield.

The muscadine grapes had been ripe for about a week. She liked them almost as much as figs but thought they were in the same category as grapefruit as far as ease of eating. One had to squeeze the pulp out of the thick skin, then strain the seeds away with the teeth. Too much work for someone running a business and keeping house. Uncle Rory was more than willing to come out and pick them for jelly. He usually left a half-filled grocery bag hanging on the Paynes' carport door for the children.

The sprinkles thickened to light rain as Carley drove. She dashed to the café back door with umbrella raised, then stood beneath the eaves to shake away excess drops.

Brooke, she thought, switching on kitchen lights. She could hear thunder rumbling in the distance. Should she telephone, advise her to have Mildred drive her? Or if that was an impossibility, tell her to wait it out? *Seven miles,* she thought.

What if Mr. Kimball answered and had another temper tantrum? *He can't hurt you over the phone,* she reminded herself.

Still, she was relieved when the shrill female voice answered.

"She's already went."

"But it's raining."

The woman let out a profanity, which Carley thought was directed toward her until it was followed by "GIT DOWN FROM THERE!"

"Cat chased a roach up the cabinet," she muttered next.

"Ah . . . may I have directions to your house?" Carley was not sure if the bicycle would fit into her GL, but she had to at least try.

"Well, where are ye comin from?"

"Main Street. Wait, please." Carley held the phone, listened to a now familiar pattern of knocking. "Thank you anyway. She's here."

Brooke's hair had turned into dripping ringlets because the hood of her raincoat had flapped backward, and her legs were so sodden that her tennis shoes squished. She was in a surprisingly good mood, under the circumstances. But then, she probably figured that having an excuse to leave the house for the day outweighed any physical discomfort.

"What size shoes do you wear?" Carley asked as the girl took her uniform from the office closet.

"But there's no place to buy any here."

"Dollar General has some canvas sneakers for three dollars."

When the girl wrinkled her nose, Carley said, "They'll be dry. Those wet feet will make you sick."

"Then wait, let me get—"

"You can pay me later if you like. Just get dressed, and let everyone else in if I'm not back in time."

The rain had melded into puddles on the concrete when Carley left Dollar General with the sneakers and a pair of socks. She went home for her hair dryer, and by the time she returned to the café, Lisa and Rachel were already setting out cutting boards and cutlery, having left their houses early in case the rain were to slow them down.

"Here," Carley said, handing the bag and dryer to the girl. "You may use my office."

"Thank you," Brooke murmured.

The remaining staff filtered in, with Troy typically last, but even he signed in five minutes early. Carley flipped the *Open* sign with a tiny knot of anxiety. This was Annabel Lee Café's first day to open after USM's thirty-one-point-deficit loss in Berkeley. It was no secret about town that she came from California. Would die-hard USM fans stay away?

She need not have worried. Still, she *was* teased.

"You must have slept with your windows locked," quipped Maggie Sherwood, owner of Odds and Ends.

"I hope the sounds of our sobs didn't intrude upon your victory party," drawled Marianne Tate's husband, Jim.

"Did you say she's from California?" said one of the three firemen at the table next to Jim's, with a feigned look of shock.

"I'm surprised you didn't call in sick today," drugstore owner Chester Templeton said.

Who would I call? Carley thought. *Myself?*

Her stock reaction was to laugh obligingly and then explain that she was more of a basketball fan than a football fan. And really, she was flattered by the ribbing. In one of Linda's few attempts at mothering, she had said when Carley came home from first grade in tears because boys on the bus called her *Carrot-head*, that people only tease the people they like.

That was not always true, Carley had later learned, just as Alton Terris had learned. But in today's case, it seemed to fit. And the ribbing was not all one-sided.

"Do you serve humble pie?" asked Mr. Marshall of the hardware store.

Troy Fairchild paused at the counter at the end of his shift to say in a low voice, "Brooke was crying a little while ago. When we asked her why, she said it was nothing. But she doesn't want you to know."

Carley looked at the double doors, then over at Danyell writing up a ticket for two women who would be at the counter any minute.

"Want me to run the register for you?" Troy offered.

"Thank you. I'll add it to your time sheet."

Stupid rain, stupid seven miles, stupid parents who don't give a flip about their children! Carley thought on her way across the dining room. Obviously, the dry socks and shoes had been too little, too late. Paula and Danyell would have to pull double-duty, hosting and waiting tables while she took over the dishwashing and continued the bathroom cleaning forays.

You wanted to be your own boss, Carley reminded herself.

Rachel, stirring soup, gave Carley a meaningful nod, and Lisa raised eyebrows and looked over at the sink.

"Brooke." Carley touched the girl's shoulder.

"Hmm?" The girl turned.

"Dry your hands and come with me."

In the office, Carley closed the door. "I'm going to call my Uncle Rory and ask him to drive you home."

The girl gave her an odd look. "Why? I was working hard."

"You work great. But if you take care of yourself now, maybe you won't come down with something more serious later."

"Huh?"

"Don't you feel sick?"

"No." Brooke shook her head.

Carley raised her hand to her own throat. "Not sore?"

"I'm fine, Carley."

"Then, why were you crying?"

The girl drew in a deep breath, blew it out. "My eyes got all teary for a minute, that's all. I didn't think it was such a big deal. I told them not to tell you."

Teenage angst. Carley could understand that. "They did it because they care about you, so don't be put out at them. All right?"

She shrugged. "All right."

"Then, I'll let you get back to work. I have to relieve Troy at the counter."

"Sure."

But when Carley reached for the doorknob, Brooke said from behind, "Carley?"

Carley turned.

Brooke gave her a sheepish little smile. "At the sink . . . I was noticing how just having your feet warm and dry makes you feel better all over. That was the nicest thing anybody's ever done for me. Fussin' over me like that."

Before Carley could respond, the girl shook her head. "Well, giving me this job was real nice too, but you needed a dishwasher the same time I needed a job."

Touched, Carley said lightly, "And so I don't get as many brownie points for that one?"

That made the girl laugh.

Brooke Kimball was a remarkable creature, Carley thought. Abandoned by her mother, living with an alcoholic father, little formal education, few friends, minimal chances for the future, and yet when she laughed it was as if she had not a care in the world.

Back in the dining room, a memory nudged her. *"That's what I like most about you . . . your sense of humor,"* Dale had said. Could a sense of humor be God's compensation for the bad stuff? Because He would not take away Huey Collins or even her mother's freedom to make their own choices, had He provided her with the equipment that would help ease the pangs of childhood abuse and neglect?

Was this why Brooke had such a ready laugh? How many stand-up comedians had easy childhoods, she wondered?

Almost a month ago, Aunt Helen had advised her to wait until she was one hundred percent sure before offering Brooke a room in her house. She respected her aunt's advice, or else she would have brushed it aside. While she had not reached the one-hundred percent point yet, she was in the nineties, and perhaps that was close enough. There was risk in everything. If she had waited until she was one hundred percent sure about opening a café, she would not be welcoming customers today.

She did not have to ask Brooke to wait around after work, for the girl was consistently last to leave.

"Do you really mean it?" Brooke asked when Carley issued the invitation.

"Wait," Carley said, holding up a hand, for the girl looked ready to seize her. "As long as you understand that I can't treat you any differently here than I treat any of the other staff."

"Sure!"

"And that it's my house you'll be staying at, not a hotel."

"Ah . . . okay," the girl said with expression fading.

Carley sighed. The sharp Brooke could morph into the dull Brooke with dizzying speed. "What I mean is, you would have to promise to share the chores, refrain from playing loud music, and not smoke inside."

"I don't smoke. It gives me headaches."

"Really?" Carley stared at her for a second and then continued. "And no boys over."

The girl colored, just a bit. "My boyfriend's in Oakley. So he won't be coming around. And I'll pay rent . . ."

"No, let's just keep it the way I said. I keep a list of weekly chores. We'll divide it up. As for rent, I'd rather you put that money in a savings account. The house isn't costing me anything."

That was when Carley was struck by a thought. Brooke was a juvenile. All this would be moot if her father withheld permission.

He granted it easily, Brooke said, arriving for work the following morning.

"You're kidding," Carley said.

"Well, Mildred's been naggin' at him to get me out of the house for ages anyway. I just had to promise some things."

"Of course." Carley's estimation of Mr. Kimball edged up a notch. "I hope you assured him I plan to keep a close eye on you. And if he'd like to meet me . . ."

"Oh, not that." The girl shook her head. "I had to promise to buy Mildred a washer and dad six cases of Old Milwaukee."

Throw in a mule, and someone could have proposed marriage, Carley thought.

———

Business did not suffer so much Friday night, with the high school game played in Richton, but there were long faces in Annabel Lee Café Saturday morning after the 14–6 loss. Dale's was among them. "Those boys played their hearts out."

"I'm sorry," Carley said.

"You could cheer me up by coming with me to Barnhill's tomorrow," he said cautiously.

"Sure," she said. "But no movie. I have paperwork to finish."

She had also offered to help Brooke move during the two days off, but the girl said that Mildred would be bringing her things Monday on her way to Hattiesburg for the washer and beer.

"You're making a big mistake," Dale said Sunday afternoon, while dousing a baked potato with olive oil and balsamic vinegar. "I wish you would have discussed this with me before you invited her."

"Pardon me?" Carley said.

He waved a hand. "This isn't a control issue. I'm just worried for your safety. What if she has boys over in spite of your rules?"

"She said her boyfriend lives out of town."

"Out of town . . . did the town sound something like Oakley?"

"I think so."

He sighed. "Carley, that's a juvenile detention facility near Jackson. She must mean Brad Travis. I arrested him last spring for breaking into a house while the owners were on vacation."

That was disappointing. But then, what kind of role model of a decent man did Brooke have? *And your first boyfriend stole his father's van,* she reminded herself.

"If he's locked away, I have nothing to worry about," Carley reasoned.

"For how long? I can't recall his sentence off the cuff, but even so, they get out when they turn eighteen."

That sent a little shudder up Carley's spine. *You should have waited for the one hundred percent,* she told herself. Should she rescind the invitation? One mental picture of the disappointment on Brooke's face was all it took to abandon that notion. "You'll know when they're going to let him out . . . right?"

"Well, yes."

"Then you'll be able to warn me."

He sighed. "Don't tell me. You're still determined to do this?"

"I have to, Dale."

Pathetically, Brooke was dropped off on Monday with a black garbage bag of clothing, the bicycle, a battered cosmetic bag, and a toy china tea set in its original pasteboard box.

"Everything's so clean," she breathed.

Carley showed her to the middle bedroom—she could not bring herself to offer her grandmother's room. As an afterthought, she had placed her wicker chair in the corner. Unless teenage girls had changed since she was one, they spent a lot of time in their rooms. These days she only went into her own to change clothes and sleep, so the chair only served as a catchall.

"This is wonderful," Brooke breathed, running a hand reverently over the quilt.

"Sorry it's only a twin."

"But it gives me more space to move around the room."

Carley smiled, imagining that if she had apologized for a hole in the middle of the floor, Brooke would have found something good to say about it. "I emptied the closet and put in some hangers. You might want to fluff up your clothes in the dryer first."

"You don't mind?"

"Of course not. Use anything in the house you need."

As much as she told herself she was simply helping a young employee get back and forth to work more easily, the day had the feel of a special occasion. She made pizza from scratch, a task too troublesome to do for just herself, and taught Brooke how to toss the dough.

"I thought they only did that on TV," the girl said, gingerly giving the center of the mound of dough little flips so that the sides hung over both palms.

"Don't worry, we're not going to throw it overhead or anything like that. But it puts gravity to work and stretches it better than pulling at it in a pan."

Eventually they had it topped with sauce, pepperoni slices, and mozzarella cheese. "I have to warn you, it won't be as good as Tommy's Pizza," Carley said, sliding it into the oven. "Their oven's much hotter."

"That's okay. It's still gonna be good."

And you'd say that if I topped it with dog biscuits, Carley thought.

"Was that back bedroom your grandmother's?" Brooke asked.

"Yes, it was." It was arranged the same way, though the clothing and a lamp had gone to the Salvation Army. Carley did not consider it a shrine or such, but the fact that it made her feel connected to her grandmother's memory was reason enough to keep it that way for a little while longer.

Brooke began washing the dough bowl. "And you never met her."

"I did when I was very young. But I hardly remember it."

"That's so sad. Did your family move away or something?"

"Sort of. My mother left Washington with me."

"You never visited?"

Carley took the bowl and began drying it. "My mother was afraid they'd take me away from her."

Brooke turned off the tap, her eyes wide. "Why would they do that?"

"Because she was . . . not a fit mother."

"She drank, you mean."

"Yes."

"Where is she now?"

"She died last year."

"Oh." Brooke sighed. "My mom left when I was a baby."

"I know, Brooke," Carley said. "Do you hear from her?"

"I get Christmas cards from Chicago. I kept them when I was little. Now I throw them away. They're just cards with her name signed. Only the picture changes every year, so one's enough." The girl studied her face. "I thought you must have been like one of those girls with nice clothes and a nice little family. But you're kind of like me, aren't you?"

"Pretty much."

"I'm sorry."

"I'm not." Carley said, realizing it as she spoke. "If we had had those privileged childhoods, we wouldn't be as strong as we are."

"You think I'm strong?"

"I do." She smiled at the girl. "And so you have to be special to get into our club."

She ate one third of the pizza, Brooke wolfed down the rest. Between the two of them, cleaning the kitchen took less than five minutes. "I have some work to do at the computer," Carley said. "But it won't disturb me if you'd like to watch television."

"Are you sure?"

"I'm sure." Carley sighed. "Look, I know you're out of your comfort zone here . . ."

"I'm very comfortable," Brooke said. "This house is great."

Carley shook her head. "Your 'comfort zone' is what you're used to. It doesn't even have to be comfortable. If you were raised in a cave and suddenly given a high-rise apartment, you would have some adjustment issues after the newness wore off."

"Wow. How do you know all that?"

"Well, from my college psych class. Anyway, what I started to say is, you're going to have to make yourself at home or this isn't going to work. If I have to reassure you every time you want to use something, I'll go insane."

The girl winced. "Okay."

It took her only seconds to figure out the remote control. "You've got cable!"

"There was a sale when I had cable Internet installed," Carley said from her desk. "But I hardly ever have time to watch it."

"We live too far out for it." Brooke flipped one channel after another. "Did I thank you for inviting me to stay here?"

Carley smiled as her fingers clicked the keyboard. "A thousand times."

chapter 25

"Would you consider leaving work a little early and going to the game with me Saturday?" Dale asked at the counter on Tuesday while paying for his bowl of mushroom soup and mixed green salad. USM was to play Memphis, a fact discussed by almost every regular patron whose conversation Carley overheard.

"I'm sorry," Carley said. "Saturdays are busy. And Troy has already asked to leave early."

"Okay," he sighed. "I'll see if Garland wants to go."

"Or maybe Marti?" Carley suggested.

He looked around, leaned closer, and lowered his voice. "I can't ask her. She has a crush on me."

"Are you sure that's not male ego talking?" Carley said, lowering her own voice.

"Ego didn't write *Mrs. Dale Parker* a dozen times on a paper I came across in the trash while looking for my coffee spoon."

"Oh. Well, she's a nice person."

"Yes, very nice. But it's just not going to happen."

Aren't teenagers supposed to sleep late? Carley thought when she caught a glance of Brooke's made bed on her way to the bathroom. She put the teakettle on and went back through the living room. Micah and Kimberly stood on the steps in school clothes and backpacks, and Brooke sat on the porch swing in pajama pants and gray

T-shirt, eating a bowl of cornflakes.

"Hi, Miss Carley," Micah said, his sister echoing a half beat behind.

"Hi, kids. Heading to school?" Carley said to be sociable, even though the answer was obvious.

"We're waiting for Mom and Lane," Kimberly replied. "He poured his juice down his shirt. Now Mom has to change his clothes and wipe out the stroller."

"I could change real quick and walk you," Brooke offered.

"I'll ask," Micah said. He was halfway to the driveway when Gayle stepped from behind Carley's car with stroller wheels humming on concrete.

"Have a good day!" she called while beckoning to the children.

Annabel Lee Café did only a fair amount of business that day, but enough to keep Carley from becoming discouraged. Stanley and Loretta Malone brought another couple for lunch—his brother Dennis and his wife, Toni, from Savannah. A total of only seven antique shoppers filtered in at odd times, but nine people from First Baptist's senior citizen group made up for that slack.

"You must be bringing your father his lunch," Carley said when Mona Bryant came for her telephone takeout order of a beef Wellington sandwich and chicken mushroom pasta. The beef sandwich was proving itself to be the most popular menu item with male patrons, and Emmit White was no exception, stopping by for one at least three times since opening day.

Still, it was a silly thing to say, Carley realized after the words left her mouth. It was none of her business, and the fact that Mona made her nervous was no excuse to blather on.

Mona's stony look proved that point. "I have the twenty-seven cents," she said, digging into her jeans pocket.

Carley salved her wounded ego by reminding herself of something Jane Austen had written: *I do not want people to be very agreeable, as it saves me the trouble of liking them a great deal.*

That only made her feel guilty. She would probably be a grump herself if her husband had left her for another woman.

No I wouldn't, she decided after more thought. *I've had just as many hard knocks, and I'm nice.*

After work, Carley was in the back room of her house, ironing a shirt and skirt for the next morning when Brooke sang out from the living room, "CAR-LEY! MISS GAYLE'S HERE!"

Carley winced and set the iron on its end. On her way through the kitchen she heard Brooke saying, "Your kids are so sweet."

"Thank you." Gayle Payne was perched on the edge of a chair, and rose when Carley entered. "I hate to bother you, but can you step over for a minute? There's something I'd like to show you."

"Sure," Carley replied.

The "something" lay half curled on the dining room table, a poster of *The Singing Butler* by Jack Vettriano, which her neighbor could have easily carried over. Carley could hear the television in the den, and Micah and his father carrying on a conversation.

"I was cleaning out a closet and came across this, from a garage sale ages ago," Gayle said, a shade nervously. "I'll never get around to framing it. Can you use it?"

Carley touched a curled corner. "I've always loved this print. Are you sure?"

"Yes. I want you to have it." Gayle cleared her throat. "Carley . . . forgive my asking, but you have to be so careful when you have children. As you know, they like to drift over to your place. Is the Kimball girl, well, safe for them to be around?"

"I really believe she is," Carley replied, not surprised by the question, for her neighbor had seemed unnaturally nervous. "Do you know Arleen Fielding?"

"Vaguely. She's a nurse?"

"She spoke highly of Brooke as a baby-sitter. I can give you her number if you like."

"Oh, no. I don't need a baby-sitter. I just . . ."

She gave Carley a helpless look.

"I understand," Carley said. "As much as I trust Brooke, I

wouldn't leave my *own* children alone with her until I got to know her much better."

Gayle sighed, smoothed back her ash-blonde hair. "I hate to be ugly, but I've seen her in town so many times, riding around on that bike barely dressed."

"You're right about that. But she has a good heart, and shows so many signs of wanting to have a better life."

"I'm glad to hear it. Thank you for not being angry."

"I could *never* be angry at a mother who protects her children," Carley assured her.

"That poster's awesome," Brooke said from a living room chair when Carley unrolled it. "Are you gonna buy a frame?"

"Not with it curled like this." She set it on the coffee table. "I'll drop it off at the frame shop on my way to work tomorrow. What are you reading?"

The girl held up *The International Thesaurus of Quotations*, thumb inside to mark her place. "I'm just flippin' through the pages. I've never seen this kind of book before. There's some pretty good stuff in here."

"Well, read something to me," Carley said, settling on the sofa.

"Now?"

"No, yesterday," she teased.

Brooke laughed and opened the book again. "Okay, this one's cute: 'The fog comes on little cat feet.'"

"Carl Sandburg," Carley said.

"How did you know?"

"I was an English major."

"Then you know everything in here?"

"Goodness, no. Probably not even one percent. Read another one."

She had a reason for asking. Judging by the painstakingly printed résumé and Brooke's having dropped out of school, she was curious as to her level of literacy. And the cat-feet line, clever as it was, could have been at home in any second-grade reader.

"'The house praises the carpenter,'" Brooke read. "By someone named Emerson. I guess that means your work shows how good you are at it?"

"Um-hmm. It doesn't even have to be a house." Carley thought about an example. "A well-written book tells how good the author is; a mannerly child is proof of good parents. Read something else?"

"You don't want to listen to me all night."

"Just one more, something longer. Look up Longfellow."

"Longfellow?"

"He's my favorite poet."

Pages rustled. Brooke's eyes stopped traveling, and she held the book up again.

> "'The heights by great men reached and kept,
> Were not . . .'"

She screwed up her mouth.

> "''at-tained . . . by sudden flight,
> But they, while their com-pan-ions slept,
> Were toiling upward in the night.'"

"That's a good one," Carley said. "You read very well, Brooke."

The girl shrugged, but looked pleased. "My fourth-grade teacher, Mr. Young, taught me it's not that hard when you divide up the syllables. Dad reads cowboy books, and Mildred gets *National Enquirer*, but I've always been too antsy for a long story. That's why I like these sayings."

"That was my grandmother's."

"Oh." Brooke stared at the book as if it had transformed into breakable crystal.

"It's all right," Carley assured her. "In fact, I'd like you to have it."

She shook her head. "I can't—"

"Please take it. I think it would have made her happy."

Aunt Helen stopped by after closing her shop Friday evening, when most of Tallulah was at the stadium watching the game against the high school's biggest rival, Seminary. Eyeing the three tables occupied, she said, "You must despise home games."

"Well, you know, it evens out," Carley said. "The place was hopping earlier."

"That's good. Rory called before I left and said to invite you and Brooke over for omelets when you close."

"I'm surprised he's not at the game," Carley said.

"Only those the grandchildren play."

Brooke politely declined, saying she would rather walk on to the house, make a sandwich, and prop up her feet. Carley insisted on driving her. It pleased her that the girl did not intend to shadow her, especially with their both working at the same place. Perhaps she needed her own space as well.

And what pleased Aunt Helen was that she was wrong about inviting Brooke to move in, she said in the Hudson kitchen.

"But you weren't wrong," Carley corrected. "You said to wait until I was sure."

"Well, thank you for saying that. But I feel so badly about that girl, that we failed her."

"Why would you possibly think that?"

"Because it was obvious from looking at her that she needed help. I've been too wrapped up in my shop and family and church to extend a hand, and then here you come . . ."

"A heathen, you mean?"

"Carley! To say such a thing."

Carley grinned and patted her hand. "I'm just kidding, Aunt Helen."

The remorse deepened in Aunt Helen's face. "Still, it's true that Christians have a mandate to help people like Brooke. What does she need?"

"Well, decent clothes, obviously. I plan to have a talk with her about that next payday. She had to buy some things for her father before he'd allow her to move, so I think she's broke for the moment."

"Rory?" Aunt Helen turned to say to the man breaking eggs into a stainless steel bowl.

"The checkbook's in the china-cabinet drawer," he said.

"You don't have to do that," Carley said as her aunt pushed out her chair. "When payday comes . . ."

"Please don't rob us of the joy of helping. And Brooke should be saving as much as she can, to build some sort of future. This is no slur against your café, but surely she doesn't plan to wash dishes for the rest of her life. If she builds up a nice nest egg, perhaps you can encourage her to go back to school next fall."

"That's a good idea. Thank you both for doing this."

When Aunt Helen returned she wrote out a check and handed it to Carley.

"Two hundred dollars?" Carley said. "Aunt Helen . . . Uncle Rory . . ."

"With winter just around the corner, you might see if she has a decent jacket."

"This is so generous," Carley said, on the verge of tears. "And I'll take her shopping myself, make sure it's used wisely."

"Good idea. But please wait a few days, so she won't suspect it came from us."

"Why?"

"Because we'd rather not let the left hand know what the right is doing."

"Come again?"

"It's from the book of Saint Matthew. It means it's better to give secretly."

"Okay, little girl, what do you want in your omelet?" Uncle Rory asked.

Carley exchanged smiles with her aunt. "Everything but the kitchen sink and onions."

———

The Singing Fairchilds not only performed Sundays at Tallulah Pentecostal, but in churches as far away as Natchez and Corinth. That explained the half dozen fresh-faced girls with long hair and long skirts who began making Annabel Lee Café their Saturday lunch ritual. Without even asking, Carley knew to seat them at one of Troy's tables. Paula and Danyell called him "Romeo" in the kitchen, which made him blush so charmingly that Carley wanted to pinch his cheeks.

When the last customers left on Saturday, Paula turned up the radio in the kitchen to listen to the USM game against Memphis. Carley continued listening in her car on the way home, then on Ruby Moore's screened back porch, while Brooke stayed home to watch a rerun of a detective show.

For a treat, Ruby had a popular local dish Carley had managed to evade for the past week: newly harvested peanuts, boiled in their shells in salt water and Creole seasonings. They were soggy and looked disgusting, but the one she tried for the sake of politeness was the equivalent of one potato chip, and she did not protest when Ruby handed her a filled bowl.

"How's it working out, having the Kimball girl staying with you?" Ruby asked during commercials.

"She's good company," Carley replied, not feeling the need to share the minor adjustment issues, such as having to teach the girl to empty the dryer filter with each use, and that drinking directly from the orange juice carton was unhygienic and just plain gross. "I've lived alone since graduating from college, and I'd forgotten how nice it is to have someone to come home to."

Carley's cheeks went hot. "Oh, Ruby," she said, laying a hand on her neighbor's arm. "I'm sorry."

Ruby patted her hand. "Please, don't be. I feel the same way.

But it's better to come home to an empty house than to a man with a wandering eye."

"I understand."

"And I don't hold it against Brooke. If we were held responsible for what our relatives did, I'd be in Parchman Prison for life, with those jailbirds on my mother's side."

"What do you mean?" Carley asked.

"Nothing," Ruby said, shaking her head. "My mouth gets away with me. Brooke had a cousin living with them a few years ago, and I learned she was one of Don's conquests. Or he was one of hers. Anyway, that's ancient history. Whoops—the game's back on."

"We won, twenty-three to six," Carley said to Brooke in her living room afterward.

"Yay," Brooke said politely, following her into the kitchen. "You should have seen this show. The detective wears a rumpled old raincoat and pretends to be kind of dense. That makes the murderer relax and think he got away with it. Columbo's his name."

"The murderer?"

"No, the detective."

Carley filled a water glass from the refrigerator. Thankfully, there were no longer crumbs floating in the pitcher. She held it out. "You?"

"No, thank you. It comes on weekdays at eleven. If I buy some blank tapes, can I start taping it when we're at work?"

"You don't have to ask."

Brook screwed up her face. "I'm sorry. I'll get used to this before I drive you crazy. I promise."

"You're doing just fine," Carley said. "And I've had a three-pack of tapes unopened for months. Help yourself."

———

Sunday afternoon Carley went over to the café to record the week's invoices for Mr. Laird. When she returned to the house,

Brooke stood on the porch with a broom in her hands, chatting with Mrs. Templeton over the railing.

"Did you know Miss Byrle here played basketball in school?" Brooke asked as Carley joined them.

"I didn't," Carley confessed, to her own shame. What had she thought, that her neighbor was born stooped and fragile?

"We were just a little team," Mrs. Templeton said, face glowing with recollection. "If one of us got sick, we had to forfeit."

After a few more stories of her youth, Mrs. Templeton said she needed to check on a cake she had in the oven, so Carley and Brooke went inside.

"That was nice of you," Carley said in the living room as she turned on the computer. "Taking up time with her."

"She's interesting," the girl said. "You should have seen *Columbo* today. This guy murdered his uncle because he was about to get married and change his will. He threw an electric mixer in his bathtub. It turned out he had a twin brother, and they both blamed each other. But see, the housekeeper was watching TV when the murder happened, and her screen . . ."

"Brooke," Carley cut in, looking up from the computer monitor.

"Hmm?"

Carley rolled her eyes. "Don't make me go through the labor. Just show me the baby. Which twin did it?"

The girl laughed. "Both. One threw the mixer, the other fixed the switch when it blew. That's why the housekeeper's TV blinked out for a few seconds." She leaned her head. "I thought you went to the café to do your computer work."

"I'm thinking of ordering some books." It took so long to finish one these days, that library books, with their silent nagging due dates, were too stress inducing.

"There's a Books-A-Million."

"It's easier online." Carley looked up. The girl stood watching her with both hands in her jeans pockets.

"But you know, checking out some stores might be a better idea." She was not sure if enough time had passed since Aunt Helen wrote the check, but then, she halfway hoped the girl would figure it out anyway. "Tomorrow, we could go into town, maybe hang out at the mall for a little while, have a bite to eat."

Brooke's face was a mingling of anticipation and uneasiness. "I only have seven dollars left from payday. But at least that's enough to buy my meal. I don't guess it hurts to look, does it?"

"It doesn't hurt to look," Carley said. *Unless you're broke, and you'll find out tomorrow that you're not.*

"That looks too small," Carley said when Brooke held up a pink knit shirt in JCPenney at Turtle Creek Mall. "You want room to move around in. And the dryer shrinks cotton."

The girl's nod lacked enthusiasm. "Loose clothes aren't, well, sexy."

Why does a seventeen-year-old want to look sexy? Carley asked herself, then thought of the thirteen-year-olds she had seen walking down the sidewalk looking as if they had stepped out of a rock video. What were their parents thinking?

You're getting old, she told herself. She dug a size large from the rack. "Humor me. Just try it on. Anyway, feminine's more attractive than sexy."

Brooke gave her an odd look. "Huh?"

Carley sighed. "If you show off your *body,* guys only think about one thing when they look at you. You could have the brains of an amoeba and it wouldn't matter."

Whether to appease her or not, Brooke tried on the larger clothes.

"You look great," Carley said every time she stepped from the dressing room.

With an embarrassed little smile, the girl conceded at the mirror that she did. She selected three shirts large enough to allow for shrinkage, a pair of black slacks, jeans she could actually move around in, a khaki skirt that fell to a modest just-above-the-knee length, brown loafers, and to save for cooler weather, a hooded fleece jacket.

"You're still not gonna tell me who gave you the money?" Brooke asked at the checkout.

"Nope." Nor did she need to know that Carley had added almost seventy dollars of her own.

"Won't you give me a hint?" the girl said on the way to the car. "This is so nice. Was it your aunt? Or Miss Byrle?"

Carley unlocked the trunk. "The person—or persons—wishes to remain anonymous."

"Anono—?"

"Anonymous. Means 'doesn't want you to know.' And I'm going to say that every time you ask me."

"But I want to say thank you."

"You can, by wearing the clothes."

After browsing for a half hour in Books-a-Million, they went next door to China Garden. Carley allowed Brooke to spend her own money. She didn't want to make the girl feel like a complete pauper.

"My first Chinese food," Brooke said, raising lo mein noodles with her fork. "Dad said he wouldn't give a dime to Chinks."

"Brooke!" Carley hissed, and looked over her shoulder. Fortunately, the waiter was pointing something out on the menu to a foursome several feet away. "Not a good word."

The girl colored. "I'm sorry."

She apologized again on the drive home. "Really, Carley. It just slipped out."

Eyes on Highway 98 unrolling before her, Carley said, "I'm not angry. But just as a future thought, most slang words for a person's race are offensive."

"But people call us rednecks."

"Well, that's wrong too," Carley said, wincing inside.

"I'll try to do better."

Carley smiled at her. "Me too."

Headlights came from the opposite direction when she turned onto Third Street. She recognized Dale's Mustang coupe as they passed, and in the rearview mirror saw the lights swing into a driveway and out again. He parked behind her.

"I thought I'd missed you," he said, closing his car door. He was dressed in jeans, sneakers, and a black knit shirt. "Hi, ladies."

"Hi," Brooke mumbled. To Carley she said, "I'm gonna put away my clothes now."

Carley handed her the keys, thinking it was time to trust the girl with the extra one in her desk. She smiled at Dale. "We've been shopping."

"What did you buy me?" he said, raising brows playfully.

"Well, a fifty-pound sack of sunflower seeds."

"Ah . . . thanks. You shouldn't have."

"Or maybe we'll just give it to Mrs. Templeton. You can help me unload it."

He flexed his biceps. "Pretty lady, stand aside. Let strong man work."

As Carley directed, he carried it over to the neighbor's porch and propped it beside the door. "Should we knock?"

"No. She goes to bed early."

On their way back through the yard, he nodded toward Carley's house. "She doesn't like me."

"I'm sure you're mistaken. She hardly knows you."

"She knows I busted her boyfriend. Have you asked about him yet?"

"No. But she doesn't get letters from anybody."

Dale gave her a sidelong look. "He's not the literary sort."

They sat side-by-side on her top step. Lowering her voice, Carley said, "As long as he's in reform school, he's not a problem. Right?"

"That's why I'm here," Dale said. "I checked. He'll be released in three weeks."

"I'll have a talk with her."

"You ought to send her back to her old man. There's no way she's not gonna see him."

Carley shook her head. "I have to give her a chance. But I'll warn her that if she even *meets* him anywhere for a date, she'll have to leave. I wouldn't be able to leave the house without worrying that he could come over and steal something. Not to mention being afraid to sleep. I don't need the added stress."

"I just hope it works," Dale said doubtfully. "You're too trusting, Carley."

"I'm not as trusting as you think."

"Oh yeah?"

"I can be very cynical."

"I'm glad to hear it." He hesitated. "You're not cynical about *me,* are you?"

"I don't know." Carley gave him a measured look. "You claim to be this big-time land baron, but I haven't seen proof of it yet."

"All right, all right," he said, holding up both palms in surrender. "Picnic? Sunday?"

"That sounds nice." Carley smiled. "And thank you for looking out for me, Dale."

He rested a hand upon her shoulder. "I like looking out for you."

It was the most natural thing in the world, to close her eyes and meet his kiss halfway.

"M-m-m, nice," Dale said when they drew apart again.

What are you doing? managed to pierce Carley's light-headedness. *Too soon.* The friendship stage should not involve kisses that made her toes curl.

"I'd better go inside," she said, albeit regretfully. "I have some things to do to prepare for work in the morning."

"All right," he said with regretful voice, getting to his feet as well. "See you tomorrow."

"You mean Sunday."

"The cafe's not open this week?"

"Oh . . . yeah." *You need to come down to earth,* she told herself.

One of the advantages—or disadvantages—of an attic fan was that for a room to be ventilated the door had to be open. Brooke was seated in the wicker chair, painting her fingernails with a paper towel over her lap.

"May I come in?" Carley said at the door.

The girl shrugged. "Your house."

"It's your room as long as you're staying here."

"Ah . . . okay. Then, come in."

Carley sat on the side of the bed. The tea set was out of the package, arranged on the dresser beside the flat Christmas-decorated Oreo cookie tin in which Brooke kept her earrings. The crumpled JCPenney bag peeked from the top of the trash basket. "You've already hung up your clothes."

"I didn't want them to get wrinkled. Are you dating him?"

Right to the point, Carley thought. Why not? Better to jump into a cold pool, adjusting all at once, instead of a few inches at a time. "Sort of. Why don't you like him?"

"I never said I didn't." Brooke blew at the fingernails of her left hand.

"Oh, so you *do* like him?"

The girl twisted open the bottle again. "I shouldn't have asked you. It's none of my business."

"Don't shut me out now, Brooke," Carley said. "I'll never be angry at you for telling me what you think. And I'm going to tell you what *I* think. You don't like him because he arrested your boyfriend."

She did not reply right away, seemingly concentrating on painting the pinkie nail of her right hand. "Brad said he hit him."

"Then, there was probably a struggle. Some seventeen-year-old boys are as big as men."

"How do you know how old he is?"

"Because he's getting out in three weeks, when he turns eighteen."

Brooke looked up, visibly shaken. "I didn't know."

"Do you plan to see him?"

"He's my boyfriend."

"Then, you have some time to think about this," Carley said. "If you do, you'll have to move back home."

After a hesitation, Brooke said, "What if he doesn't come here?"

"Doesn't matter. I need to feel safe, more than you need the company of a thief."

Anger flashed in the green eyes. "Then I'll move back tomorrow."

"I hate to hear that."

"Why?"

"Because I like having you here," Carley said.

"You mean that?" Brooke said, expression softening a bit.

"I do. You're good company."

"But if you're telling me who I can date . . ."

"I'm trying to look out for you, even though you can't see it." Carley massaged her temples. "Look, did you really mean it all those times you thanked me for inviting you here, or were you just schmoozing me?"

The girl's face clouded as if she would weep. "I meant it, Carley."

"Then, I'm asking you to repay me. Simply take the three weeks and think about this. We won't even discuss it unless you bring it up. That's what I'm asking for in return."

————

"Would you like to come to the Hudsons with me after work?" Carley asled Brooke on Thursday morning. Aunt Helen and Uncle Rory's son, Ken, and wife, Glenda, had arrived from Raleigh the day before, fleeing Hurricane Isabel.

"Thanks for asking," the girl replied, smiling, "but I think I'd rather just prop up my feet and watch *Columbo*."

A *détente* had existed between the two since Monday. They got along fine, but Brad Travis was an ever-present, almost palatable witness to every smile they exchanged, to every *please* and *thank-you*.

After dropping the girl off at the house, Carley brought a gallon of tomato basil soup and container of field green salad over to Fifth Street, to go with the fried chicken the Kemps were picking up from Henderson's deli. Ken Hudson was a compact-looking man with thinning salt-and-pepper hair. Glenda, taller than her husband, wore a more sober demeanor, but then, her home had been assaulted by a hurricane hours earlier. The family spent most of the evening in front of the television, watching news accounts of the deadly storm's aftermath, particularly in North Carolina.

During a commercial break, Uncle Rory related how Carley had given Brooke a job and a room in her house.

"How kind of you," Glenda said.

"Thank you. I enjoy having her there." She blew out a long breath. "But it's not without its frustrations."

Ken laughed. "In other words, she's a teenager."

"All young people should be forced to play basketball," Blake said. "By the time Patrick comes in from practice, his hormones are too worn out to act up."

"*Dad* . . ." the boy said, blushing.

Aunt Helen smiled and turned to Carley. "Would you mind if we invited her to church Sunday?"

"Of course not. But don't get your hopes up. She probably won't go."

"Why? Have you discussed it?"

"Not at all." Religion was one subject Carley avoided studiously around the girl. Her own experiences gave her no right to embitter a child. "For all her bravado, I think she's self-conscious when out of her element."

"It never hurts to ask," Aunt Helen said.

"Brooke, we're pretty busy out here," Carley said in the kitchen Friday afternoon. "I need you to check the bathrooms."

Besides the usual Tallulah High pre-home-game influx, a church van from Yazoo City had arrived with eleven women and men on an antique shopping outing.

The girl released the lever to the sprayer nozzle and quickly dried her hands. "Got it, Carley!"

Affable and helpful as always, Brooke still didn't look her in the eyes.

Had she erred in simply giving the girl time to think over the matter? Carley mulled it over that evening, while the attic fan pulled in football game sounds on a sixty-degree breeze.

She well understood how a teenage girl with zero sense of self-worth could cling to any male who would pay her a compliment, just to feel that she mattered. But did Brooke understand that? Would three weeks of simply avoiding the subject cause the girl to reach some sort of epiphany? What if Janelle Reed would have simply allowed her to stew in her own juices?

You have to talk with her.

"Want me to make you some?" Brooke asked Saturday morning while studying the measuring instructions on a box of pancake mix.

Carley, in the middle of a yawn, waited to reply. "I'm just going to make toast."

The girl eyed her. "You didn't sleep?"

"I slept like a log—once I finally *fell* asleep. And you?"

"The same."

"We need to talk."

Brooke sounded relieved. "Okay."

"Let's finish making breakfast. I can't concentrate if you're flipping pancakes." She went over to the refrigerator for the butter. "Would you like to try maple syrup this time?"

"Nope. Will you get out the cane, please?"

Carley made a face behind the open refrigerator door. Brooke had bought a quart can of Steen's 100% Pure Cane Syrup from Henderson's. Just a shade lighter than molasses, it had a strong flavor that dominated anything it was poured upon. She realized it was popular here—Uncle Rory ate it with biscuits almost every morning—but her California taste buds simply could not tolerate it.

Once Carley's tea and toast, Brooke's pancakes and milk, were assembled on the table, Carley pulled out chairs and waded into the subject on both their minds.

"I said I wouldn't discuss Brad Travis unless you brought it up. But I have to ask you why you chose him for a boyfriend."

"I didn't choose him." Brooke slathered butter on three pancakes. "He chose me."

"And you were flattered. He must be very cute."

Brooke colored, but she nodded. "He made a mistake. I'll bet you made mistakes when you were young. Maybe you didn't steal, but—"

"Oh, I stole."

The girl's mouth parted.

"Lipsticks, earrings, even a pair of jeans one time. I'm ashamed to admit it—and by the way, I've never told anyone this besides the pack of friends I roamed with back then. But I never considered it a *mistake*. I knew what I was doing was wrong. I just didn't care."

"But you straightened up, stopped doing it."

"Yes."

"Well, maybe Brad knows it was wrong too. Maybe he wants to change, like you did."

Carley's ears picked up a subtle shade of doubt in Brooke's voice, but she did not call her on it. "I would be happy to hear that. But you shouldn't want to be the guinea pig."

"What do you mean?"

"It's not enough for a person to *say* he wants to change. He has to prove it, not only to others, but to himself."

"How?"

"Well, if he works hard at a job for a few years, pays his bills, obeys the law, treats everyone decently . . ."

"A few *years?*"

"What's your hurry, Brooke? You're *seventeen.* Is your whole life centered on waiting for this guy? You're willing to stake your future on someone who hasn't proven himself trustworthy?"

"Easy for you to say." Brooke doused her pancakes with syrup. "I don't have that many boys wanting to date me, if you haven't noticed."

"So what? Are only the girls with boyfriends worthy of the good things in life? There's so much more out there for you. If only you could see it."

A thought entered her mind from another direction, and Carley went with it. "Let me ask you, Brooke. How did Brad treat Neal Henderson?"

"Neal?" Brooke glanced away for the telltale fraction of a second. "He treated him okay."

"What did he call him behind his back?"

Brooke's expression was saturated with *How did you know?*

Tears spiked the girl's lashes. She looked so much better without all the eyeliner, Carley thought, but she was the *last* person to lecture a girl about dependence upon makeup.

"He loves me, Carley."

"Oh, Brooke . . ." Carley groaned. "Don't you know? Boys will say anything to a girl to sleep with them. Did he ever ask you about your dreams, your goals? There's so much more out there for you than being some guy's amusement park."

Brooke swallowed, whispered, "What's out there for me, Carley? I appreciate my job, but I'm a dishwasher."

Carley spread her hands. "Everything, Brooke. You're young and bright, and a hard worker. What do you want?"

"I don't know."

"That's okay. You don't *have* to know right now. But right now is when you start preparing yourself, so that when you *do* know, you haven't locked yourself into a life-style that's impossible to change."

A very small degree of hope mingled with the resignation in Brooke's expression. "How would I do that? Prepare myself, I mean."

"Education, Brooke. Why did you drop out of school?"

"I *hated* it." Her face hardened. "The other girls called me a skank. I won't go back."

Carefully, gently, Carley said, "So you're going to let them win?"

"What?"

"You'll set your sights low, while they go on to college, just so you don't have to associate with them for a couple more years?" She was well aware that she had not offered the same advice to Alton Terris. But Brooke did not have Alton's advantage of a wealthy family, hence, more choices.

"I'd rather *die* than go back there, Carley."

"Okay." Carley sighed again and opened a jar of Uncle Rory's muscadine jelly. "Look, our breakfast is getting cold. Why don't we save this discussion for later?"

"Okay."

But halfway through her sodden pancakes, Brooke gave her one cautious look, then another.

"What?" Carley asked.

"I want to be a nurse."

"Really?" Wary of such a quick decision, Carley said, "That just came to you?"

"No. I've been thinkin' about that ever since I was little—how good it would feel to help make people well. I used to pretend-doctor our dogs and cats. And then when I'd see Miss Arleen go off to work in her uniform, I wished I could be like her."

"Why didn't you mention it when I asked?"

She shrugged. "I don't know how to become one."

"No one is born knowing anything about anything. How about if I find out? Ruby Moore works for the school board and has all sorts of contacts."

"You won't tell her why you're asking, will you?"

"Well, that might be difficult."

"I don't want anybody laughing at me."

Carley touched Brooke's scarred arm. "All right, no names."

The telephone rang while Carley was towel-drying her hair in the bathroom.

"I'LL GET IT!" Brooke called.

Carley could not help but smile at the sound of bare feet thumping. For all the emotional ups and downs of having a teenager in the house, it was not boring.

The kitchen wall telephone was just around the corner past the short hall. Through the door, Carley overheard, "I don't know. I think I'd be embarrassed."

After a short silence "You wouldn't mind?"

Another silence, then, "Okay, I'll be ready."

"You're not gonna need me for anything tomorrow mornin', are you?" Brooke asked when Carley walked out in her robe.

"No. I'm going out."

"Oh," Brooke said with flat voice. "With Chief Dale?"

"Brooke . . . we're just going on a picnic. As friends. Who was on the phone?"

The girl took in a breath. "Miss Helen invited me to church. She said it's mostly just old people, and that if I get uncomfortable, they'll take me home. And we'll go to the Old Grist Mill afterward."

"It's good of you to agree," Carley said with a twinge of guilt. "That'll mean a lot to them." She walked on into the kitchen, where her teakettle was sending out a tinny little whistle. "Thanks for putting on the water."

"You're welcome," Brooke said, following. "Anyway, I have a feeling they're the ones who bought the clothes, so I couldn't really say *no*. But it might be interesting. I've never been inside a church."

Carley set the Natchez Trace mug on the breakfast table. "Not even for a funeral or wedding?"

"We didn't go to any of my grandparents' funerals. And my kin aren't really into marrying. Anyway, Dad chased away the Vacation Bible School bus. He says his folks beat religion into him when he was a boy, and that church people are hypocrites."

"He shouldn't judge people he hasn't even met," Carley said before thinking. *Wonderful,* she told herself. *You're in league with Melvin Kimball.*

———

"Sour-Bessie plain, egg-pie, Popeye," Paula sang to Rachel and Lisa in the kitchen of Annabel Lee Café.

It both disturbed and amused Carley that she was able to figure out their verbal shorthand. Roast beef on sourdough with no mayonnaise, quiche Lorraine, and spinach salad. Whatever helped to break the monotony, though there was little monotony on this Saturday, with most or all tables filled at any given time.

When Carley squeezed in time to telephone Ruby, her neighbor insisted she and Brooke come over after work for German chocolate cake and a game of UNO.

"Now, what did you want to ask me?" Ruby asked, dealing cards at her dining room table.

"Oh, just something I'm curious about," Carley replied without looking at Brooke. "With two hospitals in Hattiesburg, there must be some nursing education available in this area?"

"Absolutely," Ruby replied. "And the newspaper often mentions a nursing shortage. It would be a good field for a young person to look into. But I thought you were happy with running a restaurant."

"It's for me, Miss Ruby," Brooke said, having either decided Ruby could be trusted, or that this was worth risking being mocked.

Carley had to restrain a smile at the pretend surprise in Ruby's expression. "What a good idea. You'd make a fine nurse."

Brooke flushed with pleasure. "Why do you say that?"

Ruby winked at her. "Because you're not a wimpy little girly-girl. When I had my hysterectomy nine years ago, my favorite nurses were the tough ones."

"Thank you." The girl hesitated. "The problem is, I dropped out of school. And I don't want to go back."

"Can you read on an eighth-grade level?"

"I think so."

"She can," Carley said.

Ruby rose to write *Pearl River Community College* on an index card. "It's in Poplarville, not too far away. You can get into the LPN program with your General Education Diploma, and the state gives free online courses to help prepare you for it. Check out both Web sites."

Carley did, in her own living room an hour later with Brooke hovering at her shoulder. The girl would be required to score an average of forty-five on her General Education Diploma exam, and then an eighteen composite score on the ACT.

"But you have to be tested first, to see which GED courses you need to take," Carley said. "You'd have until July to get all this in, if we're thinking about next fall."

When Brooke did not comment, Carley turned and caught the panic in her eyes.

"It says I have to be eighteen to take the GED."

"But not the online courses, Brooke. And you'll be eighteen in January, right?"

"Well, yeah. But what about my job?"

"The courses are available twenty-four hours a day. And *I* can help you as much as time allows."

Cautious hope entered the girl's expression. "When you see the steps all laid out like this, it . . . doesn't seem impossible, does it?"

"I won't lie. It won't be a cakewalk. Not with your job." A way to lighten that load came to Carley's mind. Mentally she pushed it away, but it bounded back. Stifling a sigh, she said, "And we'll cut your hours to part-time."

Panic flashed again in her eyes. "Please don't."

"But why not? You have minimal expenses here, and eight hours is a long time to stand at a sink anyway. You'll burn out if you don't have time to take a break now and then, even watch a little *Columbo.*"

"But what about the dishes when I'm not there?"

"I'll hire a high schooler to come in at four. They're always applying. You'll still have five hours every day—enough to put away some money for nursing school."

Brooke bit her lip.

Carley smiled at her. "Teal green uniform with *Brooke* on the badge? Making sick people feel better?"

The girl smiled back, said dreamily, "Wouldn't that be something?"

"It would." Carley's fingers returned to the keyboard. "But horse before cart, remember? Let's find out the date for the next test."

———

"Did you know Poloma is Choctaw for *Bow?*" Dale said, driving the Mustang across the bridge north of Tallulah, where Main Street melded into Highway 589.

"No." With new eyes Carley looked to the right and the left, where the sandy-banked river dipped southward several hundred feet past the bridge. "But I see how it fits."

They rode in companionable silence, passing a field of sugar cane with four-foot-high green stalks. Carley smiled and thought of Brooke and her cane syrup. The girl had actually seemed pleased when Aunt Helen and Uncle Rory came for her this morning. She was dressed modestly in her khaki skirt and a sea green knit top that enhanced her green eyes. Her hair still stood out in spikes, but that was Brooke.

"Brooke's being tested to see if she qualifies for GED online courses the Friday after next," Carley said.

"Why doesn't she just go back to school?" Dale asked.

"She said she'd rather die."

"Are all teenage girls so dramatic?"

She smiled. "Yep. Pretty much. Anyway, we're aiming toward nursing courses at Pearl River Junior College next fall. If she qualifies, I'll hire a high schooler to share her shift."

"Does that mean she agreed to dump Brad Travis?"

"Yes." Or at least Carley thought that was the agreement.

About six miles past the bridge, Dale slowed and turned left, onto a black tar road with no signpost. "Tent Road," he said, and motioned to the pasture on his right. "I was told the name comes from a regiment of Tennessee riflemen who camped there in 1814, on their way to meet Andrew Jackson in New Orleans to fight the British."

"Interesting," Carley said.

"What can I say? I should go on *Jeopardy*. That's a game show, by the way."

She wrinkled her nose at him. "I know what *Jeopardy* is."

Tall pines shaded the road, some behind strands of barbed-wire fencing. Goldenrod and black-eyed Susans proliferated on either side.

"How far does this go?"

"Six miles, then it meets Black Creek Road, which eventually links up with Highway 42. It would be a great shortcut from highway to highway, but Black Creek Road is gravel, hard on the paint job."

A wood frame house appeared in the near distance on the right.

Surely vacant, Carley thought, even though a dust-coated red truck was parked in a driveway of gravel, clay, and clumps of weeds.

"I guess you know who lives there," Dale said.

"Uh-uh. Should I?"

"You're kidding. That's the Kimballs' mansion."

"Really?" She reached out to touch his sleeve. "Slow down, please?"

The house was apparently white, ages ago. Now dingy alkaline-looking paint flaked from weathered gray boards. The porch roof sagged where a post had been replaced with the trunk of a young cedar tree. Its limbs were hacked off, leaving knobs on which bits of rope and chain and an aluminum pot were hanging. A peach basket overfilled with newspapers sat between two wooden rockers.

National Enquirer? Carley thought.

Out in what could only loosely be called a yard, the body of a rusted-out Volkswagen was sinking into a bed of weeds. A washing machine lay on its side. In the long grass beyond the porch was a glittering pyramid of brown bottles.

Poor Brooke, Carley thought. She understood, now, why the girl had not accepted the offer to help her move or to drive her home to beat the rain.

"You'd better move on," she said to Dale, fearful someone would come to the window. As he accelerated, she said, "Why haven't you ever told me your property is on the same road?"

He shrugged. "It never came up. But is there some reason I should have?"

"I guess not."

"Anyway, here we are," he said, slowing again about a mile farther down the road. He made a left turn onto a patch of weed-choked ground. A six-foot-wide metal gate hung from posts from which three strands of barbed wire stretched out on either side. A red *Posted* sign hung on the gate, two more on trunks of pines.

"Hunters," he said, inserting a key into a padlock attached to a chain looped around the gate post.

"Are they a big problem?"

"Well, the good ol' boys out here assume any unoccupied patch of land is fair game. No pun intended." He looked at her. "Will you get that can of WD–40 from the glove compartment? I figured this might be rusted. It's been a long while since I've been out here."

"Sure." She had never heard of WD–40, but the *can* part was a good clue. She found the blue and yellow spray can and brought it over to him, stepping carefully over weeds with her sandals.

"Do the signs and lock keep them out?"

"Pretty much." He sprayed the lubricant up into the lock and handed the can back to her. "*And* the fact that most folks know who owns this land. One of the perks of being chief of police."

Back in the Mustang, he drove slowly down two rutted wheel tracks, following another barbed-wire fence leading down into the property. Weeds brushed the underside of the car. After what seemed a hundred and fifty, perhaps two hundred, feet, the trees thinned and Carley caught sight of water.

"I forgot about the pond," she said, sitting straighter.

He drove a few feet farther into a clearing and turned off the engine. "Pretty, isn't it? I'll get the ice chest."

While he went around to the trunk, Carley walked to the edge. The surface was a mirror, reflecting trees, cloudy sky, and hazy sunlight. A fish flipped near the center, sending ripples. Pine needles and grass-covered banks sloped down naturally from the woods, around three-quarters of the pond's circumference. Almost directly opposite from where she stood rose a steep, brush-covered bank. Over her shoulder she called, "How big is it?"

"Three and a half acres." He came around carrying an ice chest by the handles. "It's not a natural pond. The previous owners dammed a stream running through a valley."

"Is that the dam?" Carley said, pointing across.

"Yep. I brought a beach towel. I hope it's big enough for a picnic blanket."

"It'll be fine. I can't believe you never come here," she said, helping spread the towel. "You could keep a boat tied up, paddle around, go fishing. Can you swim here?"

"Why? Would you like to?"

While his tone was not suggestive, his blue eyes seemed to undress her. The look disappeared a fraction of a second later, absorbed by an affable smile.

You're imagining things, Carley told herself. Wasn't she?

"I meant in general."

"Well, it probably wouldn't be a good plan. The deepest part's fourteen feet, but the water gets pretty warm in summer, especially in the shallow parts. I wouldn't know about the bacteria count." He handed her a six-pack of canned apple juice. "Okay, are we going to eat or talk?"

"Well, preferably both." Carley sat and started pulling cans from the plastic holder. "Where will you build the deck?"

"The what?"

"Your deck. When you build your retirement home." She pointed to her right, where about thirty feet away, a red clay bank rose about five feet out of the water. "I vote there."

"I haven't given it much thought. I still have quite a few years before that happens."

A voice crackled over the portable radio unit. He unclipped it from his belt. "What is it, Garland?"

". . . way . . . park . . . shots," were the only words Carley could pick out amidst static garble.

"Can't hear you," Dale said, frowning.

". . . Lockwood . . . almost . . ."

"Look, I don't know if you can hear me, but I'm coming in."

"Just leave me," Carley said.

"No." He took her arm, hurried her toward the car. "But we'll have to come back for all that. Reception's lousy out here. I hope no one's hurt."

As the Mustang sped up Tent Road, Carley clenched her teeth

and held onto the armrest. A mile down the highway, the unit crackled to life again.

"Speak to me, Garland."

". . . control . . . boys . . . fireworks . . ."

Carley let out the breath she was holding. Dale smiled, started decelerating. "Okay, Garland. I'll check in with you later."

He had packed peanut butter on whole wheat sandwiches, guacamole, baked tortilla chips, baby carrot sticks, and a plastic container of cantaloupe chunks. "I could probably snare you a rabbit," he teased, arranging containers on the towel.

"I think I can manage," she said, though she wished he didn't have such a thing against sugar, for she preferred her peanut butter sandwiches with jelly. The guacamole more than made up for it, though. She finished before he did, and started walking away from the bank, toward the gray remains of a house or barn she could see between the trees.

"Careful," he called.

"I won't go far enough to get lost," she called back over her shoulder.

"I mean, of snakes."

She turned, and her sandals covered the distance between them in seconds. He was grinning up at her, a half sandwich in his hand.

"Not funny," she said.

"You're right," he said, sobering. "I shouldn't have scared you. It's just that cottonmouth moccasins are territorial."

Folding her arms to her chest, she looked around. Her surroundings became suddenly ominous. "Maybe we should leave?"

"If you like, but we're fine here, out in the open." He rewrapped the rest of his sandwich and put it in the ice chest. "Let's take a walk first."

"Well . . ."

"I'll get my gun."

He returned the ice chest to the trunk and strapped on his holster. They walked half the pond's circumference, hand-in-hand. In the shade of a dogwood tree, he took her in his arms. "I love you, Carley."

She put a hand to his chest. "I'm sorry, Dale."

"What is it?" He looked hurt, and cupped a hand to his mouth. "My breath?"

"Of course not."

"Has Brooke said something against me?"

"I understand about the boyfriend," Carley said. "I told her if you hit him, it was probably during a struggle."

There was uncertainty in the blue eyes, as if he was debating whether to say more. After a fraction of a second it faded, and he said with wounded voice, "I thought you were beginning to feel the same way I do."

"Let's walk some more," she said.

"All right." He did not resist when she took his hand.

"You remember the talk we had that day Steve Underwood was in the café?"

He blew out his cheeks. "Yes, the day I acted like a lunatic. I thought you'd forgiven me."

"Of course I have. And I appreciate how honest you were with me about your feelings. I hope I can be the same with you."

"Absolutely, Carley. Tell me anything. Only . . . please be gentle?"

That made her smile. And made what she had to say even more difficult, for she truly liked him. "Back to that day . . . you admitted you've had a lot of girlfriends."

"They're nothing to me, Carley. Ancient history."

"But how can you be sure all of that is out of your system?"

"My system? What do you mean?"

"How do you know you won't eventually miss the thrill of the chase—or the thrill of having them chase you?"

"Because I told you. I'm tired of all that." Squeezing her hand, he said, "I want to be with you."

The temptation was strong, just to throw caution to the wind and melt into his arms. She had to force her mind to focus on the thoughts that had kept her awake half the night, alone in her room, insulated from the effect of his presence.

"I'm flattered, Dale," she said. "And I believe you mean it. But long-standing habits are more tenacious than you think. My mother tried to give up smoking a hundred times. Sometimes she lasted as long as a whole week."

He gave her a sidelong look. "I think I'm a little stronger than your mother was, Carley."

"Exactly, Dale. So your breaking point may be months, if you have one. Let's wait awhile. See if you . . . if *we* still feel the same way after some time has passed. I don't want to get hurt."

Halting, he turned to face her, pulled a twig from her hair. Gently he said, "I'll never hurt you, Carley."

She hesitated, caught up in the urge to forget all this nonsense. But she made herself ask, just as gently, "Am I the first woman you've ever said that to?"

"I mean it this time," he said, and sighed. "What can I say to make you believe me?"

"I do believe you," Carley replied. "You're a good person. And . . . I believe you meant it the other times."

He stared at her, his expression unreadable.

"Dale?"

"We'd better get back. Looks like it might rain."

His pride was wounded, of course. Without speaking they climbed into the Mustang.

But after locking the gate again, he fastened his seat belt and looked over at her. "I love you, Carley. But if you need some space, I won't pester you for any more dates until you tell me you're ready. And I won't be seeing anyone else, either. You're worth waiting for."

"Thank you, Dale."

"Does this mean we can't speak to each other?"

"I *hope* it means we can be friends."

"Friends," he muttered, and sighed theatrically. "Sure."

But at length he smiled and reached over to brush her cheek softly with the back of his hand. "I guess I've had worse friends."

From her bed Carley heard an automobile turning into the driveway. A car door opening. Voices. The same car backing out. Footsteps across the porch. A key turning in the lock.

"Carley?"

Carley closed her eyes.

The footfalls from Brooke's new loafers continued through the house, growing fainter, along with "Carley?"

Eventually the footfalls grew loud again, ending with four light raps on her door.

"I'm taking a nap, Brooke," Carley called.

"Oh! Sorry!"

This time, silence. Carley gathered her pillow beneath her neck.

She heard the doorknob ease open behind her, a soft, "Are you all right?"

"I'm all right."

"You *never* nap. Do you have a headache? Do you need to take something?"

"No. I'm just tired. I didn't sleep well last night."

"Okay. Sorry to bother you."

"It's okay." Carley rolled to the other side, propping herself on her elbow. "How was church?"

The girl smiled and took a couple of steps closer. "You know, it wasn't as boring as I thought it would be. Everybody was so nice. When I'm a nurse, I want to work with old people. Maybe in one of those old folks' homes."

"You'd be good at that. I see how you are with Mrs. Templeton."

"And the Old Grist Mill was neat, with all those pictures and stuff on the walls. We sat out on the screened porch, over the river."

"Well, sit down and tell me about it. What did you eat?"

Gingerly, the girl came over to perch on the side of the bed. "Fried shrimp. They were so good—I didn't even ask for ketchup. I told Miss Helen and Mr. Rory I was gonna study for my GED so I can be a nurse, and they said they were proud of me. Your cousins—the Kemps—came after we got our tea. I wasn't happy about them sittin' with us because Patrick was in my same grade, even though he wasn't ever a jerk. But then his dad, Mr. Blake, told such funny jokes that I forgot to be uncomfortable."

Carley sat up, wrapping her arms around her knees. "He's a comedian, all right."

The girl's face sobered. "We were all worried about you after we heard those shots. Uncle Rory asked the manager about it, and he came back and said the police told him some boys had been lighting cherry bombs. Patrick said that was pretty stupid, to do that with the chief of police around."

"It was sweet of you to worry. We heard about the fireworks."

"Well . . . you *heard* them too, didn't you?"

"We weren't at the park," Carley said.

"I thought you went on a picnic."

"Yes. We did."

"You went to his land, didn't you?" Her eyes narrowed.

What happened to the girl who was too meek to use the dryer without asking? Carley asked herself.

"Brooke," she said in her best schoolteacher voice. "I never lived in any mansion when I was a girl. I've seen rats as big as cats, and once we lived across the street from a crack house. And anyway, look at Abe Lincoln, probably our greatest president. *He* was born in a one-room log cabin."

She paused to gauge the effect of her words.

The girl's face was slack with puzzlement. "Huh?"

Patience, Carley thought. "Don't you see? It's where you *end up* that matters."

"You think I didn't want you to go because I'm ashamed of the dump I lived in?"

"Well, I wouldn't call it a *dump,*" Carley lied.

Sadness washed over the girl's face. She pressed fingertips against her lips.

"What is it?" Carley said.

After a hesitation, Brooke said, "If I tell you something, will you promise never to tell a soul?"

"All right."

She looked at the open window. "Not here."

The sagging velveteen sofa in the back room had long-ago gone to the Salvation Army. In its place were a steel frame futon with purple mattress from Ruby's garage, and a glider rocker with scratched arms and country-blue plaid upholstery from Byrle Templeton's attic. Carley sat in the rocker, while Brooke fetched something from her room.

"My cousin, Tracy Knight," she said, returning, handing over a snapshot. A woman who appeared to be Carley's age sat on the steps of a familiar-looking porch, long bare legs crossed and long golden-brown hair draped over one shoulder. She wore what could only be described as a seductive smile. The blonde girl beside her wore a more innocent smile as she held two kittens up for the camera, one tiger-striped and one calico.

"You?" Carley said, even though it was obvious.

"I was eleven. Mr. Steve took that."

Disappointment surged through Carley. "Steve Underwood?"

"Yes. Tracy had one of those disposable cameras she bought at Dollar General. That's where she worked."

"Wait." Carley looked up at her. "Look, sit down please, you're making me nervous."

The girl flopped onto the futon and folded her arms.

"They were dating?" Carley asked.

"No. He came by that day to give her a ride to Soso, and Tracy asked him to take our picture. She liked him a lot, but I don't think they ever went on a date, or she would have told me. She didn't have many friends, and Dad wouldn't speak to her. I think he let her come stay with us just to tick off my mother's kin. She's my Uncle Alvin's girl."

"I'm still lost, Brooke. What is Soso?"

"It's a town that makes Tallulah look like New York, Tracy said. That's where her great-grandma Willa on her mother's side lived. She was ninety-eight years old; she's most likely dead by now. Mr. Steve was writing a paper about Jones County so he could become a professor."

"A dissertation."

"I guess so. Tracy struck up talking with him at Dollar General, and he asked if he could meet her grandma. Something about Jones County not wanting to be part of the South during the Civil War. Even though her Grandma Willa wasn't alive in those days, Mr. Steve said she might have heard stories passed down."

Brooke frowned and shook her head. "But that's not what I have to tell you."

"All right." Carley glanced at the picture again. "Tell me."

"Okay." The girl unfolded her arms to hold up both palms. "First, I already *know* it wasn't right for Tracy to be runnin' around like she did. Even when I was eleven, I knew that."

She was poised for argument. Carley said gently, "Why was she living with you, Brooke?"

"Uncle Alvin caught her in the house with some neighbor man and kicked her out. So she hitchhiked over to us."

"She became your friend."

"My *only* friend," Brooke replied. "She was good to me—

brought home treats from Dollar General, and even the tea set on my dresser. Dad still had his job roofing houses back then, and on Tracy's days off we'd slip over to Chief Dale's pond so she could swim. The gate wasn't up in those days. We didn't think we were hurting anybody."

"Didn't you swim too?" Carley asked.

"I can't. I sat on the bank."

"You're kidding."

The girl shrugged. "I don't like being in water. That's why I only take showers. My mother answered the phone and forgot about me in the tub when I was little. I don't remember, but Dad said he had to give me CPR. That was before Dad started drinking."

"I'm sorry, Brooke."

"It's not your fault." The girl fell silent, face clouding.

"What is it?" Carley asked.

"Remember, you promised not to tell."

"I won't break my word."

"I think Chief Dale killed Tracy."

Carley studied her face for any sign of jest, but her expression was as grave and sincere as any face could wear.

"Okay, Brooke," she said wearily. "This time, don't show me the baby yet. Bring me through the labor."

The girl nodded, drew breath. "It was the day after Fourth of July, I remember because the skins from our firecrackers were still in the road. Dad was putting up a roof somewhere, and Tracy called in to Dollar General that she had a headache. Only she told me someone was on his way to take her swimming. I asked to go, and she laughed and said not this time, that they wouldn't be wearing swimsuits. I thought she was kidding, but all she carried was a towel and her purse. I watched from Dad's bedroom window while she waited in the yard. After a minute, an old green car stopped out front. The windows were down, so I could see a man driving. She got in, and then they went on up the road."

"In the direction of the pond," Carley said.

Brooke swallowed audibly. "I heard two shots about five minutes later. I was in the house, but it sounded like they came from that direction. I didn't know what to do. If I called the police and Chief Dale—or anybody else—went back there and caught them, Tracy would never speak to me again. About an hour later, I was so worried that I put on my shoes and walked up there."

"What did you see?" Carley asked, even though she knew the outcome of this story. Brooke's cousin had run away with Emmit White's son-in-law.

"I heard something first. A car, coming real fast. That made me feel better. But I knew Tracy would get mad, so I hid behind a tree. After it passed, I looked. It was a police car."

"Dale's car, you mean?"

"I couldn't tell who was driving," Brooke admitted. "I jumped out in the road and waved my arms in case he'd look back in the mirror, but he didn't even slow down. So I kept going. I could tell by the weeds bending forward between the tracks that a car had been on Chief Dale's land."

"Well, you had just seen the patrol car."

"But there could've been more than one car, right? I went on back to the pond, but there was no one there. And no one's ever heard from Tracy again."

And that's all you have? Carefully, Carley said, "Surely you know she was with Emmit White's son-in-law. His family hasn't heard from him either."

The girl's face clouded again. "Rick Bryant. Yes, everybody says they ran off together. Even Dad, but he always said Tracy was a tramp."

"What else could have happened? Why would you think Dale did anything to them?"

"Well, they were swimming . . . without clothes on his land."

"That's no reason to kill anybody. Especially when you're—"

"I know," the girl said wearily. "When you're the chief of police, and everybody says you're such a hero. But he has a temper. Just ask Brad."

"The word of a thief," Carley said.

"Tracy wouldn't have lied to me about swimming. And if she *did* run off, she would've called to let me know she was all right."

Carley tried to place herself in the scenario. "You're still seeing this through eleven-year-old eyes. Tracy was probably afraid you would try to stop her, perhaps call someone before they got far away. And once they were gone, Rick Bryant may have pressured her so he couldn't be hunted down. People get arrested for not paying child support."

"Why didn't she pack anything but her purse?"

"Well, she couldn't have *had* many belongings," Carley reasoned. "Not if she hitchhiked her way over. And anyway, why would she even have needed her purse, if she was just going up the road to swim?"

"Her comb. She was fussy about her hair." Finally the girl looked away. "And she kept birth control stuff in there. I saw it when I was looking for gum."

This has been one long day, Carley thought, rubbing her temple.

"You have a headache?" Brooke asked.

"No." Carley gave her a sympathetic smile. "I know you miss your cousin. But I have to tell you, if you're suggesting Dale shot Tracy and Rick, where did he . . . hide the bodies? Did you look?"

"Well, not that day. I figured I'd made a mistake. There's another swimming place miles farther down, where Black Creek Road crosses the creek at a rickety old bridge, and Tracy hadn't actually said they were going to the *pond*. I worried that the bridge might have caved in. Dad wouldn't drive me—he said it was good riddance to bad rubbish. So I rode down there on my bike the next day, and the bridge was still there."

"Did you tell anyone?"

She nodded. "When Mr. Rick's wife called, screamin' bad things about Tracy, I told her about the swimming—but not the part about no swimsuits—so she would get somebody to look for them."

"And. . . ?"

Brooke's shoulders rose, fell. "The police looked for tire tracks at all the creeks, even the river."

"And did they look around the pond too?"

"Well, yeah," the girl replied with hopeless tone. "But Chief Dale would be smart enough to cover the tracks. And besides, with him being the chief, how hard do you think he looked?"

Carley said, gently, "Everything you've said points to their running away, Brooke."

Brooke blew out her cheeks. "I know that, Carley. I started thinking everybody else was right, and then a couple of days later, I walked down to Chief Dale's property to have another look, and there was this big gate with a lock, and *Posted* signs all over the place. And the *For Sale* sign was gone. That was how I cut my arm, climbing through the barbed wire."

"And what did you find?"

"Nothing," the girl conceded. "It was snake season, so I didn't go too deep in the woods. But I looked over every inch when the weather cooled, lots of times."

Carley could only stare at her. "Then, why are we having this conversation?"

Tears filled Brooke's eyes. "Because that pond's deep enough to hide a car."

Rising, Carley went into the kitchen for a paper napkin, returning to sit next to the girl.

"Here now," she said, dabbing her face gently, then handing it over so that Brooke could blow her nose. "I understand. Tracy was good to you, and you miss her. But when we feel very strongly about something—or someone—our emotions can cloud the facts. Dale took the land off the market because he decided he'd like to live on it when he retires. And just today he complained about hunters, which would explain the gate. You mentioned snakes. Perhaps he came across one—*if* it was him indeed who fired the shots. He joined the police force because he respects the law, Brooke. He's no murderer."

Brooke turned to her, eyes red-rimmed and smeared with liner, her expression bleak with *you too?*

"I *know* he did it," she said thickly, shaking her head. "Every time I look at him, it's like I can see it in his eyes, and he *knows* I know."

"Brooke . . ."

The girl sighed, blew her nose again. "You think I'm crazy now."

"No. I understand that feeling. But that's not enough. *My* intuition says he's a good person who couldn't have done it. We can't both be right. Our emotions can lie to us."

She combed her mind for an example. "Okay, Brooke, this is not to be repeated, but during my first few times around Blake Kemp, whom you say is so funny, I had a creepy feeling that told me not to trust him. It went away as I got to know him better."

"This is more than creepy, Carley."

"Okay, then, let's do something about it."

"No! You promised!"

Carley shook her head. "So, you'll just go on the rest of your life, believing Dale killed Tracy and Rick, and not try to find out if it's really true?"

"I *tried.*"

"Then there's another way. We find Tracy."

Brooke blinked at her. "How do we do that?"

"I have a private investigator's card in my wallet. We'll call him, ask his advice."

This is going to cost you, Carley's frugal side jumped in to say.

It's only money. And business is great, argued the side of her that wanted to put to rest the torment her young friend had lived under for years. *He wouldn't even have to visit Tracy, just give us a phone number so Brooke can hear her voice. How much can that cost?*

The frugal side was too ingrained to be totally ignored. She would determine the amount she was willing to spend ahead of time, and then Brooke would just have to let it go once that was reached.

chapter 29

"The reason Mr. Malone hired me to find you, Miss Reed,"
Dennis Wingate said over the telephone, "is that he was able to
trace your late mother to Sacramento with her social security number. But not having *your* number, and the fact that she lost custody
of you when you were fourteen, led him to a dead end. He needed
someone to do the footwork. I'm working another case now, but if
you'll e-mail me this Tracy Knight's social security number, driver's
license number, anything else you have, I can probably find you at
least an employment address by the end of the week, just with the
Internet and a few phone calls."

Carley smiled at Brooke, hanging close to the kitchen telephone.

"We'll try."

"Also," Mr. Wingate went on, "Any information you can give me about Rick Bryant would be
helpful. They may still be together."

"That's probably going to be impossible," Carley said.

"Then, we'll wait and see if we need it." His
voice warmed. "So, you moved to Tallulah, did
you?"

"I even opened up a little café here with my inheritance."

"Well, you've made my day, Miss Reed. Most of my searches
don't have such happy endings."

"I'm glad you found me," Carley told him.

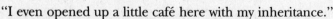

After hanging up, she said to Brooke, "You're going to have to call Tracy's father and get her social security and driver's license numbers. Can you do that?"

The girl frowned, rubbed a mosquito bite on her upper arm. "She didn't have a driver's license. I don't know if he'll give me the other number. He was put out with us for taking her in . . . and then letting her disappear."

"But if you explain what it's for, surely he'll cooperate. It can't hurt to try."

After identifying herself, and making the request, Brooke held the telephone to her ear, nodding, tears making new dark tracks down her face. Eventually she made writing motions, and Carley took the grocery list pad and magnetic pen from the refrigerator.

"He says please let him know what we find out," Brooke said, hanging up.

Carley still had a café to run. The Moores were coming to clean in the morning. Now that the place was used and maintained, the process took only three to four hours—not counting her office, where she would be immersed in paperwork until after four, when she was expecting a delivery of produce from Fresh Pickin's.

"I'll come and help," Brooke offered while Carley made a turkey sandwich to take along.

"No. The floors here need dust mopping and the refrigerator should be cleaned out. That would help me most."

The Moores brought their CD player as usual. It was not as intrusive, coming through office walls, and Carley actually found the music pleasant, though the lyrics were sometimes depressing.

". . . Dan and I with throats burned dry and souls . . . that cry . . . for water. . . ."

At 1:45, she completed her last bit of paperwork, the income statement for the week of September 16 through 20. *Maybe we should open Mondays too,* she thought, seeing how good the numbers looked on the computer screen. She rocked back in her chair. That would require hiring more people, spacing out schedules. The apple cart was rolling along just fine for the moment.

Give it more time, she told herself at length. Easier to work with what she *had,* than realize she had made a mistake and have to lay off people. That notion put aside for the present, she checked her e-mail. There was a message from Dennis Wingate.

I've reached a dead end with Tracy Knight.

Carley clicked on Reply and typed, *I'll try to get Rick Bryant's information.*

Two hours until the produce was due. She took out her telephone book and found Emmit White's number. Mona answered on the fourth ring.

"May I come over for a few minutes?" Carley asked after identifying herself.

"Why?"

"I really can't talk about it over the phone. Please?"

"Oh, all right."

The GL's windshield was flecked with drops when Carley let herself out the back door, and there were a few puddles in the gravel ruts. The Whites lived on First Street, east of Main, in a two-story home of mellow tan brick and blue shutters. "Over here," Carley heard when she was just a few feet from the wood-stained front door.

She followed a path of round cement stepping-stones through the damp grass to the side of the house, where a colorful garden about twenty-by-twenty was enclosed by a natural-colored picket fence. Birdhouses were stuck on high posts, and wind chimes tinkled from metal staffs. Small puddles glimmered on three concrete benches. A bay window revealed a kitchen breakfast nook, and steps led up to a side door. Mona Bryant, on her knees at a mound of dirt, said without preliminaries, "What do you want?"

To the back of Mona's denim shirt, Carley said, "Would you mind if we talked face-to-face?"

"Whatever." Mona rose and turned with exaggerated motions, brushing at the damp knees of her jeans.

"What are you planting?" Carley asked, not that she remotely cared, but in the hopes of getting the intimidating scowl off Mona's face.

"Sweet alyssum." No change in scowl.

"This is a beautiful garden. Did you plant it yourself?"

There seemed a tiny softening of the stone-faced demeanor. "Mom started it, before she got sick. She potters in it sometimes, but I tend most of it. She likes to sit out here."

"You must be a very good daughter," Carley said, sincerely.

A smile flickered and disappeared. "I'm not as good at this as she was. What do you want?"

Carley took a breath. "Brooke Kimball—I guess you know she lives with me now?"

Mona pulled a pack of cigarettes from her pocket, tapped the end against her palm. "What about her?"

"I'm trying to help her find her cousin. And it would help if I had information on your husband."

The oath Mona spat out was predictable.

"I'm sorry about what happened," Carley said. "But Brooke was only eleven when Tracy Knight disappeared. She had nothing to do with what happened. She just wants to make sure she's all right, or at least have some closure."

"Closure," Mona said thoughtfully, and lit her cigarette. Smoke jetted from her lips. "What's that mean?"

"Well, just knowing what happened, so she can stop thinking about it. We would share the information with you. You might be able to go after your husband for back pay on child support."

Mona shrugged. "All right."

"Really?" Carley said.

"If the girl wants closure."

Wednesday after closing, Carley gave in to Brooke's urging and watched a prerecorded *Columbo* episode, sharing the sofa.

"I think you're required to go to bad-grammar school to make your own car commercials," Carley said during a break in which a Hattiesburg dealer shouted his wares.

Brooke chuckled. "That must be where they learn to say 'dollahs.'"

In spite of herself, Carley was drawn into the detective show plot, in which a rare-orchid grower murders his nephew after convincing him to pretend to be kidnapped so that they could tap into his trust fund. "This show is pretty cynical about nephews and uncles, isn't it?"

"Sh-h-h."

The telephone rang. Brooke hit the Pause button.

"Hello?" Carley said.

It was Dennis Wingate, with bad news. "It's as if they both dropped off the face of the earth."

"Meaning, they're . . ." She looked at Brooke.

"Not necessarily. In fact, if this Bryant fellow's trying to avoid child support, they may have ditched the car as soon as possible and gotten new social security numbers. For the right price and with the wrong people, that can be done."

"So, what should we do now?"

"Well, I can fly out to Jones County when I finish this other case, start from square one. But we're talking thousands of dollars."

"No, thank you," Carley said. "I'll put a check in the mail tomorrow. How much do I owe you?"

"This one's on the house, Miss Reed."

"I can't let you do that."

"I made enough looking for you to throw in a bonus," he said. "I hope this case turns out to have a happy ending too."

"That would be a pleasant surprise," Carley said, thanking him.

When she related the conversation to Brooke, the girl shook her head. "They can get new social security numbers for the right price? That means lots of money. If Mr. Rick had lots of money, why would he pick her up in a dented old car?"

"Well, if they were going to ditch it later, an old car would make sense. We don't know how much he had with him. Maybe they had planned this for a long time."

The girl sighed. "We're never going to know what happened, are we?"

"I don't know," Carley confessed. "But when you don't have a concrete answer, all you can do is go with the one with the most evidence to support it."

Brooke did not respond, but turned off the television a minute later and eyed Carley.

"What?" Carley said with heart sinking.

"Okay, please hear me out. Dad has a long chain with a hook that he used to pull shingles up onto roofs. And his old aluminum fishing canoe is still in the shed too. It's light enough for two people to carry. He's got life vests too. If we could get it back there, you could paddle while I drag the chain and see if it catches on anything."

Carley pulled herself to her feet. "I think you've had enough *Columbo* for tonight."

The girl looked up at her, blinking tears. "What can it hurt? Chief Dale won't arrest his girlfriend for trespassing."

"I'm not his *girlfriend*. And making spectacles of ourselves would be *worse* than being arrested."

"Please, Carley. If I could just know for sure that Tracy's not down there, then I could stop thinking about it."

Folding her arms, Carley said, "Okay. I'll compromise. I'll ask Dale about taking a boat back there, if you'll allow me to give him the real reason."

"No way," Brooke said.

"Why not?"

"Because I'm afraid of him." She glanced at the front door.

"You have no reason to be," Carley said wearily. "I know you get tired of hearing the hero bit, but it's a fact that the man risked his life to save who-knows-how-many women from a serial killer. I'm going to bed."

She was at her bedroom door when she heard the sniff behind her. She turned.

"So, he's just gonna get away with it," Brooke said miserably.

"Look," Carley said as gently as her battered patience would allow. "I'm sorry Tracy never contacted you. It was wrong of her. But just because people treat us well, doesn't always mean they're good people. Sometimes it means they're using us."

————

"You've sure made my life easier," Dale said at the counter Thursday while paying for his spinach wrap and soup. "I can hardly remember what it was like to have to pack my own lunch every day."

Carley smiled and handed over change from his ten. "Thank you."

After a glance toward the occupied tables where the patrons were absorbed in conversations, he leaned a fraction closer and lowered his voice. "We had a call from a private detective a couple of days ago, looking for information on Tracy Knight and Rick Bryant."

"Um-hmm?" Carley said with sinking feeling. So certain that the adulterous couple were far away from Mississippi that she had given Mr. Wingate all the information he needed, she had not considered that he might try to get more from *local* authorities.

But then, why would Dale assume *she* had hired Mr. Wingate, and not Mona Bryant?

Evasive action seemed best. "Why are you telling me this?"

"Because he's from Sacramento."

Carley sighed. "Brooke misses her cousin, and wants to make sure she's all right."

"I figured that. I'm just wondering what he found out. He refused to agree to keep me posted, and as the person in charge of the search when they disappeared, I'd like to know for the record."

That made sense. And filled Carley with relief. She leaned a bit closer herself. "He thinks they may have changed their identities. And as much as I like Brooke, I'm not willing to pay him to chase that theory."

"Of course not." He nodded. "You did what you could."

———

When the Underwoods walked into the café with Marti Jenkins at half-past three Saturday, Carley spared them the early-dinner, late-lunch joke. She visited their table after Danyell took their orders, and sensed from Marti a coldness not related to the overhead vent.

"Business is obviously going well, Carley," Vera said.

"It is," Carley replied, smiling. "How about the woodworking business?"

"Buzzing along," Clifford said, which made everyone, including Marti, smile.

Steve, clad in a plaid shirt that brought out the bronze of his skin, asked, "But are you enjoying yourself?"

"Very much. You know, for years I thought teaching was my calling."

"From what I hear, it still is."

"I beg your pardon?"

"Brooke Kimball," he said, and his mother nodded.

"Why, thank you," Carley said, and warmth from their smiles stayed with her through the rest of the day.

She happened upon Steve again in Henderson's parking lot the following afternoon, while Brooke was still with the Hudsons' at an after-church covered-dish dinner. Stashing one bag into a maroon Honda Accord, he said, "I always bring a quart of their chicken salad back to my apartment. I'm hooked on it."

Carley smiled. "There are worse addictions. Have you ever tried it on raisin bread?"

"Are you joking?"

She shook her head. "I can tell better jokes than that."

His laugh was nice, spontaneous and warm. "I believe you."

"Hi, Carleyreed! Hi, Mister Steve!"

They both waved at Neal, pushing a loaded cart for Mrs. Oswald of Timeless Collectibles.

"Do you come to town every weekend?" Carley asked before realizing how much that sounded like a hint. *Well, wasn't it?*

Steve's dark eyes were studying her, as if wondering the same thing.

Don't blush, don't blush, don't blush! she ordered her cheeks.

"I'm afraid not," he replied at length. "Dad bit off more than he could chew by promising a cupboard before the end of the month. We finally finished late last night. I'll probably not be back around until Thanksgiving."

"Of course." Mortified, Carley took a backward step, nodded, pushed her purse strap back up to her shoulder. "Well, it was good seeing—"

"I don't suppose you're able to get away for any USM home games?" Steve asked tentatively, as if feeling a bit awkward himself.

Carley's embarrassment evaporated. "I'm afraid Saturdays are our biggest days."

"Of course." He hesitated. "I need to get back to Hattiesburg and grade papers, but I have time for coffee and dessert over at the Old Grist Mill. . . ."

"What about your chicken salad?"

"I'll just bring it inside."

Several people exchanged nods and greetings with either Carley or Steve as they trailed behind the hostess through the vast dining room. Carley only recognized some faces by sight, either from the streets or in her café. She was relieved when the face she had hoped *not* to see did not materialize. This would probably reach Dale's ears, sooner or later, but she did not care to have his brokenhearted expression casting a pall over the afternoon.

And for the same reason, she was glad when the hostess laid down menus at a small table back in the corner.

The Old Grist Mill's specialty was warm peach cobbler with a scoop of vanilla ice cream. Carley had had it twice before, but it was no less of a treat. Still, owning a café had ruined her ability to dine casually. She found herself looking around, mentally testing the service and atmosphere.

"You feel guilty for sitting?" Steve asked, stirring creamer into his coffee.

"How did you know?"

"You have an expressive face."

"I never realized that. Is that a bad thing?"

"No, not at all." He smiled back. "Unless you play poker."

He asked about the day-to-day operations of the café, and she asked about his lectures. Time flew by, and it seemed like only a few minutes had passed when the waitress was taking their dishes and asking about refills on his coffee and her tea.

"No, thank you," Carley said.

"Yes, for me," Steve said. "And the check too, please."

"Don't you have papers waiting?"

"After this. Promise to make me leave. But maybe you're in a hurry to get back to Henderson's?"

"Not at all. Just need eggs and milk. One of the benefits of owning a café is that we have so many meals there that it cuts down on personal cooking and shopping."

"What made you decide to invite Brooke to stay with you?"

"Well, her having to ride her bike through the rain. You know how far out she lives."

"Yes." He nodded, spooning sugar and creamer into his refilled cup. "I once went out there to drive her cousin, Tracy Knight, over to Jones County to visit her relatives. Her great-grandmother was very helpful when I was writing my thesis."

"On Jones County."

Surprise briefly crossed his face. "Yes. Specifically, my thesis was

that the anti-Confederates living there were more interested in sup-
porting the Union than forming their own independent republic,
as is commonly thought." He clucked his tongue at himself. "Sorry.
This isn't a classroom."

"No, I'm interested," she said, meaning it. "May I read it?"

"You're sure?"

"Yes."

"I'm flattered. I'll bring it Thanksgiving. And then . . . maybe
you'd enjoy seeing some of the places I wrote about? They're not
too far for a day-trip."

"I'd like that," Carley said.

"Really?"

She smiled. "Why do you look so surprised?"

"I didn't think I looked surprised. I thought I looked pleased. I
assumed you and Chief Parker were . . ."

"Just friends."

The distaste that entered in the brown eyes at his mention of
Dale's name brought back memories of the two other times Carley
had witnessed the same. "You don't care for him, do you?"

He took a sip of coffee. "I'm sure he's a decent guy, but no, he's
not on my Christmas list."

As much as she would like to flatter herself, she suspected the
dislike had a deeper reason than Dale's interrupting two conversations. Partly to shut up Brooke's voice in her head saying *I told you
so,* partly for her own curiosity, she said, "May I ask why?"

"Sure. I know a very nice person who adores him, but he hardly
gives her the time of day."

Marti, Carley thought.

"I can't help but think if she were as beautiful as other women
he's dated, he would give her a chance." He set down the cup, gave
her a worried look. "I hope I didn't just offend you."

By calling me beautiful? Carley shook her head.

When Brooke arrived home from church, she was oddly silent,

except to say that she'd had a good time, and that those old people sure could cook. All afternoon Carley expected the other shoe to drop, to be drawn into another debate. But the girl spent most of the day at the kitchen table with pencil, paper, and *Practical Algebra*, in preparation for Friday's TABE—Test of Adult Basic Education—to determine if she qualified for online GED courses.

"Everything okay?" Carley asked before going to bed.

Brooke, chewing on her pencil eraser, nodded. "Um-hmm. Sleep well."

When Brooke had not risen by ten the next morning, Carley lifted the girl's notebook and counted seven pages of equations and fractions written in haphazard fashion, as well as a pretty decent sketch of a rabbit in one corner.

The telephone rang while she was rolling meatballs. She grabbed a paper towel to pick up the receiver.

"I have to run to JCPenney and return a catalog order," Aunt Helen said. "Why don't you come with me, and I'll treat you to lunch?"

"That sounds nice," Carley said. "But I have a busy day ahead. I've already started a pot of spaghetti sauce, and this afternoon I'll be interviewing some high school kids to share Brooke's job."

"Hmm, have you anything there Brooke can make her own lunch with?"

"Well, yes." Odd, that her aunt would not sug-
gest simply inviting the girl, as the two seemed to be building rapport. "I brought some leftover minestrone from work Saturday."

"There you are! Just wrap whatever you've done so far for the refrigerator. We won't be long, and when we return, I'll finish the spaghetti for you."

"Well, okay," Carley said. "But I'll pick *you* up."

She did not know if creeping along below the speed limit was peculiar to her aunt, or if it just came with aging in general—like crow's feet—but she wanted to ensure returning in time.

The temperature had dipped to a lovely forty-seven last night, but the thermometer was now at sixty-five, so Carley changed into her coral knit shirt with three-quarter sleeves, black capris, and sandals.

"I've asked Rory to help Pam in the shop while I'm up at Canton," Aunt Helen said as Carley turned the GL onto Highway 589 South.

Aunt Helen and her friend Marianne Tate would be away from October seventh through tenth, setting up and working a booth at the Canton Flea Market Arts and Crafts Show.

"By the way, it's the same Canton where *A Time to Kill* was filmed," she added.

Carley was impressed. "But can Uncle Rory handle four days on his feet?"

"Pam knows to coddle him. It's either that, or he'll insist on coming with us and end up in bed for a month like he did two years ago. Marianne has a nephew up there we're hiring to do the heavy lifting."

Her aunt seemed to have more to say but was saving it for an appropriate time. And Carley was not surprised when that time turned out to be at the table at Barnhill's.

"Brooke accepted Christ yesterday and would like to be baptized."

Carley dabbed butter into a split sweet potato. "Why couldn't she tell me herself?"

"Because I asked her to let me. I was afraid you'd think we pressured her into it."

"I don't think that at all." Carley could well understand the pull of the Gospel to a girl just finding out that someone loved her enough to die for her. Hadn't it been the same with her?

She felt a twinge of melancholy. How trusting she had been in those days. She likened herself to the seed in the parable that sprang up among thorns that eventually choked her.

But had the seed really died? She could see how God had been looking out for her, weaving strands of gold through the frayed places in her life, even while she, like the animals Mrs. Templeton nurtured, ran away every time she felt His presence.

Forgive me, Father, she found herself praying.

"Well, what do you think?"

Her aunt's voice drew her back to the present.

"About Brooke being baptized?" Carley said. "I'm surprised. She's afraid of water."

"Afraid of water?" Aunt Helen smiled, obviously thinking she was joking. "She washes dishes."

"But she doesn't climb into the sink. She didn't tell you?"

Aunt Helen shook her head. "What should we do?"

Carley had to think. "Nothing, I guess. She's pretty independent. Maybe she wants to try. When is it?"

"You'll come?" Aunt Helen said cautiously.

"Of course. You think I'd stay away?"

"It's next Sunday. Thank you, Carley."

"No, thank *you.* For caring about her soul while I was licking my wounds. Is it okay to mention that you told me?"

"Absolutely. If you say nothing, she'll think you don't approve."

When Carley parked outside JCPenney at Turtle Creek Mall, Aunt Helen gathered her parcel from the back seat. "Are you coming in? I'll just be a minute."

Carley looked at her watch. A little over two hours until her first interview. "Let's do a little shopping."

She found the perfect outfit for Brooke in the junior department at McRae's—a peacock-blue knit shirt with coordinating tweed skirt.

When they arrived back at the house, Brooke was reading a history text from the library. While Aunt Helen opened the refrigerator to make good on her agreement to finish the sauce, Carley rested her left hand on the girl's shoulder. "Aunt Helen told me. I'm happy for you."

Brooke looked up at her. "Thanks, Carley."

Low-key, understated, Carley would have thought, had it not been for the glistening in her green eyes. She put the McRae's bag on the table. "I thought you might like something special to wear Sunday."

The girl pushed out her chair, and Carley was caught up in an embrace. Smiling at Aunt Helen over Brooke's shoulder, Carley understood why women chose to be mothers.

———

October 1 rolled in Wednesday with a deficit—less than an inch and a half of rain had fallen over the latter half of September. Pollen from the pine trees, ragweed, and goldenrod caused noses and eyes to redden. Lawn sprinklers were common sights up Third Street, and Carley felt for the soybean farmers on the outskirts of town.

Against Carley's advice, Brooke had stayed up late nights over the past week pouring over *Practical Algebra*.

"What time did you turn out your light?" Carley asked on Friday, the morning of the test, as she put a plate of scrambled eggs and bacon before the bleary-eyed girl.

Brooke blinked up at her. "Hmm?"

"Brooke . . ."

"No, I'm okay." She picked up her fork. "I wasn't gonna turn out my light until the light went *on* in my head about that ratio-and-proportion stuff."

Carley smiled, went to the refrigerator for orange juice. "Well, did it?"

The girl finished a yawn. "At about two, I think. Thanks for breakfast."

"You're welcome. A nice long shower will help wake you." Carley had already lit the wall heater for her own shower, for the thermometer had dipped to forty-five last night. "And when you get back to town, have Uncle Rory drop you off here."

"Are you sure?"

"Yes. The agency said the temp won't mind washing dishes."

Tyler Sibley, a bookish sophomore, was to begin three-hour daily shifts on the tenth, when Brooke would know if she qualified for online courses. But Carley needed someone all day today. The temp was a stout black woman named Karen Orr, whose uncomplaining dedication to her dishes earned her a twenty-dollar tip.

Brooke was watching *Columbo* with feet propped up on the coffee table when Carley walked into the house that evening.

"How was it?" Carley asked.

"It was easy." Brooke pressed the Pause button, freezing Peter Falk holding what appeared to be a stopwatch. "I'm sure glad I crammed on algebra."

"Good. Did you nap?"

"Slept like a hound under the porch."

———

Sunday morning, it seemed fitting that Carley should wear the outfit she had worn on her first flight to Tallulah—or at least the taupe skirt and white blouse, for the blazer was not appropriate for the eighty-plus degrees expected today. Brooke looked very nice in her new clothes. Fresh-faced even, for Carley had convinced her to leave off the eyeliner.

"It'll only smear."

"Okay," Brooke had conceded. "But I'm still wearing mascara."

Leaving the steps on their way to the driveway, Carley could no longer put off saying, "You know, no one will think ill of you, if you decide you can't handle it."

"I can handle it," Brooke said, with telltale forced bravado.

Carley found herself sending up another prayer. *Help her, Father.*

Grace Community Church met in a brick building the size of a large house, past Lockwood's Red Barn Emporium on Second Street. The bricks were painted almost an oyster white, the door and shutters were varnished oak. There was no steeple, but a cross was attached to the peak of the roof, and the windows were stained glass.

Besides Aunt Helen and Uncle Rory, there were several recognizable faces in the sanctuary, including those of Stanley and Loretta Malone. Everyone knew Brooke, obviously. Carley smiled to herself. The girl had come from having no grandparents to having at least a dozen.

The minister's name was James Kelly, a blonde, Nordic-looking man of about fifty, who had played football for Ole Miss before attending seminary. The theme of the sermon was "A Life Changed by God," based upon Saint Paul's conversion in the ninth chapter of Acts. So fascinated was Carley in hearing Scripture read in a lyrical drawl, that she had to remind herself to pay attention to its meaning and not just the delivery. During the closing hymns, Brooke left for the back with an older woman Carley recognized as one of Mrs. Templeton's senior citizen center friends. When the baptistery curtains parted, Brooke stood with the minister in white robes.

Carley dabbed her eyes with a fingertip.

"Need a tissue?" Aunt Helen whispered.

"No, thank you."

Brooke was lowered into the water. When she came up out of it again, she wore such a smile of wonderment that Carley's throat thickened and her eyes began smarting again. She nudged her aunt's elbow. "Okay, I'll take one."

――――――――

"You've *really* never played Candyland?" Carley heard Micah Payne say through her bedroom window Monday afternoon. The day had warmed to the high seventies, and so the attic fan was rotating again. She put away the rest of her folded laundry and crept over to the window, leaned over the headboard. Brooke sat on the porch floor in a square with the older Payne children, the game board open in the center.

"This is the first time I've even *seen* Candyland," Brooke said.

"What did you play when you were a girl?" Kimberly asked.

"Lots of things. Jump rope, jacks. And jigsaw puzzles some-times."

"They all start with *J*!" the girl chortled.

"Were you joking?" Micah asked suspiciously.

"No. But come to think of it, that starts with a *J* too!"

The children chortled as if that were the funniest thing ever. Carley smiled and backed away from the curtain. She brought water out the back door to Patrick, who was operating the leaf blower with headphones in his ears. Next door, Gayle was taking towels down from the clothesline, dropping them into a basket, while Lane played with a yellow toy truck at her feet.

"I heard about Brooke's baptism," Gayle called.

Carley walked over, out of range of leaf blower noise. Delicately, she said, "Is that why you're allowing the children near her?"

Discomfort washed across Gayle's pretty face. "I'm sorry for that. I was wrong."

"No, you were right. You didn't know her."

Glancing back at Patrick, blissfully caught up in his music, Car-ley said, "I've only told one other person this, first, because I was ashamed, and now, because I don't care to carry around a 'victim' banner. But my stepfather abused me when I was a girl. And he was a deacon and choir member."

Gayle shook her head. "Oh . . . Carley . . ."

"For most of my life, I've pegged Christians as hypocrites. I'm learning just how wrong I was. Even so, you must never assume your children are safe around someone, based solely on his or her church standing. My Aunt Helen once said there were wolves among the sheep. She's right."

"Thank you for telling me." Gayle directed a worried looked toward Carley's house. "Ah . . . should I . . ."

Carley gave her an understanding smile, then knelt to look at Lane's truck. "You have nothing to worry about, Gayle. They're just playing Candyland on the porch. And Brooke's definitely no wolf."

The telephone rang after supper, when Carley sat sideways on the sofa with feet propped, reading the October issue of *Restaurant Hospitality*. She stretched out for the telephone on her desk.

"Hello?"

A male voice said, "Brooke."

Carley's dormant English-teacher side took immediate issue. "I beg your pardon?"

"I wanna speak to Brooke."

She was tempted to hang up, make the problem go away. But if the voice on the other end indeed belonged to Brad Travis, Brooke was going to have to be the one to break the news that she could not see him.

Or *not* break the news. Carley was well aware of the control a young man could have over a girl starved for love.

But she's not starved for love, she corrected herself.

"Hold on, please." She held her hand over the phone, called, "Brooke?"

Brooke came out of her room in her gold USM Eagles shirt, pajama pants, and fuzzy slippers. Carley nodded and held out the receiver. The girl gave her a vague look and went into the kitchen. Carley heard chair legs against the wooden floor, then the metallic sound of the receiver being lifted.

"Hello?"

Carley hung up. About eight seconds of silence passed.

"I'm glad you're out too," she finally heard Brooke say. "Was it rough?"

The silence lasted much longer.

"No, I'm sorry. I need to sleep. I have work tomorrow."

Still more silence.

"No, I really can't."

Carley heard her throat clearing.

"Well, maybe you should give your mom a chance. See, I'm

gonna be taking online courses for my GED real soon, and I'm not gonna have time for—"

When Brooke spoke again, after the lengthiest silence yet, her voice shook. "No, I don't want to! That's a crazy plan!" The chair sound came again, sharper. "I have to go now!"

As soon as the receiver clicked again, Carley got to her feet and went into the kitchen. "I'm sorry," she said, patting Brooke's back. "I know that was hard, but trust me, you did the right thing."

Brooke blinked tear-spiked lashes. "It was only hard hearing him yell at me, that's all. You're right, Carley, he's bad news. He wants me to hitchhike to Las Vegas with him to see if some cousin will find him a job there. Is that crazy or what?"

The telephone began ringing again.

"I'm sure that's him again." Brooke said.

"Let the machine pick it up."

But when that happened, the ringing stopped, only to start again seconds later. After the sixth go-round, Carley turned off the ringer and the answering machine.

"I'm going to have to tell Dale."

"No," Brooke said quickly, fear filling her eyes. "Brad might do something. He has a temper."

Carley lifted her brows. "Oh? Meaning . . . a policeman might have to use physical force to subdue him?"

"I don't know," the girl mumbled, and went to her room.

chapter 31

The almost-half-inch of rain that had fallen Tuesday morning brought on a festive mood in the dining room of Annabel Lee Café. Carley recognized Brad Travis as soon as he sauntered inside— brown hair ruffled with pillow indentations, shirt buttoned only halfway, a homemade swastika tattoo on one forearm, a skull on the other. Eyes as hard as pebbles traveled the dining room and stopped at her face.

"Brooke here?"

"I'm afraid she's working."

He gave her a smug smile, turned, and headed for the kitchen doors. Carley hurried around the counter and caught up with him. "I'm sorry. You can't go back there."

When his steps did not slow, she reached for his arm. She let go immediately when the muscles tightened.

He turned a thunderous face to her. "Keep out of this, you—"

"Please," Carley cut in, trying to stay calm for the sake of her customers.

But he pushed on ahead. Helplessly, she looked at the table Garland Smith, off duty, shared with his wife, Amy, and their two girls. He was already getting to his feet. Mr. Lockwood of the nursery did the same from the opposite corner, and Troy dropped his order pad on a table. The commotion coming from the kitchen was easily heard over Mozart's *Flute and Harp Concerto*. Carley followed the men. Within seconds, Garland had an arm wrapped around Brad's neck from behind; Mr. Lockwood had one arm, and Troy the other.

Lisa and Rachel and Brooke stood in a huddle with ashen faces.

"Amy's calling Marti on the cell," Garland said between grunts as the men dragged the cursing young man through the storeroom. The siren was already wailing when Carley unlocked and pushed open the door. Within seconds the boy was cuffed and inside the squad car, kicking his feet against the window. Garland decided to help book him, saying Dale had the night shift, and it would only take a few minutes.

"Are you all right?" Carley asked her staff. "Do we need to close?"

"Don't close," was the consensus, with Brooke, the most shaken, agreeing.

"I'm sorry you had to witness this," Carley announced back in the dining room, particularly to the five older women who were first-time customers. "The young man's been taken into custody and will not return. And as our way of apology, we'll be bringing around dessert trays—on the house."

That brought smiles, even from the five new customers.

As for Garland and Mr. Lockwood, their whole tickets would be on the house. Troy's reward would come in his next paycheck.

Almost immediately people started dropping by, to reassure themselves that everything was back to normal: Uncle Rory, on his first day filling in for Aunt Helen, hurried over from Auld Lang Syne Antiques. Danyell's mother. Pastor James Kelly. Loretta Malone, apologizing that Stanley had to stay clear just in case he was appointed counsel for the defense. Mayor Coates. Ruby Moore. Several shop owners from both sides of Main. Most visitors were too busy to stay longer than a minute or two. Thanks to Brad Travis, today would probably be the weakest day of the month, profit-wise. But a strong day, friendship-wise.

Carley heard knocking after the last customers had left, and unlocked the door to allow Dale inside.

"Are you all right?" he said, the same question she had asked her staff.

"Yes, I'm fine."

"I'm sorry I wasn't here."

"You can't be everywhere," she said.

"But I should have expected something like this when the boy got out."

"You can't *know* everything."

Finally he smiled. "Thanks, Carley. I need to speak with you and Brooke about pressing charges. Would you like to come to the station now, or should I just wait for you and Brooke here?"

"Please wait," Carley said.

He exchanged greetings with the staff on their way out. When Carley and Brooke joined him at a table, he said to the girl, "Did he lay a hand on you?"

"No sir," she mumbled with eyes focused on the salt and pepper shakers.

You could at least look at the man when he's expressing concern, Carley thought, wishing there was some way to send the message via brain waves to Brooke's head.

Dale gave Carley a helpless look, probably mirroring the one on her own face.

"Good," he replied. "We can hold him for a week for disturbing the peace and trespassing, give him time to cool off and refresh his memory about what a drag it is to be incarcerated. If you'd like to press charges for harassment, we can hold him until it goes to trial, unless his mother is willing to post bail—which I doubt."

Carley felt sudden pity for the boy. What kind of life had led to his being this way? But she did not have the power to help him, especially not with Brooke under her wing.

"I'm afraid of him," she admitted. "Afraid what he'll do to Brooke. If there was just some other way . . ."

Brooke nodded agreement, grimly.

Dale folded his arms and sat back in his chair. "Well, hear me out. His father, up in Little Rock, is willing to wire money for a bus ticket. He sounds like he regrets his failings. So, what I can do is, tell the young punk you'll not press charges if he'll agree to go on up to Little Rock. I'll drive him to the bus station myself, after he serves his time."

Maybe they could help the boy after all, if only in this small way, Carley thought. "You'll make sure he gets on?"

"I'll buy the ticket, watch him leave."

"What do you think, Brooke?" Carley said.

"He told me he wants to hitchhike to Las Vegas."

"Well, either way we'd be rid of him," Dale said. "But I'd have a week to convince him it's in his best interest to stay on the bus."

"All right," Brooke said, facing Carley, not Dale. "Besides, if we make him stay in jail longer, he'll only be madder when he gets out."

During the short drive home, Carley asked, "Couldn't you have been a little nicer?"

Brooke, staring out the window, replied, "All your talk about there being more important things than having a boyfriend, and here you are, wanting Chief Dale to like you so much that you believe every word that comes out of his mouth."

"Brooke!"

The girl turned to her. "I *know* he did something to Tracy!"

"You know no such thing! You just can't accept that she didn't care enough to call you, so you found someone else to blame."

"That's not true!" Brooke shot back, sniffed, and said thickly, "I'll pack my stuff and call Mildred."

Carley steered left on Third Street. "Is that what you want?"

Another sniff, then, " 'Course not. But . . ."

"People don't just drop out of each other's lives because they disagree. But I don't have the energy to argue with you about Dale any more. Understand?"

There was silence, then Brooke said in a small voice, "All right."

———

Dale stopped by the house in uniform Wednesday evening, a half hour after Carley and Brooke returned from work.

"Just want to make sure you're both all right," he said after Carley let him in.

"That's very thoughtful of you," Carley said.

"I'm fine," Brooke said with the animation of a robot. She clicked the remote control, sending *Columbo* to black screen. Aiming her face in Dale's direction, she stretched her lips into a grimace-like smile and said, "Thank you. I'm kinda tired—think I'll go to bed now."

You wouldn't turn off Columbo *even if you hadn't slept all week!* Carley thought, eyes following Brooke toward the hall. She turned to Dale. "I'm sorry."

He smiled, nodded toward the porch. "May we sit outside for a minute?"

"Sure." This time she had no qualms about sharing the swing with him. The chains creaked softly, and crickets sang their pleasure at the fifty-nine-degree October air.

"This is my favorite time of year," he said absently.

"We'll have to start closing our windows at night soon," Carley said, and turned to him. "Look, I'm sorry about Brooke."

"It's all right, Carley. But for what it's worth, please tell her when she's in a more receptive mood, how impressed I am with her for giving Brad Travis the brush-off. You're a good influence on her."

"Thank you for saying that," she said, and thought if only Brooke could see this side of Dale, she would not be imagining homicidal looks in his eyes.

There was a way to stop this obsession—a plan she had treated with scorn when Brooke suggested it only a couple of weeks ago.

"You know, now that you mention mood," she said offhandedly. "That gives me an idea. That might be part of her problem—the whole Brad thing—and I know she's anxious about the GED. Remember how I said you should put a boat on your pond?"

He nodded. "It was a good idea. And I just might do that, when we can afford to hire a couple more deputies, and I can slow down the pace a bit."

"Well, for now, would you mind if Brooke and I borrowed her dad's canoe and paddled around? A change in routine would be good for both of us."

"You mean, without me?"

"Just a girlfriend outing." She smiled. "No boys allowed."

Dimples creased his cheeks. "All right, be that way. I'll get the gate key over to you before . . ." He paused thoughtfully. "You should bring a gun along for snakes. A shotgun would be best, and Kimball probably has—"

"Shotgun?" Carley cut in.

"If you're not comfortable with that, I can lend you a Beretta revolver I have at the house."

The idea of snakes *and* being in charge of a gun made Carley queasy. "Won't they be hibernating in another month or so?"

"Well, yes."

"Then, we'll wait." Not that she even remotely planned to follow through with this outing, for paddling around while a girl dragged a chain ranked high on her list of things *never* to do. She had the answer she wanted. That was enough.

"Thank you, Dale."

"Sure, Carley. And now I'd better make my rounds."

As they got to their feet and started ambling toward the steps. Carley asked, "How many nights will you be on duty?"

"Three more. Then I'll go on days again."

"I wouldn't think the chief of police would have to work the night shift."

He shrugged. "I just couldn't see making Garland and Marti carry that whole load. I'm optimistic that we'll be hiring another deputy next fiscal year. Successful new businesses like yours bring in more tax money, so we'll see."

"Then I'll try to have a better attitude when I send in my next quarterly payment," she quipped. "It must be difficult, rearranging your body clock."

"It's not too bad. I keep a little window air-conditioning unit in my bedroom and have two layers of dark curtains, so it's like a tomb." He stretched his arms, covered a yawn, and grinned self-consciously. "Of course, no system is perfect."

"Okay, you can stop hiding," Carley said, knocking on Brooke's closed door.

The girl opened it. She had dressed for bed, in her long T-shirt and fuzzy slippers, though she had not yet removed her makeup. "I wasn't hiding."

Carley folded her arms. "Oh, so you really are going to bed. I guess you'll catch up with *Columbo* tomorrow."

The girl gave her a sheepish smile. "Well, tomorrow I might not have time."

"Imagine that," Carley said, stepping aside.

Brooke settled on the sofa, picked up the remote from the coffee table, and propped her feet in the same spot. "Aren't you gonna finish watching it with me?"

"Sure," Carley said, sitting on the sofa and kicking off her shoes. "But first, some news."

"Um-hmm?"

"I asked Dale about our taking your dad's boat out for a ride. He said fine, that he would give me the gate key."

Brooke sat up, stared at her. "Really?"

"Really."

"Monday okay?"

Now it was Carley who stared. "You still want to go?"

"Well, yeah."

"Sorry. No way."

"But, *Carley* . . ."

Carley shook her head. "That's *not* gonna happen, Brooke."

The animation left the girl's face. "Then why did you—?"

"To prove to you he has nothing to hide. Doesn't that tell you something . . . that he gave permission without so much as the blink of an eye?"

Brooke sank back into the cushions, clicked on the remote. Naturally, Lieutenant Columbo exposed the senatorial candidate who was manufacturing death threats against himself. When the tape was finished, the girl switched the remote again.

"I couldn't stand the idea of Tracy runnin' off and leaving me like that," she murmured, staring at the blank screen. "I wanted to believe she loved me as much as I loved her. But you know . . ."

She swallowed audibly, tears filling her eyes.

"She wasn't always nice. She called me 'fatso' whenever she was in a grumpy mood. She threw a box of macaroni and cheese at me one time. And she never helped with the dishes or the laundry. . . ."

"I understand, sweetie." Carley moved closer to put an arm around her shoulders. "You were grateful for every scrap of affection. For just being noticed, period."

"So, I need to put her out of my mind."

Thank you, Father, Carley prayed. "Life's too short to be torturing yourself over what might have been. Besides, you're going to be super busy, starting tomorrow."

"*If* I passed," the girl said with a worried little smile.

"We can take that *if* out of the equation. You said it was easy."

"Well . . . yeah . . ." Brooke's smile grew more genuine, more confident. "Okay, I passed."

"That's the spirit."

"I hope."

Carley laughed, cuffing her lightly on the arm. "Okay, whatever works for you."

A Mrs. Tucker from the Mississippi Adult Education Project put an end to the suspense at 9:10 Friday morning. Over the telephone she informed Brooke, "You may begin your first online course at any time."

"So, the second step is completed," Carley said, smiling as the girl hopped around the living room hugging a sofa pillow.

Brooke paused. "You mean the *first* step."

"Studying for the test was the first step. Passing it, the second. Beginning the courses is the third. And *you* need to finish getting dressed."

"Okay," Brooke said, but halfway to her room she turned around and went back to the telephone. "The *third* step is calling Mr. Rory and thanking him for taking me there."

Carley smiled again. Knowing Brooke, the girl had thanked him to distraction on the day of the test. But better an overdose of gratitude than too little.

"Did you pass?" was the first question on the lips of each arriving member of the staff. It turned out to be an all-round good-news day: Morning showers fed South Mississippi's thirsty soil almost an inch and a half of water. Danyell had a letter from her husband. While pulling up carpeting, Paula's husband had found a cameo pin her grandmother had given her, wedged between carpeting and floorboards. Lisa was going to have a baby.

Mona Bryant actually wished Carley a good day when she paid for a takeout meal.

Odd though, Carley thought, that she did not ask what Dennis Wingate had discovered about Rick. Perhaps the marriage was so bad that she didn't care if she found out—child support or not.

Aunt Helen telephoned that evening upon her return from Canton. "Rory said Brooke called this morning about passing her test. He also told me about the Travis boy. Are you both all right?"

"We're fine. He's going to join his dad in Arkansas, and hopefully get some direction. How was Canton?"

"Lots of fun. But I think we dealers spent as much at each other's booths as the customers did. I found Sherry a salt-glazed pitcher for her collection and you something for the café."

"How sweet. What is it?"

"Sorry, you'll have to see it for yourself. I'll bring it to the shop tomorrow, and you can come by before you open."

Saturday morning, Pam Lipscomb was dusting a display of vintage toys when Carley entered Auld Lang Syne.

"How's your daughter?" Carley asked.

A smile briefly transformed the solemn face. "Coming home from Iraq next month!"

The gift was a cross-stitch in an ebony frame, expertly stitched on faded light brown linen with a sentiment from an English essayist of the late eighteenth century.

> *Thank God for tea!*
> *What would the world do*
> *without tea?*
> *How did it exist?*
> *I am glad I was not*
> *born before tea.*
>
> *Sydney Smith*

"Judging by the frame, it was probably stitched in the thirties," Aunt Helen said. "I thought you might want to put it somewhere in the kitchen."

"Are you kidding?" Carley said as they embraced. "This goes in the dining room. Mr. Smith would have felt right at home in Tallulah."

"If he could learn to drink it iced," Pam said behind the counter.

"Car-ley," came faintly over the roar in Carley's ears Sunday morning. Or was she hearing things?

She switched off the blow-dryer. A second later, Brooke appeared in her doorway.

"Miss Helen wants to know if you want to meet us at the Grist Mill after church. What are you doing?"

"Getting dressed for church."

"You're kidding."

Carley ignored the stunned look. "Tell Aunt Helen they don't need to come by. I'll drive us."

She smiled at the sound of barefoot thumps, then overheard, "You'll never believe this!"

The decision had cost her very little sleep. It was time to return to the fold, to stop holding the majority of good Christians responsible for the failings of their errant brothers and sisters.

James Kelly's sermon, from the book of Nehemiah, was appropriate for the occasion. When the children of Israel returned to a destroyed Jerusalem after exile in Babylonia for half a century, their first order of business was to rebuild the temple.

The temple needed rebuilding in her own life.

But then, perhaps any sermon would have fit? Perhaps God's word fed each seeker exactly what was needed that day? Another reason to search the Scriptures. The soft worn leather of her grandmother's Bible felt comfortable in her hands.

In the Old Grist Mill, hostess Robbie Gibson gathered menus and asked the foursome, "Will the Kemps be joining you?"

"They will," Uncle Rory replied.

Later, after Blake, Sherry, and Patrick were seated, the waitress asked Carley, before she could specify which side she wanted with her baked trout, "You want double mashed potatoes with no gravy, right, honey?"

"I love small-town living," Carley said, exchanging waves with Kay Chapman and her husband.

"If we just had a Wal-Mart," Sherry sighed.

"Home Depot," said Uncle Rory.

"A movie theater," Patrick said.

"A mall," Brooke added.

Aunt Helen shook her head. "If we had all those things, we wouldn't be small-town."

"We had a theater once." Blake's straw swirled the ice in his tea. "Where the post office sits. When I was eight, Angela and I walked there on opening day to see *To Kill a Mockingbird*. Dad gave us fifty cents for a box of popcorn and two Cokes, and we watched it three times in a row."

Aware that Blake's older sister had died of breast cancer as a young woman, Carley was touched by the sentiment in his expression. "What a pleasant memory."

"Yes." Eventually, humor glinted his eyes. "Dollars to donuts says you haven't seen it."

She shrugged. "You'd win that bet. But I read it twice in high school."

"You *have* to see the movie," Sherry said. "Gregory Peck was *born* to play Atticus Finch. You too, Brooke. We'll lend it to you."

"When will you start your online classes?" Patrick asked Brooke after the food arrived. Initially timid in each other's company, the two were beginning to converse in small degrees.

"I started Friday night," Brooke said.

Uncle Rory gave her a sage smile. "The day you found out you passed the test, eh?"

The girl flushed with pleasure.

"She's at the computer every morning when I wake up," Carley said.

"You mean she's a teenager who doesn't like to sleep in?" Blake said with a wink at his son.

Still flushing, Brooke said, "Dad said I slept through a tornado that took the barn when I was seven. I guess I sleep so deep that I'm all rested up when morning comes."

———

Monday, CPA Bruce Laird confirmed Carley's optimism about being able to give her employees a portion of the profits next month, at the end of the first quarter. "It was wise of you not to borrow money," the elderly man drawled. "Every penny above your expenses is gravy. Unfortunately, Uncle Sam loves gravy, but you're still doin' just fine. Enough to hire that hostess whenever you're ready."

Brooke was enthusiastic about her classes, and new employee Tyler showed signs of being just as diligent at the sink in the afternoons. On Tuesday, as Dale paid for his hummus, pita bread, and mixed-green salad, plain, he leaned over the counter to say, "As of two hours ago, Brad Travis is on a Greyhound headed north. He'll be in Little Rock tonight."

Carley thanked him. Brad, hovering in the back of her mind, had been the only barrier to a perfect week.

The latent stress of the whole Brad Travis episode finally caught up with Carley at 4:00 the following morning, when her right temple throbbed as if a nail were imbedded in it. She made it to the bathroom in time to throw up, and when there was nothing left but dry heaves, she rinsed her face with cold water and sat on the side of the bathtub, wishing she could die.

Eventually, slowly, she got to her feet. With slow, measured steps she went to Brooke's door and opened it.

"Brooke." She panted, leaned against the frame. "Brooke!"

In the dark there was rustling, feet thumping to the floor. "Carley?"

"Need you."

The light flicked on. Carley closed and shielded her eyes.

"Sorry," Brooke said. "What's wrong?"

"Migraine. Fix me some oatmeal and tea?"

The girl took her arm. "Do I need to call Doctor Borden?"

"No. Need . . . eat something."

She sat in the kitchen trying to keep her head level while the girl clanged about at the sink and stove. "No butter," Carley panted. "Fats . . . worse."

Just a teaspoon first. She moved the oatmeal around in her mouth, swallowed. Little by little, she downed a half cup. If she could keep down the half-tablet of Dramamine for fifteen minutes or so, the nausea would clear, and then she could keep down the Excedrin.

"Thanks, Brooke," she said forty minutes later, while lying on the sofa with an ice bag at her temple.

The girl bent over her. "Is it gone?"

"No. But it's bearable."

"You're not gonna go to work, are you?"

"Got to. I think it's time to hire another hostess." She gave the girl a weak smile. "I'll be all right. Now, go back to bed while you can."

"My clock's gonna go off in less than an hour," Brooke said, sending a longing glance toward the computer.

"No way. Set it back another hour and go back to bed."

"But—"

"But nothing," Carley said. "If you can't sleep, lie there and count sheep."

The girl gave her an odd look. "Why would I want to do that?"

"It's just a saying."

She was able to do more than count sheep, for Carley had to rouse her to dress for work. Forty-five-degree air felt good on Carley's face as they walked out to the car.

"Want me to drive?" Brooke asked.

Carley laughed in spite of the pain. "That would be a trip."

Brooke got in on the passenger side. "Hey, I've known how since I was fourteen. It's just I can't get my license 'til I take driver's ed, and I figured what was the point without a car? And Mildred would have a fit if I tried to drive her truck."

Maybe you should give her the lessons, Carley thought. Once Brooke started college, she would need a little car too.

Later . . . think later.

At the café, she sent Brooke on in to start the tea, and went next door to the drugstore.

Chester Templeton's thick lenses made him resemble pictures of aliens with huge eyes. "You've never taken prescription medicine?"

"I've tried everything . . . self-injections, nose sprays, everything. They work, but then a rebound headache kicks in an hour or so later. I gave up four or five years ago."

"Well, there you are, Miss Reed. There are better medicines on the market now."

And . . . that's why I'm here, she thought. Short temper was a common migraine side effect.

He smiled as if reading her thoughts and said kindly, "I'll call Doctor Borden's office and see if they can squeeze you in. I'm afraid he will not prescribe anything until he sees you."

"No, thank you," Carley said. "I'll call and make a Monday appointment."

Even though the migraine would be history by then, there was always another waiting in the wings. It was time to be proactive instead of reactive.

"How long do they last?"

She rubbed her temple. "Normally, less than a day. But one this fierce usually hangs on for two, three days."

"What are you taking now?"

"A half-tablet of Dramamine with two Excedrin. They take away the nausea, but only dull the pain."

"Take a whole Dramamine tonight," Chester suggested. "Maybe it'll help you sleep it off."

"Okay. Thank you."

She slogged through the hours.

"I can take your place," Brooke told Carley when Tyler arrived for his shift.

"No, thank you. Three more hours, and I'll crash."

"Well, you don't have to drive me home now. I'll walk."

"Thank you."

"Maybe I should start riding my bike here again?"

"Let's talk about it later?" Carley said weakly.

When she finally arrived at home, Brooke rose from the computer to show her a fig cake Byrle Templeton had brought over. "She said she hopes you start feeling better."

"That sweet lady," Carley mumbled. She wondered idly if pharmacists were held to the same confidentiality rules as doctors. Not that she cared, in this instance.

"Want some?" Brooke asked.

"Yes, please."

"Milk?"

"Um-hmm. And then I'm going to bed."

"I'll light the bathroom heater."

"Thanks." Carley washed the Dramamine and Excedrin down with the milk. By the time she was in her pajamas, she was yawning. From her bed she could see the pencil of light beneath the door. She had to smile. Brooke had been attentive all evening. She could just imagine the girl racing for the computer as soon as she was free.

Sleep's gauzy net drew her in without a struggle.

It's about time! Dale thought in the shadow of Mrs. Templeton's utility shed, as the middle bedroom window next door went black. The soles of his running shoes easing into the grass, he crossed Carley's backyard. The living room windows were dark as well.

Not yet. He would need to give Brooke time to fall asleep, for it was logical that she was the one staying up late.

On his way back to the shed, he wiped his nose on his sleeve. The dark sweat suit was warm enough insulation for the run over here in forty-five degree weather, but not for lurking in shadows. But he had had to dress the part, just in case anyone happened to spot him.

And he *would* be running back home. After it was done.

The shiver passing through him had nothing to do with the cold. He felt the sting of tears, and blinked. He had tried to convince himself that he was paranoid, that Brooke Kimball had not infected Carley with her suspicions, that the request to take the boat out was as innocent as Carley had tried to make it sound.

And perhaps he *could* have convinced himself, had he not run into waitress Tiffany Hogan at the bank last Thursday. Obviously she had assumed that relating seeing a certain couple getting cozy at a secluded table in the Old Grist Mill would better her own chances with him. No way. Not when she could barely conceal the zeal in her eyes as she delivered the news that would break his heart.

He allowed another half hour to pass before easing Mrs. Templeton's ladder from her shed. The same ladder he had borrowed last year.

Which window?

He chided himself for not figuring that out during the long wait. But what was there to figure out? Transom windows made entering through the enclosed back porch impossible. The kitchen window was small, and he would have to clamber over the sink. He was not sure if Carley slept in the front or back bedroom.

Living room. A good plan, anyway. Give the gas enough time to build, before it hit the stove's pilot light.

————————

Bright light burned into Carley's eyes. Noise assaulted her ears. Brooke was opening the window on the east side, flooding the bedroom with cold air.

"Carley, get up!"

"Why are you—"

"Get up now!"

The girl hopped up on the bed and got on her knees to open the front window. Carley eased up on the pillow, and Brooke grabbed her arm. "We have to go outside!"

"What happened?" Dean Payne asked, answering his carport door in a dark terry cloth robe over striped pajama pants.

"There's gas leaking!" Brooke said.

Dean looked at the door Brooke had left open. "Gas? Where did it come from?"

"I don't know," Brooke said. "I woke up to answer the phone and smelled it."

"Who was it?" Carley asked, lifting one bare foot and then the other on the cold concrete.

"Wrong number."

"Come on in the house while we call the utility company," Dean said.

Within five minutes, a truck from Mississippi Power sat behind the GL, and one from Tallulah Volunteer Fire Department was parked on the side of the street. Several porch lights were shining down Third Street, and Carley could vaguely make out the forms of neighbors standing at the ends of their driveways.

"The gas to the living room heater was on," said a utility worker with *Larry* on his pocket badge. "You're lucky it didn't reach the stove pilot light, or you'd both be toast by now. You must have bumped the lever?"

Carley, with a coat she borrowed from Gayle over her pajamas and her feet warm in Dean's socks and tennis shoes, had to take a moment to replay her actions of the evening.

"Ma'am?" Larry said.

"She's on medication," Brooke said defensively, also wearing clothes borrowed from the Paynes.

Larry sent a meaningful glance toward the three waiting firemen. "I see."

Carley recognized two as customers and lifted a hand in greeting. "I don't remember going near the heater."

"She didn't," Brooke said. "And I turned it off after I shut down the computer."

"What time was this?" a fireman asked.

"About midnight."

"Brooke," Carley scolded. "You're going to work yourself sick . . ."

"You think you might have accidentally turned the lever the wrong way?" Dean asked Brooke.

"No sir. I remember turning it off."

"But you had to have been sleepy, right?" Larry asked.

"Well, yes, sir."

Another siren sounded, closer, and then the squad car was stopping at the end of the driveway. Garland got out. "What happened?"

After a fireman explained, Garland asked Larry, "You didn't touch the lever, did you?"

"Well, yeah. I had to turn it off."

"Yeah," Garland sighed, and said to Carley, "I'll need to look for signs of forced entry."

"Forced entry?" Carley said. "That's impossible. Who would do this?"

"I still have to look."

"We don't lock the windows," Brooke said. "We're always raising and shutting them."

The deputy nodded understanding. This was, after all, Tallulah. "Then, I'll check the screens."

Gayle came out, bearing a tray. "Would ya'll care for hot chocolate?"

When Carley answered the door at 8:10 in the morning, Dale walked in and rested both hands on her shoulders. "I just came on duty and blasted Garland out for not calling me."

"Well, there was nothing you could do," Carley said, tightening the belt to her robe.

"Hey, Chief Dale," Brooke said from the kitchen doorway. "I'm making pancakes. Want some?"

A smile diluted some of the worry on Dale's face, "No, thank you. Good for you, smelling that gas."

"Thank you," she said, sending him a smile before returning to the stove.

Dale gave Carley an incredulous look, mouthed the word, *Wow.*

Then he got down to the bad news. "I called Greyhound. Brad evidently got off the bus somewhere between here and Jackson Tuesday, because he didn't make the transfer. I called his dad up in Little Rock and got the machine, so I left a message."

"Why didn't *he* call, when Brad didn't get off the bus Tuesday night? Or didn't his mother call up there to see if he arrived?"

"I don't know, Carley," Dale admitted. "The boy was furious when his mother wouldn't bail him out of jail, and anyway, we're not talking about the Parents of the Year. Marti's coming in a little while to dust the outsides of your windows for prints. If it *was* Brad, I don't expect to find anything. He was clever enough to wear gloves that time he broke into a house. If I hadn't seen his flashlight in a window during my rounds, I probably wouldn't have caught him."

"So, he just gets away with it?"

"Well, we're still at the *if* stage. I've already put out a statewide all-points bulletin on him, and naturally we're looking here. But you see? This might be coincidence. He could be hitchhiking to Las Vegas this very minute. Brooke *could* have accidentally bumped the lever. According to Garland's report, it was late when she turned off the heater, and she *had* gotten up early with you the previous morning."

Faced with such logic, Carley could only nod. They might never learn what happened. But at least she took comfort in the fact that Dale was taking charge of the situation.

chapter 33

Carley taped a sign—*Now Hiring Waiter or Waitress. Inquire Within*—to a corner of the café window on Saturday, October 18. Rather than hire a hostess, she had decided to have Danyell and Paula rotate hostessing and waiting tables on a weekly basis. Both had great rapport with customers. She would have more time for the paperwork and would still be able to oversee the dining room without the pressure of being tied to the counter.

But she would still be tied to the bathroom stalls, for it was only expedient that she be the one to continue the checks and cleanings.

Three women and one young man came in to ask for applications. If none impressed her during interviews this coming Monday, she would take that as a sign that she should continue hosting for a while.

Not a bad problem to have. Looking over the dining room of her own café, she prayed, *God, you're so good!* Could she ever have imagined that she could be so happy?

Sunday was the one-year anniversary of her grandmother's death. There was no grave to visit, but Carley had ordered a bouquet of daisies, chrysanthemums, alstroemeria, bells of Ireland, and baby's breath for the podium of Grace Community Church. After the worship service, she and Brooke followed the Hudsons to their house, where Uncle Rory had a roast waiting in the oven.

Beef, not venison.

The Kemps arrived twenty minutes later, when the table was set and tea glasses iced. Everyone, even Blake, was in a quiet mood as befitting the significance of the day. After lunch Patrick, recently shed of his braces, and Brooke played checkers. There was no hint of a romance between the two, even though Tara had recently dumped Patrick for a football linebacker. It was good for Brooke to learn that she could simply be friends with a boy, Carley thought.

Dale stopped by the house Monday morning to tell her that Brad Travis had finally contacted his dad after linking up with a cousin in Las Vegas. Peeling a banana at the table, he said, "It *could* conceivably take six days to hitchhike to Las Vegas, especially when you look like a hoodlum. But if he hustled, he would have had time to come back here for one last bit of revenge."

Carley spread some of Uncle Rory's muscadine jelly on her toast. "So, what does all that mean?"

He sighed, pulled a string from the banana pulp, and placed it on a paper napkin. "Well, we didn't find any of his fingerprints, as expected, and no one here has seen him since I drove him to the bus station. We can bring him back here for questioning if you like, but I'd be tempted to keep this on the back burner until we uncover some concrete evidence. If we found no cause to hold him, he would be right back here among us, and might decide to stay this time."

Carley shuddered. "No. Let's do it your way. I'm sure Brooke will agree."

"Pity we don't have the very latest fingerprinting technique yet. I'm going up to Jackson next month for a presentation of crime-detecting equipment. For example, there's a nanoparticle dust being developed in England, that's drawn like a magnet to even the tiniest traces of oil, even through latex gloves."

"Interesting," Carley said after a bite of toast.

He gave her a dry smile. "I'd be more interested if they hadn't scheduled it the same day as the Tulane game. There's no way it'll be over by two, and then there's still the drive."

Brooke came out of her room, tilting her head to insert an earring. She was dressed for shopping, in jeans and a short-sleeved coral top appropriate for the mid-eighties temperature expected today. Her brown leather purse hung from her shoulder by a narrow strap.

"Hi, Chief Dale."

"Hi, Brooke."

"Can you sit a minute?" Carley asked. "Dale has some information about Brad."

"I heard in my room. That's fine with me, waiting." The girl took a glass from the cabinet and opened the refrigerator. Holding out the carton of Minute Maid, she said, "Juice?"

"No, thank you," Carley and Dale answered in unison.

A horn honked. Brooke chugged down the glass and laid it in the sink. "Okay if I leave?"

"Go on," Carley said. "And remember to get the iron. Make sure it has a clear water-level gauge."

"Okay, see you!"

The front door closed behind her, and the sounds of her footfalls faded.

"My iron died," Carley said. "I bought it when I started college, so I guess it served its time."

Dale smiled. "You were one hundred percent right."

"Well, thank you. But anyone could tell it was broken. It wouldn't heat."

"No, silly. About Brooke."

Returning his smile, Carley said, "I knew what you meant. And thank you. But *Brooke* had more to do with that, than my simply being right."

"Who's taking her shopping? Miz Hudson?"

"No, Mildred Tanner. Wednesday is Mr. Kimball's birthday, and they're going in together for a television for his bedroom."

This time it was Dale who shuddered. "I'd rather be tortured than sit in a closed car with that woman. Not only the body odor, but that mouth . . ."

"I've only seen her from a distance. She and Brooke aren't close, but I guess they need each other on this project."

———————

November wafted in on cool breezes that coaxed leaves wearing their most splendid colors—red dogwood, tan oak, brown hickory, and yellow sweet gum—to loosen their grips and sail.

At Annabel Lee Café, the month got off to a bumpy start, brought on by Carley's hiring Dana Hughs as the replacement wait-ress with no other qualification than that she was Paula's second cousin. New employees were expected to make mistakes, but she took out her frustration on customers who complained about order mix-ups. Pep talks in the office boosted Dana's productivity and atti-tude for only an hour or so.

"Believe me, I would do the same thing if I was you," Paula said when Carley drew her aside before opening on Thursday the sixth. But Dana spared Carley the task of firing her by simply not showing up that day.

"Can you come in to work tomorrow?" Carley asked Gladys Jef-fers over the telephone. A sixty-two-year-old homemaker, widowed only five weeks ago, she was looking for something to take her out of the house. Carley had liked her immediately, but wondered about her staying power if the job was to be just an outlet, a hobby.

"I'll be there," Gladys said. "Or I can come today if you like."

"Come on, then," Carley said.

One week later, Gladys was becoming a fixture in the place. She brought bran or blueberry muffins for the staff every morning, passed on compliments about the food to the cooks, and knew the names of everybody in town.

"Quick . . . the man with the mustache sitting with the lady in the blue sweater," Carley whispered during one foray from her office.

"Jim and Eileen Graham. They live off Old Mill Creek Loop and raise cattle."

Brooke was coming along well with her courses, which were laid out so well that Carley was only called upon twice so far for grammar advice.

"If a gerund is a verb ending in 'ing' that acts like a noun," Carley said in the second instance, "then a gerund *phrase* acts the same way. For example . . . Spending all her free time at the computer makes Brooke a dull girl. What is the subject here?"

The girl looked up with a dry smile. "Spending all her free time at the computer. Right?"

Carley patted her shoulder. "Right."

"But it also makes Brooke a nurse."

The girl had checked out a couple of books on health from the library in anticipation of her studies. An added benefit of her reading was that she had decided to eat healthy—no more pancakes, bacon, fried foods, or sweets—and more vegetables and salads.

Slowly, an inch at a time, Carley was feeling more at home at Grace Community Church. She agreed to donate three hours every Monday morning to work in Nearly New Thrift Shop on First Street, a ministry maintained by four Tallulah churches.

Dale came in for pita bread and hummus on Friday, and dropped by the office while the cooks were preparing his takeout order of two spinach wraps with mixed-field-green salad.

"There won't be a single thing I can eat up at that conference tomorrow," he said. "*That's* why I keep an ice chest in both cars."

"We're printing up new menus in January, adding four new dishes," Carley told him. "A veggie burger will be one."

He came around the desk and wheeled out her chair.

"Hey!"

Spinning her around, he grabbed her shoulders and planted a kiss on her forehead. "You angel, you!"

She smiled up at him. "It's because the vegan foods have done well."

"Aw, come on. It's because you like me."

"Maybe a little," she conceded. "And now you have to let me work. If I don't send my supply order in by three, it'll come a day later."

"Point taken." But he paused at the door, studied her thoughtfully.

"What?" Carley said.

"Are you . . . up to a movie tonight? *Master and Commander* just opened at Turtle Creek."

"I can't. Sorry," she answered. "I promised to go to Ruby's Tupperware party."

"Whoa . . . and here I am only offering dinner and a movie."

That made her laugh. "A promise is a promise."

"I know. It was just a thought. Hope you get your order in."

He was halfway through the door with his hand on the knob when she said, "I'm free tomorrow night. If you're back in time."

He turned, his smile bringing out the dimples. "Pick you up here?"

"Okay."

"Thanks, Carley."

Thanking me for going out with him, Carley thought, turning again to her keyboard. And in spite of lingering misgivings about his experiences with other women, she believed he absolutely meant it.

"Hello?" Carley said into the receiver with sleep-thickened voice the following morning.

"Carley! Did I wake you?" Dale said.

"Ah, well . . ."

"I'm sorry. I waited until it was time for me to leave. I thought you got up around eight."

"It's okay." She stifled a yawn. "The Tupperware party went a little long."

"I just wanted to say that you might want to dress up a little tonight. We'll go to Magnolia House restaurant, if you like, then catch the late show."

"Is there anything there you can eat?"

"Sure, not to worry."

"Then you'd better pick me up at the house so I can change."

"That's fine. I'll have to change from my uniform. Don't know why they expect us to wear them just to sit in meetings, but that's the way it is."

Odd, Carley thought, hanging up, that Brooke was not at her usual early morning spot at the computer. *She needs to catch up on her sleep anyway.*

She returned to the bedroom for her slippers and padded toward the kitchen to put the teakettle on low flame. On her way to the bathroom she realized Brooke's door was open, so she reached in to close it and buffer some of the noise from her moving around in the bathroom and kitchen. Eastern light from the window slanted in on an empty bed.

No sound came from behind the closed bathroom door. Gently, Carley knocked. "Brooke? You okay?"

When there was no reply, she turned the knob and eased open the door. With typical consideration, the girl had left the heater on low flame.

"Brooke?" Carley went back through the living room and opened the front door, though she did not expect the girl to be taking breakfast outdoors. The swing was empty. And her bicycle was not in its usual spot against the wall.

Exercising? That would fit in with her newfound health consciousness. Or maybe she decided to blow the diet for Dixie Burger sausage biscuits. Either way, she would come back to a lecture. No matter that the girl was almost eighteen, housemates weren't supposed to cause each other worry. She could have at least left a note.

She has her good points, Carley reminded herself, opening the bathroom medicine cabinet.

A sheet of folded paper formed a tent over her tube of Colgate. Carley took it out, opened it.

> Please don't be mad. I bought a rubber boat when Mildred took me to Hattiesburg for Dad's birthday. I'm going to take it out to Chief Dale's pond. I called Tyler last night and he said he would work both shifts. Don't worry about me! I'll be careful!
> Love,
> Brooke

"You hardheaded girl!" Carley groaned.

When she was able to corral her racing thoughts a few seconds later, she went to her desk for her phone number list. Let Melvin Kimball rant! Perhaps Brooke had not yet arrived, and he still had a moral responsibility to keep his daughter from acting so foolishly.

Eight unanswered rings later, she hung up and changed into jeans and a sweatshirt and fleece jacket. She had a loafer on her left foot when she thought of her black suede boots in the back of her closet. They were more dressy than practical with the two-inch heels, but gave her a measure of security, just in case some water moccasins had not gotten the word about hibernating.

As she pulled out of the driveway, she wondered whether she should have telephoned the police. But what if Dale had not yet left for his conference? Even if he had, Garland or Marti would be sure to tell him about Brooke's little caper. How would she explain it?

Well, Brooke wanted to drag a chain around your pond because she believes you killed Tracy and Rick Bryant.

The red truck was not in the Kimball driveway. How in the world had Brooke conned her father and Mildred into this? But how else would she have gotten the canoe over to the pond? Carley struck the steering wheel with the heel of her hand. Maybe Brooke needed to see a psychiatrist. *Obsessive-compulsive disorder.* Wasn't that the term?

The red truck was not parked at Dale's gate. Only a blue bicycle, leaning against a post. Carley honked her horn five times in a row, then another five before getting out of the car. She heard only wind sifting through pine branches, the tapping of a woodpecker, the *jeee!* of a wood duck.

She cupped both hands to her mouth. "BROOKE!"

It would not occur to a person like Mildred Tanner to glance back and notice a man holding a bag of ice, as she unloaded from her cart a box of donuts, twelve-pack of cream soda, pound package of bologna, some sort of crayon-yellow cheese, loaf of white bread, giant size bag of barbecue potato chips, and copy of *National Enquirer.* Dale glared at the back of her perfectly coifed hair and then shrugged when cashier Anna Erwin sent him a helpless smile.

"Hey, Miss Mildred! Where's Brooke?"

Neal Henderson, bagging Mildred's combination of trans-fats and preservatives, artificial dyes and gossip, was all smiles until the woman shrilled, "The ig-nert girl woke me up at six, lookin' for the box with the blow-up boat! Then she took off with it on her bike! She's up to some mis-cheef, likely as not!"

"Brooke's not ig-nert," the boy said, face flooded with hurt. "She's my friend."

"Well, *you* don't have to put up with her foolishness. Gonna be a nurse? She's more'n likely to kill somebody, give 'em the wrong pill."

"Honey," Anna said to the crestfallen boy, "Run and tell your momma I'm gettin' low on quarters."

The burning in the pit of Dale's chest had raced up to his face. *Just put the ice back and leave.*

But on second thought, it might be best to continue as planned. At least until he got behind the wheel of the patrol car and could think.

"Sorry about that, Chief Dale," Anna said when he finally placed the ice on the belt.

He forced a smile, realizing the flush he could feel in his cheeks could be explained by Mildred's inconsiderateness, his haste to get on the road. "That's okay. I don't guess she had deodorant in that cart, did she?"

"Shame on you, Chief," Anna scolded, but with a smile, and scanned the ice. "That'll be ninety-four cents."

"Don't worry about the change," Dale said, handing her a dollar. "I've got to get on to a meeting up in Jackson."

For once, Dale was glad the Hendersons had built their grocery on the town's outskirts. It was a simple matter to continue down Highway 42 and take the long way up Black Creek Road. Traffic was light, no school buses on a Saturday, most folks just now stirring. Even if he crossed paths with someone who recognized him, he could say that Mildred's comments had caused him to wonder if Brooke Kimball was in danger paddling around on his pond.

If he happened to pull her body from the water, there was not a soul in Tallulah who would assume he did anything less than try to save her.

At least he *hoped* not, especially in the case of one particular soul.

It was encouraging that he had spoken to Carley at her house just minutes ago. Perhaps his intuition had failed him after all. Maybe Carley *had* simply wanted a pleasant outing. Had it not been the day of their picnic when she first suggested he get a boat?

And was it so outrageous, to think that Tiffany Hogan could have lied about Steve and Carley being together at the Old Grist Mill? If they *were* dating, Steve would have shown himself around town these past several weeks. Dale had kept close tabs on Carley—no trips to Hattiesburg.

For the first time in his life, he was relieved to consider that he may have been wrong. It would have been hard to live with—knowing he had mistakenly consigned the woman he loved to a fiery death.

And it would have been premeditated, making him a full-blown criminal instead of a man dogged by unfortunate coincidence.

Two unfortunate coincidences, as a matter of fact.

The second had occurred only days after Gwen Stillman's death, as he was attempting to hide the accursed red Mustang. He banged his kneecap making the jump from the dam, but every inch of water lapping up to meet the sun-glinted windows and firethorn-red hood, took more of the load off his shoulders.

And then, the sound of a vehicle speeding up the track, red dust rising through the trees. He had sprinted for all his life, ignoring the fire in his knee, hoping to reach the intruder soon enough to wave him away. But Rick Bryant's battered green Dodge Colt rolled to the edge of the water. The engine died. Even from forty feet and gaining, Dale could hear a male voice through the open window.

"Look! What's that?"

No . . . Dale had groaned inside.

Still, Rick had not looked in his direction.

"Rick, let's get out of here!" said a female voice.

Dale could hear the rapid clicking of a solenoid that had failed to engage the old Dodge's starter. His feet pounded the ground. He could explain the Mustang, somehow.

I just got here myself . . . did you see anyone running away?

Yes, that would work! Had he not destroyed all identification?

His heart sank. *Fingerprints can be taken under water!* Why had he not worn gloves? His footprints would be the only ones on the dam. Even the chief of police could only hide so much evidence, especially in a case that had the whole town enraged.

They'll hang you, he told himself as he approached the car. Rick's crimson-faced attention was absorbed by the impotent revs of the engine. But then he turned, met Dale's eyes.

The puzzlement in Rick's expression changed rapidly to awareness. And then terror.

"We didn't see nothin, Chief!"

It was that terror, accompanied by the scream from the passenger seat, that pumped Dale with so much horrible adrenaline that he drew his service pistol. He could no more stop himself than fly.

But not all reasoning had vanished. While Rick's hands were fluttering up in surrender, Dale reached in and shot him in the chest so that blood splatter and the bullet would be confined to the upholstery. By now he recognized the screaming woman as Tracy Knight. She was struggling for the door handle. He ran around the front of the car. Never, had he purposely hurt a woman. He *saved* women's lives.

He had had to close his eyes as he pulled the trigger.

One sleepless night later, he had dredged up *some* consolation by reminding himself that the two would not have met with such a tragedy if they had not been fooling around.

And at least *their* suffering was over. His was just beginning. He would have to take his land off the market, be tied to Tallulah for decades, if not forever. He could not leave the land under the protection of gate and "Posted" signs without the intimidation factor of his position. Nor could he have the pond filled in; even if he had a plausible explanation, it would first have to be drained. As for selling the timber, he was not comfortable with the idea of having the pond visible from the road. The trees would have to shield his secret.

And now another domino had fallen. He could see how wrong he had been, to have ignored the accusation in Brooke Kimball's eyes all these years and to have naively allowed himself to think he had won her over after the Brad Travis ordeal. If he had found a way to take care of her years ago, he would be on his way to Jackson with no heavier thought than whether his favorite shirt was clean for his date with Carley tonight.

But then, he was not a cold-blooded killer, he reminded himself. It was only when cornered that he had had to act.

His heart fell at the sight of the blue Ford GL blocking the gate, just inches from a familiar blue bicycle.

This may not be as bad as it looks, he thought, stepping out of the patrol car. Carley must have discovered the girl was missing when his phone call woke her up, and put two and two together. If she had simply come out here to bring Brooke back home, then he could deal with the girl later.

Not too much later, though.

Carley's keys were in the ignition.

Good girl, he thought, opening the door.

————

Hope came with the sound of a car roaring up the lane.

Thank you, Father!

But it died just as quickly. The six-foot inflatable boat still rested in the shallow end, where Carley had waded into the soft mud to flip it right-side up.

She'll never be a nurse. Fresh tears stung her swollen eyes. The back of her throat felt raw. She would never hear Brooke's chirpy good-mornings as her fingers rested on the computer keyboard, or her dishes rattling in the kitchen while relating every detail of the latest *Columbo.*

Why didn't I guess it would come to this?

She heard the car door opening. Footfalls on the ground, racing toward her. "Carley?"

Carley turned and fell into Dale's arms, sobbing. "Can't . . . find . . . her, Dale. I think she got caught in the chain! She can't swim!"

"Brooke, you mean?"

"I should have known!"

"Poor baby," he said into her hair, stroking her back. "But you're going to have to calm down now, help me. What chain? What was she doing here?"

"She thinks . . ." Carley pulled in a shuddering breath. "*Thought* . . . her cousin's down there."

It had to come out now. The situation was too serious for sparing feelings.

Strong arms tightened around her. Carley was too wracked with guilt and grief to take comfort from them.

"Why would she think that?" Dale asked, close to her ear.

"She wouldn't let it go. Thought maybe you . . ."

The arms loosened, and Carley backed out of them. Grabbing his sleeves, she shouted, "The water's cold! You hear about people reviving! Call for help!"

"I tried the radio on my way here and just got static. But I'll find her!"

He unfastened his belt, dropping holster to the ground, then key chain and wallet. As he was pulling off his left shoe, Carley reached down and scooped up his keys.

"And I'll call from the Kimballs'!"

Four steps toward the patrol car, and then her right arm was grabbed. She was jerked around so violently that her teeth bit her tongue.

He shouted in her face, "I need you here!"

"We have to call, Dale! I'll be back in five minutes! I'll break a window if they're not home!"

But he had her by her other arm. His grip was tightening painfully.

"Oh, Carley . . ." he groaned.

The bleak resignation creeping into his face terrified her. They could not give up yet!

"*Please*, Dale! We have to try."

"I *told* you not to take her in!" He shook his head. "If you would have just listened!"

"What are you talking about?"

But he looked away, muttered, "Just come help me." With an arm around her shoulder, he began leading her down the slope.

"No!" Her sodden boots took unwilling steps. "What are you doing, Dale?"

"Stop fighting me!"

She started dragging her heels through the pine straw, and then mud of the shallow end. "Please!"

"I'm sorry, Carley!" he muttered, crimson-faced, forcing her deeper and deeper into the pond.

The plunge was heart-shocking cold. A hand pushed her head under, causing water to rush into her throat and nostrils. Her lungs burned. Kicking was useless, for she could not gain footing in the soft mud. She clamped both hands around his wrist, but he was much stronger.

And then, the pressure on her head ceased. She found footing and rose in chest-deep water, coughing and shivering and blinking. Dale still held her arm, but his attention was drawn by something over the bank. A squad car was braking to a gentle stop. The door opened, Marti stepped out and squinted in their direction.

"Chief?"

Dale released her, started moving toward the bank where his holster lay.

"No!" Carley screamed, pushing feet against the sloping bottom, following, reaching out for his shoulders in vain. "He tried to kill me! He wouldn't let me get help for Brooke!"

"She's crazy, Marti!" Dale called. They were in waist-deep water now, the gap between them widening. "I'll explain, just let me get out of—"

"He'll kill us both!" Carley cried. "Don't let him get his gun!"

Marti hesitated, drew her revolver, and hustled over to where Dale's lay in the pine straw.

"Stay right there for now," she said with uncertain voice. "Okay?"

Knee-deep in the water, Dale picked up speed, sloshing forward. "You're not gonna believe *her*, are you, Marti? It's me . . . Dale. I *rescue* women!"

He was going to win. Carley could see it in the deputy's expression, the slight lowering of her gun.

Over the sob filling her throat, Carley called desperately, "Please, Marti! Why would I make it up?"

Dale wheeled around, gave her a thunderous look. "SHUT UP!"

Carley flinched, gave a little cry, and was backing away, when the rage left Dale's face as quickly as it had come. He blinked, gave her a brief, stunned look, and turned.

Marti had crouched to pick up his holster with one hand. Twisting, she flung it underhand, toward the patrol car. She lowered her own revolver slightly. A shot roared, and the water six feet to Dale's left dimpled. He froze.

Evenly, the deputy called out, "Come up on the bank and lie face down, Dale."

After several tense seconds, he obeyed almost meekly, shoulders slumping. Carley thought she heard a sob as he lay on the pine straw. Still, she gave him wide berth as she came out of the water, trembling with cold and grief. Too late for Brooke. She had to be dead by now.

"I need you to go to the car and radio Garland," Marti said gently. She did not take her eyes off Dale. "Crank the engine and warm yourself up. Hurry now!"

The latter command prompted Carley into action. She jogged over to the patrol car and got inside. Fortunately, she had watched Dale operate his radio.

"Garland?" she said. "This is Carley Reed. Can you hear me?"

"What . . . Marti . . . wrong?" Carley heard through the static.

She forced herself to speak slowly, sharply. "Marti needs you right now on Dale Parker's property on Tent Road. Emergency! Emergency! Can you hear me?"

"Got . . . coming."

On impulse, even though it was too late, she added, "We need the search and rescue team too."

The heater began blowing warm air. Carley closed her eyes and leaned her head against the window. It occurred to her to wonder how the deputy knew to come back here, but she was too drained from the ordeal to ask.

She heard a vehicle racing up the lane. *Garland,* she thought dully. Only, she had radioed barely a minute ago. Sirens were sounding, but faintly, far in the distance.

Carley turned to look through the dusty far window. Mildred Tanner's red truck was braking to a stop. The only thing she could make out about the driver was a familiar head of blonde-orange hair.

Incredulously, Carley opened the door and stepped out. She was seized by a pair of young arms.

"I heard a shot!" Brooke sobbed. "I thought Chief Dale was out of town! Oh, Carley, I'm so sorry!"

"Brooke?" Carley could only mumble as her mind made the transition from one reality to another. "You're here."

"You mean you staged this whole thing?" Garland said, somber-faced, after leading a sullen, handcuffed Dale Parker to the back seat of his patrol car.

"I thought she wouldn't wake up until after Chief Dale was gone." Brooke swiped her knuckles across her sodden makeup-free eyes. "Then she'd call you, and you'd have to drag the pond when you saw the raft."

Draped with a blanket someone from the search and rescue team had brought over from the fire truck, Carley asked the girl, "Where were you?"

The girl looked to the ground. "In my dad's shed. I walked back after I put the boat in the water."

Marti's hands rested on her hips. "Tell me why we shouldn't arrest you for criminal mischief?"

No kidding! Carley thought, but then something clicked into place. "Dale tried to kill me only *after* I tried to go for help. He didn't want anyone else going into that water. Shouldn't that tell you something?"

The two deputies exchanged looks. Garland looked over his shoulder at the fire truck, "As long as they're out here, I guess it wouldn't hurt to give the boys a chance to practice."

The air had warmed to the midsixties when, a few minutes after 11:00, one of the pair of divers bobbed to the surface and pushed back his mask. "We got a car down here!"

Ten feet away at the outer edge of the ripples, the second diver surfaced. "We got a car down here!"

"Are you talking about the same car?" Garland shouted back.

The divers looked at each other, lowered their masks, and submerged. Both came back up holding up two fingers.

"Two!"

All eyes went to Brooke. The girl shook her head. "I don't know."

Automatically, gazes shifted to the back of Garland's patrol car. Dale, apparently lying down, was no longer visible.

"It's gonna take some time to get them up," Garland said. "I'll book him and come back."

As Garland started the engine, Marti said to Carley, "And I may as well drive you on home so you can change. We'll come by later for statements."

"I'll be able to drive," Carley said.

"I'd like to stay," Brooke said. She gave Carley a worried look. "If you think you'll be okay?"

Carley understood. "Yes, sure."

"No," Marti said. "Go on back with Carley. It might not be a pretty sight."

They decided Brooke would drive Carley down the lane to her car, and they would ride home together after dropping off the truck. But Carley had just opened the truck's passenger door when her earlier question struck her again. She turned to ask Marti, "How did you know we were back here?"

The deputy gave her an apologetic smile. "Blake Kemp called, asked me to check on you. I would've gotten here sooner if he'd said it was urgent. I don't guess he had any way of knowing."

"But how did he know we were out here at all?"

She shrugged. "Something about a note. We'll have to ask him."

The truck bounced across ruts in the wake of the dust from the patrol car. Gripping the armrest, Carley could not stop looking at Brooke.

"You're furious, aren't you?" the girl said. "I don't blame you."

"No." Carley shook her head. "I still can't believe you're alive."

"Thank you, Carley," she murmured. When they reached Tent Road, they got out to load the bicycle into the truck bed.

"Maybe Mildred'll drop it off at the house for me one day, when she gets over her mad," Brooke said.

"Why do you think she's angry?"

"Well, after I heard the shot, I didn't exactly ask permission to use the truck." She slammed the tailgate.

Carley started the GL and took the lead. A half mile up the road, a man was hustling toward them, red-faced and unshaven, with the gait of a fifty-year-old and skin of a seventy-year-old. She eased down on the brake pedal, but he ignored Carley and waved down Brooke.

He's angry about the truck too. Carley watched in the rearview mirror as he jerked open the door. She would have to help explain. Slowing to a complete stop, she shifted into park.

But the side mirror told the rest of the story. Melvin Kimball held his daughter in his arms, weeping profusely.

As Carley waited in the Kimballs' driveway. Mildred, wearing a wrinkled housedress, slammed the door, stalked across the porch and down the steps.

Carley rolled down the window. "Brooke's okay."

"That girl took my truck! I aughter call Chief Parker!"

"Suit yourself," Carley said, nodding her head forward. "He's probably at the station by now."

chapter 35

Two Mississippi state troopers on motorcycles manned a road-
block at the end of Tent Road, and waved Carley on through. But
almost immediately after making the right turn onto Highway 49,
she noticed a white Roadmaster and silver minivan parked on the
shoulder. She pulled in line behind the van, and she and Brooke
got out. Hurrying toward her were Aunt Helen and Uncle Rory,
Sherry and Patrick.

"We're fine," Carley said as her aunt embraced her.

It was nice to be fussed over.

"The sirens have the whole town astir," Uncle Rory said.

"But how did you know it was us out here?"

"With the police and firemen involved, word gets back."

"And we checked your house after Blake called me," Sherry
said, punching buttons on her cell phone.

Carley wondered again, *How did he. . . ?*

"I SAID . . . THEY'RE ALL RIGHT!" Sherry
shouted into her phone with a finger in her other
ear.

Brooke, obviously assumed to be the one who
had been in the gravest danger, was passed from
one set of arms to another. Even Patrick patted her
shoulder. Still, there were confused expressions.

"What happened?" Aunt Helen asked. "And what's going on
now?"

Carley looked over her shoulder and felt a chill go up her spine.
"May we talk about it at the house?"

"Good idea," Uncle Rory said. "But let Helen drive you. I'll take your car and go help Pam in the shop."

In the midst of the drama, all thought of Annabel Lee Café had been pushed aside. Carley fully expected it to be closed, with no one to let in her staff. But ahead to her right, she could see a group of women entering.

"It's open!" Brooke said from the backseat.

"After word got out you were in some kind of trouble out there, Emmit White came and unlocked the door," Aunt Helen explained, slowing even beyond her normal snail's pace to give them a good look. "Would you like to stop in for a second?"

"No, thank you." Carley had not the energy for explanations en masse, especially with so many questions of her own. Beneath a hanging English ivy in the window, she recognized three of her regular patrons. The dark-skinned man and woman sat across from each other, while the little girl with braids stared out at the street, an arm draped over the back of her chair. Meeting the child's eyes, Carley touched the glass of the car window. The girl smiled and lifted her hand.

While Brooke explained as much as she could in the living room, Carley took a long hot shower. It felt good to dig her fingers in her scalp, wash away the lingering feel of Dale's forceful hand. She turbaned her head in a towel and wrapped herself in her robe. Sherry made room for her on the sofa, and Aunt Helen brought her a mug of tea.

Sherry had a piece of the puzzle. Determined to clean out the catchall basket on their entrance table, she had asked Blake to deliver the *To Kill a Mockingbird* video *and* Carley's extra house key on his way to the barbershop that morning. He had gotten out of his car in her empty driveway, intending to leave the tape at the door, but then he realized he could not do the same with the key. The teakettle was whistling when he let himself inside. After turning off the burner, he was curious enough to look around the house.

The open medicine chest, toothbrush in the sink, and note he picked up from the floor made him uneasy enough to call the police.

"It's probably nothing serious," he had said to Marti. "But if you have time to run down there and check it out . . ."

When Blake came over at 4:10 after closing up shop, Carley stood on tiptoe to kiss his cheeks, and then Brooke did the same.

"Aw, it wasn't anything," he said, but then repeated his part in the saga for Gayle and Mrs. Templeton, and then again for Uncle Rory. Carley did not mind. She would probably be dead right now if not for him; saving a person's life covered a multitude of personality quirks.

Only Aunt Helen remained at the house when Marti and Garland arrived at 5:30 to take statements.

"There were . . . remains of two people in the Dodge," Garland said over a bowl of potato soup from the pot Troy Fairchild had delivered from the café. Neither deputy had eaten for hours. "They're on their way to the crime lab in Jackson."

Brooke's green eyes filled.

"And the second car?" Aunt Helen asked, while the girl blew her nose.

The significance of that one had escaped Carley. Had Dale planted other bodies?

"I'm afraid we can't discuss that one until the lab looks it over." Garland hesitated. "We suspect it was used in another crime."

"Did you ask . . ." Carley could not say his name.

Garland nodded understanding. "He's not saying anything. By the way, we're going to transfer him to Hattiesburg after we take your statements. Just a precaution. We suspect everyone's gonna be upset as more information comes out."

"And maybe knowing he's out of town will help you sleep better tonight," Marti said.

"It will," Carley agreed.

Marti turned to Brooke. "How did you know Chief Parker's secret?"

The girl told them everything: the two shots, the speeding patrol car, the gate and Posted signs. "But mostly, it was the way he looked at me whenever I saw him in town. I just knew."

"You didn't tell anyone?"

She shrugged. "Who'd believe me?"

Carley felt a stab of regret.

"What gave you the raft idea?" Garland asked.

"When I thought it might be Chief Dale who turned on the gas—"

"Whoa," he said, lowering his soup spoon. "Let's backtrack. What made you assume that?"

"Because I know Carley and *I* didn't turn the lever, and neither did Brad. That's what woke me up that night; he called from a pay phone in Phoenix. I noticed the gas smell while he was talking, and hung up on him." She turned to Carley. "I'm sorry I lied about it being a wrong number. I didn't want to upset you."

"It's okay," Carley said, and reached out to cover her hand.

"Go on?" Marti said.

Brooke nodded. "A couple of days later, when I got home from my shift, Brad called from Las Vegas. I thought if I talked to him, he'd leave me alone. He was laughing about how Chief Dale was a sucker for giving him fifty dollars to help him get a new start, not figuring that if he had money in his pocket he would hitchhike to his cousin's."

"I'm sorry, Brooke." Garland rubbed his forehead. "I'm lost. Dale gave him *money?*"

"That's what Brad said."

The deputy sent Marti a bewildered glance. "Go on?"

"Well, I told myself Chief Dale should have *known* that that's what Brad would do with the money. We *told* him Brad wanted to go to Las Vegas. And so I got to thinking . . . what other reason would he have, other than just being nice? I remembered that Carley had asked him about taking Dad's canoe on his pond just a few days earlier, and realized he knew what we were thinking."

"What *you* were thinking," Carley corrected, to give credit where it was due.

The girl gave her a grateful look. "Anyway, I figured he needed Brad to be out on the road just in case the gas didn't catch fire, so everyone would think he did it. That was why I started pretending to trust Chief Dale, so he wouldn't try anything like that again."

Apparently out of questions, both deputies stared at Brooke. Garland blew out his cheeks. "You're studying to be a nurse? You ought to think about the police academy, girl. You could become a detective."

"You mean like Columbo?" Brooke asked.

Marti looked bemused, but Garland laughed. "Yeah, that's it."

She smiled and shook her head. "Once was enough."

———

By Monday noon, all of Tallulah knew Tracy Knight and Rick Bryant's fates, and of the dented Mustang with enough red paint remaining in the rust for the crime lab to link it to Gweneth Stillman's hit-and-run death.

Averil Stillman knocked at Carley's door that evening, carrying a bouquet of pink camellias. "These came from a bush Gwen planted by our church steps," the pastor said in the living room with glistening eyes. "She loved her flowers."

"Then you should give them to the real heroine," Carley said gently, and fetched Brooke from her room.

Tuesday, reporters for the *Hattiesburg American, Clarion Ledger, Times Picayune,* and Channel 7 were waiting outside Annabel Lee Café before opening. Because of the life-and-death struggle at the pond, each wanted to interview Carley. But she was quick to correct them. *Her* only intention that morning, she explained, was to stop a teenager from making a fool of, or killing, herself. Brooke's intention was to find justice.

"You may have her for thirty minutes, if she's willing," Carley added, an arm around the girl's shoulders. "And if you'll excuse me, I have a business to run."

She actually did not mind the commotion. It was good to have a distraction, to keep her mind from wandering in an unpleasant direction.

Newly appointed Chief of Police, Garland Smith, stopped by the café to say Dale had hired a Hattiesburg attorney and that the Lamar County prosecutor would be presenting evidence against him in front of the grand jury in two weeks.

Thank you, Father, for protecting me from that man, Carley prayed silently.

Knocks sounded at Carley's door when she and Brooke were attempting to ease back into their normal evening routines—she at the computer filling in an invoice register, Brooke at the coffee table finishing an algebra self-quiz.

"Please don't be a reporter," Carley said in low voice as she got to her feet.

"Unless he's cute," Brooke said, chewing on her pencil.

It felt good to laugh again. Carley pressed her face against the glass. Steve Underwood stood in the dim amber light pouring out onto the porch.

"I thought Thanksgiving vacation didn't start until Thursday," Carley said as she let him inside.

"It doesn't. But when Mom called, I had to come."

"Hi, Mr. Steve!" Brooke chirped.

"Hi, Brooke. My mom says you're all over the news. I didn't even realize." He turned again to Carley, "Are you all right?"

She smiled. "We're getting there."

"I'm glad."

Their eyes locked. He seemed on the verge of embracing her, but then he glanced over at Brooke and cleared his throat. "I was worried . . ."

"Thank you." Impulsively, Carley reached for his hand. "I'll bet you haven't had supper."

He smiled as his fingers, calloused from years of familiarity with woodworking tools, folded over hers. "Well, no . . . I planned to stop by Dixie Burger."

She exchanged smiles with Brooke and began leading him through the living room.

"Please stay. We have six casseroles from the ladies of Mount Olive Church."

epilogue

The Lamar County Grand Jury found enough evidence to indict Dale Parker. To escape the certainty of first-degree murder convictions, he pleaded guilty to felony hit-and-run, two cases of second-degree murder, and one count of attempted murder. Carley did not even have to testify beyond giving her statement to the county attorney. As part of his plea bargain, Dale was sent to a federal correctional institution in Coleman, Florida.

When the crime lab released Tracy and Rick's remains in early December, Steve accompanied Carley and Brooke and Melvin Kimball to a tiny Baptist church in Soso for Tracy's funeral. Rick's was held in Lockwood Funeral Home two days later. Out of respect for her landlord, Carley was one of the handful of attendees.

Mona Bryant, dressed in black, drew Carley aside after the burial in Tallulah Cemetery. "I'm sorry I weren't any help when you were looking."

"But you were. You gave me his social security number and birth date."

Mona gave her a dry smile. "The private eye Dad hired three years ago said it looked like Rick had got himself a new identity. But if I told you that, your man would know to start from there instead of backtracking. I was afraid you'd find him."

"But, why? Wouldn't you have wanted child support?"

"He would've found some way to get out of it." She shrugged. "That's the sort of things he did. We were gonna let seven years pass and try to have him declared dead for the insurance. Now we don't have to. And I'd better get back to my boy."

Emmit merely nodded at her, but he did visit Carley in her office three days later. "Thank you for helpin' us put this behind us," he said. "You can have the same rent, for as long as you want."

In this case, Carley did not remind him that Brooke was the true heroine.

———

Five months later, Brooke was awarded her General Education Diploma and scored a surprising twenty-three on her ACT. She was still putting most of her salary away for nurses' training, so she spent the five-thousand-dollar reward on a lemon yellow 1999 Dodge Neon, and the five hundred dollars from the Lion's Club Citizen of the Year award on her first six months' insurance.

Steve and Carley had had five dates since November, and he telephoned from Hattiesburg almost every week. She did not have to give him the "friendship" speech, for he seemed to understand her caution instinctively. But she liked him very much and could tell he felt the same way about her. Sometimes she found herself counting the weeks until he would be back in Tallulah for the summer.

Annabel Lee Café attracted even more patrons than before, perhaps due to Carley and Brooke's notoriety. The hours stayed the same. Almost losing her life had given Carley an understanding of where career should fit on the priority scale.

Certainly not before family, and having the two days off each week gave her time to be with them.

And not before worship. She had made peace with God. While she would never wish to go back and relive the wretched portions of her life, they were part of the sum total that made her who she was.

Her favorite poet, Longfellow, himself a Christian, had captured her newfound sentiments over a hundred and fifty years ago in his poem *The Ladder of Saint Augustine.*

Standing on what too long we bore
With shoulders bent and downcast eyes,
We may discern—unseen before—
A path to higher destinies.
Nor doom the irrevocable Past,
As wholly wasted, wholly vain,
If, rising on its wrecks, at last
To something nobler we attain.

CROSSINGS®
THE BOOK CLUB FOR TODAY'S CHRISTIAN FAMILY

A Letter to Our Readers

Dear Reader:

In order that we might better contribute to your reading enjoyment, we would appreciate your taking a few minutes to respond to the following questions. When completed, please return to the following:

Andrea Doering, Editor-in-Chief
Crossings Book Club
401 Franklin Avenue, Garden City, NY 11530

You can post your review online! Go to www.crossings.com and rate this book.

Title _____ Author _____

1 Did you enjoy reading this book?

❏ Very much. I would like to see more books by this author!

❏ I really liked_____

❏ Moderately. I would have enjoyed it more if_____

2 What influenced your decision to purchase this book? Check all that apply.

    ❏ Cover
    ❏ Title
    ❏ Publicity
    ❏ Catalog description
    ❏ Friends
    ❏ Enjoyed other books by this author
    ❏ Other _____

3 Please check your age range:

    ❏ Under 18   ❏ 18-24
    ❏ 25-34   ❏ 35-45
    ❏ 46-55   ❏ Over 55

4 How many hours per week do you read? _____

5 How would you rate this book, on a scale from 1 (poor) to 5 (superior)?
_____

Name_____

Occupation_____

Address_____

City_____ State_____ Zip_____